HUGO AND *NEBULA* AWARD WINNER BRIAN W. ALDISS:

"Helliconia came to mind suddenly. But something much grander emerged, a pattern buried deep in the human psyche.

"Suppose that Earth took not a year of 365 days to complete its orbit of the sun, but the equivalent of 2592 years—would not almost everything we know be transformed?

"There is not just mankind on Helliconia; there are also phagors. The two species are enemies, yet co-dependent.

"What happens when that a-human race competes for supremacy? How does that competition fare when nature requires both species to survive if either are to do so?

"The story that unfolds over generations is a dual one: we have on the one hand the growth and decay of nations, with the struggle for power which that implies. And on the other we have the intense hopes and disappointments, loves and triumphs, of individuals. . . ."

"No less than the story of a civilization's rebirth . . . completely engrossing!"
                                —Publishers Weekly

OTHER VOLUMES BY BRIAN W. ALDISS

BRIAN W. ALDISS

HELLICONIA SPRING

BERKLEY BOOKS, NEW YORK

This Berkley book contains the complete
text of the original hardcover edition.

HELLICONIA SPRING

A Berkley Book / published by arrangement with
Atheneum Publishers

PRINTING HISTORY
Atheneum edition published 1982
Berkley trade paperback edition / November 1983

ISBN: 0-425-06186-8

A BERKLEY BOOK ® TM 757,375
Berkley Books are published by The Berkley Publishing Group,
200 Madison Avenue, New York, New York 10016.
The name "BERKLEY" and the stylized "B" with design
are trademarks belonging to Berkley Publishing Corporation.

PRINTED IN THE UNITED STATES OF AMERICA

My dear Clive,

In my previous novel LIFE IN THE WEST, I sought to depict something of the malaise sweeping the world, painting as wide a canvas as I felt I could confidently tackle.

My partial success left me ambitious and dissatisfied. I resolved to start again. All art is a metaphor, but some art forms are more metaphorical than others; perhaps, I thought, I would do better with a more oblique approach. So I developed Helliconia: a place much like our world, with only one factor changed—the length of the year. It was to be a stage for the kind of drama in which we are embroiled in our century.

In order to achieve some verisimilitude, I consulted experts, who convinced me that my little Helliconia was mere fantasy; I needed something much more solid.

Invention took over from allegory. A good thing, too. With the prompting of scientific fact, whole related series of new images crowded into my conscious mind. I have deployed them as best I could. When I was farthest away from my original conception—at the apastron of my earliest intentions—I discovered that I was expressing dualities that were as relevant to our century as to Helliconia's.

It could hardly be otherwise. For the people of Helliconia, and the non-people, the beasts, and other personages, interest us only if they mirror our concerns. No one wants a passport to a nation of talking slugs.

So I offer you this volume for your enjoyment, hoping you will find more to agree with than you did in LIFE IN THE WEST—and maybe even more to amuse you.

Your affectionate
Father

Begbroke
Oxford

CONTENTS

Why have so many heroic deeds recurrently dropped out of mind and found no shrine in lasting monuments of fame? The answer, I believe, is that *this world is newly made*; its origin is a recent event, not one of remote antiquity.

That is why even now some arts are still being perfected: the process of development is still going on. Yes, and it is not long since the truth about nature was first discovered, and I myself am even now the first who has been found to render this revelation into my native speech. . . .

Lucretius: *De Rerum Natura*
55 BC

PRELUDE:
Yuli

This is how Yuli, son of Alehaw, came to a place called Oldorando, where his descendants flourished in the better days that were to come.

Yuli was seven years old, virtually a grown man, when he crouched under a skin bivouac with his father and gazed down the wilderness of a land known even at that time as Campannlat. He had roused from a light doze with his father's elbow in his rib and his harsh voice saying, "Storm's dying."

The storm had been blowing from the west for three days, bringing with it snow and particles of ice off the Barriers. It filled the world with howling energy, transforming it to a grey-white darkness, like a great voice that no man could withstand. The ledge on which the bivouac was pitched afforded little protection from the worst of the blast; father and son could do nothing but lie where they were under the skin, dozing, once in a while chewing on a piece of smoked fish, while the weather battered away above their heads.

As the wind expired, the snow arrived in spurts, twitching in feather-like flurries across the drab landscape. Although Freyr was high in the sky—for the hunters were within the tropics—it seemed to hang there frozen. The lights rippled overhead in shawl after golden shawl, the fringes of which seemed to touch the ground, while the folds rose up and up until they vanished in the leaden zenith of heaven. The lights gave little illumination, no warmth.

Both father and son rose by instinct, stretching, stamping their feet, throwing their arms violently about the massive barrels of their bodies. Neither spoke. There was nothing to say. The storm was over. Still they had to wait. Soon, they knew, the yelk would be here. Not for much longer would they have to maintain their vigil.

Although the ground was broken, it was without feature, being covered with ice and snow. Behind the two men was higher ground, also covered with the mat of whiteness. Only to the north was there a dark grim greyness, where the sky came down like a bruised arm to meet the sea. The eyes of the men, however, were fixed continually on the east. After a period of stamping and slapping, when the air about them filled with the foggy vapour of their breath, they settled down again under the skins to wait.

Alehaw arranged himself with one befurred elbow on the rock, so that he could tuck his thumb deep into the hollow of his left cheek, propping the weight of his skull on his zygomatic bone and shielding his eyes with four curled gloved fingers.

His son waited with less patience. He squirmed inside his stitched skins. Neither he nor his father was born to this kind of hunting. Hunting bear in the Barriers was their way of life, and their fathers' before them. But intense cold, exhaled from the high hard hurricane mouths of the Barriers had driven them, together with the sick Onesa, down to the gentler weather of the plains. So Yuli was uneasy and excited.

His ailing mother and his sister, together with his mother's family, were some miles distant, the uncles venturing hopefully towards the frozen sea, with the sledge and their ivory spears. Yuli wondered how they had fared in the days-long storm, if they were feasting even now, cooking fish or hunks of seal meat in his mother's bronze pot. He dreamed of the scent of meat in his mouth, the rough feel of it meshed in saliva as it was gulped down, the flavour. . . . Something in his hollow belly went *whang* at the thought.

"There, see!" His father's elbow jabbed his biceps.

A high iron-coloured front of cloud rose rapidly in the sky, dimming Freyr, spilling shade across the landscape. Everything was a blur of white, without definition. Below the bluff on which they lay stretched a great frozen river—the Vark, Yuli had heard it called. So thickly covered in snow was it that nobody could tell it was a river, except by walking across it. Up to their knees in powdery drift, they had heard a faint ringing beneath their heels; Alehaw had paused, putting the sharp end of his spear to the ice and the blunt end to his ear, and listened to the dark flow of water somewhere beneath their feet. The far bank of the Vark was vaguely marked by mounds, broken here and there by patches of black, where fallen trees lay half-concealed by snow. Beyond that, only the weary plain, on and on, until a line of brown could be made out under the sullen shawls of the far eastern sky.

Blinking his eyes, Yuli stared at the line and stared again. Of course his father was right. His father knew everything. His heart swelled with pride to think that he was Yuli, son of Alehaw. The yelk were coming.

In a few minutes, the leading animals could be discerned, travelling solidly on a wide front, advancing with a bow wave preceding them, where their elegant hoofs kicked up snow. They progressed with their heads down, and behind them came more of their kind, and more, without end. It appeared to Yuli that they had seen him and his father and were advancing directly upon them. He glanced anxiously at Alehaw, who gestured caution with one finger.

"Wait."

Yuli shivered inside his bearskins. Food was approaching, enough food to feed every single person of every tribe upon whom Freyr and Batalix ever shone, or Wutra smiled.

As the animals drew nearer, approaching steadily at something like a man's fast walking pace, he tried to comprehend what an enormous herd it was. By now, half of the landscape was filled with moving animals, with the white-and-tan texture of their hides, while more beasts were appearing over from the eastern horizon. Who knew what lay that way, what mysteries, what terrors? Yet nothing could be worse than the Barriers, with its searing cold, and that great red mouth Yuli had once glimpsed through the scudding wrack of cloud, belching out lava down the smoking hillside. . . .

Now it was possible to see that the living mass of animals did not consist solely of yelk, although they made up the greater part. In the midst of the herd were knots of a larger animal, standing out like clumps of boulders on a moving plain. This larger animal resembled a yelk, with the same long skull about which elegant horns curled protectively on either side, the same shaggy mane overlying a thick matted coat, the same hump on its back, situated towards its rump. But these animals stood half as tall again as the yelk which hemmed them in. They were the giant biyelk, formidable animals capable of carrying two men on their backs at the same time—so one of Yuli's uncles had told him.

And a third animal associated itself with the herd. It was a gunnadu, and Yuli saw its neck raised everywhere along the sides of the herd. As the mass of yelk moved indifferently forward, the gunnadu ran excitedly to either flank, their small heads bobbing on the end of their long necks. Their most remarkable feature, a pair of gigantic ears, turned hither and thither, listening for unexpected alarms. This was the first two-legged animal Yuli had seen; below its long-haired body, two immense pistonlike legs propelled it. The gunnadu moved at twice the speed of the yelk and biyelk, covering twice as much ground, yet each animal remained where it was in relation to the herd.

A heavy dull continuous thunder marked the approach of the herd. From where Yuli lay against his father, the three species of animal could be distinguished only because he knew what to look for. They all merged with one another in the heavy mottled light. The black cloud-front had advanced more rapidly than the herd, and now covered Batalix entirely: that brave sentinel would not be seen again for days. A rumpled carpet of animals rolled across the land, its individual movements no more distinguishable than currents in a turbulent river.

Mist hung over the animals, further shrouding them. It comprised sweat, heat, and small winged biting insects able to procreate only in the heat from the burly-hoofed flock.

Breathing faster, Yuli looked again and—behold!—the creatures in the forefront were already confronting the banks of the snowbound Vark. They were near, they were coming nearer—the world was one inescapable teeming animal. He flicked his head to look in appeal at his father. Although he saw his son's gesture, Alehaw remained rigidly staring ahead, teeth gritted, eyes clenched against the cold under his heavy eye ridges.

"Still," he commanded.

The tide of life surged along the riverbanks, flowed over, cascaded over the hidden ice. Some creatures, lumbering adults, skipping fauns, fell against concealed tree trunks, dainty legs kicking furiously before they were trampled under the pressure of the march.

Individual animals could now be picked out. They carried their heads low. Their eyes were staring, white-rimmed. Thick green trails of saliva hung from many a mouth. The cold froze the steam from their upthrust nostrils, streaking ice across the fur of their skulls. Most beasts laboured, in poor condition, their coats covered with mud, excrement, and blood, or hanging loose in strips, where a neighbour's horns had stabbed and torn them.

The biyelks in particular, striding surrounded by their lesser brethren, their shoulders enormous with grey-bunched fur, walked with a kind of controlled unease, their eyes rolling as they heard the squeals of those who fell, and understood that some kind of danger, towards which they were inevitably to progress, threatened ahead.

The mass of animals was crossing the frozen river, churning snow. Their noise came plain to the two watchers, not solely the sound of their hoofs but the rasp of their breath, and a continued chorus of grunts, snorts, and coughs, a click of horn against horn, the sharp rattle of ears being shaken to dislodge ever persistent flies.

Three biyelks stepped forth together on the frozen river. With sharp resounding cracks, the ice broke. Shards of it almost a metre thick reared up into view as the heavy animals fell forward. Panic seized the yelk. Those on the ice attempted to scatter in all directions. Many stumbled and were lost under more animals. The cracking spread. Water, grey and fierce, jetted into the air—fast and cold, the river was still flowing. It rushed and broke and foamed, as if glad to be free, and the animals went down into it with their mouths open, bellowing.

Nothing deterred the oncoming animals. They were as much a natural force as the river. They flowed ever on, obliterating their companions who stumbled, obliterating too the sharp wounds opened in the Vark, bridging it with tumbled bodies, until they surged up the near bank.

Now Yuli raised himself on to his knees and lifted his ivory spear, his eyes blazing. His father seized his arm and dragged him down.

"See, phagors, you fool," he said, giving his son a furious, contemptuous glare, and stabbing ahead with his spear to indicate danger.

Shaken, Yuli sank down again, as much frightened of his father's wrath as by the thought of phagors.

The yelk herd pressed about their outcrop of rock, lurching by on either side of its crumbling base. The cloud of flies and stinging things that sang about their twitching backs now enveloped Yuli and Alehaw, and it was through this veil that Yuli stared, trying to get a sight of phagors. At first he discerned none.

Nothing was to be seen ahead but the avalanche of shaggy life, driven by compulsions no man understood. It covered the frozen river, it covered the banks, it covered the grey world back to the far horizon, where it tucked itself under the dun clouds like a rug under a pillow. Hundreds of thousands of animals were involved, and the midges hung above them in a continuous black exhalation.

Alehaw dragged his son down and indicated a spot to their left with one shaggy eyebrow. Half-hidden beneath the skin that served as their bivouac, Yuli stared at the advance. Two giant biyelks were lumbering towards their coign of vantage. Their massive white-furred shoulders were almost on a level with the ledge. As Yuli blew the midges away from before his eyes, the white fur resolved itself into phagors. Four of them, two riding on each biyelk, clung tight to the hair of their mounts.

He wondered how he had missed sighting them before. Though they merged with their giant steeds, they exhibited the presence of all who ride while others travel on foot. They clustered on top of the biyelks' shoulders, directing their moody bull faces ahead towards the higher ground where the herd would stop and graze. Their eyes glared out under upward-curving horns. Every now and again, one would shoot out his white milt, curving it up the slot of his powerful nostrils, to remove plaguing midges.

Their clumsy heads pivoted above the bulk of their bodies, which were completely covered with long white hair. The creatures were all white, except for their pink-scarlet eyes. They rode the striding biyelks as if they were part of them. Behind them, a crude leather carrier holding clubs and weapons swung to and fro.

Now that Yuli was alert to the nature of the danger, he discerned other phagors. Only the privileged rode. The rank and file of their nation went on foot, proceeding at a walking pace matching that of the animals. As he watched, so tense he dared not even brush the flies from his eyelids, Yuli saw a group of four phagors pass within a few metres of where he and his father lay. He would have had no difficulty in spearing the leader between the shoulder blades, had Alehaw given the command.

Yuli looked with particular interest at the horns that passed him, two by two. Smooth though they appeared in the dull light, the inner and outer edges of each horn were sharp from base to tip.

He coveted one of those horns. Horns of dead phagors were used as weapons in the savage recesses of the Barriers. It was for their horns that learned men in distant towns—couched in dens remote from storm—referred to phagors as the ancipital race: the species with two sharp edges.

The leading ancipital strode along dauntlessly. Lack of an ordinary knee joint made his an unnatural-looking stride. He marched mechanically as he must have done for miles. Distance was no obstacle.

His long skull was thrust forward in typical phagor fashion, low between his shoulders. On either arm he wore hide straps, to which were attached outward-pointing horns, their extremities tipped with metal. With these, the creature could prod away any animal that walked too close to him. Otherwise, he was unarmed; but to a nearby yelk, a bundle of possessions had been tied, a bundle including spears and a hunting harpoon. Adjacent animals also involuntarily carried baggage belonging to the other phagors in the group.

Behind the leader were two more males—so Yuli assumed—followed by a female phagor. She was of slighter build, and carried some kind of bag tied round her middle. Under her long white hair, pinkish dugs swung. On her shoulders rode an infant phagor, clutching uncomfortably at its mother's neck fur, its head clamped down on her head. Its eyes were closed. The female walked automatically, as though in a daze. It was a matter for conjecture for how many days she and the others had been walking, or how far.

And there were other phagors, spread thinly round the outskirts of the moving concourse. The animals took no notice of them, accepting them as they accepted the flies, because there was no alternative to acceptance.

The noise of the drumming hoofs was punctuated by laboured breathing and coughing and breaking wind. Another sound rose. The phagor who led the small group was emitting a kind of hum or growl, a rough noise delivered over a vibrating tongue which varied in pitch; perhaps it was intended to cheer the three who followed. The sound terrified Yuli. Then it was gone, and the phagors too. More animals streamed by and eventually more phagors, continuing stanchlessly. Yuli and his father lay where they were, occasionally spitting flies from their mouths, waiting for the time to strike and win the meat they desperately needed.

Before sunset, the wind got up again, blowing as before off the ice-caps of the Barriers, into the faces of the migratory army. The attendant phagors marched with their heads down, eyes slitted, and long trails of saliva fanned from the corners of their mouths and froze across their chests, as fat freezes when thrown out on the ice.

The atmosphere was iron. Wutra, god of the skies, had withdrawn his shawls of light and shrouded his domain with overcast. Perhaps another battle had been lost to him.

From under this dark curtain, Freyr became visible only when it reached the horizon. Blankets of cloud rumpled back to reveal the sentinel smouldering in a perspective of golden ashes. It shone out with spirit over the wastes—small but bright, its disc no more than a third as large as that of its companion star, Batalix, yet Freyr's light was greater, fiercer.

It sank into the eddre of the ground and was gone.

Now was the time of dimday, which prevailed in summer and autumn, and which almost alone distinguished those seasons from even less merciful times. Dimday suffused a dazed half-light across the night sky. Only at times of New Year would Batalix and Freyr rise and set together. At present their lives were solitary, hidden frequently behind cloud which was the billowing smoke from Wutra's war.

In the manner of day's turning to dimday, Yuli read the weather omens. Driving winds would soon be conjured up with snow on their breath. He recalled the rhyme they chanted in Old Olonets, the tongue of magic, of past things, of red ruin, the tongue of catastrophe, fair women, giants, and rich food, the tongue of an inaccessible yesterday. The rhyme had been recalled in the croupy caves of the Barriers:

> Wutra in sorrow
> Will put Freyr to barrow
> And us to the billow

As if responding to the changing light, a general shudder passed across the mass of yelk, and they stopped. Groaning, they settled where they were upon the trampled ground, tucking their legs beneath their bodies. For the enormous biyelk, this manoeuvre was not possible. They stood where they were and slept, ears across eyes. Some of the phagor groups gathered themselves together for companionship; most simply flung themselves down indifferently and slept where they fell, jamming their backs against the flanks of supine yelk.

Everything slept. The two figures sprawled on the rock ledge dragged their sheltering skin over their heads and dreamed, empty-bellied, with their faces buried in their folded arms. Everything slept, except for the mist of biting and sucking insects.

Things that were capable of dreams struggled through the uneasy mirages that dimday brought with it.

In general, the view, with its lack of shadow and constant level of suffering, might have appeared to anyone scrutinising it for the first time to represent not so much a world as a place awaiting formal creation.

At this stage of quiescence, there was a motion in the sky hardly more energetic than the unfolding of the aurora which had hung above the scene earlier. From the direction of the sea came a solitary childrim, sailing through the air some metres above the prostrate mass of living things. It looked to be no more than a great wing, glowing red like the embers of a dying fire, beating with a steady lethargy. As it passed over the deer, the animals twitched and heaved. It skimmed over the rock where the two humans lay, and Yuli and his father twitched and heaved, like the yelk seeing strange visions in their sleep. Then the apparition was gone, heading on lonely for the mountains in the south, leaving behind it a trail of red sparks to die in the atmosphere like an echo of itself.

After a while, the animals woke and rose to their feet. They shook their ears, which bled from the attentions of the gnats, and again started forward. With them went the biyelks and gunnadus, scuttling here and there. With them too went the phagors. The two humans roused, and watched them go.

Throughout another day the great progress continued, and blizzards raged, plastering the animals with snow. Towards evening, when wind was blowing tattered cloud across the sky and the cold held a whistling edge, Alehaw sighted the rear of the herd.

The rear was not as tight as the vanguard had been. Stragglers from the herd trailed back several miles, some limping, some coughing pitifully. Behind and beside them scurried long furry things with bellies near the ground, waiting the chance to nip a fetlock and bring a victim crashing down.

The last of the phagors marched past the ledge. They did not walk at the rear, either from respect for the low-bellied carnivores or because the going was difficult over such trampled ground, piled with scumble.

And now Alehaw rose, motioning his son to do likewise. They stood, clutching their weapons, and then slithered down to level ground.

"Good!" said Alehaw.

The snow was strewn with dead animals, in particular round the banks of the Vark. The break in the ice was plugged with drowned bodies. Many of those creatures who had been forced to lie down where they stood had frozen to death as they rested, and were now turned to ice. The lumps of which they composed the red core were unrecognisable in shape after the blizzard.

Delighted to be able to move, young Yuli ran and jumped and cried aloud. Dashing to the frozen river, he skipped dangerously from one unidentifiable lump to another, waving his hands and laughing. His father called him sharply to heel.

Alehaw pointed down through the ice. Black shapes moved, obscurely seen, partly defined by trails of bubbles. They streaked the turbid medium in which they swam with crimson, boring up beneath the frozen layers to attack the banquet provided for their benefit.

Other predators were arriving by air, large white fowl coming in from the east and the sullen north, fluttering heavily down, brandishing ornate beaks with which they bored through the ice to the flesh underneath. As they devoured, they fixed on the hunter and his son eyes heavy with avian calculation.

But Alehaw wasted no time on them. Directing Yuli to follow, he moved to where the herd had stumbled across fallen trees, calling and waving his spear as he went, to frighten off predators. Here dead animals were readily accessible. Although badly trampled, they still preserved one part of their anatomies intact, their skulls. It was to these that Alehaw addressed his attention. He prized open the dead jaws with the blade of a knife, and adroitly cut out their thick tongues. Blood spilled over his wrists onto the snow.

Meanwhile, Yuli climbed among the tree trunks, collecting broken wood. He kicked the snow away from one fallen trunk, contriving a sheltered place in which he could make a small fire. Wrapping his bowstring round a pointed stick, he rubbed it to and fro. The crumbled wood smouldered. He blew gently. A tiny flame sprang up, as he had seen it do often under the magical breath of Onesa. When the fire was burning well, he set his bronze pot on it, and piled snow in to melt, adding salt from a leather pocket he carried in his furs. He was ready when his father brought seven slimy tongues in his arms, and slipped them into the pot.

Four of the tongues were for Alehaw, three for Yuli. They ate with grunts of satisfaction; Yuli trying to catch his father's eye and smile, to show satisfaction; but Alehaw kept his brows knit as he chewed, and his gaze down at the trampled ground.

There was work still to be done. Even before they had finished eating, Alehaw got to his feet and kicked the smouldering embers aside. The scavenger birds nearby rose momentarily, and then settled again to their feast. Yuli emptied the bronze pot and secured it to his belt.

They were almost at the place where the great herd of animals reached the western limit of its migration. Here, on higher ground, they would seek out lichen under the snow, and graze on the strands of shaggy green moss that wrapped the larch forests about. Here, too, on a low plateau, some of the animals would reach their due term and bring forth their young. It was to this plateau, no more than a mile off, that Alehaw and his son made their way through the grey daylight. In the distance, they saw groups of other hunters, heading in the same direction; each group deliberately ignored the others. No other group consisted of two people only, Yuli noted; that was the penalty his family paid for being not of the plain, but of the Barrier. For them, everything was more arduous.

They walked bent double, up the incline. The way was strewn with boulders, where an ancient sea had once withdrawn in the face of encroaching cold—but of that aspect of affairs they knew and cared nothing; only the present was of importance to Alehaw and his son.

On the lip of the plateau they stood, shielding their eyes against biting cold in order to peer forward. Most of the herd had disappeared. All that remained of its still active numbers were occasional swarms of flying insects and the pungent smell. It had left behind on the plateau those of its members who were propagating.

Among these fated individuals were not only yelk but the flimsier gunnadu and the bulky bodies of giant biyelk. They lay inert, covering a wide area, dead or almost dead, sometimes with sides heaving. Another party of hunters was moving closer among the dying animals. Grunting, Alehaw gestured to one side, and he and Yuli moved over in the direction of a broken cluster of pines, near which a few yelk lay. Yuli stood over one to watch his father kill the helpless beast, already labouring its way into the grey world of eternity.

Like its monstrous cousin, the biyelk, and the gunnadu, the yelk was a necrogene, giving birth only through its death. The animals were hermaphrodite, sometimes male, sometimes female. They were too crudely designed to have within them the apparatus of mammals such as ovaries and wombs. After mating, the spurted sperm developed within the warm interior into small maggotlike forms, which grew as they devoured the stomach of their maternal host.

A time came when the maggot-yelk reached a main artery. It could then spread in its numbers like seed in the wind throughout the host animal, causing death within a short while. This event occurred unfailingly when the great herds reached the plateau at the western limit of their range. So it had done throughout ages that no one could count.

Even while Alehaw and Yuli stood over the beast, its stomach collapsed like an old bag. It threw up its head and died. Alehaw plunged in his spear, in ceremonial fashion. Both men dropped to their knees in the snow, and with their daggers ripped up the belly of the animal.

The maggot-yelk were within, no bigger than a fingernail—almost too small to see but collectively delicious to taste, and highly nourishing. They would help Onesa in her illness. They died on exposure to the freezing air.

Left to themselves, the maggot-yelk would live in safety inside the skins of their hosts. Within their little dark universe, they would not hesitate to devour each other, and many were the bloody battles fought in aorta and mesenteric arteries. The survivors grew through successive metamorphoses, increasing in size as they decreased in numbers. At length, two or possibly three small rapid-moving yelks would emerge from throat or anus, to face the starveling world outside. And this emergence would be achieved just in time to avoid death by trampling, as the herds moved slowly into position on the plateau for their return migration northeastwards towards far Chalce.

Dotted over the plateau, among the animals simultaneously procreating and dying, stood thick stone pillars. The pillars had been set there by an earlier race of men. On each pillar was carved a simple device: a circle or a wheel with a smaller circle at its centre. From the centre circle, two opposed curved spokes radiated to the outer one. Nobody present on the sea-sculpted plateau, animal or hunter, attended to these decorated pillars in the least degree.

Yuli was engrossed with their catch. He tore off strips of hide, weaving them crudely into a bag, into which he scraped the dying maggot-yelk. Meanwhile his father was dissecting the carcass. Every bit of the dead body could be utilised. From the longest bones, a sledge would be built, lashed together with strips of hide. Horns would serve as runners, to ease their having to pull the sledge all the way home. For by then the little carriage would be loaded high with good solid joints of shoulder and rib and rump, covered over with the rest of the skin.

Both worked together, grunting with effort, their hands red, breath in a cloud above their heads where midges gathered unnoticed.

Suddenly, Alehaw gave a terrible cry, fell backwards, tried to run.

Yuli looked round in dismay. Three great white phagors had crept from a place of concealment among the pines, and stood over them. Two sprang on Alehaw as he got up, and clubbed him to the snow. The other struck out at Yuli. He rolled aside, yelling.

They had completely forgotten about the dangers of phagors, and had neglected to keep any watch. As he rolled and sprang and avoided the swinging club, Yuli saw the other hunters nearby, working calmly on the dying yelk just as he and his father had been doing. So determined were they to get on with the work, to build their sledges and be off—so near was starvation—that they continued about their business, glancing up at the fight only now and again. The story would have been different had they been kin of Alehaw and Yuli. But these were plainsmen, squat unfriendly men. Yuli yelled to them for help, without avail. One man nearby hurled a bloody bone at the phagors. That was all.

Dodging the swinging cudgel, Yuli started to run, slipped, and fell. Up thundered the phagor. Yuli fell into an instinctive defensive pose, resting on one knee. As the phagor dived at him, he brought up his dagger in an underarm movement and sank it into the broad gut of his attacker. He watched with shocked amazement his arm disappear into stringy stiff pelage and that coat immediately belch into thick gold gore gushing everywhere. Then the body smote him, and he went rolling —rolling then by volition, rolling out of harm's way, rolling into what shelter offered itself, rolling panting behind an upthrust shoulder of dead yelk, from where he looked out on a world suddenly turned enemy.

His assailant had fallen. Now he picked himself up, nursing that golden patch in his gut with enormous horned paws, and staggering mindlessly, crying "Aoh, aoh, aohhh, aohhhh. . . ." He fell head first and did not move again.

Behind the fallen body, Alehaw had been beaten to the ground. He lay crumpled, but the two phagors immediately seized him and one of them arranged him over his shoulders. The pair looked about, stared back at their fallen comrade, glanced at each other, grunted, turned their backs on Yuli, and began to march away.

Yuli stood up. He found his legs, bound inside his fur trousers, were shaking. He had no idea what to do. Distractedly, he skirted the body of the phagor he had killed—how he would boast of that to his mother and uncles—and ran back to the scene of the scuffle. He picked up his spear and then, after some hesitation, took his father's spear as well. Then he set off to follow the phagors.

They were trudging ahead, making heavy weather of getting uphill with their burden. They soon sensed the boy following them, and turned now and again, halfheartedly trying to drive him off with threats and gestures. Evidently they did not think him worth expending a spear on.

When Alehaw recovered consciousness, the two phagors stopped, set him on his feet, and made him walk between them, encouraging him with blows. Uttering a series of whistles, Yuli let his father know that he was nearby; but whenever the older man ventured to look over his shoulder, he received a clout from one of the phagors that sent him reeling.

The phagors slowly caught up with another party of their own kind, consisting of a female and two males; one of the latter was old and walked with a stick as tall as himself, on which he leaned heavily in his progress uphill. Every now and again, he stumbled in the piles of yelk droppings.

Eventually, the scatters of scumble appeared no more, and the smell died from their nostrils. They were moving along an upward path the migratory herd had not taken. The winds had dropped, and spruce trees grew on the slope. There were now several knots of phagors climbing up the hillside, many of them bowed beneath carcasses of yelk. And behind them trailed a nine-year-old human being, fear in his heart, trying to keep his father in sight.

The air grew thick and heavy, as if under enchantment. The pace was slower, the larches closer, and the phagors were forced to bunch more closely. Their rough song, scraped across their horny tongues, sounded loudly, a hum that on occasions rose to a scalding crescendo and then died again. Yuli was terrified, and fell further behind, darting from tree to tree.

He could not understand why Alehaw did not break from his captors and run back downhill; then he could grasp his spear again, and together the two of them would stand side by side and kill all the shaggy phagors. Instead, his father remained captive, and now his slighter figure was lost among the crowding figures in the twilight under the trees.

The humming song rose harshly and died. A smokey greenish light glowed ahead, promising a new crisis. Yuli sneaked forward, running doubled up to the next tree. Some kind of building stood ahead, fronted by a double gate, which opened slightly. Within, the faint fire showed. The phagors were shouting, and the gate opened more. They began to crowd in. The light was revealed as a brand, which one of their kind held aloft.

"Father, Father!" screamed Yuli. "Run, Father! I'm here."

There was no answer. In the murk, which the torch further confused, it was impossible to see whether or not Alehaw had already been pushed inside the gate. One or two phagors turned indifferently at the shouts, and shooed Yuli away without animosity.

"Go and zzhout at the wind!" one cried in Olonets. They wanted only full-grown human slaves.

The last burly figure entered the building. Amid more shouting, the gates closed. Yuli ran to them crying, banging against their rough wood as he heard a bolt being shot home on the other side. He stood there for a long while with his forehead against the grain, unable to accept what had happened.

The gates were set in a stone fortification, the blocks of which were crudely fitted into each other and patched with long-tailed mosses. The edifice was no more than an entrance to one of the underground caves in which the phagors, as Yuli knew, had their existence. They were indolent creatures, and preferred to have humans working for them.

For a while, he ranged round about the gate, climbing up the steep hillside, until he found what he expected to find. It was a chimney, three times his height and of impressive circumference. He could climb it with ease, because it tapered towards the top and because the blocks of stone of which it was made were crudely set together, allowing plenty of foothold. The stones were not as freezingly cold as might have been expected, and free of frost.

At the top, he incautiously stuck his face over the lip, and was immediately jerked backwards, so that he lost his hold and fell, landing on his right shoulder and rolling in the snow.

A blast of hot, foetid air, mixed with wood smoke and stale exhalation, had erupted at him. The chimney was a ventilator for the phagor warrens below ground. He knew he could not climb in that way. He was shut out, and his father was lost to him forever.

He sat miserably in the snow. His feet were covered by skins, laced in place up the legs. He wore a pair of trousers and a tunic of bear fur, stitched in place by his mother with the fur next to his skin. For additional warmth, he had on a parka with a fur hood. Onesa, during a period when she was feeling well enough, had decorated the parka with white scuts of an ice rabbit round the shoulders, three scuts to each shoulder, and had embroidered the neck with red and blue beads. Despite which, Yuli presented a forlorn sight, for the parka was stained with the remains of food and fat drippings, while dirt caked the fur of his garments; they smelt strongly of Yuli. His face, a light yellow or beige when clean, was wrinkled brown and black with dirt, and his hair straggled greasily about his temples and collar. He had a flat-nostrilled nose, which he began to rub, and a broad, sensuous mouth, which began to pucker, revealing a broken front tooth among its white neighbours, as he started to cry and punch the snow.

After a while, he rose and walked about among the forlorn larches, trailing his father's spear behind him. He had no alternative but to retrace his steps and try to return to his sick mother, if he could find his way back through the snowy wastes.

He realised also that he was hungry.

Desperately forsaken, he started a hullabaloo at the closed gates. There was no kind of response. Snow began to fall, slowly but without cease. He stood with fists raised above his head. He spat, the gob landing on the panels. That for his father. He hated the man for being a weakling. He recalled all the beatings he had received from his father's hand— why had his father not beaten the phagors?

At last, he turned away through the falling snow in disgust, and began to walk downhill.

He flung his father's spear away into a bush.

Hunger battled with fatigue and got him back as far as the Vark. His hopes were immediately dashed. None of the dead yelk remained undevoured. Predators had arrived from every corner and torn away their meat. Only carcasses and piles of bare bones by the river awaited him.

He howled in wrath and dismay.

The river had frozen over and snow lay on the solid ice. He scraped the snow away with his foot and stared down. The bodies of some of the drowned animals still remained in the ice; he saw one where the head of the yelk hung down into the dark current below. Large fish ate at its eyes.

Working strenuously with his spear and a sharp horn, Yuli bored a hole in the ice, enlarged it, and waited, standing above it with spear poised. Fins flashed in the water. He struck. A blue-flecked fish, its mouth open in amazement, shone at the spearpoint as he pulled it forth dripping. It was as long as his two hands outstretched and placed thumb to thumb. He roasted it over a small fire and it tasted delicious. He belched, and slept for an hour, propped between logs. Then he started to trek southwards, along a trail the migration had all but obliterated.

Freyr and Batalix changed sentry duty in the sky, and still he walked, the only figure moving in the wilderness.

"Mother," cried old Hasele to his wife, before he even got back to his hut, "Mother, see what I found by the Three Harlequins."

And his ancient crone of a wife, Lorel, lame since childhood, hobbled to the door, stuck her nose out in the biting cold air, and said, "Never mind what you found. There's gentlemen from Pannoval waiting to do business with thee."

"Pannoval, eh? Wait till they see what I found by the Three Harlequins. I need help here, mother. Come, it's not cold. You waste your life stuck in that house."

The house was rude in every extreme. It consisted of piles of boulders, several of them taller than a man, interspersed with planks and timbers, and roofed over with hides on top of which turfs grew. The interstices of the boulders were stuffed with lichen and mud, to make the interior windproof, while spars and whole tree trunks propped the edifice at many points, so that the whole affair most resembled a defunct porcupine. To the main structure, additional rooms had been added in the same spirit of improvisation which had prompted the original. Bronze chimneys thrust up into the sour sky, smoking gently; in some rooms, pelts and hides were dried, in others sold. Hasele was a trader and trapper, and had made enough of a living so that now, towards the end of his life, he could afford a wife and a sledge pulled by three dogs.

Hasele's house perched on a low escarpment which curved away eastwards for several miles. This escarpment was strewn with boulders, in some places split, in others piled one on top of the other. These boulders provided shelter for small animals, and so made good hunting grounds for the old trapper, who was no longer inclined to wander as far afield as he had done in the days of his youth. On some of the more monumental piles of stone, he had bestowed names, the Three Harlequins being one. At the Three Harlequins, he dug in salt deposits for the mineral he needed to cure his hides.

Smaller stones littered the escarpment, each subtending from its eastern side a raked cone of snow, its size varying according to the nature of the stone, pointing precisely away from the point from which the west wind whistled off the distant Barriers. This had once been a beach, belonging to a long-vanished sea coast, the north coast of the continent of Campannlat, when times had been more favourable.

To the eastern side of the Three Harlequins grew a little thicket of thorn bushes, taking advantage of the shelter of the granite to thrust forth an occasional green leaf. Old Hasele valued these green leaves in his pot, and set snares all round the bushes in order to keep off animals. Unconscious and entangled in the sharp twigs lay the youth he had discovered, whom he now dragged with Lorel's aid into the smokey sanctuary of his hut.

"He's no savage," said Lorel admiringly. "See here how his parka is decorated with beads, red and blue. Pretty, ain't they?"

"Never mind that. Give him a mouthful of soup, mother."

She did so, stroking the lad's throat until the soup went down, when her patient stirred, coughed, sat up, and whispered for more. As Lorel fed him she looked down, pursing her lips, at the swollen cheeks and eyes and ears, where countless insect bites had caused blood to flow and mat beneath his collar. He took more soup, then groaned and slumped back again into a coma. She held him to her, putting an arm round him, under his armpit, rocking him, remembering ancient happinesses to which she could no longer give a name.

Guiltily looking round for Hasele, she found he had padded off already, eager to do business with the gentlemen from Pannoval.

She laid the youth's dark head down, sighing, and followed her husband. He was sipping spirits with the two large-built traders. Their parkas steamed in the warmth. Lorel tugged at Hasele's sleeve.

"Maybe these two gentlemen will take this sick youth you've found back with them to Pannoval. We can't feed him here. We're starving as it is. Pannoval is fat and rich."

"Leave us, mother. We're negotiating," Hasele said, in a lordly way.

She hobbled out the back of the building, and watched as their captive phagor, shuffling under his chains, secured their dogs in the snow kennel. She looked beyond that bowed back to the gritty grey landscape to the miles of desolation that faded into a desolate sky. From somewhere out in that wilderness, the youth had come. Perhaps once or twice a year, people, alone or in pairs, straggled dying from the ice deserts. Lorel could never gain any clear impression of where they came from, only that beyond the desert were mountains colder still. One fugitive had babbled of a frozen sea that could be crossed. She made the holy circle over her dry breasts.

In her younger days, it had teased to have no clearer picture. Then she had gone wrapped to stand on the escarpment and stare northwards. And childrims flew overhead, waving their solitary wings, and she had fallen to her knees with a dazed impression of men—massed and holy, rowing the great flat wheel of the world to some place where the snow did not always fall or the wind always blow. She went indoors crying, hating the hope the childrims brought her.

Though old Hasele had dismissed his wife in a lordly way, he took note of what she said, as he always did. When his deal with the two gentlemen from Pannoval was concluded, and a small pile of precious herbs and spices and wool fibres and flour balanced against the skins the men would load on their sledge, Hasele raised the question of their taking the sick youth with them back to civilization. He mentioned that the youth wore a good decorated parka, and therefore—just possibly, gentlemen—might be someone of importance, or at least the son of someone important.

Rather to his surprise, the two gentlemen agreed that they would be very happy to take the youth with them. They would have to make a small charge of an extra yelk skin, to cover the youth and defray the extra expense. Hasele muttered a bit, and then gave in with a good grace; he could not afford to feed the boy if he lived and, if he died— it never pleased him to feed human remains to his dogs, and the native habit of mummification and aerial burial was not his way.

"Done," he said, and went to fetch the least good skin he could quickly lay his hands on.

The youth was awake now. He had accepted more soup from Lorel, and a warmed leg of snow rabbit. When he heard the men coming, he lay back and closed his eyes, one hand tucked inside his parka.

They surveyed him only casually, then turned away. Their plan was to load the sledge with their acquisitions, spend some hours here being entertained by Hasele and his wife, getting drunk, sleeping it off, and then set out on the challenging journey south to Pannoval.

All this was done, and a fine noise was made as Hasele's spirits were consumed. Even when the gentlemen slept on a pile of skins, their snores were loud. And Lorel secretively tended Yuli, feeding him, bathing his face, smoothing his thick hair, hugging him.

In early dimday, when Batalix was low, he was gone from her, still feigning unconsciousness as the gentlemen lifted him on to their sledge, cracked their whips, scowled to achieve some fortification between their hangovers and the brow-clamping cold, and were off.

The two gentlemen, whose lives were hard, robbed Hasele and any other trapper they visited to the maximum extent that the trappers allowed themselves to be robbed, knowing as they did so that they would themselves be robbed and cheated when, in their turn, they had to trade in the skins. Cheating was one of their methods of survival, like wrapping up well. Their simple plan was, as soon as they were out of sight of Hasele's ramshackle edifice, to slit the windpipe of their newly acquired invalid, to pitch his body into the nearest snowdrift, and to see to it that only the good decorated parka—together possibly with the under tunic and trousers—reached the safety of the market in Pannoval.

They halted the dogs and braked the sledge. One of them drew a gleaming metal dagger and turned back towards the prostrate figure.

At which moment the prostrate figure rose up with a yell, hurling the skin that had covered him over the gentleman's head, kicking him ferociously in the stomach, and running furiously into the distance, taking a zigzag course to avoid any speeding spears.

When he considered himself far enough away, he turned, crouching behind a grey stone, to see if he was followed. In the dull light, the sledge had already disappeared from view. There was no sign of the two gentlemen. Save for the whistle of the west wind, all was still. He was alone in the frozen waste, some hours before Freyr-rise.

A great horror came upon Yuli. After the phagors had taken his father to their underground lair, he had wandered for more days than he could count through the wilderness, dazed by cold and lack of sleep, crazed by insects. He had completely lost his way, and was close to death when he collapsed into the thorn bush.

A little rest and nourishment had quickly restored his health. He had allowed himself to be loaded onto the sledge, not because he at all trusted the two gentlemen from Pannoval, who smelt all wrong to him, but because he could not bear the old crone who insisted on touching him in a way he disliked.

Now, after that brief interlude, here he was, in the wilds again, with a sub-zero wind plucking at his ears. He thought once more of his mother, Onesa, and of her illness. The last time he had seen her, she had coughed, and blood bubbled out of her mouth. She had looked upon him in such a ghastly way as he left with Alehaw. Only now did Yuli realise what that ghastly look meant: she had never expected to see him again. It was useless seeking to get back to his mother if she were a corpse by now.

Then what?

If he was to survive, there was only one possibility.

He rose, and at a steady jog trot followed in the wake of the sledge.

Seven large horned dogs of the kind known as asokins pulled the sledge. The leader was a bitch called Gripsy. They were known collectively as Gripsy's team. They rested for ten minutes in every hour; at every other rest period, they were fed foul-smelling dried fish from a sack. The two gentlemen took it in turn to trudge beside the sledge and to lie on it.

This was a routine Yuli soon understood. He kept well back down the trail. Even when the sledge was out of sight, as long as the air was still his keen nose could detect the stink of men and dogs running ahead. Sometimes he drew near to watch how things were done. He wanted to see how to handle a dog team for himself.

After three days' continuous travelling, when the asokins were having to take longer rests, they reached another trapper's post. Here the trapper had built himself a small wooden fort, decorated with horns and antlers of wild animals. Lines of skins flapped stiffly in the breeze. The gentlemen stayed here while Freyr sank from the sky, pale Batalix also died, and the brighter sentinel rose again. The two gentlemen screamed with the trapper in their drunkenness, or slept. Yuli stole some hardtack from the sledge and slept fitfully, rolled in a skin, in the sledge's lee side.

On they went.

Two more stops were made, interspersed with several days' journeying. Always Gripsy's team drove roughly southward. The winds became less chill.

At last, it became apparent that they were getting close to Pannoval. The mists towards which the team pulled proved solid stone.

Mountains rose from the plain ahead, their flanks deeply covered with snow. The plain itself rose, and they were working through foothills, where both gentlemen had to walk beside the sledge, or even push it. And there were stone towers, some with sentries who challenged them. The sentries challenged Yuli too.

"I'm following my father and my uncle," he called.

"You're lagging behind. The childrims will get you."

"I know, I know. Father is anxious to get home to Mother. So am I."

They waved him on, smiling at his youth.

At last, the gentlemen called a halt. Dried fish was thrown to Gripsy and her team, and the dogs were staked out. The two gentlemen picked a snug little corrie on the hillside, covered themselves with furs, applied alcohol to their insides, and fell asleep.

As soon as he heard their snores, Yuli crept near.

Both men had to be disposed of almost at the same time. He would be no match for either in a fight, so they must have no warning. He contemplated stabbing them with his dagger or bashing their brains in with a rock; either alternative had its dangers.

He looked about to see that he was not watched. Removing a strap from the sledge, he crept close to the gentlemen, and managed to tie a strap round the right ankle of one and the left ankle of the other, so that whoever jumped up first would be impeded by his companion. The gentlemen snored on.

While undoing the strap from the sledge, he noticed a number of spears. Perhaps they had been for trade and had not sold. He did not wonder at it. Removing one from its confining strap, he balanced it and judged that it would throw badly. For all that, the head was commendably sharp.

Returning to the corrie, he nudged one of the gentlemen with his foot until the gentleman rolled with a groan onto his back. Bringing the spear up as if he were about to transfix a fish, Yuli transfixed the gentleman through his parka, his rib cage, and his heart. The gentleman gave a terrible convulsive movement. Expression horrible, eyes wide, he sat up, grasped at the shaft of the spear, sagged over it, and then slowly rolled back with a long sigh that ended in a cough. Vomit and blood seeped from his lips. His companion did no more than stir and mutter.

Yuli found that he had sunk the spear so fiercely it had driven through the gentleman and into the ground. He returned to the sledge for a second spear and dealt with the second gentleman as he had with the first—with equal success. The sledge was his. And the team.

A vein throbbed at his temple. He regretted the gentlemen were not phagors.

He harnessed up the snarling and yelping asokins and drove them away from the spot.

Dim shawls of light rippled in the skies overhead, to be eclipsed by a tall shoulder of mountain. There was now a distinct path, a track that broadened mile by mile. It wound upwards until it negotiated a towering outcrop of rock. Round the base of the rock, a sheltered high valley was revealed, guarded by a formidable castle.

The castle was partly built of stone and partly hacked out of the rock. Its eaves were wide, to allow snow to avalanche from its roofs to the road below. Before the castle stood an armed guard of four men, drawn up before a wooden barrier which barred the road.

Yuli halted as a guard, his furs decorated with shining brasses, marched up.

"Who're you, lad?"

"I'm with my two friends. We've been out trading, as you see. They're away behind with a second sledge."

"I don't see them." His accent was strange: not the Olonets to which Yuli was accustomed in the Barriers region.

"They'll be along. Don't you recognise Gripsy's team?" He flicked the whip at the animals.

"So I do. Of course. Know them well. That bitch is not called Gripsy for nothing." He stepped to one side, raising his sturdy right arm.

"Let her up, there," he shouted. The barrier rose, the whip bit, Yuli hollered, and they were through.

He breathed deep as he got his first sight of Pannoval.

Ahead was a great cliff, so steep that no snow clung to it. In the cliff face was carved an enormous representation of Akha the Great One. Akha squatted in a traditional attitude, knees near his shoulders, arms wrapped round his knees, hands locked palms upward, with the sacred flame of life in his palms. His head was large, topped with a knot of hair. His half-human face struck terror into a beholder. There was awe even in his cheeks. Yet his great almond eyes were bland, and there was serenity as well as ferocity to be read in that upturned mouth and those majestic eyebrows.

Beside his left foot, and dwarfed by it, was an opening in the rock. As the sledge drew near, Yuli saw that this mouth was itself gigantic, possibly three times taller than a man. Within, lights could be seen, and guards with strange habits and accents, and strange thoughts in their heads.

He squared his young shoulders and strode forward boldly.

That was how Yuli came to Pannoval.

Never would he forget his entry into Pannoval, and his passing from the world under the sky. In a daze, he steered the sledge past guards, past a grove of beggarly trees, and stopped to take in the roofed expanse before him under which so many people lived out their days. Mist compounded with darkness, as he left the gate behind, to create a sketchy world with forms but no outlines. It was night; the few people moving about were wrapped in thick clothes which in their turn were wreathed by nimbi of fog, encircling them, floating about their heads, moving after them in slow swirls like threadbare-cloak trails. Everywhere was stone, stone carved into walls and divisions, stalls, houses, pens, and flights of steps—for this great mysterious cave tipped away up towards the interior of the mountain, and had been hewn over the centuries into small level squares, each separated from the next by steps and flanking walls.

With forced economy single torches fluttered at the head of each flight of steps, their flames oblique in a slight draught, illumining not the concourse but the misty air, to which their smoke contributed further opacity.

Ceaseless action of water through long eons had carved out a number of linked caves in the rock, in various sizes and on various levels. Some of these caves were inhabited, and had become regularised by human endeavour. They were named, and furnished with the necessities of rudimentary human life.

The savage halted, and could proceed no farther into this great station of dark until he found someone to accompany him. Those few outsiders who, like Yuli, visited Pannoval, found themselves in one of the larger caves, which the inhabitants knew as Market. Here much of the necessary work of the community was carried out, for little or no artificial light was required, once one's eyes had become accustomed to the dimness. By day the place rang with voices, and with the irregular knock of hammers. In Market, Yuli was able to trade the asokins and the goods on the sledge for things necessary to his new life. Here he must stay. There was nowhere else to go. Gradually he became accustomed to the gloom, to smoke, to smarting eyes, and to the coughing of the inhabitants; he accepted them all, along with the security.

It was his fortune to fall in with a decent fatherly trader called Kyale, who, with his wife, ran a stall in one of the small squares of Market. Kyale was a sorrowful man with a downward-turning mouth partly concealed by blackish moustaches. He befriended Yuli for reasons Yuli could not understand, and protected him from swindlers. He also went to some trouble to introduce Yuli to this new world.

Some of the echoing noises of Market were attributable to a stream, the Vakk, which ran through the rear end of Market, deep in its own chasm. This was the first free-flowing stream Yuli had ever seen, and it remained for him one of the wonders of the settlement. The splashing waters filled him with pleasure and, with his animistic faith, he regarded the Vakk as almost a living thing.

The Vakk had been bridged, so that access was gained to the end area of Market, where increasing steepness of the ground necessitated many steps, which culminated in a wide balcony housing a huge statue of Akha, carved from the rock. This figure could be seen, its shoulders rising from shadows, even from the far side of Market. Akha held in his outstretched hands a real flame, which a priest replenished at regular intervals, appearing from a door in Akha's stomach to do so. The people of Akha presented themselves to the feet of their god regularly; there they offered up all manner of gifts to him, which were accepted by the priests, unobtrusive in black-and-white-striped robes. The supplicants prostrated themselves, and a novice swept the ground with a feathery brush, before they dared gaze hopefully up at the black stone eyes high above them in the web of shadow, and retreat to less holy ground.

Such ceremonials were a mystery to Yuli. He asked Kyale about them, and received a lecture that left him more confused than before. No man can explain his religion to a stranger. Nevertheless, Yuli received a strong impression that this ancient being, represented in stone, fought off the powers raging in the outer world, particularly Wutra, who ruled the skies and all the ills associated with the skies. Akha was not greatly interested in humans; they were too puny for his concern. What he wanted was their regular offerings, to keep him strong in the struggle with Wutra, and a powerful Akhan ecclesiastical body existed to see that Akha's desires in this respect were carried out, in order that disaster did not descend on the community.

The priesthood, in alliance with the militia, had the governance of Pannoval; there was no one overall ruler, unless one counted Akha himself, who was generally supposed to be out prowling the mountains with a celestial club, looking for Wutra and such of his dreadful accomplices as the worm.

This was surprising to Yuli. He knew Wutra. Wutra was the great spirit before whom his parents, Alehaw and Onesa, offered prayers in time of danger. They had represented Wutra as benevolent, the bringer of light. And, as far as he recalled, they never mentioned Akha.

Various passages, as labyrinthine as the laws issued by the priesthood, led to various chambers adjoining Market. Some of these chambers were accessible, some forbidden of entry to common folk. About the forbidden regions, people were reluctant to talk. But he soon observed wrongdoers being dragged off there, hands tied behind their backs, winding up dark stairways into the aularian shadows, some to the Holies, some to a punishment farm behind Market called Twink.

In due course of time, Yuli traversed a narrow passage choked with steps which led to a large regularised cave called Reck. Reck also contained its enormous statue of Akha, here seen with an animal hanging on a chain about his neck, and dedicated to sport; Reck was the site at which mock battles, displays, athletic contests, and gladiatorial combats were held. Its walls were painted crimson and sang-de-boeuf, with swirling decorations. Much of the time Reck was almost empty, and voices boomed through its hollow spaces; then citizens with an especial bent for holiness came and wailed up into the high-vaulted dark. But on the glowing occasions of the games—then music sounded, and the cavern was crowded to overflowing.

Other important caverns opened from Market. At its eastern side, a nest of small squares or large mezzanines led up between flights of steps impeded by heavy balustrades to an extensive residential cavern called Vakk, after the stream that surfaced here, sunk deep in its gurgling ravine. Over Vakk's great entrance arch was much elaborate carving, with globular bodies entwined between flowing waves and stars, but much of it had been destroyed in some forgotten roof-fall.

Vakk was the oldest cavern after Market, and was filled with "livings," as they were called, dating back many centuries. To one arriving on its threshold from the outer world, viewing—or rather, guessing at—its mounting and confused terraces that climbed back into obscurity, Vakk in the uncertain light was a daunting dream where substance could not be distinguished from shadow, and the child of the Barrier felt his heart quail in his chest. A force like Akha was needed to save anyone who trod in such a thronged necropolis!

But he adapted with the flexibility of youth. He came to look on Vakk as a prodigal town. Falling in with guild apprentices of his own age, he roamed its muddle of livings which were clustered on many floors, often leading one from another. Cubicle was stacked on cubicle in profusion, the furniture in each fixed because carved from the same rock as floors and walls, all in one flowing line. The story of rights of ways and privacies in these organic warrens was complex, but always related to the guild system of Vakk, and always, in case of dispute, to be settled by the judgement of a priest.

In one of these livings, Tusca, Kyale's kindly wife, found Yuli a chamber of his own, only three doors from where she and Kyale lived. It was roofless and its walls curved; he felt as if he had been set down within a stone flower.

Vakk sloped steeply, and was dimly lit by natural light—more dimly than Market. The air was sooty with the exhalations of fat lamps, but clerics collected tax on every lamp, which had numbers stamped on their clay bases, so that they were used sparingly. The mysterious fogs which afflicted Market had less power in Vakk.

From Vakk, a gallery led direct to Reck. There were also, on lower ground, ragged arches leading to a high-roofed cavern called Groyne, which had good clean air, although the inhabitants of Vakk thought the inhabitants of Groyne rather barbarous, chiefly because they were members of more lowly guilds, slaughterers, tanners, diggers of chert and clay and fossil wood.

In the honeycombed rock adjoining both Groyne and Reck was another large cavern full of habitations and cattle. This was Prayn, which many avoided. It was being energetically extended by the sappers' guild when Yuli arrived. Prayn collected all the night soil from the other suburbs and fed it to swine and noctiferous crops, which thrived on heat. Some of the farmers in Prayn bred as a sideline a strain of bird called a preet, which had luminous eyes and luminescent patches on its wings. Preets were popular as cage birds; they added a little brightness to the livings of Vakk and Groyne—though they also were the subject of taxes collected by priests for Akha.

"In Groyne they are gruff, in Prayn pretty tough," went a local saying. But Yuli found the people lifeless, except when roused by the games, rare exceptions being those few traders and trappers living in Market in terraces of their own guild, who regularly had occasion to be blessed by Akha and sent on business in the outside world, as had been the case with the two gentlemen of his acquaintance.

From all the major caverns, and from smaller ones, paths and tunnels led into the blind rock, some ascending, some descending. Pannoval was full of legends of magical beasts that came in from the primordial dark of the rock, or of people who were spirited away from their livings into the mountain. Best to stay put in Pannoval, where Akha looked after his own with his blind eyes. Better Pannoval, too, and taxes, than the cold glare of outside.

These legends were kept alive by the sayers' guild, members of which stood on every stairway, or waited on terraces, and spun fantastic tales.

In this world of nebulous gloom, words were like lights.

To one other section of Pannoval, which figured largely in people's whispered discourse, Yuli was not allowed to make his way. That was the Holies. The Holies could be reached by gallery and stair from Market, but it was guarded by the militia, and set apart by repute. No one went voluntarily through its winding approaches. In the Holies lived the militia, forever guarding the law of Pannoval, and the priesthood, forever guarding its soul.

All these arrangements were so magnificent to Yuli that he could not see their meanness.

It took Yuli little time to find how closely the people were governed. They expressed no surprise in a system to which they had been born; but Yuli, accustomed to open spaces and the easily comprehended law of survival, was astonished at the way in which their every movement was circumscribed. Yet they thought themselves uniquely privileged.

With his legitimately acquired stock of skins, Yuli planned to purchase a stall next to Kyale, and set up shop. He discovered that there were many regulations that forbade anything so simple. Nor could he trade without a stall—unless he had a special licence—and for that he would have to have been born a member of a hawkers' guild. He needed a guild, an apprenticeship, and certain qualifications—a kind of exam—that only the priesthood could confer. He also needed a two-part certificate from the militia, together with insurance and references. Nor would he be able to trade until he owned a living. Yet he could not possess the room Tusca had rented for him until he was fully accredited with the militia. He was unable to meet even the most elementary qualification: a belief in Akha and a proof of regular sacrifices to the god.

"It's simple. First you, as a savage, must attend a priest." That was the dictum of a sharp-faced militia captain before whom Yuli had to appear. He confronted Yuli in a little stone room, the balcony of which was a metre or so above one of Market's terraces, and from which one might survey the whole animated scene.

The captain wore a floor-length cloak of black and white over the customary skins. On his head he wore a bronze helmet displaying the holy symbol of Akha, a kind of two-spoked wheel. His hide boots came halfway up his calf. Behind him stood a phagor, a black and white woven band tied round its hairy white brow.

"Pay attention to me," growled the captain. But Yuli found his eyes ever drifting towards the silent phagor, wondering at its presence.

The ancipital stood with an air of taciturn repose, ungainly head thrust forward. Its horns were blunt; they had been sawn short, and their cutting edges dulled with a file. Yuli saw that it had a leather collar and thong about its throat, half-concealed under white hair, a sign of its submission to man's rule. Yet it was a threat to the citizens of

Pannoval. Many officers appeared everywhere with a submissive phagor beside them; the phagors were valued for their superior ability to see in the dark. Ordinary people went in fear of the shambling animals that spoke basic Olonets. How was it possible, Yuli wondered, for men to form liaisons with the same beasts who had imprisoned his father—beasts that everyone in the wilds hated from birth?

The interview with the captain was dispiriting, and worse was to come. He could not live unless he obeyed the rules, and they appeared interminable; there was nothing for it—as Kyale impressed upon him—but to conform. To be a citizen of Pannoval, you had to think and feel like a Pannovalian.

So he was consigned to attend the priest in the alley of livings where he had his room. This entailed numerous sessions at which he was taught a ritualised history of Pannoval ("born from Great Akha's shadow on the eternal snows . . .") and forced to learn many of the scriptures by heart. He also had to do whatever Sataal, the priest, told him to do, including the running of many tedious errands, for Sataal was lazy. It was no great consolation to Yuli to find that the children of Pannoval went through similar courses of instruction at an early age.

Sataal was a solidly built man, pale of face, small of ear, heavy of hand. His head was shaven, his beard plaited, in the manner of many priests of his order. There were twists of white in the plaits. He wore a knee-length smock of black and white. His face was deeply pocked. It took Yuli some while to realise that, despite the white hairs, Sataal was not past middle age, being only in his late teens. Yet he walked in a round-shouldered way suggesting both age and piety.

When he addressed Yuli, Sataal spoke always kindly but remotely, keeping a gulf between them. Yuli was reassured by the man's attitude, which seemed to say, This is your job and mine, but I shall not complicate it by probing into what your inner feelings are. So Yuli kept quiet, applying himself to the task of learning all the necessary fustian verses.

"But what do they mean?" he asked at one point, in bewilderment.

Sataal rose slowly in the small room, and turned about, so that his shoulders loomed black in a distant source of light, and all the rest of him flowed into encompassing shadow. A dull highlight gleamed on his pate as he inclined his head towards Yuli, saying, admonishingly, "Learning first, young fellow, then interpretation. After learning, then less difficulty in interpretation. Get everything by heart, you hardly need it by head. Akha never enforces understanding from his people, only obedience."

"You said that Akha cares nothing for anyone in Pannoval."

"The important point, Yuli, is that Pannoval cares for Akha. Now then, once again:

> "Whoso laps Freyr's bane
> Like a fish swallows ill bait:
> When it groweth late
> Our feeble frames he will burn."

"But what does it mean?" Yuli asked again. "How can I learn it if I don't understand it?"

"Repeat it, son," said Sataal sternly. " 'Whoso laps . . .' "

Yuli was submerged in the dark city. Its networks of shadows snatched at his spirit, as he had seen men in the outer world catch fish with nets under the ice. In dreams, his mother came to him, blood flying from her mouth. Then he would wake, to lie in his narrow cot staring up, far up, far beyond the confines of his flower-shaped room, to the roof of Vakk. Sometimes, when the atmosphere was fairly clear, he could see distant detail, with bats hanging up there, and stalactites, and the rock gleaming with liquid that had ceased to be liquid; and he wished he could fly away from the traps he found himself in. But there was nowhere else to go.

Once, in midnight desperation, he crawled through to Kyale's home for comfort. Kyale was annoyed at being woken, and told him to go away, but Tusca spoke to him gently, as if he were her son. She patted his arm and clutched his hand.

After a while, she wept softly, and told him that indeed she had a son, a good kind lad of about Yuli's age, Usilk by name. But Usilk had been taken from her by the police for a crime she knew he had never committed. Every night, she lay awake and thought of him, concealed in one of those terrifying places in the Holies, guarded by phagors, and wondered if she would ever see him again.

"The militia and the priests are so unjust here," Yuli whispered to her. "My people have little to live on in the wilds, but all are equal, one with another, in the face of the cold."

After a pause, Tusca said, "There are people in Pannoval, women as well as men, who do not learn the scriptures and think to overthrow those who rule. Yet without our rulers, we should be destroyed by Akha."

Yuli peered at the outline of her face through the dark. "And do you think that Usilk was taken . . . because he wanted to overthrow the rulers?"

In a low voice she replied, holding tightly to his hand, "You must not ask such questions or you'll meet trouble. Usilk was always rebellious—yes, perhaps he got among the wrong people. . . ."

"Stop your chatter," Kyale called. "Get back to your bed, woman—and you to yours, Yuli."

These things Yuli nursed in himself all the while he went through his sessions with Sataal. Outwardly, he was obedient to the priest.

"You are not a fool, even if you are a savage—and that we can change," said Sataal. "Soon you shall progress to the next step. For Akha is the god of earth and underground, and you shall understand something of how the earth lives, and we in its veins. These veins are called land-octaves, and no man can be happy or healthy unless he lives along his own land-octaves. Slowly, you can acquire revelation, Yuli. Maybe, if you are good enough, you could yourself become a priest, and serve Akha in a greater way."

Yuli kept his mouth shut. It was beyond his ability to tell the priest that he needed no particular attentions from Akha: his whole new way of life in Pannoval was a revelation.

The days followed one another peacefully. Yuli became impressed with the never varying patience of Sataal, and began disliking his instruction periods less. Even away from the priest, he thought about his teaching. All was fresh and curiously exciting. Sataal had told him that certain priests, who undertook to fast, were able to communicate with the dead, or even with personages in history; Yuli had never heard of such things, but hesitated to call them nonsense.

He took to roving alone through the suburbs of the city, until its thick shadows took on for him colours of familiarity. He listened to people, who often talked of religion, or to the sayers who spoke at street corners, who often laced their stories with religion.

Religion was the romance of the darkness, as terror had been of the Barriers, where tribal drums warded off devils. Slowly, Yuli began to perceive in religious talk not a vacuum but a core of truth: the way in which people lived and died had to be explained. Only savages needed no explanation. The perception was like finding an animal's trail in the snow.

Once he was in a malodorous part of Prayn, where human scumble was poured into long trenches on which the noctiferous crops grew. Here, the people were pretty tough, as the saying had it. A man with short-cropped free-flowing hair, and therefore neither a priest nor a sayer, ran up and jumped onto a scumble barrow.

"Friends," he said, standing before them. "Listen to me for a moment, will you? Just stop your labours and hear what I have to say. I speak not for myself but for the great Akha, whose spirit moves inside me. I have to speak for him although I put my life in danger, for the priests distort Akha's words for their own purposes."

People stopped to listen. Two tried to make a joke at the young man's expense, but the others stood in submissive interest, Yuli included.

"Friends, the priests say that we have to sacrifice to Akha and nothing more, and he will then keep us safe in the great heart of his mountain. I say that is a lie. The priests are content and do not care how we the ordinary people suffer. Akha tells you through my lips that we should do more. We should be better in ourselves. Our lives are too easy—once we have made sacrifices and paid taxes, we care nothing. We merely enjoy, or go to the games. You hear so often that Akha cares nothing for us and everything for his battle with Wutra. We must make him care— we must become worthy of his care. We must reform ourselves! Yes, reform! And the easy-living priests must reform themselves also. . . ."

Someone called to say that the militia were coming.

The young man paused. "My name is Naab. Remember what I say. We too have a role in the great war between Sky and Earth. I will be back to speak if I can—speak my message to all Pannoval. Reform, reform!—Before it is too late . . ." As he jumped down, there was a surge among the crowd that had gathered. A great tethered phagor rushed forward, with a soldier at the other end of his leash. It reached forward and grabbed Naab's arm with its powerful horned hands. He gave a cry of pain, but a hairy white arm went round his throat and he was led away in the direction of Market and the Holies.

"He shouldn't have said such things," a grey man muttered, as the crowd dispersed.

Yuli followed the man on impulse, and grasped his sleeve.

"The man Naab said nothing against Akha—why should the militia take him away?"

The man looked furtively about. "I recognise you. You're a savage, or you wouldn't ask such stupid things."

For answer, Yuli raised his fist. "I'm not stupid or I would not ask my question."

"If you weren't stupid, you'd keep quiet. Who do you think has power here? The priesthood, of course. If you speak out against them—"

"But that's Akha's power—"

The grey man had slipped away into the dark. And there in that dark, that ever watchful dark, could be felt the presence of something monstrous. Akha?

One day, a great sporting event was to be held in Reck. It was then that Yuli, acclimatised to Pannoval, underwent a remarkable crystalisation of emotion. He hurried along to the sports with Kyale and Tusca. Fat lamps burned in niches, leading the way from Vakk to Reck, and crowds of people climbed through the narrowing rock passages, struggled up the worn steps, calling to one another, as they filed into the sports arena.

Carried along by the surge of humanity, Yuli caught a sudden view ahead of the chamber of Reck, its curved walls flickering with light. He saw but a slice of the chamber to begin with, trapped between the veined walls of the passage along which the rabble had to pass. As he moved, so into that framed distant view moved Akha himself, high above the heads of the crowd.

He ceased to listen to what Kyale was saying. Akha's gaze was on him; the monstrous presence of the dark was surely made visible.

Music played in Reck, shrill and stimulating. It played for Akha.

There Akha stood, broad and horrible of brow, its large stone eyes unseeing yet all-seeing, lit from below by flares. Its lips dripped disdain.

The wilderness held nothing like this. Yuli's knees were weak. A powerful voice inside him, one he scarcely recognised as his own, exclaimed, "Oh, Akha, at last I believe in you. Yours is the power. Forgive me, let me be your servant."

Yet alongside the voice of one longing to enslave himself was another, speaking simultaneously in a more calculating manner. It said, "The people of Pannoval must understand a great truth which it would be useful to get to comprehend by following Akha."

He was astonished at the confusion within himself, a war that did not lessen as they entered the chamber and more of the stone god was revealed. Naab had said, "Humans have a role in the war between Sky and Earth." Now he could feel that war alive within him.

The games were intensely exciting. Running races and spear throwing were followed by wrestling between humans and phagors, the latter with their horns amputated. Then came the bat shoot, and Yuli emerged from his pietistic confusions to watch the excitement. He feared bats. High above the crowd, the roof of Reck was lined with the furry creatures, dangling with their leather wings about their heads. Archers came forward and shot in turn at the bats with arrows to which were attached silken threads. The bats, when hit, fell fluttering down, and were claimed for the pot.

The winner was a girl. She wore a bright red garment tight at the neck and long to the ground, and she pulled back her bow and shot more accurately than any man. And her hair was long and dark. Her name was Iskador, and the crowd applauded her wildly, none more so than Yuli.

Then there were the gladiatorial combats, men against men, men against phagors, and blood and death filled the arena. Yet all the time, even when Iskador was tensing her bow and her lovely torso—even then, Yuli thought in terms of great joy that he had found an amazing faith. The confusions within would be banished by greater knowledge, he assumed.

He recalled the legends he had listened to round his father's fire. The elders had spoken of the two sentinels in the sky, and of how the men on earth had once offended the God of the Skies, whose name was Wutra. So that Wutra had banished the earth from his warmth. Now the sentinels watched for the hour when Wutra returned, to look again with affection on the earth, and see if the people behaved better. If he found they did, then would he remove the frosts.

Well, Yuli had to acknowledge that his people were savages, just as Sataal claimed; how else would his father have allowed himself to be dragged away by phagors? Yet there must be a germ of truth in the tales. For here in Pannoval was a more reasoned version of the story. Wutra was now merely a minor deity, but he was vengeful, and he was loose in the skies. It was from the skies that peril came. Akha was the great earth god, ruling underground, where it was safe. The Two Sentinels were not benign; being in the sky, they belonged to Wutra, and they could turn against mankind.

Now the memorised verses began to make sense. Illumination shone from them, so that Yuli muttered with pleasure what had previously given him pain, gazing upon Akha's face as he did so:

> *"Skies give false prospects,*
> *Skies shower extremes:*
> *Against all such schemes*
> *Akha's earth overhead protects."*

Next day, he went humbly to Sataal and told the man that he had been converted.

The pale heavy face of his priest regarded him, and Sataal drummed his fingers on his knees.

"How were you converted? Lies fly about the livings these days."

"I looked at Akha's face. For the first time I saw it clear. Now my heart is open."

"Another false prophet was arrested the other day."

Yuli smote his chest. "What I feel inside me is not false, Father."

"It's not so easy," said the priest.

"Oh, it is easy, it is easy—now everything will be easy!" He fell at the priest's feet, crying his delight.

"Nothing's so easy."

"Master, I owe you everything. Help me. I want to be a priest, to become as you."

During the next few days, he went about the lanes and livings noticing new things. No longer did he feel himself encased in gloom, buried underground. He was in a favoured region, protected from all the cruel elements that had made him a savage. He saw how welcome the dim light was.

He saw too how beautiful Pannoval was, in all its chambers. In the course of their long habitation, the caves had been decorated by artists. Whole walls were covered with painting and carving, many of them illustrating the life of Akha and the great battles he had fought, as well as the battles he would fight when again enough humans had faith in his strength. Where the pictures had grown old and faint, new ones had been painted on top of them. Artists were still at work, often perched dangerously on top of scaffolding that reached towards the roof like the skeleton of some mythical long-necked animal.

"What's the matter with you, Yuli? You attend to nothing," Kyale said.

"I'm going to be a priest. I've made up my mind."

"They'll never let you—you from outside."

"My priest is speaking to the authorities."

Kyale pulled at his melancholy nose, slowly lowering his hand until the tugging operations were taking place at one end of his moustache, as he contemplated Yuli. By now, Yuli's eyesight had so adjusted to the dimness that every nuance of expression on his friend's face was clear. When Kyale moved without a word to the back of his stall, Yuli followed.

Again grabbing his moustache for security, Kyale placed his other hand on Yuli's shoulder. "You're a good lad. You remind me of Usilk, but we won't go into that. . . . Listen to me: Pannoval isn't like it was when I was a child, running barefoot through the bazaars. I don't know what's happened, but there's no peace any more. All this talk of change—nonsense, to my mind. Even the priests are at it, with wild men ranting about reform. I say, let well enough alone. Know what I mean?"

"I know what you mean, yes."

"Well, then. You may think that it would be soft, being a priest. So it might. But I wouldn't recommend it at present. It's not as—as secure as it used to be, if you follow me. They've become restive. I hear they often execute heretical priests in the Holies. You'd do better here indentured to me, making yourself useful. Understand? I'm speaking to you for your own good."

Yuli looked down at the worn ground.

"I can't explain how I feel, Kyale. Sort of hopeful . . . I think things ought to change. I want to change myself, I don't know how."

Sighing, Kyale removed his hand from Yuli's shoulder. "Well, lad, if you take that attitude, don't say I didn't warn you. . . ."

Despite Kyale's grumpiness, Yuli was touched that the man cared about him. And Kyale passed on the news of Yuli's intentions to his wife. When Yuli went to his little curved room that evening, Tusca appeared in his doorway.

"Priests can go anywhere. If you become an initiate, you'll have the run of the place. You'll come and go in the Holies."

"I suppose so."

"Then you may find what has happened to Usilk. Try to, for my sake. Tell him I still think of him. And come and tell me if you can find any news of him."

She put a hand on his arm. He smiled at her. "You are kind, Tusca. Don't your rebels who want to bring down the rulers of Pannoval have any news of your son?"

She was frightened. "Yuli, you will change in all ways when you're a priest. So I'll say no more, for fear of injury to the rest of my family."

He lowered his gaze. "Akha strike me if I ever harm you."

On the next occasion when he appeared before the priest, a soldier was also present, standing behind Sataal in the shadows with a phagor on a leash. The priest asked Yuli if he would give up everything he possessed to walk in the path of Akha. Yuli said that he would.

"Then it shall be done." The priest clapped his hands, and off marched the soldier. Yuli understood then that he had now lost his few possessions; everything but the clothes he wore and his knife which his mother had carved would be taken by the military. Speaking no further word, Sataal turned, beckoning with one finger, and began to walk towards the rear of Market. Yuli could do nothing but follow, pulse beating fast.

As they came to the wooden bridge spanning the chasm where the Vakk leaped and tumbled, Yuli looked back, beyond the busy scene of trade and barter, out through the far archway of the entrance, catching a glimpse of snow.

For some reason, he thought of Iskador, the girl with the dark hair flowing. Then he hurried after his priest.

They climbed the terraces of the worship area, where people jostled to leave their sacrifices at the feet of the image of Akha. At the back were screens, intricately painted. Sataal whisked past them, and led into a narrowing passage, up shallow steps. The light became rapidly dimmer as they turned a corner. A bell tinkled. In his anxiety, Yuli stumbled. He had reached the Holies sooner than he had bargained for.

Just for once in crowded Pannoval, nobody else was about. Their footsteps echoed. Yuli could see nothing; the priest ahead of him was an impression, nothing, blackness within blackness. He dared not stop or reach out or call—blind following was what was now demanded of him and he must treat all that came as a test of his intentions. If Akha loved chthonic darkness, so must he. All the same, the *lack* of everything, the void that registered itself on his senses only as a whispered noise, assaulted him.

They walked forever into the earth. So it seemed.

Softly, suddenly, light came—a column of it appearing to strike down through a stagnant lake of darkness, creating on its bed a circle of brightness towards which two submerged creatures advanced. It silhouetted the heavy figure of the priest, black and white garb swirling about him. It allowed Yuli some sense of where he was.

There were no walls.

It was more frightening than total darkness. He had already grown so accustomed to the confines of the settlement, to having a cliff, a partition, a fellow's back, a woman's shoulder, always within jostling distance, that agoraphobia seized him. He went sprawling, uttering a gasp as he fell to the paving.

The priest did not turn. He reached the place where the illumination fell and marched steadily on, shoes clack-clacking, so that his figure was lost almost immediately behind the misty shaft of light.

Desperate at being left, the youth picked himself up and ran forward. As the shaft of light impaled him, he stared up. High above him was a hole through which ordinary daylight shone. Up there were the things he had known all his life, the things he was renouncing for a god of darkness.

He saw ragged rock. Now he could comprehend that he was in a chamber larger than the rest of Pannoval, and higher. At a signal—perhaps the tinkling bell he had heard—someone somewhere had opened a high door onto the outside world. As warning? As temptation? Or merely as a dramatic trick?

Maybe all three, he thought, since they were so much more clever than he, and he hurried on after the priest's disappearing figure. In a moment, he sensed rather than saw that the light behind him faded; the high door had closed. He was again in unbroken darkness.

They at last reached the far side of the gigantic chamber. Yuli heard the priest's steps slow. Without faltering, Sataal had reached a door, on the panel of which he rapped. After some delay, the door opened. A fat lamp floated in the air, borne above the head of an ageing woman who sniffed continuously. She allowed them to pass into a stone corridor before fastening the door behind them.

Matting covered the floor. Several doors confronted them. Along both walls, hip high, ran a narrow band of carving, which Yuli wanted to look at more closely but did not dare to; otherwise the walls were undecorated. The sniffing woman knocked at one of the doors. When response came, Sataal pushed it open and motioned Yuli in. Bowing, Yuli passed his mentor's outstretched arm and marched into the room. The door closed behind him. That was the last he saw of Sataal.

The room was furnished with detachable furniture of stone, covered with coloured rugs. It was lit by a double lamp standing on an iron holder. Two men sat at a stone table, and looked up without smiling from some documents. One was a militia captain, his helmet with its wheel insignia resting on the tabletop by his elbow. The other was a thin grey priest with a not unfriendly face, who blinked as if the mere sight of Yuli's face dazzled him.

"Yuli of the Outside? Since you have come this far, you have taken one step on the way to becoming a priest of Great Akha," the priest said in a reedy voice. "I am Father Sifans, and first of all I must ask you if you have any sins that destroy your peace of mind, to which you wish to confess."

Yuli was disconcerted that Sataal had left him so abruptly, without even a whispered farewell, though he understood that he must now give up such worldly things as love and friendship.

"Nothing to confess," he said sulkily, not looking the thin priest in the eye.

The priest cleared his throat. The captain spoke.

"Youth, look at me. I am Captain Ebron of the North Guard. You entered Pannoval on a sledge teamed by asokins called Gripsy's team. It was stolen from two renowned traders of this city named Atrimb and Prast, both of Vakk. Their bodies were found not many miles from here, with spears through them, as if they had been done to death in their sleep. What say you about this crime?"

Yuli stared at the floor.

"I know nothing of it."

"We think you know everything. . . . Had the crime been committed within the territory of Pannoval, it would carry the penalty of death. What do you say?"

He felt himself shaking. This was not what he had expected.

"I have nothing to say."

"Very well. You cannot become a priest while this guilt lies on you. You must confess the crime. You will be shut up until you speak."

Captain Ebron clapped his hands. Two soldiers entered and grasped Yuli. He struggled for a moment, to test their strength, had his arms sharply wrenched, and allowed himself to be led away.

Yes, he thought, the Holies—full of priests and soldiers. They've got me properly. What a fool I am, a victim. Oh, Father, you abandoned me. . . .

It was not even as if he had been able to forget about the two gentlemen. The double murder still lay heavy inside him, although he always tried to rationalise it by reminding himself that they had attempted to kill him. Many a night, as he lay on his cot in Vakk, staring up at the distant vault, he saw again the gentleman's eyes as he sat up and tried to pull the spear from his entrails.

The cell was small and damp and dark.

When he recovered from the shock of being alone, he felt cautiously about him. His prison was featureless except for an ill-smelling gutter and a low shelf on which to sleep. Yuli sat on it and buried his face in his hands.

He was given plenty of time to think. His thoughts, in the impenetrable darkness, took on a life of their own, as if they were the figments of delirium. People he knew, people he had never seen, came and went about him, engaged in mysterious activities.

"Mother!" he exclaimed. Onesa was there, as she had been before her illness, slender and active, with her long serious face that readily broke into a smile for her son—though it was a guarded smile with lips scarcely parted. She bore a great bundle of twigs on her shoulder. A litter of little horned black piglets walked before her. The sky was a brilliant blue; both Batalix and Freyr shone there. Onesa and Yuli stepped along a path out of a dark larch forest and were dazzled by the brightness. Never had there been a blue like that; it seemed to tint the piled snow and fill the world.

Ahead was a ruined building. Although it had been solidly built in the long past, weather had broken it open like an old tree fungus. Before it stood a flight of shallow steps, now ruined. Onesa flung down her twigs and sprang so eagerly up the steps that she almost skipped. She raised her gloved hands as she went, and even offered a snatch of song to the crisp air.

Rarely had Yuli seen his mother in such spirits. Why did she feel like that? Why not more often? Not daring to put these questions direct, yet longing to have some personal word from her, he asked, "Who built this place, Mother?"

"Oh, it's always been here. It's as old as the hills. . . ."

"But who built it, Mother?"

"I don't know—my father's family, probably, long ago. They were great people, with stores of grain."

This legend of his mother's family's greatness was well-known to him, and the detail of the store of grain. He marched up the ruined steps, and pushed open a reluctant door. Snow scattered in a cloud as he shouldered his way inside. There was the grain, golden, piles of it, enough for them all for ever more. It started running towards him in a river, great piles of it cascading down, over the steps. And from under the grain, two dead bodies heaved to view, struggling blindly towards the light.

He sat up with a great cry, sprang to his feet, stood up, paced to the cell door. He could not understand where these alarming visions came from; they seemed not to be a part of him.

He thought to himself, *Dreams are not for you, dodger. You're too tough. You think of your mother now, yet you never showed her affection. You were too afraid of your father's fist. You know, I really believe I hated my father. I believe I was glad when the phagors carried him off—weren't you?*

No, no. . . . It's just that my experiences have made me hard. You're hard, dodger, hard and cruel. You killed those two gentlemen. What are you going to be? Better to confess to the murders and see what happens. Try and love me, try and love me. . . .

I know so little. That's it. The whole world—you want to find out. Akha must know. Those eyes see everything. But me—you're so small, dodger—life's no more than one of those funny feelings when the childrim flies overhead.

He marvelled at his own thoughts. Finally he cried for the guards to open his door, and found that he had been incarcerated for three days.

For a year and a day, Yuli served in the Holies as a novice. He was not allowed to leave the halls, but dwelt in a monastic nocturne, not knowing whether Freyr and Batalix swam separately or together in the sky. A wish to run through the white wilderness gradually left him, erased by the penumbral majesty of the Holies.

He had confessed to the murder of the two gentlemen. No punishment followed.

The thin grey priest with the blinking eyes, Father Sifans, was the charge-father over Yuli and other novices. He clasped his hands and said to Yuli, "That unhappy incident of the murders is now sealed behind the wall of the past. Yet you must never allow yourself to forget it, lest, in forgetting, you come to believe that it never happened. Like the many suburbs of Pannoval, all things in life are interwoven. Your sin and your longing to serve Akha are of a piece. Did you imagine that it was holiness that led a man to serve Akha? Not so. Sin is a more powerful mover. Embrace the dark—through sin you come to terms with your own inadequacy."

"Sin" was a word often on Father Sifans' lips at one period. Yuli watched it there with interest, with the absorption pupils devote to their masters. The way the lips moved was something he imitated to himself later, alone, using the movements to repeat all that he had to learn by heart.

While the father had his own private apartment to which he withdrew after instruction, Yuli slept in a dormitory with others of his kind, in a nest of dark within the dark. Unlike the fathers, they were allowed no pleasures; song, drink, wenches, recreation were forbidden, and their food was of the most spartan kind, selected from the offerings made by supplicants of Akha daily.

"I can't concentrate. I'm hungry," he complained once to his charge-father.

"Hunger is universal. We cannot expect Akha to fatten us. He defends us against hostile outside forces, generation by generation."

"Which is more important, survival or the individual?"

"An individual has importance in his own eyes, but generations have priority."

He was learning to argue the priest's way, step by step. "But generations are made up of individuals."

"Generations are not only the sum of individuals. They contain also aspirations, plans, histories, laws—above all, continuities. They contain the past as well as the future. Akha refuses to work with individuals alone, so individuals must be subdued—quenched, if necessary."

Slyly, the father taught Yuli to argue. On the one hand, he must have blind faith; on the other, he needed reason. For its long journey through the years, the entombed community needed all defences, needed both prayer and rationality. The sacred verses claimed that at some time in the future, Akha, in his lonely battle, might suffer defeat and the world undergo a period of intense fire descending from the skies. The individual must be quenched, to avoid the burning.

Through the entombing halls went Yuli, with all these ideas declaiming themselves in his head. They stood his understanding of the world upside down—but therein lay much of their attraction, since every revolutionary new insight only emphasised his previous ignorant state.

Among all the deprivations, one sensory delight stole upon his bewilderment to soothe him. The priests found their way through the dark labyrinth by wall-reading, an arcane mystery in which Yuli was soon to be initiated. There was also another directional clue, intended to delight. Music. At first, Yuli in his innocence imagined that he heard the sound of spirits overhead. He could make nothing of the tickling line of melody played on a one-stringed vrach. He had never seen a vrach. If not a spirit, could it be the wail of wind through a crevice somewhere in the rock?

His delight was so secret that he asked no one about the sounds, not even his fellow novices, until walking one day unexpectedly with Sifans into a religious service. Choirs were important, and monody even more so, with a single voice launched into the hollows of the dark; but what Yuli came to love most were the interventions by inhuman voices, those of the instruments of Pannoval.

Nothing similar was ever heard in the Barriers. The only music the besieged tribes there knew was a prolonged drumming, on a drum made of hide; clacking, of animal bones struck together; and clapping, of human hands, accompanied by a monotonous chant. It was the luxurious complication of the new music that convinced Yuli of the reality of his still awakening spiritual life. One great tune in particular took him by storm, "Oldorando," which had a part for an instrument that soared about all others, then dived into their midst, finally to retreat into a secure melodic refuge of its own.

Music became almost an alternative to light for Yuli. When he talked to his fellow novices, he found that they felt little of his exhilaration. But they—he came to realise—all carried a much greater central commitment to Akha himself than he. Most of the novices had loved or hated Akha from birth; Akha was nature to them as he was not to Yuli.

When he wrestled with such matters during the sparse hours allotted to sleep, Yuli felt guilt that he was not as the other novices. He loved the music of Akha. It was a new language. But was not music the creation of men, rather than of . . .

Even when he choked off the doubt, another doubt sprang up. How about the language of religion? Wasn't that also the invention of men —perhaps pleasant, ineffectual men like Father Sifans?

"Belief is not peace but torment; only the great War is peace." That part of the creed at least was true.

Meanwhile, Yuli kept his own council, and fraternised only superficially with his fellows.

They met for instruction in a low, damp, foggy hall named Cleft. Sometimes they went in utter darkness, sometimes in the glow of wicks carried by the fathers. Each session ended with the priest pressing his hand to the novice's forehead, gesturing at his brain, an action at which the novices laughed later in their dormitory. Priests' fingers were rough, from the wall-reading by which they navigated briskly about the labyrinths of the Holies even in the most pitchy blackness.

Each novice sat in a curiously shaped dock, built of clay bricks, facing his instructor. Each dock was decorated in individual low-reliefs, to make their identification in the dark easier. Their instructor sat opposite and above them, astride a clay saddle.

When only a few weeks of the novitiate had lapsed, Father Sifans announced the subject of heresy. He spoke in a low voice, coughing as he did so. Worse than nonbelief was to believe wrongly. Yuli leaned forward. He and Sifans had no light, but the charge-father in the next box did, a fluttering flame which served to throw a foggy orange nimbus about Sifans' head and shade his face. The old man's white-and-black gown further disintegrated his outlines, so that he merged with the dark of the chamber. Mist rolled about them, trailing anyone who walked slowly by, practising wall-reading. Coughs and muttering filled the low cavern; water dripped ceaselessly, like small bells.

"A human sacrifice, Father, did you say a human sacrifice?"

"The body is precious, the spirit expendable. One who has spoken against the priesthood, saying they should be more frugal to aid Akha . . . You are far enough on with your studies to attend his execution. . . . Ritual from barbarous times . . ."

The nervous eyes, two tiny points of orange, flickered in the dark like a signal from a remote distance.

When the time came, Yuli walked through the lugubrious galleries, nervously trying to wall-read with his fingers. They entered the largest cavern in the Holies, called State. No light was allowed. Whispering filled the air as the priesthood assembled. Yuli surreptitiously took hold of the hem of Father Sifans' gown in order not to lose him. Then a voice of a priest, declaiming the history of the long war between Akha and Wutra. Night was Akha's, and the priests were set to protect their flock through the long night's battle. Those who opposed the guardians must die.

"Bring forth the prisoner."

There was much talk of prisoners in the Holies, but this one was special. The tramp of the militia's heavy sandals could be heard, a shuffling. Then brightness.

A shaft of light blazed down. The novices gasped. Yuli recognised that they stood in the vast chamber through which Sataal had led him, a long while ago. The light source was as before, high above the multitude of heads; it appeared blinding.

At its base stood a human figure, tied to a wooden framework, legs and arms spread. It was in the upright position, and naked.

Even as the prisoner gave a cry, Yuli recognised the dense impassioned face, square, and framed by short-cropped hair. It was the young man he had once heard speak in Prayn—Naab.

His voice and message were also recognisable. "Priests, I am not your enemy, though you treat me like one, but your friend. Generation by generation, you sink into inaction, your numbers grow less, Pannoval dies. We are not just passive votaries of Great Akha. No! We must fight with him. We must also suffer. In the great war between Sky and Earth, we must play our part. We must reform and purify ourselves."

Behind the bound figure were militiamen in gleaming helmets, guarding him. Others arrived, bearing smoking brands. With them marched their phagors, checked by leather leads. They halted. They turned inward. They hoisted their brands high above their heads, and the smoke rose in leisurely braids upwards. Forward creaked a stiff cardinal, bowed under black-and-white garb and an elaborate mitre. He struck a golden staff against the ground three times, crying shrilly in the Priestly Olonets, "Have done, have done, have done. . . . O Great Akha, our Warrior God, appear to us!" A bell tinkled.

A second pillar of the brilliant white light, solidifying rather than banishing the surrounding night. Behind the prisoner, behind the phagors and the soldiers, Akha appeared, reaching upwards. A murmur of expectation came from the crowd. It was a skeletal scene, the militia and the massive white beasts all but transparent, Akha chalky in the column of light, the whole embedded in obsidian. In this representation, the semihuman head of the god thrust forward, and his mouth was open. The eyes were as sightless as ever.

"Take this unsatisfactory life, O Great Akha, and use it for Thy satisfaction."

Functionaries moved smartly forward. One began to crank at a handle set in the side of the frame holding the prisoner. The frame began to creak and shift. The prisoner cried softly once, as his body was forced to bend backwards. As the hinges on the framework opened, his body arched back, exposing his helplessness.

Two captains marched forward with a phagor between them. The great beast's blunted horns had been capped with silver and reached almost to the height of the soldiers' eyebrows. It stood in the ungainly customary stance of a phagor, head and prow of chest thrust forward, its long white hair stirring slightly in the draught that blew through State.

Music sounded again, drum, gongs, vrachs, drowning out Naab's voice, and the sustained warble of a fluggel rising high above them. Then everything stopped.

The body was bent double now, legs and feet twisted somewhere out of sight, head right back, exposing throat and thorax, gleaming pale in the column of light.

"Take, O Great Akha! Take what is already Thine! Eradicate him."

At the priest's scream, the phagor stepped a pace forward and bent down. It opened its shovel mouth and applied rows of blunt teeth to either side of the proffered throat. It bit. It raised its head, and a great morsel of flesh came up with it. It moved back into place between the two soldiers, swallowing noncommittally. A trickle of red ran down its white front. The rear column of light was cut off. Akha disappeared back into his nourishing darkness. Many of the novices fainted.

As they jostled out of State, Yuli asked, "But why use those devilish phagors? They're man's enemy. They should all be killed."

"They are the creatures of Wutra, as their colour shows. We keep them to remind us of the enemy," said Sifans.

"And what will happen to the—to Naab's body?"

"It will not be wasted. Every item is of some application. The whole carcass may go for fuel—perhaps to the potters, who always need to fire their kilns. I really don't know. I prefer to keep myself aloof from administrative details."

He dared say no more to Father Sifans, hearing the distaste in the old priest's voice. To himself, he said over and over again, "Those evil brutes. Those evil brutes. Akha should have no part of them." But the phagors were all over the Holies, padding patiently along with the militia, their noctilucent eyes peering here and there under their craggy brows.

One day Yuli tried to explain to his charge-father how his father had been caught and killed by phagors in the wild.

"You do not know for sure they killed him. Phagors are not always entirely evil. Sometimes Akha subdues their spirit."

"I'm sure he's dead by now. There's no way of being certain, though?"

He heard the father lick his lips as he hesitated, and then leaned towards Yuli in the blackness.

"There is a way of being sure, my son."

"Oh, yes, if you mounted a great expedition from Pannoval north—"

"No, no . . . other ways, more subtle. You will one day understand the complexities of Pannoval more fully. Or perhaps you won't. For there are entirely other orders of the priesthood, warrior mystics, of which you do not know. Perhaps I had better say no more. . . ."

Yuli urged him on. The priest's voice sank still lower, until it was almost lost under the splash of a water drip near at hand.

"Yes, warrior mystics, who forswear the pleasures of the flesh and in return gain mysterious powers . . ."

"That's what Naab advocated, and was murdered for it."

"Executed after trial. The superior orders prefer us, the administrative orders, to remain as we are. . . . But they . . . they communicate with the dead. If you were one of them, you could speak with your father after death."

Into the dark, Yuli stammered his amazement.

"There are many human and divine capacities which can be trained, my son. I myself, when my father died, fell into a fast through sorrow, and after the passage of many days saw him clear, suspended in the earth which is Akha's as if in another element, with his hands over his ears, as if he heard some sound he disliked. Death is not an end, but our extension in Akha—you recall the teaching, my son."

"I'm still angry with my father. Perhaps I have difficulty because of that. He was weak at the end. I wish to be strong. Where are these—these warrior mystics of whom you speak, Father?"

"If you do not believe my words, as I sense, it is pointless my telling you anything further." The voice held a nicely calculated shade of petulance.

"I'm sorry, Father. I'm a savage, just as you say. . . . You think the priesthood should reform itself, as Naab claimed, don't you?"

"I take a middle way." He sat leaning forward tensely for a while, blinking as if there was more to be said, and Yuli heard his dry eyelids flutter. "Many schisms divide the Holies, Yuli, as you will come to see if you take your orders. Things are less easy than they were when I was a boy. Sometimes it seems to me . . ."

The water drops went splash-splash-splash and someone coughed distantly.

"What, Father?"

"Oh . . . you have heretical thoughts enough, without my planting more. I can't imagine why I talk to you. That's the end of instruction for today, boy."

Talking not to Sifans, who liked to proceed by equivocation, but to his fellows, Yuli gradually learnt something of the power structures that held the community of Pannoval together. The administration was in the hands of the priests, and they worked with the militia, one reinforcing the other. There was no final arbitrator, no great chief, like the chiefs in the tribes of the wilderness. Behind each order of the priesthood lay another. They faded off into the metaphysical darkness, in obscure hierarchies, none finally with the power to command all the others.

Some orders, went the rumour, lived in more distant caverns in the mountain chain. In the Holies, habits were lax. Priests might serve as soldiers and vice versa. Women came and went among them. Under all the prayer and learning was confusion. Akha was elsewhere. Somewhere —somewhere there was greater faith.

Somewhere along the receding chain of command, thought Yuli, must be Sifans' order of warrior-mystics, who could commune with the dead and perform other amazing acts. The rumours, really no more to be listened to than the drip of water down a wall, whispered of an order elsewhere, set above the inhabitants of the Holies, who were referred to, when they were referred to at all, as the Keepers.

The Keepers, according to the whisper, were a sect to which admission was by election. They combined the dual role of soldiering and priesthood. What they kept was knowledge. They knew things unknown even in the Holies, and that knowledge gave them power. By keeping the past, they laid claim to the future.

"Who are these Keepers? Do we see them?" Yuli asked. The mystery excited him, and as soon as he heard of them he longed to be part of the mysterious sect.

He was speaking again to Father Sifans, almost at the end of his term. The passage of time had matured him; he no longer mourned his parents, and the Holies kept him busy. He had discovered recently in his charge-father an intense relish of gossip. The eyes blinked faster, the lips trembled, and the morsels slipped out. Every day, as the two men worked together in the prayer hall of their order, Father Sifans allowed himself a small ration of revelation.

"The Keepers can mix among us. We do not know who they are. Outwardly, they look no different from us. I might also be a Keeper, for all you know. . . ."

Next day, after prayer, Father Sifans beckoned Yuli with a mittened hand and said, "Come, since your novice term is nearly up, I'll show you something. You recollect what we were talking about yesterday?"

"Of course."

Father Sifans pursed his lips, squeezed his eyes together, raised his little sharp nose like a shrew's towards the ceiling, and nodded his head sharply a dozen times. Then he set off at a stiff mincing pace, leaving Yuli to follow.

Lights were rare in this section of the Holies and, in some places, forbidden entirely. The two men moved now with assurance through total darkness. Yuli kept the fingers of his right hand extended, lightly touching a carved skein unwinding on the wall of the corridor. They were passing through Warrborw, and Yuli was now wall-reading.

Steps were indicated ahead. Two of the luminous-eyed preets fluttered in a wicker cage, punctuating the junction between the main passage, a side one, and the steps. Yuli and his old charge-father progressed steadily upwards, *clack-clack-clack*, up stairs, along passages punctuated by more stairs, avoiding by habit others who walked in the limestoned dark.

Now they were in Tangwild. The wall-scroll on the rock under Yuli's fingers told him so. In a never repeating design of intertwined branches sported small animals which Yuli considered must have been figments of some long dead artist's imagination—animals that hopped and swam and climbed and rolled. For some reason, Yuli imagined them all in vivid colours. The band of wall-scroll carving ran for miles in all directions, never more than a hand-span wide. This was one of the secrets of the Holies; nobody could get lost in the labyrinthine dark once he had memorised the various patterns that identified the sectors and the coded signs signalling turns or steps or corridor divisions, all woven into the design.

They turned into a low gallery which the resonance of sound told them was otherwise unoccupied. Here, the wall-scroll was of quaint men squatting with out-turned hands among wooden huts. They must be outside somewhere, Yuli thought, enjoying the scenery beneath his palm.

Sifans halted, and Yuli bumped into him. As he apologised, the old man rested against the wall.

"Be silent and let me enjoy a good pant," he said.

In a moment, as if regretting the severity of his tone, he said, "I'm getting old. On my next birthday, I shall be twenty-five. But the death of an individual is nothing to our Lord Akha."

Yuli feared for him.

The father fumbled about the wall. Moisture ran down the rock and soaked everything.

"Hah, yes, here . . ."

The charge-father opened a small shutter, permitting light to blaze in upon them. Yuli had to shield his eyes for a moment. Then he stood by Father Sifans and looked out.

A grunt of astonishment escaped him.

Below them lay a small town, built on a hill. Crooked lanes ran up and down, sometimes fronted by quite grand houses. They were intersected by alleys, where riotous building concocted a maze of dwellings. To one side, a river ran in a chasm, and livings perched dangerously on its very edge. People, tiny as ants, moved among the lanes and jostled inside roofless rooms. The noise of their traffic rose faintly to where the men stood peering down.

"Where are we?"

Sifans gestured. "That's Vakk. You've forgotten it, haven't you?"

He watched with some amusement, his nose screwed up, as Yuli stared down, open-mouthed.

How simple he was, he thought. He should have recognised it was

Vakk without having to ask, like a savage. He could see the far archway leading to Reck, faint as ice in the distance. Nearer, squinting, he made out familiar livings and the alley where his room had been, and the home of Kyale and Tusca. He recalled them—and the beautiful black-haired Iskador—with longing, but his feelings were muted, because there was no point in yearning for a bygone world. Kyale and Tusca would have forgotten him, as he had them. What chiefly struck him was how bright Vakk appeared, for he remembered it as a place of deep shadow, lacking all colour. The difference marked how greatly his sight had improved during his stay in the Holies.

"You recollect that you asked me who the Keepers were," said Father Sifans. "You asked if we saw them. Here is my response." He indicated the world below them. "The people down there do not see us. Even if they look upward, they are still unable to spot us. We are superior to them. So are the Keepers superior to mere members of the priesthood. Within our fortress there is a secret fortress."

"Father Sifans, help me. Is that secret fortress . . . is it friendly towards us? Secrecy is not always friendly."

The father blinked his eyes. "The question should be rather, Is the secret fortress necessary to our survival? And the answer to that is, Yes, whatever it costs. You may find that a strange answer, coming from me. I am for the middle way in everything but this. Against the extremities of our life, against which Akha seeks to defend us, extremes are called for.

"The Keepers keep Truth. According to the scriptures, our world has been withdrawn from Wutra's fire. Many generations ago, the people of Pannoval dared to defy Great Akha and went to live outside our sheltering holy mountain. Towns like Vakk which we see before us were built under the naked skies. Then we were punished by fire, which Wutra and his cohorts sent down. A few survivors lived to return to our natural home, here.

"This is not merely scripture, Yuli. Forgive the blasphemy of that 'merely.' This is scripture, I should say. It is also a history that our people have lived. The Keepers in their secret fortress keep that history, and many things that still survive from the period of naked skies. I believe they see uncloudedly what we see clouded."

"Why are we in the Holies not considered fit to know these things?"

"Enough to know them as scripture, a parable. Myself, I believe that the naked knowledge is kept from us, first, because those in power always prefer to hoard knowledge, which is power, and second, because they believe that armed with such knowledge we might again attempt to return to the outside world of naked skies at such time as Great Akha banishes the snows."

Yuli thought with racing thoughts. Father Sifans' frankness aston-ished him. If knowledge was power, where stood faith? It occurred to him that he was possibly being tested, and was aware of the priest awaiting his answer with alert interest. Playing safe, he brought in the name of Akha again.

"Surely, if Akha banishes the snows, that is his invitation to return to the world of skies? It is not natural for men and women to be born and die in darkness."

Father Sifans sighed. "So you say—but you were born under the skies."

"I hope to die there, too," Yuli said, with a fervour that surprised himself. He feared that his unpremeditated response would provoke his charge-father's anger; instead, the old man placed a mittened hand on his shoulder.

"We all desire conflicting desires. . . ." He struggled with himself—either to speak or to stay silent—then said calmly, "Come, we will return, and you shall lead the way. Your reading of the wall-scrolls is becoming excellent."

He closed the shutter on Vakk. They regarded each other as the night rushed back. Then they returned through the dark sleeve of the gallery.

Yuli's initiation as a priest was a great event. He fasted for four whole days, and came light-headed before his cardinal in Lathorn. With him went three other young men of Yuli's own age, also due to take all the vows of a priest, also to sing for two hours, standing in stiff clothes and unaccompanied by music, the liturgies memorised for the occasion.

Their voices rose thinly in the great dark church, hollow as a cistern.

> Darkness be our guise
> Ever, and sting the sinner within
> To sing. Bremely we begin
> Priests, priests, of great rate,
> Golden in ancient Akha's gaze,
> Armoured in ancient right.

A solitary candle stood between them and the figure of the seated cardinal. The old man remained motionless throughout the ceremony; perhaps he slept. A breeze blew the candle flame fluttering in his direction. In the background stood the three charge-fathers who had sponsored the young men to priesthood. Yuli could see Sifans dimly, his nose wrinkled upwards like a shrew's in pleasure, nodding to the chant. No militia were present, or phagors.

At the end of the initiation, the stiff old figure decked out in its black and whites and chains of gold rose to its feet, raised its hands above its head, and intoned a prayer for the initiates:

". . . and grant finally, O Ancient Akha, that we may move ever more deeply into the caverns of thy thought until we discover within ourselves the secrets of that illimitable ocean, without bound or dimension, which the world calls life, but which we privileged few know to be Everything that is beyond Death and Life. . . ."

Fluggels began to play, swelling music filled Lathorn and Yuli's heart.

Next day, he was given his first task, to go among the prisoners of Pannoval and listen to their troubles.

For newly ordained priests there was an established procedure. They served first in the Punishment area, and then were transferred to Security before being allowed out to work among the ordinary people. In this process of hardening off, they were fortified in the distancing between them and the people implied in their ordination.

Punishment was full of noise and burning brands. It also had its quota of warders, drawn from the militia, and their phagors. It was situated in a particularly wet cavern. A light rain fell most of the time. Anyone who looked up could see the beads of moisture swinging downwards on a crooked path, teased by wind from stalactites far overhead.

Warders wore heavy soles to their boots, which sounded on the pavements. The white-coated phagors which accompanied them wore nothing, able to rely on their natural protection.

Brother Yuli's job was to work duty spells with one of the three guard lieutenants, a coarse thick man called Dravog, who walked as if he were crushing beetles and spoke as if he were chewing them. He constantly beat his leggings with his stave, making an irritating drumming noise. Everything that concerned the prisoners—including the prisoners themselves—was meant to be banged. All movements were executed to gongs, any delay was punished by application of a stave. Noise was the order of the day. The prisoners were a sullen lot. Yuli had to legitimise any violence and frequently patch its victims.

He soon found himself opposed to Dravog's mindless brutality, while the unremitting hostility of the prisoners eroded his nerves. The days spent under Father Sifans had been happy even if he had not always appreciated that at the time. In these harsh new surroundings, he missed the dense dark, the silences, the piety, and even Sifans himself, with his cautious friendliness. Friendship was not a quality Dravog recognised.

One of the sectors of Punishment was a cavern called Twink. In Twink, squads of prisoners worked at demolishing the rear wall to enlarge the work space. The toil was endless. "They're slaves, and you've got to beat them to keep them going," Dravog said. The remark gave Yuli an uncomfortable glimpse into history—probably much of Pannoval had been opened up in this way.

The rubble from the excavation was carried away in clumsy wooden carts, which needed the efforts of two men to shift. The carts trundled to a place somewhere in the warrens of the Holies where the Vakk ran far below ground level and a deep pit waited to receive the rubble.

Twink contained a farm worked by the prisoners. Noctiferous barley was grown for bread, fish were farmed in a pool fed by a stream which poured from the rock. A quota of larger fish was culled every day. Diseased fish were dug into long banks where enormous edible fungi grew. Their pungent odour cut across the senses of anyone entering Twink.

Nearby, in other caverns, were more farms, and chert mines. But Yuli's movements were almost as circumscribed as those of the prisoners; Twink formed the limit of his beat. He was surprised when Dravog, in conversation with another warder, mentioned that one of the side passages leading from Twink would take him into Market. Market! The name conjured up a jostling world he had left behind in a different life, and he thought nostalgically of Kyale and his wife. "You'll never be a proper priest," he told himself.

The gongs were struck, the wardens shouted, the prisoners strained their grudging bodies. The phagors shambled back and forth, sticking their milts up their slotted nostrils, and occasionally exchanging a grunted word with each other. Yuli hated their presence. He was watching four prisoners under the eye of one of Dravog's warders trawl in the fish pool. To do this, the men were forced to get into the freezing water up to their stomachs. When their net was full, they were allowed to climb out and drag the catch onto the bank.

The fish were gout. They were a pale strawy white, with blind blue eyes. They struggled hopelessly as they were dragged from their natural element.

A rubble cart was passing, pushed by two prisoners. One of its wheels struck a stone. The prisoner shouldering the nearside shaft staggered and fell. As he went, he struck one of the fishers, a youth stooping to get a hold on the end of the net, who plunged head first into the water.

The warder began to shout and struck about him with his stave. His phagor hopped forward and grasped the prisoner who had slipped, lifting him off his feet. Dravog and another warder came running up in time to beat the young prisoner about his head as he dragged himself from the pool.

Yuli grasped Dravog's arm.

"Leave him alone. It was an accident. Help him out."

"He's not allowed in the pool on his own," Dravog said savagely, elbowing Yuli out of the way and striking again.

The prisoner climbed out with blood and water pouring from his head. Another warder rushed up, his brand hissing in the rain, his phagor behind him, eyes pink in the shadows. He shouted, sorry to have missed the excitement. He joined with Dravog and the other warders in booting the half-drowned prisoner back to his cell in the next cavern.

When the commotion had died and the mob disappeared, Yuli cautiously approached the cell, in time to hear a prisoner in the adjoining cell call, "Are you all right, Usilk?"

Yuli went to Dravog's office and collected the master key. He unlocked the cell door, took a fat lamp from a niche in the passage, and entered.

The prisoner sprawled on the floor in a pool of water. He was supporting his torso with his arms, so that the outline of his shoulder blades stuck painfully through his shirt. Head and cheek were bleeding.

He turned a sullen look at Yuli, then, without change of expression, let his head droop again.

Yuli looked down at the soaked and battered skull. Tormented, he squatted by the man, setting the lamp down on the filthy floor.

"Scumb off, monk," the man growled.

"I'll help you if I can."

"You can't help. Scumb it!"

They remained in the same positions, without moving or speaking, and water and blood mingled in the puddle.

"Your name's Usilk, I believe?"

No response. The thin countenance remained pointing down at the floor.

"Is your father's name Kyale? Living in Vakk?"

"Leave me alone."

"I know—I knew him well. And your mother. She looked after me."

"You heard what I said. . . ." With a sudden burst of energy, the prisoner flung himself on Yuli, beating at him rather feebly. Yuli rolled over and disengaged himself, jumping up like an asokin. He was about to fling himself into the attack when he paused. With an effort of will, he controlled himself and pulled back. Without a word more, he collected the lamp and left the cell.

"A dangerous one, that," Dravog said to him, permitting himself a sly grin at the priest's expense, seeing his flustered appearance. Yuli retreated to the brothers' chapel, and prayed in the dark to an unresponsive Akha.

There was a story Yuli had heard in Market, a story not unknown to the ecclesiastics in the Holies, about a certain worm.

The worm was sent by Wutra, wicked god of the skies. Wutra put the worm into the labyrinth of passages in Akha's holy mountain. The worm is large and long, its girth being about equal to that of a passageway. It is slimy, and it slides along noiselessly in the dark. Only its breathing can be heard, issuing from its flabby lips. It eats people. They are safe one moment; the next, they hear the evil breathing, the rustle of long whiskers, and then they are swallowed.

A spiritual equivalent of Wutra's worm was now at large in the labyrinths of Yuli's thought. He could not prevent himself seeing, in the thin shoulders and blood of the prisoner, the gulf that lay between preachments and practice in Akha. It was not that the preachments were so pious, for mainly they were practical, stressing service; nor was it that life was so bad; what troubled him was that they were at odds.

There returned to his memory something that Father Sifans had said to him. "It is not goodness and holiness that lead a man to serve Akha. More often it is sin such as yours." Which implied that many among the priesthood were murderers and criminals—little better than the prisoners. Yet they were set over the prisoners. They had power.

He went about his duties grimly. He smiled less than he had. He never felt happy working as a priest. The nights he spent in prayer, the days in thought—and in trying, when possible, to forge some sort of contact between himself and Usilk.

Usilk shunned him.

Finally, Yuli's time in Punishment was completed. He entered a period of meditation before going to work with the Security Police. This branch of the militia had come under his notice while working in the cells, and he found within himself the ghost of a dangerous idea.

After only a few days in Security, Wutra's worm became ever more active in his mind. His task was to see men beaten and interrogated and to administer a final blessing to them when they died. Grimmer and grimmer he became, until his superiors commended him and gave him cases of his own to handle.

The interrogations were simple, for there were few categories of crime. People cheated or stole or spoke heresy. Or they went to places that were forbidden or plotted revolution—the crime that had been Usilk's. Some even tried to escape to Wutra's realm, under the skies. It was now that Yuli realised that a kind of illness gripped the dark world; everyone in authority suspected revolution. The illness bred in the darkness, and accounted for the numerous petty laws that governed life in Pannoval. Including the priesthood, the settlement numbered almost six and three quarter thousand people, every one of whom was forced into a guild or order. Every living, guild, order, dormitory, was infiltrated by spies, who themselves were not trusted, and also had an infiltrated guild of their own. The dark bred distrust, and some of its victims paraded, hangdog, before Brother Yuli.

Although he loathed himself for it, Yuli found he was good at the work. He felt enough sympathy to lower his victim's guard, enough destructive rage to tear the truth out. Despite himself, he developed a professional's taste for the job. Only when he felt secure did he have Usilk brought before him.

At the end of each day's duty, a service was held in the cavern called Lathorn. Attendance was compulsory for the priesthood, optional for any of the militia who wished to attend. The acoustics of Lathorn were excellent: choir and musicians filled the dark air with swelling veins of music. Yuli had recently taken up a musical instrument. He was becoming expert on the fluggel, a bronze instrument no bigger than his hand, which he at first despised, seeing other musicians play enormous peetes, vrachs, baranboims, and double-clows. But the tiny fluggel could turn his breath into a note that flew as high as a childrim, soaring up to the clouded roof of Lathorn above all conspiring melody. With it, Yuli's spirit also flew, to the traditional strains of "Caparisoned," "In His Penumbra," and, his favourite, the richly counterpointed "Oldorando."

One evening, after service, Yuli left Lathorn with an acquaintance, a shriven fellow priest by the name of Bervin, and they walked together through the tomblike avenues of the Holies, to run their fingers over new carvings even then being created by the three Brothers Kilandar. It chanced that they encountered Father Sifans, also strolling, reciting a litany to himself in a nervous undertone. They greeted each other cordially. Bervin politely excused himself, so that Yuli and Father Sifans could parade and talk together.

"I don't enjoy my feelings about my day's work, Father. I was glad of the service."

As was his fashion, Sifans responded to this only obliquely.

"I hear marvellous reports of your work, Brother Yuli. You will have to seek further advancement. When you do, I will help you."

"You are kind, Father. I recall what you told me"—he lowered his voice—"about the Keepers. An organisation for which one can volunteer, you said?"

"No, I said one could only be elected to the Keepers."

"How could I put my name forward?"

"Akha will aid you when it is necessary." He sniffed with laughter. "Now you are one of us, I wonder . . . have you heard a whisper of an order above even the Keepers?"

"No, Father. You know I don't listen to whispers."

"Hah, you should. Whispers are a blind man's sight. But if you are so virtuous, then I will say nothing of the Takers."

"The Takers? Who are they?"

"No, no, don't worry, I will say not a word. Why should you bother your head with secret organisations or tales of hidden lakes, free of ice? Such things may be lies, after all. Legends, like Wutra's worm."

Yuli laughed. "Very well, Father, you have worked me up to sufficient interest. You can tell me everything."

Sifans made tsking noises with his thin lips. He slowed his step, and sidled into an alcove.

"Since you force me. Very regrettable . . . You may remember how the rabble lives in Vakk, its rooms all a huddle, one on top the next, without order. Suppose this mountain range in which Pannoval lives is like Vakk—better, like a body with various interconnected parts, spleen, lungs, vitals, heart. Suppose there are caverns just as large as ours above us and below us. It's not possible is it?"

"No."

"I'm saying it is possible. It's a hypothesis. Let us say that somewhere beyond Twink there exists a waterfall, falling from a cavern above ours. And that waterfall falls to a level below ours, some way below. Water plays where it will. Let us say that it falls into a lake, the waters of which are pure and too warm for ice to form on them. . . . Let us imagine that in that desirable and secure place live the most favoured, the most powerful, the Takers. They take everything of the best, the knowledge and the power, and treasure it for us there, until the day of Akha's victory."

"And keep those things from *us* . . ."

"What's that? Fillips, I missed what you said, Brother. Well, it's just an amusing story I tell you."

"And does one have to be elected to the Takers?"

The father made little clicking noises with his tongue. "Who could penetrate such privilege, supposing it existed? No, my boy, one would have to be born to it—a number of powerful families, with beautiful women to keep them warm, and perhaps secret ways to come and go, even beyond Akha's domains. . . . No, it would need—why, it would need a revolution to get near such a hypothetical place."

He stuck his nose in the air and giggled.

"Father, you tease the poor simple priests below you."

The old priest's head went to one side, judicially. "Poor you are, my young friend, and will most like remain so. Simple you are not—and that is why you will always make a flawed priest, as long as you continue. That is why I love you."

They parted. The priest's declaration troubled Yuli. Yes, he was a flawed priest, as Sifans said. A music lover, nothing more.

He washed his face in icy water as his thoughts burned. All these hierarchies of priesthoods—if they existed—led only to power. They did not lead to Akha. Faith never explained precisely, with a verbal precision to rival the precision of music, how devotion could move a stone effigy; the words of faith led only to a foggy obscurity called holiness. The realisation was as rough as the towel on which he dried his cheeks.

Lying in the dormitory far from sleep, he saw how old Sifans' life had been stripped from the old man, real love had been starved from him, until he was left only with teasing ghosts of affection. He did not really care—had perhaps ceased to care a while ago—whether those beneath him had faith or not. His hints and riddles expressed a deep-rooted dissatisfaction with his own life.

In sudden fear, Yuli told himself that it would be better to die a man in the wilderness than a dry mouth here in the shadowy safeties of Pannoval. Even if it meant leaving behind his fluggel and the strains of "Oldorando."

The fear made him sit up, casting off his blanket. Dark winds, the restless inhabitants of the dormitory, blew about his head. He shivered.

With a kind of exultation matching the exultation he had experienced on entering Reck long ago, he whispered aloud, "I don't believe, I believe nothing."

Power over others he believed. He saw it in action every day. But that was purely human. Perhaps he had actually ceased to believe in other than human oppression during that ritual in State, when men had allowed a hated phagor to bite the words from young Naab's throat. Perhaps Naab's words might still triumph, and the priests reform themselves until their lives held meaning. Words, priests—they were actual. It was Akha that was nothing.

Into the moving dark he whispered the words, "Akha, you are nothing!"

He did not die, and the winds still rustled in his hair.

He jumped up and ran. Fingers unwinding the wall-scroll, he ran and ran until he was exhausted, and his fingertips raw. He turned back, panting. Power he wanted, not subjection.

The war in his mind was stilled. He returned to his blanket. Tomorrow, he would act. No more priests.

Dozing, he started up once again. He was back on a frozen hillside. His father had left him, taken by the phagors, and he flung his father's spear contemptuously into a bush. He recalled it, recalled the movement of his arm, the hiss of the spear as it embedded itself among the tattered branches, the knife-sharp air in his lungs.

Why did he suddenly recollect that insignificant detail?

Since he had no powers of self-analysis, the question remained unanswered as he drifted into sleep.

The morrow was the last day of his interrogation of Usilk; interrogations were permitted for only six days consecutively, then the victim was allowed to rest. Rules in this respect were strict, and the militia kept a suspicious eye on the priesthood in all these matters.

Usilk had said nothing useful, and was unresponsive alike to beating and cajolery.

He stood before Yuli, who was seated on an inquisitorial chair carved elaborately from a solid chunk of timber; it served to emphasise the difference between the state of the two men, Yuli outwardly at ease, Usilk half-starved, ragged, shoulders bowed, face wan and without expression.

"We know that you were approached by men who threaten the security of Pannoval. All we wish is their names and then you can go free, back to Vakk."

"I did not know them. It was a word in the crowd."

Both question and answer had become conventional.

Yuli rose from his chair and walked round the prisoner, giving no sign of his emotions.

"Usilk, listen. I feel no enmity for you. I respect your parents, as I told you. This is our last session together. We shall not meet again, and you will certainly die in this miserable place, for no reason."

"I have my reasons, monk."

Yuli was surprised. He had expected no response. He lowered his voice.

"We all have reasons. . . . I will put my life in your hands. I am unfit to be a priest, Usilk. I was born in the white wilderness under the skies far to the north of Pannoval, and to the wilderness I wish to return. I will take you with me, I will help you to escape. That's true speaking."

Usilk raised his gaze to Yuli's. "Scumb off, monk. That trickery won't work on me."

"It's true speaking. How can I prove it? You wish me to blaspheme against the god to whom I made my vows? You think I can say these things lightly? Pannoval has shaped me, yet something in my inner nature makes me rebel against it and its institutions. They bring shelter and content to the multitude, but not to me, not even in the favoured role of priest. Why not, I cannot say, except that it is how I am made. . . ."

He choked back his flow of words.

"I'll be practical. I can get a spare monk's cassock for you. When we go from this cell later, I will help you slip into the Holies and we will escape together."

"Scumble on your tricks."

Yuli fell into a rage. It was all he could do to stop himself attacking and beating the man. He flew in fury to the instruments hanging on the wall, and lashed at his chair with a whip. He seized the fat lamp that stood on the table and thrust it under Usilk's eyes. . . . He hit himself on the chest.

"Why should I lie to you, why betray myself? What do you know, after all? Nothing, nothing worth having. You're just a thing, snatched up from Vakk, your life without meaning or importance. You have to be tortured and killed, because that is your destiny. Fine, go ahead with it, enjoy feeling your strength die day by day—it's the price you pay for pride, and for being a cretin. Do what you will, die a thousand times. I've had enough. I can't bear the torment. I'm off. Think of me as you lie in your own scumble—I'll be out, free, free, under the sky where Akha's power can't reach."

He shouted these words, careless who heard him, blazing before the beaten pallor of Usilk's face.

"Scumb off, monk." Just the same sullen phrase he had used all week.

Jumping back a pace, he brought up the whip and struck Usilk with the stock across his broken cheek. All his force and rage went behind the blow. His glaring gaze saw by the lamp's uncertain light exactly where on the cheek under the eye and across the bridge of Usilk's nose the stock struck. He stood with whip half-raised, watching as Usilk's hands came up towards the injury, how his knees buckled. He swayed and fell to the floor, resting on knees and elbows.

Still clutching the whip, Yuli stepped over the body and quitted the cell.

In his own confusion, he was scarcely aware of the confusion round him. Warders and militia were running here and there in an unexpected manner—the normal progress through the dark veins of the Holies was a funereal walking pace.

A captain came along briskly, holding a flaring torch in one hand and shouting orders.

"You're one of the priest-interrogators?" he demanded of Yuli.

"What of it?"

"I want all these rooms cleared of prisoners. Get them back to their cells. The injured are going to be put in here. Look sharp."

"Injured? What injured?"

The captain roared his annoyance. "Are you deaf, Brother? What do you think all the shouting's been about this last hour? The new borings in Twink have collapsed, and many good men are buried. It's like a battlefield down there. Now, get moving and get your prisoner back in his cell, fast. I want this corridor cleared in two minutes."

He moved on, shouting and cursing. He was enjoying the excitement.

Yuli turned back. Usilk still lay crumpled on the floor of the interrogation room. Stooping, he seized him under the shoulders and dragged him into an upright position. Usilk moaned and appeared semiconscious. By levering one of the prisoner's arms over his shoulder Yuli could persuade him to walk after a fashion. In the corridor, where the captain still roared, other interrogators were removing their victims, hustling excitedly, nobody exactly looking displeased at this interruption to routine.

They headed into the dark like shadows. Now was his chance to disappear, while the excitement was on. And Usilk?

His rage was dying, his guilt returning. He was aware of wishing to show Usilk that he was sincere in his earlier offer of help.

The decision was made. Instead of heading towards the prison cells, he turned towards his own quarters. A plan grew in his mind. First, he had to revive Usilk, to prepare him for escape. It was useless to think of taking him to the brothers' dormitory, where they would be discovered; there was a safer place.

Wall-reading, he turned off before the dormitories, propelling Usilk up a winding stair, off which, in a warrenlike arrangement, the chambers of some of the fathers led. The band of carving under his hand kept him informed of where he was, even when the darkness grew so intense that phantasmal crimsons drifted through it like submerged weeds. At Father Sifans' door, he tapped and entered.

As he had calculated, there was no response. At this time of day, Sifans should be engaged elsewhere. He pulled Usilk in.

He had stood outside this door many times, but had never entered it. He was at a loss. He helped Usilk to sit, leaning with his back against a wall, and groped about for the lamp bracket.

After some blundering against furniture, he found it, and spun the chert wheel attached to the bracket. A spark flew, a tongue of light grew, and he lifted the lamp from its socket and looked about him. Here were all Father Sifans' worldly goods, few in number. In one corner stood a small altar with a statue of Akha, greasy with handling. There was a place for ablutions. There was a shelf supporting one or two objects, including a musical instrument, and a mat on the floor. Nothing more. No table or chairs. Lost in shadow was an alcove which Yuli knew without looking would contain a cot where the old father slept.

He moved into action. With water from the basin, piped from the rock, he washed Usilk's face and tried to revive him. The man drank a little water, puking as he did so. On the shelf in a tin was some doughy barley bread; Yuli fed some to Usilk and ate a chunk himself.

He shook Usilk's shoulder gently. "You'll have to forgive my temper. You provoked it. I'm only a savage at heart, not fit to be a priest. Now you see that I spoke truth—we are going to escape from here. With a rockfall in Twink, it should be easy to get away."

Usilk merely moaned.

"What do you say? You're not that bad. You'll have to move for yourself."

"You will never trick me, monk." He looked at Yuli through slitted eyes.

Yuli squatted down beside him. The movement made Usilk flinch away. "Look, we have already committed ourselves. I have committed myself. Try and understand. I'm asking nothing from you, Usilk—I'm just going to help you get out of here. There must be some way to escape through the north gate dressed as monks. I know an old trapper woman called Lorel, not many days journeying north from here, who will allow us shelter while we grow used to the cold."

"I'm not moving, man."

Smiting his forehead, Yuli said, "You'll have to move. We are hiding in a father's room. We can't stay here. He's not a bad old boy, but he'd surely report us if he discovered us."

"Not so, Brother Yuli. Your not-so-bad old boy is a grave of secrets."

Jumping up, Yuli turned and stood face to face with Father Sifans, who had emerged quietly from the alcove. He put forward a papery hand in a protective gesture, fearing attack.

"Father . . ."

The gesture became one of reassurance as Father Sifans blinked at him in the wan light.

"I was resting. I was in Twink when the roof fell in—what a mess! Fortunately, I was not in great danger, but a piece of rock flew and hit my leg. I can advise you that there will be no escape through the north gate; the guard have closed it and declared a state of emergency, just in case the worthy citizens do something unwise."

"You're going to report us, Father?" From the olden days, the days of his adolescence, he had kept one possession, the bone knife which his mother had carved in her well days. His hand crept beneath his cassock and grasped the knife as he asked his question.

Sifans sniffed. "Like you, I shall do something unwise. I am going to advise you on the best route to take to leave our country. I am also going to advise you not to take this man with you. Leave him here, I'll see to him. He's close to death."

"No, he's tough, Father. He'll recover quickly when the idea of freedom really sinks in. He's been through much, haven't you, Usilk?"

The prisoner stared up at them, across a blackened cheek which had already swollen enough to close one eye.

"Also, he is your enemy, Yuli, and will remain so. Beware of him. Leave him to me."

"It's my fault he is my enemy. I will make amends and he will forgive me when we are safe."

The father said, "Some men do not forgive."

As they stood regarding each other, Usilk made clumsy movements to rise to his feet, and stood gasping, resting his forehead against the wall.

"Father, I hardly can ask you this," Yuli said. "For all I know, you are a Keeper. Will you come with us to the outer world?"

The eyes blinked rapidly. "Before my initiation, I felt I could not serve Akha, and I attempted once to leave Pannoval. But I was caught, because I was always one of the docile kind, and not savage like you."

"You never forget my origins."

"Oh, I envied savagery. I still do. But I was defeated; my wish was subverted by my nature. I was caught and treated—well, as to how I was treated, let me merely say that I also am a man who cannot forgive. That was long ago. Since then I have gained promotion."

"Come with us."

"I will remain here and nurse my injured leg. I always have my excuses, Yuli."

Taking a stone from the floor, the father drew a sketch on the wall for Yuli, explaining an escape route to him. "It is a long journey. You must travel beneath the Quzint Mountains. You will find yourself at last not in the north but the more clement south. Stay well, and prosper." Spitting on his hand, he erased the marks on his wall and tossed the stone into a corner.

Finding nothing to say, Yuli put his arms round the old man, so that his frail arms were pinned to his side, and hugged him. "We'll go at once. Farewell."

Usilk said, speaking with difficulty, "You must kill this fellow, kill him now. Or, as soon as we leave, he will give the alarm."

"I know him and I trust him."

"It's a trick."

"You and your damned tricks, Usilk. I won't let you touch Father Sifans." This was said in some agitation, as Usilk came forward and Yuli put out a detaining arm to keep him from the old priest. Usilk struck at his arm, and for a moment the two wrestled together, until Yuli pushed him off as gently as possible.

"Come on, Usilk, if you're fit enough to struggle. Let's go."

"Wait. I see I'll have to trust you, monk. Prove yourself true by freeing a comrade of mine. His name's Scoraw and he worked with me at the fish pool. He'll be in Cell 65. Also fetch a friend of mine from Vakk."

Stroking his chin, Yuli said, "You're in no position to dictate anything." Every delay meant danger. Yet he saw that it was necessary to make some gesture to placate Usilk, if they were to agree at all. Sifans' plan made it clear that they had a dangerous journey ahead.

"All right, Scoraw. I remember the man. He was your revolutionary contact?"

"Are you still trying to interrogate me?"

"Very well. Father, may Usilk stay here with you while I collect this Scoraw? Good. And who is the man in Vakk?"

A kind of smile moved briefly over Usilk's broken face. "Not a man, a woman. My woman, monk. Name of Iskador, queen of archery. Lives at the Bow, Bottom Alley."

"Iskador . . . yes, yes, I know her—I knew her once by sight."

"Get her. She and Scoraw are tough. We'll see how tough you are later, monk. . . ."

The father tweaked at Yuli's sleeve, and said softly to him almost inserting his nose into Yuli's ear. "My apologies, I have changed my mind. I do not dare to be left alone with this surly and stupid person. Please take him with you—you have my assurances I shall not leave my room." He clutched fiercely at Yuli's arm.

Yuli clapped his hands together. "Very well. Usilk, we go together. I'll show you where you can steal a habit. Put it on, go and collect Scoraw. I will go down into Vakk and collect your girl, Iskador. We will meet at the inner corner of Twink, where there are two passages leading off, so that we can escape if necessary. If you and Scoraw do not come, I shall have to leave without you, knowing you have been captured. Is that clear?"

Usilk grunted.

"Is that clear?"

"Yes, let's move."

They moved. They left the shelter of Sifans' small room and launched themselves into the thick night of the corridor. Fingers to wall-scroll, Yuli led on, forgetting in his excitement even to bid farewell to his old mentor.

The people of Pannoval at this time were hardheaded. They had no great thoughts, except to keep their stomachs fed. Yet they had a kind of small change in stories, which were bartered about by storytellers from time to time.

At the great entrance, by the guardhouses, before a visitor to Pannoval came among the terraces of Market, trees grew—small in number and stunted, but definitely green trees.

They were properly prized for their rarity, and for their habit of yielding an occasional harvest of wrinkled nuts called roofers. No tree managed to crop every year, but every year one tree or other had a few lime-coloured roofers dangling from its outer twigs. Most of the roofers had maggots in them; but the dames and children of Vakk and Groyne and Prayn ate the maggots along with the flesh of the nut.

Sometimes the maggots died when the nut was cracked. The poor little story had it that the maggots died of shock. They believed that the interior of their nut was their whole world, and the wrinkled case that contained it the sky. Then, one day, their world was cracked open. They saw with horror that there was a gigantic world beyond their world, more important and brighter in every way. It was too much for the maggots and they expired at the revelation.

Yuli thought of the maggots in the roofer nuts as he left the gaunt shadows of the Holies for the first time in more than a year, and returned, dazzled, to the busy world of ordinary life. At first, the noise and the light and the bustle of so many people reduced him to a state of shock.

All the challenge and temptation of that world was epitomised by

Iskador, Iskador the beautiful. The image of her face was fresh in his mind, as if he had seen her only yesterday. Confronting her, he found her even more beautiful, and could only stutter before her.

Her father's living had several compartments and was part of a small factory for making bows; he was the grand bowmaster of his guild.

Rather haughtily, she allowed the priest in. He sat on the floor and drank a cup of water, and slowly managed to tell her his tale.

Iskador was a sturdy girl of no-nonsense appearance. Her flesh was milky white, contrasting with her flowing black curly hair and her hazel eyes. Her face was broad, with high cheekbones, and her mouth wide and pale. All her movements were energetic, and she folded her arms over her bosom in a businesslike way as she listened to what Yuli had to say.

"Why doesn't Usilk come here and tell me all this rigmarole?" she asked.

"He is collecting another friend for the journey. He could not come into Vakk—his face is a bit bruised at present, and would excite unwelcome attention."

The dark hair hung down on either side of the face, framing it with two wings. Now the wings were flicked impatiently aside with a toss of the head, as Iskador said, "Anyhow, I have an archery contest in six days, which I want to win. I don't want to leave Pannoval—I'm happy enough here. It was Usilk who was always complaining. Besides, I haven't seen him for *ages*. I've got another boyfriend now."

Yuli stood up, flushing slightly.

"Fine, if that's how you feel. Just keep quiet about what I've told you. I'll be off and take your message to Usilk." His nervousness before her made him more brusque than he intended.

"Wait," she said, coming forward with extended arm, a well-shaped hand reaching out towards him. "I didn't say you could go, monk. What you tell me is pretty exciting. You're meant to plead on Usilk's behalf, begging me to come along with you."

"Just two things, Miss Iskador. My name is Yuli, not 'monk.' And why should I plead on Usilk's behalf? He's no friend of mine, and besides . . ."

His voice tailed off. He glared angrily at her, cheeks colouring.

"Besides what?" There was a hint of laughter in her question.

"Oh, Iskador, you're beautiful, that's what besides, and I admire you myself, that's what besides."

Her manner changed. She put her hand up so as to half-hide her pale lips. "Two 'that's what besides' . . . both rather important. Well, Yuli, that does make a bit of difference. You're not unpresentable yourself, now I come to look at you. How did you get to be a priest?"

Sensing the turn of the tide, he hesitated, then said boldly, "I killed two men."

She seemed to spend a long while regarding him from under her thick eyelashes.

"Wait there while I pack a bag and a strong bow," she said at last.

The collapse of the roof had sent an anxious excitement through Pannoval. The event most dreaded in popular fancy had occurred. Feelings were somewhat mixed; with dread went a relief that only prisoners and warders and a few phagors had been buried. They probably deserved everything that Great Akha sent them.

At the rear of Market, barriers were drawn up, and the militia were out in force to keep order. Rescue teams, men and women of the physician's guild, and workers, were moving back and forth at the scene of the disaster. Throngs of onlookers pressed forward, some quiet and tense, others merry, where an acrobat and a group of musicians encouraged them to be cheerful. Yuli pushed through the melée with the girl behind him, and people gave way to a priest out of long custom.

Twink, where the disaster had occurred, had an unfamiliar look. No onlookers were allowed, and a line of brilliant emergency flares was set up to assist the rescuers. Prisoners fed powder into the flares to maintain their brightness.

The scene was one of grim action, with prisoners digging and other ranks behind waiting to take over when they rested. Phagors had been set to hauling away the rubble carts. Every so often, a shout went up; then digging became more feverish, and a body would emerge from the earth, to be passed to waiting physicians.

The scale of the disaster was impressive. With the collapse of a new boring, part of the roof of the main cave had fallen in. There had been more than one subsidence. Most of the floor was piled high with rock, and the fish and fungus farm had largely been obliterated. The source of the original weakness that led to the disaster was a subterranean stream, which now gushed from its course, adding a flood to the other difficulties.

The rock fall had almost buried the rear passages. Yuli and Iskador had to scramble over a pile of debris to get there. Fortunately, this action was concealed from enquiring eyes by a still larger pile of debris. They climbed through without being stopped. Usilk and his comrade Scoraw were waiting in the shadows.

"The black and white suits you, Usilk," Yuli commented sarcastically, referring to the priestly disguise both prisoners wore. For Usilk had come eagerly forward to clutch Iskador. Perhaps displeased by his battered face, she kept her distance, appeasing him by holding his hands.

Even in his disguise, Scoraw still looked the prisoner. He was tall and thin, with the droop to his shoulders of a man who has spent too long in a cell too small. His hands were large and scarred. His glance—

at least during this encounter—was indirect; flinching from meeting Yuli's eyes, he took little sips of sight when Yuli's attention was elsewhere. When Yuli asked him if he was prepared for a difficult journey, he merely nodded, grunted, and shrugged a bag of possessions further on to his shoulder.

It was an inauspicious start to their adventure, and for a moment Yuli regretted his impulse. He was throwing away too much to consort with two characters like Usilk and Scoraw. First, he perceived, he must assert his authority, or they would meet nothing but trouble.

Usilk evidently had the same thought in mind.

He pushed forward, adjusting his pack. "You're late, monk. We thought you'd backed out. We thought it was another of your tricks."

"Are you and your mate up to a hard journey? You look ill."

"Best to get going and not stand about talking," Usilk said, squaring his shoulders and pushing forward between Iskador and Yuli.

"I lead, you cooperate," Yuli said. "Let's get that clear, then we'll all agree together."

"What makes you think you're going to lead, monk?" Usilk said jeeringly, nodding to his two friends for support. With his half-closed eye, he looked both sly and threatening. He was feeling pugnacious again, now that the prospect of escape was offered.

"Here's the answer to that," Yuli said, bringing his bunched right fist round in a hard curve and sinking it into Usilk's stomach.

Usilk doubled up, grunting and cursing.

"Scumb you, you eddre . . ."

"Straighten up, Usilk, and let's march before we're missed."

There was no more argument. They moved after him obediently. The faint lights of Twink died behind them. But at Yuli's fingertips went a wall-scroll, serving as his sight, teasingly formed of beads and chains of tiny shells, spinning out like a melody played on a fluggel, leading them down into the enormous silences of the mountain.

The others did not share his priestly secret, and still relied on light to get about. They began to beg him to go more slowly, or to let them light a lamp, neither of which he would do. He seized on the opportunity to take Iskador's hand, which she gave gladly, and he walked in a steady delight to feel her flesh against his. The other two contented themselves with clinging to her garment.

After some while, the passages branched, the walls became rougher, and the repeating pattern gave out. They had reached the limits of Pannoval, and were truly alone. They rested. While the others talked, Yuli kept clear in his mind the plan that Father Sifans had sketched for him. Already, he regretted that he had not embraced the old man and bidden him farewell.

Father, you understood much about me, I believe, for all your odd ways. You know what a lump of clay I am. You know that I aspire to

*good but cannot rise above my own dull nature. Yet you did not betray
me. Well, I did not knife you either, did I? You must keep trying to
improve yourself, Yuli—you're still a priest, after all. Or am I? Well,
when we get out, if we get out . . . And there's this wonderful girl . . .
No, no, I'm not a priest, old father, bless you, never could be, but I did
try and you helped. Fare you well, ever. . . .*

"Get up," he called, jumping to his feet and assisting the girl to hers.
Iskador rested a hand lightly on his shoulder in the dark before they set
off again. She did not complain about being tired when Usilk and
Scoraw began to do so.

They slept eventually, huddled together at the foot of a gravelly
slope, with the girl between Usilk and Yuli. Night fears got to them; in
the dark, they imagined that they heard Wutra's worm slithering
towards them, its jaws open and its slimy whiskers trailing.

"We'll sleep with a light burning," Yuli said. It was chill, and he
held the girl tight, falling asleep with one cheek against her leather tunic.

When they woke, they nibbled frugally on the food they had brought.
The way became much more difficult. There had been a cliff fall, and
they crawled for hours on their bellies, nose to toe, each calling to the
other unashamedly, in order to keep in touch in the overmastering
night of the earth. A freezing wind whistled through the slot they had
to work their way through, icing their hair to their heads.

"Let's go back," Scoraw begged, when at last they could stand, bent-
backed, and draw in breath. "I prefer imprisonment to this." Nobody
answered him, and he did not repeat the suggestion. They could not go
back now. But the great presence of the mountain silenced them as
they proceeded.

Yuli was hopelessly lost. The rock collapse had thrown him out of
his reckoning. He could no longer remember the old priest's map and
was almost as helpless without the repeating pattern at his fingers as
the others. A whispering noise grew and he strove to follow it. Bars of
evil and unidentifiable colour drifted before his staring eyes; he felt that
he was pressing through solid rock. His breath broke from his open
mouth in sharp gasps. By mutual consent, they rested.

The way had been leading downhill for hours. They staggered on,
Yuli with one hand to the side, one arm raised above his face, so that
he did not strike his head against rock, as he had already done on several
occasions. He felt Iskador clutching his habit; in his present state of
fatigue, the touch was merely an annoyance.

With his mind rambling, he began to believe that the way he
breathed controlled the diseased colours he saw. Yet that could not be
entirely correct, for a kind of luminosity was creeping into view. He
plunged on, ever down, squeezing his swollen lids tight together and
then releasing them. Blindness was descending upon him—he was seeing
a faint milky light. Looking round, he seemed to see Iskador's face as

in a dream—or a nightmare, rather, for her eyes were staring, her mouth gaping, in the ghostly disc of her face.

At his gaze, her awareness returned. She stopped, clutching at him for support, and Usilk and Scoraw barged into them.

"There's light ahead," Yuli said.

"Light! I can see again. . . ." Usilk grasped Yuli's shoulders. "You scumbing villain, you have brought us through. We're safe, we're free!"

He laughed greatly, and rushed ahead, arms outstretched as if to embrace the source of the light. In joy, the others followed, stumbling down the rough ground through a light that never was before, unless over some unknown northern sea where icebergs swam and clashed.

The way levelled out, the roof withdrew. Pools of water lay at their feet. They splashed through, and the path led up again steeply, until they were reduced to a walk, and the light grew no stronger, though there were now fierce noises all round.

Suddenly, they were at the end of the way, and stood daunted on the lip of a fissure. Light and noise surrounded them.

"Akha's eyes," gasped Scoraw, and stuck a fist between his teeth.

The fissure was like a throat, leading down into the belly of the earth. They could look up at the gullet, some way above. From the brink of the gullet, a river burst, and plunged down into the fissure. Just below where they stood, the force of the falling water struck rock for the first time. Its energy created the intense drumming they had heard. It then cascaded into depths where it was lost to view. The water was white even where it did not foam, and shot through with livid greens and blues. Although it radiated the dim light in which they rejoiced, the rocks behind it seemed no less bright: they were coated in thick whirls of white and red and yellow.

Long before they had finished gazing upon this spectacle, and looking at the white ghosts of each other, they were drenched by spray.

"This isn't the way out," Iskador said. "This is a dead end. Where now, Yuli?"

He pointed calmly to the far end of the ledge on which they stood. "We go by that bridge," he said.

They made their way carefully towards the bridge. The ground was slimy with ropey green algae. The bridge looked grey and ancient. It had been built of chunks of stone carved from the rock nearby. Its arch curved up, then stopped. They saw that the structure had collapsed, and was no more than a stub of a bridge. Through the milky light, another stub could be seen dimly on the far side of the chasm. There had once been a way across, but no more.

For a while, they stood staring across the gulf, not looking at one another. Iskador was the first to move. Bending, she set her bag down and pulled her bow from it. She tied a thread to an arrow of a kind she had used when Yuli saw her prize-winning performance, a long time ago. Without a word, she placed herself at the edge of the chasm, a foot firm on the edge, and raised the bow. She drew back her arm as she did so, squinting along it almost casually, and let fly.

The arrow seemed to curl through the spray-laden light. It reached its zenith over an outcrop of rock, glanced against the rocky wall above the waterfall, and fell back, its power spent, until it clattered at Iskador's feet.

Usilk clapped her shoulder. "Brilliant. Now what do we do?"

For answer, she tied stout cord to the end of the thread, and then picked up the arrow and drew in the thread. Soon the leading end of the cord ran over the projecting ledge, and travelled back down to nestle in her hand. She then produced a rope on which she made a noose, drew that over the projection too, slipped the other end of the rope through the noose, and pulled the whole thing tight.

"Do you wish to go first?" she asked Yuli, passing him the rope end. "Since you are our leader?"

He looked in her deepset eyes, wondering at her cunning, and the economy of her cunning. Not only was she telling Usilk that he was not the leader, she was telling him, Yuli, to prove that he was. He chewed this over, finding it profound, then grasped the rope and squared up to the challenge.

It was alarming but not too dangerous, he estimated. He could swing across the chasm and then, walking against vertical rock, climb to the level of the lip over which the waterfall poured. As far as they could see, there was space to climb in and avoid being swept away by the water. The possibilities that followed could be assessed only when he was up there. He certainly was not going to show fear in front of the two prisoners—or Iskador.

He launched himself rather too hurriedly across the abyss, his mind in part on the girl. Striking the opposite cliff rather clumsily, his left foot slipped on green slime, he jarred against the wall with his shoulder, swung into spray, and lost his grip on the rope. Next second, he was falling down the chasm.

Amid the roar of water came their united cry—the first time they had genuinely done something in unison.

Yuli struck rock, and clung there with every fibre of his being. He squeezed his knees up under his body, fought with his toes, and gripped the rock.

His fall had been no more than two metres, though it jarred every bone in his body, and had been broken by a boulder protruding from the cliff. It afforded him little more than a foothold, but that was enough.

Gasping, he crouched in his awkward position, scarcely daring to move, his chin almost on a level with his boots.

His anguished gaze fell on a blue stone lying below his eyes. He focused on it, wondering if he was going to die. The stone would not come sharp. He felt that he might have reached out over the ledge where he crouched and picked it up. Suddenly his senses told him the truth of the matter—he was not looking at a nearby stone but a blue object far below. Vertigo seized him, paralysing him; accustomed to the plains, he had no immunity against such an experience.

He closed his eyes and clung. Only Usilk's shouts, coming from a long way off, forced him to look again.

Distantly below lay another world, to which the fissure in which he crouched served as a kind of telescope. Yuli had a view no bigger than his hand into an enormous cavern. It was illuminated in some way. What he had taken for a blue stone was a lake, or possibly a sea, since he had a glimpse only of a fragment of a whole whose size he could not attempt to guess. On the shore of the lake were a few grains of sand, now interpretable as buildings of some kind. He lay in a cataplexy, staring senselessly down.

Something touched him. He could not move. Someone was speaking to him, clutching his arms. Without will, he allowed himself to cooperate in sitting up with his back against the rock, and locking his arms about his rescuer's shoulders. A bruised face, with damaged nose, slashed cheek, and one closed black and green eye swam before his vision.

"Hang on tight, man. We're going up."

He managed then to hold himself against Usilk, as the latter worked his way slowly upwards and eventually hauled them, with enormous labour, over the rock lip from which the waterfall poured. Usilk then collapsed, flat out, panting and groaning. Yuli looked down for Iskador and Scoraw, just visible on the other side of the fissure, faces upturned. He also looked more sharply down, into the fault; but his vision of another world had disappeared, eclipsed by spray. His limbs trembled, but he could control them sufficiently to help the others to join him and Usilk.

In silence, they clutched each other thankfully.

In silence, they picked their way amid the boulders on the side of the rushing stream of the waterfall.

In silence, they went on. And Yuli kept silence over the vision of the other world he had glimpsed. But he thought again of old Father Sifans; could it have been a secret fortress of the Takers, momentarily revealed to him amid the wilderness of rock? Whatever it was, he took it inside himself and was mute.

The warrens in the mountain seemed endless. Without light, the party of four went in fear of crevasses. When they judged it to be night, they found a suitable nook to sleep, and huddled together for warmth and company.

Once, after climbing for hours along a natural passage strewn with boulders from a long-vanished stream, they found a niche at shoulder height, into which all four could scramble, to tuck themselves away from the chill wind that had been blowing in their faces all day.

Yuli went to sleep immediately. He was roused by Iskador shaking him. The other men were sitting up, whispering apprehensively.

"Can you hear?" she asked.

"Can you hear?" Usilk and Scoraw asked.

He listened to the wind sighing down the passage, to a distant trickle of water. Then he heard what had disturbed them—a continuous rasping noise, as of something moving fast against the walls.

"Wutra's worm!" Iskador said.

He clutched her firmly. "That's just a story they tell," he said. But his flesh went cold, and he grasped his dagger.

"We're safe in this niche," Scoraw said. "If we keep quiet."

They could only hope he might be right. Unmistakably, something was approaching. They crouched where they were, peering nervously into the tunnel. Scoraw and Usilk were armed with staves, stolen from the warders of Punishment, Iskador had her bow.

The noise grew louder. Acoustics were deceptive, but they thought it came from the same direction as the wind. There was a rasping element to the noise now, and a rumble as of boulders being thrust heedlessly aside. The wind died, blocked perhaps. A smell assailed their nostrils.

It was a ripe aroma of festering fish, of scumble, of rotten cheese. A greenish fog permeated the passage. Legend said Wutra's worm was silent, but now it approached with a roar, whatever it might be.

Moved more by terror than courage, Yuli peered from their lair.

There it was, coming fast. Its features could hardly be discerned behind the bank of green luminescence it pushed along in front of it. Four eyes, banked two and two, whiskers and fangs gigantic. Yuli pulled his head back in horror, choking. It was approaching irresistibly.

Next moment, they all four had a sight of its face in profile. It plunged by, eyes glaring insanely. Stiffish whiskers brushed their furs. Then their vision was blocked by scaley ribs, rippling by, blue-lit, scouring dust in upon them, choking them with filth and stink.

There were miles of it, then it was past. Clutching each other, they peered out of their hiding place to see the end of it. Somewhere at the beginning of the boulder-strewn passage was a wider cave through which they had come. A convulsion was taking place down there; the green luminescence, still visible, rippled.

The worm had sensed them. It was turning round and coming back. For them. Iskador stifled a cry as she realised what was happening.

"Rocks, fast," Yuli said. There was loose rock they could throw. He reached towards the sloping back of the niche. His hand struck something unsuspected and furry. He drew back. He struck his chert wheel. A spark flew and died—living long enough for him to see that they were keeping company with the mouldering remains of a man, of which only bones and his enveloping furs remained. And there was a weapon of sorts.

He struck a second spark.

"It's a dead shaggy!" Usilk exclaimed, using the prisoner's slang for phagor.

Usilk was right. There was no mistaking the long skull, from which the flesh had dried, or the horns. Beside the body was a staff capped by a spike and a curved blade. Akha had come to the aid of those threatened by Wutra. Both Usilk and Yuli reached out and grabbed the shaft of the weapon.

"For me. I've used these things," Yuli said, wrenching at it. Suddenly, his old life was back, he recalled facing a charging yelk in the wilderness.

Wutra's worm was returning. Again the scraping noise. More light, livid and green. Yuli and Usilk ventured a quick look out of the niche. But the monster was unmoving. They could see the blur of its face. It had turned and was facing back in their direction, but did not advance.

It was waiting.

They chanced a look in the other direction.

A second worm was bearing down on them from the direction the first had come. Two worms . . . suddenly, in Yuli's imagination the cave system was crawling with worms.

In terror, they clung to each other, as the light grew brighter and the noise nearer. But the monstrous creatures would be concerned only with each other.

Following a wave of foetid air, the head of the monster plunged by, four eyes glaring as it stared to its front. Bracing the lower half of his newly acquired spear against the side of the niche, Yuli thrust the point out beyond the rock, hanging on with both hands.

It pierced the churning side of the worm as it charged forward. From the long opening tear in its body, a thick jamlike substance gushed, and flowed down the full extent of its body. The monster was slowing before its whiskered tail had passed the shelf where the four humans sprawled.

Whether the two worms had been intending to fight or mate would never be determined. The second worm never reached its target. Its forward motion petered out. Waves of crudely telegraphed pain caused the body to ripple, the tail to lash. Then it was still.

Slowly, its luminescence died. All was quiet, save for the sough of the wind.

They dared not move. They scarcely dared change their position. The first worm was still waiting somewhere in the darkness, its presence indicated by a faint green glow, scarcely discernible over the body of the dead monster. Afterwards, they agreed that this was the worst part of their ordeal. Each supposed in his or her private thoughts that the first worm knew where they were, that the dead worm was its mate, and that it was only waiting for them to stir to plunge forward and be revenged.

Eventually the first worm did move. They heard the slither of its whiskers against the rock. It slid cautiously forward as if expecting a trap, until its head loomed over the body of its dead adversary. Then it began to feed.

The four humans could no longer stay where they were. The sounds were too terrifyingly suggestive. Jumping clear of the spilt ichor, they regained the passage, and scampered away into the dark.

Their journey through the mountain was resumed. But now they stopped frequently and listened to the sounds of the dark. And when they had need to speak, they spoke in low tremulous voices.

Occasionally, they found water to drink. But their food gave out. Iskador shot down some bats, but they could not bring themselves to eat the creatures. They wandered in the labyrinth of stone, growing weaker. Time passed, the security of Pannoval was forgotten: all that remained of life was an endless darkness to be traversed.

They began to come upon bones of animals. Once, they struck a chert and discovered two human skeletons sprawling in an alcove, one with an arm about the other; time had robbed the gesture of any gentleness it might once have possessed: now there was only bone to scrape against bone, and terrifying grin to respond to the skull's grin.

Then, in a place with a colder airflow, they heard movements, and found two red-furred animals, which they killed. Close by was a cub, mewling and poking up its blunt nose at them. Tearing the cub apart, they devoured it while the flesh was still warm and then, in a sort of raging paroxysm of awakened hunger, devoured the two parents as well.

Luminescent organisms grew on the walls. They found signs of human habitation. The remains of a shack and something that might have been a boat sprouted a crop of fungi. Nearby, a chimney in the cavern roof had encouraged a small flock of preets. With her unfailing bow, Iskador downed six of the birds, and they cooked them in a pot over a fire with fungi and a pinch of salt for flavour. That night, as they slept together, unpleasantly vivid dreams visited them, which they attributed to the fungi. But when they set off next morning, they came after only two hours of walking to a low wide cavern into which green light filtered.

In one corner of the cave, a fire smouldered. There was a crude pen, inside which were three goats, their eyes bright in the twilight. Three women sat nearby on a pile of skins, an ancient crone with white hair, and two younger women. The latter ran off squealing when Yuli, Usilk, Iskador, and Scoraw appeared.

Scoraw ran forward and jumped in with the goats. Using an old utensil lying nearby as a pail, he milked the goats into it, despite the unintelligible cries of the crone. There was little milk to be had from the animals. What there was, they shared before moving on, casting the utensil down behind them as they left before the men of the tribe returned.

They entered a passage that turned sharply and had been barricaded. Beyond lay the mouth of the cave and, beyond that, open country, mountainside and valley, and the brilliant light of the realm ruled by Wutra, god of the skies.

They stood close together, for now they felt the bonds of unity and friendship, regarding the beautiful prospect. When they regarded each other, their faces were full of merriment and hope, and they could not keep from shouting and laughing. They skipped about and hugged one another. When their eyes were accustomed sufficiently to the brightness they could shield their brows and gaze up to where Batalix flitted among thin cloud, his disc a pale orange.

The time of year must be near the spring equinox, and the time of day noon, for two reasons: Batalix was vertically overhead, and Freyr was sailing below her to the east. Freyr was several times the brighter, spilling its light over snow-covered hills. Fainter Batalix was always the faster sentinel, and would soon be setting while Freyr lingered still at zenith.

How beautiful the sight of the sentinels was! The seasonal pattern of their dance in the heavens returned fresh to Yuli's mind, making him open heart and nostrils. He leaned on the carefully wrought spear with which he had killed the worm and let his body fill with daylight.

But Usilk laid a detaining hand on Scoraw, and lingered in the mouth of the cave, looking out apprehensively. He called to Yuli, "Wouldn't we do better to stay in these caves? How are we supposed to live out there, under that sky?"

Without removing his eyes from the landscape ahead, Yuli sensed that Iskador stood halfway between him and the men at the cave mouth. Without looking back, he answered Usilk.

"Do you remember that story they told in Vakk, about the maggots in the roofer nuts? The maggots thought their rotten nut was the whole world, so that when the nut cracked open, they died of shock. Are you going to be a maggot, Usilk?"

To that Usilk had no answer. But Iskador had. She came up behind Yuli and slipped her hand into the crook of his arm. He smiled and his heart sang, but he never ceased staring hungrily ahead.

He could see that the mountains through which they had come would provide shelter southward. Stunted trees no higher than a man grew sparsely, and grew upright, which indicated that the chill west wind of the Barriers no longer had power here. He still retained his old skills, learnt from Alehaw long ago. There would be game in the hills and they could live sensibly under the sky, as the gods intended.

His spirit rose, swelling until he had to fling his arms out wide.

"We will live in this sheltered place," Yuli said. "The four of us will stay united, whatever else happens." From a snowy fold of hillside, distantly, merging into the evening sky, smoke rose. He pointed ahead. "People live there. We'll force them to accept us. This shall be our place. We'll rule them, and teach them our ways. From now on, we live under our own laws, not other people's."

Squaring his shoulders, he set off down the slope, among a shallow stand of trees, and the others followed, Iskador first, walking proudly, then the others.

Some of Yuli's intentions worked out, and some did not.

After numerous challenges, they were accepted in a small settlement sheltering under a protective fold of mountain. The people lived on a squalidly primitive level; because of their superior knowledge and their boldness, Yuli and his friends were able to impose their will on the community, to rule it, and to enforce their own laws.

Yet they never became truly integrated, because their faces looked different, and the Olonets they spoke went with a different lilt from the local variety. And they discovered that this settlement, because of its advantages, always lived in fear of raids from a larger settlement some way off on the banks of a frozen lake. Indeed, these raids were made more than once during the years that followed, with great suffering caused, and loss of life.

Yet Yuli and Usilk became cunning, and maintained their cunning because they were outsiders, and built ferocious defences against the invaders from Dorzin, as the larger settlement was called. And Iskador taught all the young women how to make bows and use them. They came to perform with great skill. The next time the invaders arrived from the south, many died with arrows in their chests, and then there were no more attacks from that direction.

Yet inclement weather beat upon them, and avalanches rolled down from the mountains. There was no end to storms. Only in cave mouths could they grow a few maggoty crops or sustain a few mangey animals to give them milk and meat, so that their numbers never grew, and they were always hungry, or seized by illnesses that could be ascribed only to the malignant gods (of Akha, Yuli allowed no mention).

Yet Yuli took the beautiful Iskador for his woman, and loved her, and looked every day on her broad strong face with comfort. They had a child, a boy they called Si, in memory of Yuli's old priest in Pannoval, who survived all the pains and dangers of childhood, and grew up wild. Usilk and Scoraw also married, Usilk to a small brown woman named Isik, curiously like his own name; Isik, despite her stature, could run like a deer and was intelligent and kind. Scoraw took a girl named Fitty, a capricious lady who sang beautifully and led him a hell of a life, and produced a baby girl who died after one year.

Yet Yuli and Usilk could never agree. Although they united in the face of common danger, Usilk at other times displayed hostility to Yuli and his plans, and tricked him when he could. As the old priest had said, some men never forgive.

Yet a deputation came from the larger settlement of Dorzin, which had suffered losses following an outbreak of disease. Having heard of Yuli's reputation, they begged him to rule them in place of their dead leader. Which Yuli did, to be away from the vexation of Usilk, and he and Iskador and their child lived by the frozen lake, where game was plentiful, and administered the laws firmly.

Yet even in Dorzin there were almost no arts to relieve the monotony of their hard life. Though the people danced on feast days, they had no musical instruments beyond clappers and bells. Nor was there any religion, except for a constant fear of evil spirits and a stoic acceptance of the enemy cold, and sickness, and death. So that Yuli became at last a real priest, and tried to instill in the people a feeling for their own spiritual vitality. Most men rejected his words because, although they had welcomed him, he was an outsider, and they were too sullen to learn new things. But he taught them to love the sky in all its moods.

Yet life was strong in him and Iskador, and in Si, and they never let die the hope that better times were emerging. He kept the vision he had been granted in the mountains, that there was possibly a way of life more enjoyable than the one immediately granted, more secure, less subject to the chances and the elements.

Yet he and his beautiful Iskador grew older for all that, and felt the cold more with the passing years.

Yet they loved the lakeside place where they lived and, in memory of another life and another set of expectations, called it by the name of Oldorando.

This is as far as the story of Yuli, son of Alehaw and Onesa can go.

The story of their descendants, and what befell them, is a far greater tale. All unknown to them, Freyr drew nearer to the chilly world: for there was truth buried in the obscure scriptures Yuli rejected, and the sky of ice would in due process of time become a sky of fire. Only fifty Helliconian years after the birth of their son, true spring would visit the inclement world that Yuli and his beautiful Iskador knew.

A new world was already poised to be born.

Embruddock

Ａnd *Shay Tal said:*
You think we live at the centre of the universe. I say we live in the centre of a farmyard. Our position is so obscure that you cannot realise how obscure.

This I tell you all. Some disaster happened in the past, the long past. So complete was it that no one now can tell you what it was or how it came about. We know only that it brought darkness and cold of long duration.

You try to live as best you can. Good, good, live well, love one another, be kind. But don't pretend that the disaster is nothing to do with you. It may have happened long ago, yet it infects every day of our lives. It ages us, it wears us out, it devours us, it tears our children from us. It makes us not only ignorant but in love with ignorance. We're infested with ignorance.

I'm going to propose a treasure hunt—a quest, if you like. A quest in which every one of us can join. I want you to be aware of our fallen state, and to maintain constant alertness for evidence as to its nature. We have to piece together what has happened to reduce us to this chilly farmyard; then we can improve our lot, and see to it that the disaster does not befall us and our children again.

That's the treasure I offer you. Knowledge. Truth. You fear it, yes. But you must seek it. You must grow to love it.

I

DEATH OF A GRANDFATHER

The sky was black, and men bearing torches came from the south gate. They were thickly wrapped in skins, and trod with a high step to get through the snow lying in the lanes. The holy man was coming! The holy man was coming!

Young Laintal Ay hid in the porch of the ruined temple, his face shining with excitement. He watched the procession trudge by between the old stone towers, each one encrusted on its east face with the snow that had arrived earlier in the day. He noticed how colour existed only at the spluttering ends of the torches, on the end of the holy father's nose, and in the tongues of the six-dog team that pulled him. In each case, the colour was red. The heavy-laden sky—in which the sentinel Batalix was buried—had leached all other colours away.

Father Bondorlonganon from distant Borlien was fat, and made fatter by the enormous furs he wore, furs of a kind not used in Oldorando. He had come alone to Oldorando—the men who accompanied him were local hunters, each one already known to Laintal Ay. It was on the father's face that the boy focussed all his attention, for strangers came seldom; he had been smaller, less tough, on the occasion of the father's last visit.

The holy man's face was oval, and massively creased by horizontal lines, into which such features as his eyes fitted as best they could. The lines seemed to compress his mouth into a long cruel shape. He sat his sledge and stared about him suspiciously. Nothing in his attitude suggested he liked being back in Oldorando. His gaze took in the ruined temple; this visit was necessary because Oldorando had killed its priesthood some generations ago, as he knew. His uncomfortable stare rested a moment on the boy standing between two square pillars.

Laintal Ay stared back. It seemed to him that the priest's look was cruel and calculating; but he could hardly expect to think well of a man who was coming to perform last rites over his dying grandfather.

He smelt the dogs as they went by, and the tarry scent of burning torches. The procession turned and was heading up the main street, away from the temple. Laintal Ay was in two minds about following. He stood on the steps and hugged himself, watching as the sledge's arrival attracted people from their towers, despite the cold.

In the murk at the far end of the lane, under the big tower where Laintal Ay and his family lived, the procession halted. Slaves appeared to deal with the dogs—they would be housed in the stable under the tower—while the holy father climbed stiffly from his perch and bundled into shelter.

At the same time a hunter approached the temple from the south gate. It was a black bearded man called Aoz Roon, whom the boy greatly admired for his swaggering air. Behind him, shackles clamped round horny ankles, trudged an ancient phagor slave, Myk.

"Well, Laintal, I see the father has arrived from Borlien. Aren't you going to welcome him?"

"No."

"Why not? You remember him, don't you?"

"If he didn't come, my grandfather wouldn't be dying."

Aoz Roon clapped him on the shoulder.

"You're a good lad, you'll survive. One day, you will rule Embruddock yourself." He used the old name for Oldorando, the name in fashion before Yuli's people came, two generations before the present Yuli, who now lay awaiting the priest's rites.

"I'd rather have Grandfather alive than be a ruler."

Aoz Roon shook his head. "Don't say that. Anyone would rule, given the opportunity. I would."

"You'd make a good ruler, Aoz Roon. When I grow up, I'm going to be like you, and know everything and kill everything."

Aoz Roon laughed. Laintal Ay thought what a fine figure he cut, as his teeth flashed between bearded lips. He saw ferocity, but not the priest's slyness. Aoz Roon was in many ways heroic. He had a natural daughter called Oyre, almost Laintal Ay's age. And he wore a suit of black skins unlike anyone else's, cut from a giant mountain bear he had slain single-handed.

Carelessly, Aoz Roon said, "Come on, your mother will want you at this time. Climb on Myk and he'll give you a ride."

The great white phagor put out his horned hands and allowed the boy to scramble up his arms onto his bowed shoulders. Myk had been in servitude in Embruddock a long while; his kind lived longer than humans. He said, in his thick, choking voice, "Come on, boy."

Laintal Ay reached up and clasped the horns of the ancipital for security. As a sign of his enslavement the sharp double edges of Myk's horns had been filed smooth.

The three figures trudged up the time-worn street, heading towards warmth as the dark closed in on another of the countless nights of winter —a winter that had ruled over this tropical continent for centuries. Wind shifted powdery snow from ledges; it drifted down on them.

As soon as holy father and dogs had entered the big tower, the onlookers disappeared, scurrying back to their billets. Myk set down Laintal Ay in the trampled snow. The boy gave Aoz Roon a cheery wave as he dashed himself against the double doors set in the base of the building.

A stench of fish greeted him in the murk. The dog team had been fed on gout hooked from the frozen Voral. They jumped up as the boy entered, barking savagely on their leashes, showing their sharp teeth. A human slave who had accompanied the father shouted ineffectually to them to keep quiet. Laintal Ay growled back, keeping his fingers wrapped under his arms, and climbed the wooden stairs.

Light filtered from above. Six floors were piled above the stable. He slept in a corner on the next floor. His mother and grandparents were on the top floor. Between lived various hunters in his grandfather's service; as the boy passed by, they turned their broad backs to him, being already busy packing. Laintal Ay saw, as he climbed to his floor, that Father Bondorlonganon's few belongings had been deposited here. The man had installed himself, and would sleep nearby. No doubt he would snore; grown-ups generally did. He stood looking down at the priest's blanket, marvelling at the strangeness of its texture, before going upstairs to where his grandfather lay.

Laintal Ay paused with his head through the hatch, staring into the room, viewing everything from the perspective of the floor. This was really his grandmother's room, the room of Loil Bry since girlhood, since the time of her father, Wall Ein Den, who had been lord of the Den tribe, Lord of Embruddock. It was filled now with Loil Bry's shadow. She stood with her back to a fire burning in an iron brazier close by the opening through which her grandson peered. The shadow loomed upon walls and low-beamed ceiling, threateningly. Of the elaborate tapestried gown that his grandmother always wore, nothing transferred to the walls but an uncertain outline, with sleeves converted to wings.

Three other people in the room appeared dominated by Loil Bry and her shadow. On a couch in one corner lay Little Yuli, his chin jutting above the furs that covered him. He was twenty-nine years old, and worn out. The old man was muttering. Loilanun, Laintal Ay's mother, sat next to him, clutching her elbows with her hands, a woebegone look on her sallow face. She had not yet noticed her son. The man from Borlien, Father Bondorlonganon, sat nearest Laintal Ay, his eyes closed, praying aloud.

It was the prayer as much as anything which halted Laintal Ay. Normally he loved to be in this room, full of his grandmother's mysteries. Loil Bry knew so many fascinating things, and to some extent took the place of Laintal Ay's father, who had been killed while on a stungebag hunt.

Stungebags contributed to the foetid honey smell in the room. One of the monsters had been caught recently, and brought home bit by bit. Broken shards of plating, chopped from its back, helped fuel the fire and keep the cold at bay. The pseudo-wood burned with a yellow flame, sizzling as it burned.

Laintal Ay looked at the west wall. There was his grandmother's porcelain window. Faint light from outside transfused it with a sullen orange glow, scarcely competition for the firelight.

"It looks funny in here," he said at last.

He came up one more step, and the bright eyes of the brazier gleamed at him.

The father unhurriedly finished his prayer to Wutra and opened his eyes. Netted among the compressed horizontal lines of his face, they were unable to open far, but he fixed them gently on the boy and said, without preliminary greeting, "You'd better come here, my lad. I've brought something from Borlien for you."

"What's that?" He held his hands behind his back.

"Come and see."

"Is it a dagger?"

"Come and see." He sat perfectly still. Loil Bry sobbed, the dying man groaned, the fire spat.

Laintal Ay approached the father warily. He could not grasp how people could live in places other than Oldorando: it was the centre of the universe—elsewhere there was only wilderness, the wilderness of ice that stretched for ever and occasionally erupted in phagor invasions.

Father Bondorlonganon produced a little hound and placed it in the boy's palm. It was scarcely longer than the palm. It was carved, as he recognised, out of kaidaw horn, with a wealth of detail which delighted him. Thick coat curled over the hound's back, and the minute paws had pads. He examined it for a while before discovering that the tail moved. When it was wagged up and down, the dog's lower jaw opened and closed.

There had never been a toy like it. Laintal Ay ran round the room in excitement, barking, and his mother jumped up to shush him, catching him in her arms.

"One day, this lad will be Lord of Oldorando," Loilanun said to the father, as if by way of explanation. "He will inherit."

"Better he should love knowledge and study to know more," said Loil Bry, almost as an aside. "Such was my Yuli's preference." She wept afresh into her hands.

Father Bondorlonganon squeezed his eyes a little more and enquired Laintal Ay's age.

"Six and a quarter years." Only foreigners had to ask such questions.

"Well, you're almost at manhood. In another year, you'll become a hunter, so you'd better soon decide. Which do you want more, power or knowledge?"

He stared at the floor.

"Both, sir . . . or whichever comes easier."

The priest laughed, and dismissed the boy with a gesture, waddling over to see his charge. He had ingratiated himself: now, business. His ear, attuned by experience to the visitation of death, had caught the sound of a change in the rate of Little Yuli's breathing. The old man was about to leave this world for a perilous journey down along his land-octave to the obsidian world of the gossies. Getting the women to aid him, Bondorlonganon stretched the leader out with his head to the west, lying on his side.

Pleased to be released from inquisition, the boy rolled on the floor, fighting with his horn dog, barking softly back at it as it furiously exercised its jaw. His grandfather passed away while one of the most savage dogfights in the history of the world was taking place.

Next day, Laintal Ay wished to stay close to the priest from Borlien, in case he had more toys hidden in his garments. But the priest was busy visiting the sick, and in any case Loilanun kept firm hold of her son.

Laintal Ay's natural rebelliousness was curbed by the quarrels that broke out between his mother and his grandmother. He was the more surprised because the women had been loving to each other when his grandfather lived. The body of Yuli, he who was named after the man who came with Iskador from the mountains, was carted off, stiff as a frozen pelt, as if his last act of will was to hold himself rigidly away from his woman's caresses. His absence left a black corner in the room, where Loil Bry squatted, turning only to snap at her daughter.

All the tribe were built solid, buttressed with subcutaneous fat. Loil Bry's once renowned stature still lingered, though her hair was grey and her head lost between her shoulder bones as she stooped over the cold bed of that man of hers—that man loved with intense passion for half a lifetime, since she first beheld him, an invader, wounded.

Loilanun was of poorer stuff. The energy, the power to love, the broad face with seeking eyes like dark sails, had missed Loilanun, passing direct from grandmother to young Laintal Ay. Loilanun was strawy, her skin sallow; since her husband died so young, there was a falter in her walk—and a falter too, perhaps, in her attempt to emulate her mother's regal command of knowledge. She was irritable now, as Loil Bry wept almost continuously in the corner.

"Mother, give over—your din gets on my nerves."

"You were too feeble to mourn your man properly! I'll weep, I'll weep till I'm taken, I'll bleed tears."

"Much good it will do you." She offered her mother bread, but it was refused with a contemptuous gesture. "Shay Tal made it."

"I won't eat."

"I'll have it, Mumma," Laintal Ay said.

Aoz Roon arrived outside the tower and called up, holding his natural daughter Oyre by the hand. Oyre was a year younger than Laintal Ay, and waved enthusiastically to him, as he and Loilanun stuck their heads out of the window.

"Come up and see my toy dog, Oyre. It's a real fighter, like your father."

But his mother bundled him back into the room and said sharply to Loil Bry, "It's Aoz Roon, wishing to escort us to the burial. Can I tell him yes?"

Rocking herself slightly, not turning, the old woman said, "Don't trust anyone. Don't trust Aoz Roon—he has too much effrontery. He and his friends hope to gain the succession."

"We've got to trust someone. You'll have to rule now, Mother."

When Loil Bry laughed bitterly, Loilanun looked down at her son, who stood smiling and clutching the horn dog. "Then I shall, till Laintal Ay becomes a man. Then he'll be Lord of Embruddock."

"You're a fool if you think his uncle Nahkri will permit that," the old woman responded.

Loilanun said no more, drawing her mouth up in a bitter line, letting her regard sink down from her son's expectant face to the skins which covered the floor. She knew that women did not rule. Already, even before her father was put under, her mother's power over the tribe was going, flowing away as the river Voral flowed, none knew where. Turning on her heel, she shouted out of the window, without more ado, "Come up."

So abashed was Laintal Ay by this look of his mother's, as if she perceived he would never be a match for his grandfather—never mind the more ancient bearer of the name of Yuli—that he hung back, too wounded to greet Oyre when she marched into the chamber with her father.

Aoz Roon was fourteen years of age, a handsome, swaggering, young hunter who, after a sympathetic smile at Loilanun and a rumple of Laintal Ay's hair, went over to pay his respects to the widow. This was Year 19 After Union, and already Laintal Ay had a sense of history. It lurked in the dull-smelling corners of this old room, with its damps and lichens and cobwebs. The very word *history* reminded him of wolves howling between the towers, the snow at their rumps, while some old boney hero breathed his last.

Not only was Grandfather Yuli dead. Dresyl also had died. Dresyl, Yuli's cousin-brother, Laintal Ay's great-uncle, the father of Nahkri and Klils. The priest had been summoned and Dresyl had gone down rigid into the dirt, the dirt of history.

The boy remembered Dresyl with affection, but he feared his quarrelsome uncles, those sons of Dresyl, Nahkri and the boastful Klils. As far as he understood these things, he expected that—no matter what his mother said—old traditions would guarantee it was Nahkri and Klils who would rule. At least they were young. He would make himself a good hunter, and then they would respect him, instead of ignoring him as at present. Aoz Roon would help.

The hunters did not leave the hamlet this day. Instead, they all attended the funeral of their old lord. The holy father had calculated exactly where the grave should be, close by a curiously carved stone, where the ground was softened enough by hot springs for burial to be possible.

Aoz Roon escorted the two ladies, wife and daughter of Little Yuli, to the place. Laintal Ay and Oyre followed, whispering to each other, with their slaves and Myk, the phagor, following them. Laintal Ay worked his barking dog to make Oyre giggle.

Cold and water created a curious stage for grief. Fumaroles, springs, geysers, burst from the ground to the north of the hamlet, pouring across naked rock and stone. Driven by the wind, the water from several geysers fanned out westwards in a curtain, to freeze before it struck the ground, building up into elaborate fanciful shapes, intertwining like rope. Hotter springs, lashing this superstructure with warm water, kept it in a perilous state of plasticity, so that chunks would break off from time to time, to fall clacking to the rock and gradually be washed away.

A hole had been dug to accommodate the old hero, once conqueror of Embruddock. Two men with leather buckets laboured to bale water out of it. Wrapped in a coarse cloth without decoration, Little Yuli was lowered in. Nothing went with him. The people of Campannlat—or those who bothered to learn the art—knew only too well what it was like down below, in the world of the gossies: there was nothing anyone could take with them to help.

Huddled about the grave was the population of Oldorando, some one hundred and seventy men, women, and children.

Dogs and geese also joined the crowd, looking on in a nervous animal way, whereas the humans stood passively, changing their weight from foot to foot. It was cold. Batalix was high, but lost in cloud; Freyr was still in the east, an hour after its rise.

The people were dark and of substantial build, with the great barrel bodies and limbs which were the heritage of everyone on the planet at this period. The weight of adults at present was close to twelve staynes in the local measure, whether male or female, with little variation; drastic changes would occur later. They huddled in two groups of roughly equal numbers, their breath cloudy about them, one group of hunters and their women, one of corpsmen and their women. The hunters wore suits of reindeer skin, the bristly pelage of which was so thickly matted that even strong blizzards could not blow the hairs apart. The corpsmen wore lighter garb, generally of ruddy deer pelts, suited to a more sheltered life. One or two hunters wore phagor pelts, boastfully; but those hides were generally reckoned too greasy and heavy for comfort.

Steam rose from both groups, to be snatched away by the breeze. Their coats gleamed with moisture. They stood unmoving, watching. Some of the women, remembering strands of the old religion, threw down a large brassimip leaf each, as being about the only green stuff freely available. The leaves blew about uncertainly, wumping as they turned over. Some trundled into the soggy hole.

Ignoring everything, Bondorlonganon proceeded with the business in hand. Squeezing his eyes shut as if he would crack them like nuts, he recited the prescribed prayer to the heathens gathered about him. Mud was shovelled into the hole.

These things were kept short, out of respect for the weather and its effect on the living. As the hole filled, Loil Bry gave a terrible cry. She ran forward, and threw herself on her husband's grave. Aoz Roon was quick to catch her up and hold her, while Nahkri and his brother looked on, arms folded, half in amusement.

Loil Bry broke away from Aoz Roon's hold. Stooping, she grasped two handfuls of mud and smeared it over her face and hair, crying as she did so. Laintal Ay and Oyre laughed with delight. It was fun to see adults doing silly things.

Although the holy man continued with the service as if nothing had happened, his face wrinkled with disgust. This miserable place, Embruddock, was known for its lack of religion. Well, their gossies would suffer, sinking through the earth to the original boulder.

Tall and old, the widow of Little Yuli ran among the crackling ice structures, through the mist, down to the frozen Voral. Geese took off in dismay before her as she went crying along the bank, a crazed hag of twenty-eight hard winters. Some of the other children laughed, until their mothers silenced them in shame.

The stricken old lady capered on the ice, with stiff, ricketty movements like a puppet. Her figure was dark grey against the greys, blues, whites of the wilderness before which all their dramas were played out. Like Loil Bry, all present there were balanced on the edge of an entropy gradient. The children's laughter, the sorrow, the madness, even the disgust, were human expressions of a war against perpetual cold. None knew it, but that war was already tipping in their favour. Little Yuli, like his great ancestor, Yuli the Priest, founder of the tribe, had emerged from eternal dark and ice. Young Laintal Ay was a precursor of the light to come.

Loil Bry's scandalous behaviour lent spice to the feasting that was held after the funeral. All celebrated. Little Yuli was fortunate, or accounted so, for he had a father to welcome him to the world of gossies. His former subjects celebrated not only his departure but a more worldly journey—the holy man's return to Borlien. For that, the priest had to be well filled with rathel and barley wine, to keep out the cold on his trip home.

Slaves—they too Borlienians, but Father Bondorlonganon overlooked that—were despatched to load the sledge and harness up the yelping dogs. Laintal Ay and Oyre went along to the south gate with a merry crowd to see him off.

The priest's face squeezed itself into something like a smile at the sight of the boy. He bent suddenly and kissed Laintal Ay on the lips.

"Power and knowledge to you, son!" he said.

Too overcome to reply, Laintal Ay lifted the toy dog in salute.

In the towers that night, over a last bottle, tales were told again of Little Yuli, and of how he and his tribe had arrived in Embruddock. And of how unwelcome they were.

As Father Bondorlonganon was drawn back, pickled, across the plain to Borlien, the clouds parted. Above him, beading the night sky, were the prodigal stars.

Among the constellations and the fixed stars was a light that crawled. Not a comet but Earth Observation Station Avernus.

From the ground below, the station appeared as no more than a point of light, casually watched by travellers and trappers as it passed overhead. Close to, it revealed itself as an irregular and complex series of units with a number of specialised functions.

The Avernus housed some five thousand men, women, children, and androids, all of the adults specialising in some aspect of the planet below. Helliconia. An Earth-like planet with particular interest for the people of Earth.

11

THE PAST THAT WAS LIKE
A DREAM

Laintal Ay, overcome by warmth and fatigue, fell asleep long before
the celebrations were over. The stories went on over his head, much
as the winds blew about the planet, in a cold fury of possession.

The stories were of the activities of men, above all of his heroism, of
the way he killed such-and-such a devil animal, of the way enemies were
defeated, and in particular—on this evening after the burial—of how
the first Yuli had come down out of darkness to found a new way
of life.

Yuli captured their imaginations because he had been a holy man, yet
had rejected faith in favour of his people. He had battled with and
defeated gods who now had no name.

An elemental quality in Yuli's character, something between ruth-
lessness and fair-mindedness, awoke a response in the tribe. His legend
grew in their minds. So that even his great-grandson, another Yuli,
"Little" Yuli, could ask himself in times of stress, "What would Yuli
have done?"

That first place he named Oldorando, to which he went with
Iskador from the mountain, did not prosper. It could do no more than
survive. It existed precariously on the edge of a frozen lake, Lake Dorzin,

and could merely bow beneath the elemental furies of winter, unaware that those furies were about to exhaust themselves. Of that, there was no hint in Yuli's lifetime. Perhaps that was another reason why the present generation in the stone towers of Embruddock liked to speak of him: he was their ancestor who lived in deep winter. He represented their survival. Their legends were the first part of their awareness to admit of the possibility of a change in climate.

Together with the towns hived in the great mountain ranges of the Quzint, that first wooden Oldorando lay close to the equator, in the middle of the extensive tropical continent of Campannlat. Of the concept of that continent, nobody in Yuli's time had knowledge; their world was limited by the hunting territory and the encampment. Only Yuli had experience of the tundras and zastrugi which stretched away to the north of the Quzint. Only Yuli had experience of the foothills of that enormous natural feature which formed the western end of the continent, known as the Barriers. There, among fast-moving frosts, volcanoes situated over four thousand metres above sea level added their own kind of intransigence to the weather, spreading a lava plateau over the ancient impact rocks of Helliconia.

He was spared knowledge of the awesome territories of Nktryhk.

To the east of Campannlat looms the Eastern Range. Hidden from the eyes of Yuli and all other men behind cloud and storm, the earth here gathers itself up into range after enormous mountain range, culminating in a volcanic shield across which glaciers grind their way down from peaks over fourteen thousand metres high. Here the elements of fire and earth and air existed almost in their pure form, held in a cold fury too great to permit a mellowing into alloys less opposed. Yet even here, at a slightly later date—by the time of the death of Little Yuli—even on ice sheets penetrating almost to the stratosphere, ancipital life might be observed, clinging to existence, rejoicing in the storm.

The howling white wilderness of the Eastern Shield was known to the phagors. They called it Nktryhk, and believed it to be the throne of a white wizard who would cast the Sons of Freyr, the hated man-things, out of the world.

Stretching north and south for almost three and a half thousand miles, Nktryhk separated the inner part of the continent from the chill eastern seas. Those seas lashed against the cliffs of Nktryhk, which reared precipitously eighteen hundred metres above the waters. The waves turned to ice as they burst upwards, bearding the cliffs with icicles or falling back to the swell as hail. Of this the scattered human tribes knew nothing.

Those generations lived by the hunt. The hunt formed the subject matter of most of the stories to be told. Although hunters hunted together and helped each other, ultimately the hunt concerned one man's courage as he faced alone the savage beast who turned to confront him. Either he lived or he died. And if he lived, then others might live, the women and children back in safety. If he died, the tribe died, very likely.

So Yuli's people, that small band by the frozen lake, lived as they had to, as committed as animals to their mode of existence. The listeners to the story enjoyed accounts of the lake settlement. There, fish were trapped in ways still so minutely described that the methods had been imitated in the Voral. Heads of deer were thrown into melt holes by the river's edge to collect much-relished eels, just as Yuli had once done.

Yuli's people also fought giant stungebags, killed deer and savage boar, and defended themselves against phagor raids. Depending on season, quick crops of barley and rye were grown. The blood of enemies was drunk.

Men and women produced few children. In Oldorando, they matured by the age of seven years and were ageing by the time they were twenty. Even when they laughed and rejoiced, frost stood by their elbows.

The first Yuli, the frozen lake, the phagors, the intense cold, the past that was like a dream: these vivid elements of legend were known to everyone, and often retold. For the little herd of people who sheltered out their lives in Embruddock were confined in ways to which that confinement blinded them. At puberty, they were each stitched into the skins of animals; the animals enfolded them. But dreams, and the past that was like a dream, gave them extra dimensions in which they could all live.

Huddled close in Nahkri's and Klils' tower, after Little Yuli's funeral, everyone took pleasure once more in sharing in the past that was like a dream. To make the past more vivid, or perhaps to dim the present, everyone drank rathel, dispensed by Nahkri's slaves. Rathel was the most highly valued liquid in Embruddock, after red blood.

Little Yuli's funeral gave them the chance to break the unvarying routine of life, and to live imaginatively. So the great tale of the past, of two tribes uniting, even as man and woman unite, was again retold. The tale was passed from mouth to mouth, much like the rathel mug, one narrator taking over from the next with hardly a pause.

The children of the tribe were present, eyes gleaming in the smouldering light, as they sipped rathel from their parents' wooden mugs. The tale they heard was called familiarly the Great Tale. At any festival, not merely at a burial or a coming of age, or at the festival of the Double Sunset, someone would be sure to cry, as darkness came slanting in, "Let's have the Great Tale!"

It was a history of their past, and much more than that. It was all the art the tribe had. Music they lacked, and painting, and literature, and almost anything fine. What had existed, the cold had devoured. But there remained the past that was a dream; that survived to be told.

No one was more responsive to this tale than Laintal Ay, when he could manage to stay awake for it. One of its themes was the union of two conflicting sides; that he understood, for the division concealed by that union, in which the tribe had to believe as an article of faith, was—had been—a part of his family life. Only later, as he grew up, did he discover how there was never union in anything, only stifled dissent. But the narrators in the fuggy hall, in this Year Nineteen After Union, gleefully conspired to tell the Great Tale as one of unity and success. That was their art.

The narrators jumped up one by one, declaiming their piece with varied assurance. The first narrators spoke of Great Yuli, and of how he came from the white wildernesses north of Pannoval to the frozen lake called Dorzin. But one generation gives place to another, even in legend, and soon another narrator rose, to speak of those, scarcely less mighty, who followed Yuli. This narrator was Rol Sakil, the midwife, who had her man and her pretty daughter, Dol, by her side; she gave a certain emphasis to the spicier aspects of her share of the tale, which was much relished by her audience.

While Laintal Ay dozed in the warmth, Rol Sakil told of Si, son of Yuli and Iskador. Si became the chief hunter of the tribe, and all feared him, because his eyes looked in different directions. He took a locally born woman called Cretha or, according to the style of her tribe, Cre Tha Den, who bore Si a son named Orfik and a daughter named Iyfilka. Both Orfik and Iyfilka were valiant and strong, in days when it was unusual for two children to survive in one family. Iyfilka went with Sargotth, or Sar Gotth Den, who excelled in catching myllk, the two-armed fish beneath the ice of Lake Dorzin. Iyfilka could crack the ice with her singing. Iyfilka bore a son to Sar Gotth whom they called Dresyl Den—a famous name in the legend. Dresyl fathered the famous brothers, Nahkri and Klils. (Laughter.) Dresyl was Laintal Ay's great-uncle.

"Oh, I adore you, my baby!" Iyfilka cried to her child, fondling him and smiling. But this was at a time when tribes of phagors were travelling in kaidaw-drawn sleighs over the ice, striking at human habitation. Both the pleasant Iyfilka and Sar Gotth were killed in a raid, running away by the bleak lake's shore. Some afterwards blamed Sar Gotth for being a coward, or for not being vigilant enough.

The young orphan, Dresyl, was taken to live with his uncle, Orfik, who by now had a son of his own called Yuli, or Little Yuli, after his great-grandfather. Although he grew enormous, he was known as Little in memory of his ancestor's greatness. Dresyl and Little Yuli became inseparable friends, and so remained through life, despite the trials that were to come. Both in their youth were great fighters, and lusty men who seduced the Den women, causing much trouble by their enjoyments. Some tales could be told on that score, were not certain folk present. (Laughter.)

One and all said that Dresyl and Yuli, the cousin-brothers, looked alike, with their powerful dark faces, hawk noses, small curling beards, and bright eyes. Both stood alertly and were of good build. Both wore similar furs with trimmed hoods. Their enemies prophesied they would meet with the same fate, but it was to prove otherwise, as the legend will relate.

Certainly, the old men and women whose daughters were in jeopardy prophesied that this pestilential pair would come to a bad end—and the sooner the better. Only those daughters themselves, lying with their legs open in the dark, and their lovers mounted on them, knew how beneficial the cousin-brothers were, and how different, one from the other; they knew that in their inward natures Dresyl was fierce and Yuli gentle, gentle as a feather and as ticklish.

At this point in the story, Laintal Ay roused. He wondered sleepily how it could ever have been that his ancient grandfather, so bent, so slow, had ever managed to tickle girls.

One of the corpsmen continued the story.

The elders and the old shaman of the lakeside tribe met together to decide how Dresyl and Yuli should be punished for their lechery. Some spat anger when they spoke, because in their hearts they were jealous. Others spoke piously since, being old, they could follow no course but virtue. (The storyteller laid this simple wisdom on thick, and assumed a piping voice, to make his audience laugh.)

Condemnation was unanimous. Although their numbers were depleted by disease and the phagor raids, and every hunter was needed, the elders decided that Little Yuli and Dresyl should be expelled from the settlement. Of course, no woman was allowed to speak in the friends' favour.

The message was conveyed. Yuli and Dresyl saw nothing for it but to leave. As they were gathering up their weapons and kit, a trapper arrived at the camp, half dead, from another tribe on the eastern fringes of the lake. He brought word that phagors were again approaching, this time in some force across the lake. They were killing any humans they came across. This was at the time of a double sunset.

Terrified, the men of the settlement promptly gathered up their women and possessions and set fire to their homes. They began at once to move southwards, Little Yuli and Dresyl among them. At their retreating backs, fire flew in robes of red and black into the sky, until eventually the lake was lost from view. They followed the Voral River, travelling day and night, for Freyr shone at night during this period. The ablest hunters travelled ahead and to either side of the main body, seeking food and safety. In the emergency, Yuli and Dresyl were provisionally forgiven their sins.

The party consisted of thirty men, including the five elders, twenty-six women, and ten children under seven, the age of puberty. They had with them their sleighs, pulled by asokins and dogs. Following were numerous birds and a variety of hounds, some little more than wolves or jackals, or crosses between the two; these last were often the playthings of the children, given to them as puppies.

Several days of travel followed. The weather was clement, although game was scarce. One Freyr-dawn, two of the hunters, Baruin and Skelit, who had been acting as scouts, returned to the main body and reported a strange town ahead.

"Where the river meets a frozen stream, water bursts into the air with great noise. And mighty towers built of stone stand up into the sky." Such was Baruin's report, and the first description of Embruddock.

He described how our stone towers stand in rows, and are decorated with brightly painted skulls, to ward off intruders.

They stood in a shallow valley full of gravel, discussing what should be done. Two more hunters arrived, dragging a trapper they had caught returning to Embruddock. They threw him to the ground and kicked him. He said that the Den tribe lived in Embruddock, and were peaceful.

Hearing there were more Dens about, the five elders immediately said that they should make a detour round the hamlet. They were shouted down. The younger men said that they should attack immediately; they could then be accepted on a basis of equality by this distantly related tribe. The women vociferously agreed, thinking it would be pleasant to live in stone buildings.

Excitement rose. The trapper was clubbed to death. All—men, women, and children—dipped their fingers in his blood and drank, that they might prevail before the day was done.

The body was thrown to the dogs and birds.

"Dresyl and I will go forward and take in the lie of the land," Little Yuli said. He stared challengingly at the men about him; they dropped their gaze and said nothing. "We will win the day for you. If we do so, then we shall be in command, and will tolerate no more nonsense from these old men. If we lose the day, then you can throw our bodies to the animals."

"And," said the next speaker to take up the story, "at Little Yuli's brave speech, the canine company looked up from their feast and yelped their agreement." The audience smiled seriously, recalling that detail from the past that was like a dream.

Now the story of that past became more tense. The audience drank less rathel as it listened to how Dresyl and Little Yuli, the cousin-brothers, planned to take the silent town. With them went five chosen heroes, their names well-remembered: Baruin, Skelit, Maldik, Curwayn, and Big Afardl, who was killed that day, and by a woman's hand.

The rest of the party remained where they were, so that the noise of their hounds did not give the game away.

Beyond the icy river was no snow. Grass grew. Hot water gushed into the air, sending curtains of steam across the area.

"It's true," murmured the audience. "It still occurs as you say."

A woman drove black hairy pigs up a path. Two children played naked among the waters. The invaders watched.

They saw our stone towers, the strong ones, the ruinous ones, all laid out in streets. And the old city wall reduced to rubble. They marvelled.

Dresyl and Yuli skirted Embruddock alone. They saw how square our towers are, with walls sloping inwards all the way up, so that the room on the top floor is always smaller than those below. How we keep our animals in the bottom floor for warmth—up the ramp to save them in case the Voral floods. They saw all the animal skulls, brightly painted and facing out, to scare intruders. We always had a sorceress, didn't we, friends? At this period, it was Loil Bry.

Well, the cousin-brothers also saw two aged sentries up on top of the big tower—this very tower, friends—and in no time they had nipped in and despatched the greybeards. Blood flowed, I have to tell.

"The flower," someone called.

Oh, yes. The flower was important. Remember how the lake people said that the cousin-brothers would meet with the same destiny? Yet when Dresyl grinned and said, "We will do well ruling this town, brother," Yuli was looking at the little flowers at his feet, flowers with pale petals—probably scantiom.

"A good climate," he said, in surprise, and plucked the flower and ate it.

They were scared when they first heard the Hour-Whistler blow, for that famous geyser, known to all, was not known to them. They recovered, and then disposed their forces so as to be prepared for the time when both sentinels were set and the hunters of Embruddock returned home, bearing with them the spoils of the chase, all unsuspecting.

Laintal Ay roused at this point. There were battles in the past that was like a dream, and one was about to be described. But the new story-teller said, "Friends, we all had ancestors in the battle that followed, and all have gone since to the world of gossies, even if they were not despatched prematurely on that occasion. Suffice it to say that all present acquitted themselves valiantly."

But he, being youthful, could not dismiss the exciting part so lightly and continued despite himself, eyes glowing.

Those innocent and heroic hunters were surprised by Yuli's stratagem. Fire suddenly bloomed from the top of the herb tower, and tall flowers of flame rose into the evening air. The hunters naturally shouted out with alarm, dropped their weapons, and ran forward to see what could be done.

Spears and stones rained down on them from the top of the neighbouring tower. Armed invaders appeared from concealment, shouting and thrusting their spears at unguarded bodies. Our hunters slipped and fell in their own blood, but some invaders they managed to slay.

Our town contained more armed men than the cousin-brothers calculated for. Those were the brave corpsmen. They appeared from everywhere. But the invaders were desperate and hid in houses they had taken over. Young boys also were forced to fight, including some of you here, now past your prime.

The fire spread. Sparks streamed overhead like husks at a winnowing, as if they would light the sky. Carnage grew in the streets and ditches. Our women took up swords from the dead to fight off the living.

All acquitted themselves valiantly. But boldness and desperation won the day—not to mention the leadership of him who this day went down to the world of the gossies to be with his ancestors. Eventually, the defenders threw down their weapons and rushed away in the gathering dark, screaming.

Dresyl's blood was up. An avenging fury rose on his brow. He had seen Big Afardl slain beside him—and from behind—and by a woman at that.

"That was my good old grandmother!" cried Aoz Roon, and laughter and cheers rose on all sides. "There was always courage in our family. We are of Embruddock stock, and not of Oldorando."

Dresyl could scarcely be recognized for his fury. His face turned black. He ordered his company to hunt down and kill every surviving man of Embruddock. The women were to be gathered into the stable of this very tower, friends. What a terrible day that was in our annals. . . .

But the victorious men, led by Yuli, took Dresyl forcibly and said to him that there must be no more killing. Killing brought bitterness. From the morrow, all must live in peace, to make a strong tribe, or there were not enough souls to survive.

These wise words meant nothing to Dresyl. He struggled until Baruin brought a bucket of cold water and flung it over him. Then he fell down as if in a swoon, and slept that dreamless sleep which comes only after battle.

Baruin said to Yuli, "You sleep too, with Dresyl and the others. I will keep watch, in case we are surprised by a counterattack."

But Little Yuli was unable to sleep. He said nothing to Baruin, but he had been wounded, and his head was light. He felt himself near to death, and staggered outside to die under Wutra's sky, into which Freyr was already preparing to ascend, for it was the third quarter. He walked down the main street here, where grass grew coarse among streams of mud. Freyr-dawn was the colour of mud, and he saw a scavenging hound slink away, full-bellied, from the corpse of one of his fellow hunters. He leaned against a crumbling wall, breathing deep.

Opposite him was the temple—ruined then as now. He stared without understanding at the decorations engraved in the stone. Remember, in those days, before Loil Bry civilized him, Yuli was by way of being a barbarian. Rats snicked in at the doorway. He moved to the temple hearing only a rushing in his ears. In his hand he held a sword taken from a fallen adversary—a better weapon than any he possessed, made of good dark metal here in our forges. This he held before him as he kicked in the door.

Inside, tethered milch sows and goats scuffled. Field implements used to be stored there in those days. Looking about, Yuli saw a trapdoor in the floor, and heard voices whispering.

Taking hold of the iron ring, he heaved up the door. Down in the pool of darkness under his feet, a smoking lamp burned.

"Who's there?" someone called. A man's voice, and I expect you know whose it was.

It was Wall Ein Den, then Lord of Embruddock, and well-remembered by us all. You can picture him, tall and upright, though his youth had fled, with a long black moustache and no beard. All remarked on his eyes, which could outstare the boldest, and his haggardly handsome face, which in its time moved women to tears. This was the historic meeting between him, the old lord, and Little Yuli.

Little Yuli went slowly down the steps to him, almost as if recognising him. Some of the masters of corps were there with Lord Wall Ein, but they did not dare speak as Yuli came down, very pale, clasping his sword.

Lord Wall Ein said, "If you are a savage, then murder is your business, and you had best get it over with. I command you to kill me first."

"What else do you deserve, hiding in a cellar?"

"We are old, and powerless in battle. Once it was otherwise."

They confronted each other. Nobody moved.

With a great effort, Yuli spoke, and his voice seemed to him to come from far away. "Old man, why do you leave this great town so poorly guarded?"

Lord Wall Ein replied with his usual authority. "It was not always thus, or you and your men would have met a different reception, you with your poor weapons. Many centuries ago, the Land of Embruddock was great, stretching north to the Quzints and south almost as far as the sea. Then Great King Denniss ruled, but the cold came and destroyed what he had wrought. Now we are fewer than ever we were, for only last year, in the first quarter, we were raided by the white phagors riding like the wind on their giant mounts. Many of our best warriors, including my son, were killed defending Embruddock, and now sink towards the original boulder."

He sighed, and added, "Perhaps you read the legend carved on this building, if you can read. It says, 'First phagors, then men.' It was for that legend and other matters that our priesthood was slain, two generations ago. Men must be first, always. Yet some days I wonder if the prophecy will not come true."

Little Yuli heard the lord's words as if in a trance. When he attempted to reply, no words rose to his bloodless lips, and he felt the power drain from his inner eddre.

One of the old men, between pitying and sniggering, said, "The youth has a wound."

As Yuli staggered forward, they backed away. Behind them was a low archway with a passage beyond, dimly lit from an overhead grating. Unable to stop now that he had started, he marched down the passage, dragging his feet. You know that feeling, friends, whenever you are drunk—as now.

It was damp in the passage, and warm. He felt the heat on his cheek. To one side was a stone stairway. He could not understand where he was, and his senses were failing.

And a young woman appeared on the stair, holding a taper before her. She was fairer than the skies. Her face swam before his vision.

"It was my grandmother!" cried Laintal Ay, shrill with pride. He had been listening excitedly, and was confused when everyone laughed.

At that time, the lady had no thought of bestowing any little Laintal Ays upon the world. She stared at Little Yuli with wild eyes, and said something to him which he could not understand.

He attempted a reply. The words would not come to his throat. His knees buckled. He sank down to the floor. Then he collapsed entirely, and all there believed him to be dead.

At this thrilling juncture, the storyteller made way for an older speaker, a hunter, who took matters less dramatically.

Wutra saw fit to spare Yuli's life on that occasion. Dresyl took command of the situation while his cousin-brother lay recovering from his wound. I believe that Dresyl was ashamed of his bloodlust and now took care to behave in a more civilized way, finding himself among civilized people like us. He may also have remembered the kindness of his father, Sar Gotth, and the sweetness of his mother, Iyfilka, killed by the hated phagor herd. He took over Prast's Tower, where we used to store salt, living at the top of it and issuing orders like a true commander, while Yuli lay in bed in a low room beneath.

Many at the time, myself included, disliked Dresyl, and treated him as a mere invader. We hated being ordered about. Yet when we understood what he intended, we cooperated, and appreciated his undoubted good points. We of Embruddock were demoralised at that time. Dresyl gave us our fighting spirit back, and built up the defences.

"He was a great man, my father, and I'll fight anyone who criticises him," shouted Nahkri, jumping up and shaking his fist. He shook it so energetically that he almost fell over backwards, and his brother had to prop him up.

None speaks against Dresyl. From the top of his tower, he could survey our surrounding country, the higher ground to the north, where he had come from, the lower to the south, and the geysers and hot springs, then strange to him. In particular, he was struck by the Hour-

Whistler, our magnificent regular geyser, bursting up and whistling like a devil wind.

I recall he asked me about the giant cylinders, as he called them, spread all over the landscape. He had never seen rajabarals before. To him they looked like the towers of a magician, flat on top, made of strange wood. Though not a fool, he did not know them for trees.

He was mainly for doing, not looking. He ordered where all his tribe from the frozen lake would be quartered, distributed in different towers. There he showed a wisdom we might all follow, Nahkri. Although many grumbled at the time, Dresyl saw to it that his people lived in with ours. No fighting was allowed, and everything fairly shared. That rule as much as anything has caused us to intermingle happily.

While he was billetting families, he had everyone counted. He could not write, but our corpsmen kept a tally for him. The old tribe here numbered forty-one men, forty-five women, and eleven children under the age of seven. That made ninety-seven folk in all. Sixty-one folk from the frozen lake had survived the battle, which made one hundred and fifty-eight people all told. A goodly number. As a boy, I was glad to have some life round the place again. After the deaths, I mean.

I said to Dresyl, "You'll enjoy being in Embruddock."

"It's called Oldorando now, boy," he said. I can still remember how he looked at me.

"Let's hear more about Yuli," someone called out, risking the wrath of Nahkri and Klils. The hunter sat down, puffing, and a younger man took his place.

Little Yuli made a slow recovery from his wound. He became able to walk out a short way with his cousin-brother and survey the territory in which they found themselves, to see how it could best be hunted and defended.

In the evenings, they talked with the old lord. He tried to teach them both the history of our land, but they were not always interested. He talked of centuries of history, before the cold descended. He told how the towers had once on a time been built of baked clay and wood, which the primitive peoples had developed in a time of heat. Then stone had been substituted for clay, but the same trusted pattern observed. And the stone withstood many centuries. There were some passages underground, and had been many more, in better times.

He told them the sorrow of Embruddock, that we are now merely a hamlet. Once a noble city stood here, and its inhabitants ruled for thousands of miles. There were no phagors to be feared in those days, men say.

And Yuli and his cousin-brother Dresyl would stride about the old lord's room, listening, frowning, arguing, yet generally respectful. They asked about the geysers, whose hot springs supply warmth to us. Our old lord told them all about the Hour-Whistler, our unfailing symbol of hope.

He told how the Hour-Whistler has blown punctually every hour ever since time began. It's our clock, isn't it? We don't need sentinels in the sky.

The Hour-Whistler helps the authorities keep written records, as the masters of corps are duty-bound to do. The cousin-brothers were astonished to find how we divide the hour into forty minutes and the minute into one hundred seconds, just as the day contains twenty-five hours and the year four hundred and eighty days. We learn such things on our mothers' laps. They also had to learn that it was Year 18 by the Lordly calendar; eighteen years had our old lord ruled. No such civilized arrangements existed by the frozen lake.

Mind, I say no word against the cousin-brothers. Barbarians though they were, they both soon mastered our system of makers corps, with the seven corps, each with different arts—the metal makers being the best, to which I'm proud to say, without boasting, I belong. The masters of each corps sat on the lord's council then, as they do now. Though, in my opinion, there should be two representatives from the metal-makers corps, because we are the most important, make no mistake.

Following a lot of jeering and laughter, the rathel was passed round again, and a woman in late middle age continued the legend.

Now I'll spin you a tale a lot more interesting than writing or time-keeping. You'll be asking what befell Little Yuli when he got better of his wound. Well, I'll tell you in a dozen words. He fell in love—and that proved worse than his wound, because the poor fellow never recovered from it.

Our old Lord Wall Ein wisely kept his daughter—poor pampered Loil Bry Den, who was in such a pother today—out of harm's way. He waited until he was sure that the invaders weren't a bad lot. Loil Bry was then very lovely, and with a well-developed figure, enough for a man to get hold of, and she had a queenly way of walking, which you will all remember. So our old lord introduced her to Little Yuli one day, up in his room.

Yuli had already seen her once. On that terrible night of the battle when, as we've heard, he nearly died of his wound. Yes, this was the black-eyed beauty with the ivory cheekbones and lips like a bird's wing, whom our friend mentioned. She was the beauty of her day, for the women from Lake Dorzin were a plain lot, to my mind. All her features were precisely drawn on the velvet of her skin, and those lips, so trimly curving, were painted in delicate cinnamon. To speak truth, I looked a bit like that myself when I was a young girl.

Such was Loil Bry when Yuli first saw her. She was the greatest wonder of the town. A difficult, solitary girl—people didn't care for her, but I liked her manner. Yuli was overwhelmed. He forever sought occasions when he could be alone with her—either outside or, better still, cloistered up close with her in her room in Big Tower where she still lives to this day, with that porcelain window. It was as if she gave him a fever. He could not control himself in her presence. He used to swagger about and boast and swear in front of her and make a real fool of himself. Many men get like that, but of course it doesn't last.

As for Loil Bry, she sat there like a little puppy, watching, smiling behind her high cheekbones, her hands folded in her lap. Of course, she encouraged him, needless to say. She wore a long heavy gown, decorated with beads, not furs like the rest of us. I heard that she wore furs underneath. But that gown was extraordinary, and reached almost to the ground. I'd like a gown like that. . . .

The way she speaks, it still is a bit of a mixture of poetry and riddles. Yuli'd never heard anything like it up on Lake Dorzin. It flummoxed him. He boasted all the more. He was bragging about what a hunter he was when she said—you know her musical voice—"We live out our lives in all kinds of darkness. Should we ignore them or explore them?"

He just goggled at her, sitting there looking lovely in her cloth garment. It had beads stitched on it, as I said, lovely beads. He asked if it was dark in her room. She laughed at him.

"Where do you think is the darkest place in the universe, Yuli?"

Poor fool, he said, "I've heard that far Pannoval is dark. Our great ancestor, whose name I bear, came from Pannoval, and he said it was dark there. He said it was under a mountain, but I don't believe that. It was just a way of speaking in those times."

Loil Bry regarded her fingertips, resting like little pink beads on the lap of that lovely garment.

"I think the darkest place in the universe is inside human skulls."

He was lost. She made a proper fool of him. Still, I must watch my tongue about the dead, mustn't I? He was a bit soft, though. . . .

She used to bemuse him with romantic talk. You know what she used to say? "Have you ever thought how we know so much more than we can ever tell?" It's true, isn't it? "I long to have someone," she'd say, "someone to whom I could tell everything, someone for whom talk is like a sea on which to float. Then I'd hoist my dark sail. . . ." I don't know what she said to him.

And Yuli would lie awake, clutching his wound and who knows what else, thinking of this magical woman, thinking of her beauty, and her troubling words. ". . . Someone for whom talk is a sea on which to float . . ." Even the way she turned her sentence seemed to him to be Loil Bry's way and no one else's. He'd long to be on that sea, sailing with her, wherever it was.

"That's enough of your womanly nonsense," cried Klils, struggling to his feet. "She put a spell about him, Father said so. Father also told us of the good things Uncle Yuli did at first, before she made him stupid." He went on to tell them.

Little Yuli got to know every inch of Oldorando while he was recovering. He saw how it is laid out, with the big tower at one end of the main street and the old temple at the other. In between, the women's house, the hunter's homes on one side, the towers of the makers corps on the other. The ruins farther out. How all our towers have the heating system of stone pipes carrying hot water from springs through them. We couldn't build anything half so marvellous today.

When he saw how the place was, he saw how it should be. With the aid of my father, Yuli planned proper fortifications, so that there would be no more attacks—especially no more phagor attacks. You've heard how everyone was set to digging a mound with a ditch on its outer side and a stout palisade on top. It was a good idea, though it cost a few blisters. Regular lookouts were drilled and posted at the four corners, as they still are. That was Yuli's and my father's doing. The lookouts were given horns to blow in case of a raid—the self-same horns we use today.

There were proper hunts as well as proper lookouts. People were almost starved before the merging of the tribes. Once the entire town was enclosed, Dresyl, my father, got the hunters breeding a proper hunting dog. Other scavengers could be kept out. Packs of hunting dogs could bring down game and run faster than we could. That was not much of a success, but we might try again some time.

What else? The guilds were able to make up their numbers. The colour-makers corps enlisted some children among the newcomers. New mugs and platters were made for everyone from a vein of clay they know about. More swords were hammered out. Everyone had to work for the common good. No one went hungry. My father nearly worked himself to death. You drunken lot ought to remember Dresyl while you're remembering his brother. He was a lot better than that one. He was, he was.

Poor Klils broke into tears. Others also began to cry, or laugh, or fight. Aoz Roon, himself staggering slightly under the weight of rathel he had drunk, grabbed up Laintal Ay and Oyre, and hustled them off to bed and safety.

He looked blurrily down at their passive faces, trying to think. Somewhere in the course of the telling of the legend of the past that was like a dream, the future of the lordship of Oldorando had been decided.

III

A LEAP FROM THE TOWER

On the day after Little Yuli's burial and the celebrations marking that occasion, everyone had to go back to work as usual. Past glories and discomforts were forgotten for the time being, except perhaps by Laintal Ay and Loilanun; they were continually reminded of the past by Loil Bry, who, when she was not weeping, liked to recall the happier days of her youth.

Her chamber was still hung with tapestries of ancient lineage, now as then. Ducts of hot water still gurgled under the floors. The porcelain window still gleamed. This was still a place of oils, powders, and perfumes. But there was no Yuli now, and Loil Bry herself had decayed into old age. Moths had got the tapestries. Her grandson was growing up.

But before Laintal Ay's time—in the days when the mutual love of his grandparents flowered—a trivial-seeming incident occurred which in its repercussions was to set a disastrous mark on Laintal Ay and on Embruddock itself: a phagor died.

When he had recovered from his wound, Little Yuli took Loil Bry as his woman. A ceremonial was held to mark the great change that had come to Embruddock, for in this union the two tribes were symbolically united. It was agreed that the old lord, Wall Ein, and Yuli and Dresyl should rule Oldorando as a triumvirate. And the arrangement worked well, because everyone had to strive hard together to survive.

Dresyl worked without cease. He took for his woman a thin girl whose father was a sword maker; she had a singing voice and a lazy glance. Her name was Dly Hoin Den. The storytellers never said that Dresyl soon grew disappointed with her; nor did they say that part of her initial attraction for Dresyl was that she represented a pretty but anonymous member of the new tribe into which he wished to integrate. For, unlike his cousin-brother, Yuli, he saw team spirit as the clue to survival. His work was never for himself; nor, in a sense, was Dly Hoin.

Dly Hoin bore Dresyl two boys, Nahkri and, a year later, Klils. Although he could spare little time apart with them, Dresyl doted on his sons, lavishing on them a sentimental love denied him by the deaths of his parents, Iyfilka and Sar Gotth. He instilled in the boys and their friends many legends concerning their great-great-grandfather, Yuli, the priest from Pannoval who had defeated gods whose names were now forgotten. Dly Hoin taught them the rudiments of annotation but nothing more. Under their father's care, both boys became adequate hunters. Their house was always full of noise and alarms. Fortunately, a clownish element in their characters—in Nahkri's, in particular—was never perceived by their fond father.

As if to defeat the predictions of those who had claimed that the cousin-brothers would meet one and the same fate, Little Yuli became self-absorbed to almost the extent that Dresyl absorbed himself in the community.

Under the influence of Loil Bry, Yuli grew soft, and hunted less and less. He sensed the hostility of the community towards Loil Bry, with her exotic ideas, and withdrew himself from it. He sat in the big tower and let the storm winds blow outside. His woman and her ancient father taught him much that was mysterious, both about the world that was past and the world below.

So it came about that Little Yuli embarked upon that sea of talk on which Loil Bry's dark sail flew free, and lost all sight of land.

Speaking of the world below, one day in the second quarter of the year, Loil Bry said to Little Yuli, gazing at him with her lustrous eyes, "My splendid one, you commune in your head with the memory of your parents. You see them sometimes as if they still walked the earth. Your imagination has the power to conjure up the forgotten sunlight in which they walked. Yet here in this empire of ours we have a method of communing direct with those who have gone before. They still live, sinking down in the world below towards the original boulder, and we can reach them, as a fish dives to feed on the riverbed."

He murmured in exchange, "I would like to talk to my father, Orfik, now that I am old enough to have sense. I would tell him of you."

"We also set store by our wonderful parents, and their parents, who had the strength of giants. You observe the stone towers in which we live. We cannot build them, yet our parents did. You see how scalding earthwater has been trapped in pipes to heat our towers. We cannot manage that art, yet our parents did. They are gone from our sight, yet they still exist as gossies and fessups."

"Teach me these things, Loil Bry."

"Because you are my lover, and my pulses rise up when I behold your flesh, I will teach you to speak direct to your father and, through him, to all your tribe who ever lived."

"Is it possible that I could speak even to my great-grandfather, Yuli of Pannoval?"

"In our children our two tribes will merge, my lover, as they do in those infants of Dresyl's. You shall learn to speak with Yuli, and mingle his wisdom with ours. You are a great person, my lover, and not a mere tribesman, like the poor fools outside; you shall be greater by speaking direct with the first Yuli."

Much though Loil Bry cared for Little Yuli, because she needed someone on whom to build a great love, she foresaw that he would fall further into her power if she taught him esoteric arts; with his protection she could remain in sumptuous idleness, as she had done before the invasion.

Much though Little Yuli loved this indolent, intelligent woman, he perceived that she might bind him to her by such devices, and resolved to learn from her all he could and not be deceived. Something in their temperaments or their situation rendered him deceived nonetheless.

Loil Bry gathered to her an old learned woman and an old learned man. With their aid, she taught Yuli the discipline of father-communing. Yuli gave up the hunt entirely in order to contemplate; Baruin and others provided their food. He began to practice pauk; in that trance state, he hoped to meet with the gossie of his father, Orfik, and commune through the gossie with fessups, the ancestral gossies sinking down through the lower world towards the original boulder, from which the world began.

At this time, Yuli rarely went out. Such unmanly behaviour was a mystery in Oldorando.

Loil Bry had roved greatly in the countryside about Embruddock when a girl, as her grandson, Laintal Ay, would come to do. She wished Yuli to see for himself how stones marking land-octaves trailed all round the continent.

Accordingly, she engaged a grey, hawkish man, by name Asurr Tal

Den. Asurr Tal was the grandfather of Shay Tal, later to play a great part in affairs. Loil Bry commanded Asurr Tal to take Yuli into the lands to the northeast of Oldorando. There she had once stood, watching day turn to dimday and dimday to brief night, and felt the pulse of the world flow through her.

So Asurr Tal took Yuli on foot in a clement season. It was early winter, when Batalix rose well to the south of east, shining there alone for less than an hour—the interval diminishing day by day—before the second sentinel also rose. A wind blew, but the sky was as clear as brass. Although Asurr Tal was withdrawn and rather bent, he managed the distance better than Yuli, who was out of training. He made Yuli ignore the distant wolves and study all he saw in terms of esoteric art. Asurr Tal showed him stone posts, such as there had been by Lake Dorzin. The posts were set solitary in wild places, each marked with a symbol of a wheel with a ring at its centre, and two lines connecting ring with wheel. He expounded their meaning in a singsong voice.

He said that the posts bore a symbol in which power radiated from a centre towards a circumference, as power radiated from ancestors to descendants, or from fessups via gossies to the living. The pillars marked land-octaves. Every man or woman born was born on one octave or another. The power in land-octaves varied with the season, determining whether infants were born male or female. The land-octaves flowed everywhere until they reached the distant seas. People lived most happily when they conformed to their own land-octaves.

Only when they were buried on their correct land-octaves could they, as gossies, hope to communicate with their living children. And their children, when their time came to make the journey to the world below, should also lie along the correct land-octave.

With his hand held like a chopper, old Asurr Tal chopped at the hills and valleys about them.

"Remember that simple regulation, and father-communing can be established. The word grows fainter, like an echo along mountain valleys, from one vanished generation to the next, throughout the kingdoms of the dead, who outnumber the living as lice outnumber men."

As Little Yuli regarded the barren mountainside, a strong revulsion rose in him against this teaching. Not long since, his interest had been only with the living, and he had felt himself free.

"This business of talking to the dead," he said heavily. "The living should have no traffic with the dead. Our place is here, travelling on this earth."

The old man snickered, caught Yuli's furred sleeve in a familiar way, and pointed downwards.

"You may think so, you may think so. Unfortunately, it is the rule of existence that our place is both here and down below, down in the grit. We must learn to use the gossies as we use animals for our benefit."

"The dead should keep in their place."

"Oh, well . . . as for that, you'll be dead one day, yourself. Besides, Mistress Loil Bry wishes you to learn these things, does she not?"

Yuli desired to shout, "I hate the dead and want nothing of them." But he bit off the words and stood silent. And so he was lost.

Although he learned how to perform the rituals of father-communicating, Little Yuli was never able to communicate with his father, much less with the first Yuli. The dead yielded no response. Loil Bry explained this by saying that his parents had been buried in an incorrect land-octave. Nobody fully understood the mysteries of the world below. In trying to understand more, he sank further under his woman's power.

All this time, Dresyl worked for the community, consulting with the old lord. He never lost his love for Yuli, even making his two sons study some of the lore that their strange aunt readily poured forth. But he never permitted them to stay long, lest they become bewitched.

Two years after Nahkri was born to Dresyl, Loil Bry presented Little Yuli with a daughter. They named her Loilanun. With the midwife's help, Loilanun was born in the tower under the porcelain window.

Loil Bry, assisted by Yuli, gave their daughter a special present. They gave her, and through her all Oldorando, a calendar.

Owing to the disruptions of the centuries, Embruddock had had more than one calendar. Of the three old calendars, the most generally known was the so-called Lordly. The Lordly simply counted years from the accession of the last lord. The other two were antiquated, and one, the Ancipital, regarded as sinister; it had been abandoned for that reason, and for that reason had never entirely died. The Denniss went in for large numbers, and was not perfectly understood since the priests had been expelled from the town.

Under these old calendars, the birth of Loilanun fell, respectively, in the years 21, 343, and 423. Now her birth date was declared to be the Year Three After Union. Henceforth, dates would be kept with reference to the number of years since Oldorando and Embruddock came together.

The population received this gift with the same stoicism they received the news that there was a band of ancipital marauders in the vicinity.

One Batalix-dawn, when the clouds were thick as phlegm and hoarfrost speckled the ancient breastworks of the hamlet, the horns of the lookout sounded from an eastern tower. Immediately, there was stir and shouting. Dresyl ordered all women to be locked in the women's tower, where many of them were already at work. He assembled his men, armed, at the barricades. His little sons came forth trembling to join him and stare towards the rising sun.

In the grey dawn distance, horns showed.

The phagors attacked in strength. Among their number were two who rode on kaidaws, their own particular animals—animals horned and mailed in fibrous red fur thick enough to withstand any cold.

As they were assailing the barricades, Dresyl had one of his men break down a small earth dam previously built to pen in the hot waters of a geyser. Phagors notoriously hate water. A scalding flood now burst upon them, swirling about their knees, causing awful confusion in their ranks. Some hunters leaped forward to press home their advantage.

One of the kaidaws went down in yellow mud, hoofs thrashing, and was killed by a well-flung spear to the heart. In panic, another of the great beasts made a standing jump, clearing the barricade. It was the legendary spring jump of the horned horse, which few humans ever witnessed. The animal came down among the warriors of Oldorando.

They clubbed the kaidaw to death and captured its rider. Many other brutes were maimed by stones. The attackers retreated at last, while only one defender had been killed. All were exhausted. Some flung themselves into hot springs to restore their energies.

This was a great victory for united action, declared Dresyl. He strode about in a kind of fury, brow dark with triumph, shouting to all that they were now one tribe, and had been blooded. Henceforth, all must work for all, and all would prosper. The women gathered round to listen, whispering while the men lay flat, recovering. It was the Year Six.

Kaidaw meat was good. Dresyl ordered a feast of celebration, to start when both sentinels had set. The kaidaw carcass was parboiled in the earthwaters, and then roasted over fires lit in the square. Barley wine and rathel were provided to celebrate the victory.

Dresyl made a speech, as did the old lord, Wall Ein. Songs were sung. The man who had charge of slaves brought forward the captured phagor.

Nobody present that evening in the Year Six had any reason for misgivings. Humans had again fought off their legendary foes and everyone intended to celebrate the occasion. The celebrations would include the putting to death of their captive.

The inhabitants of Oldorando had no way of knowing how special a personage their captive was among the ancipital race, or that his death would drift down the backwaters of the years until terrible retribution would be visited on them and their offspring.

Everyone fell silent as the monster stood among them, glaring at them with his large scarlet eyes. His arms were lashed behind his back with leather rope. His horned feet pawed restlessly at the ground. In the gathering dark, he seemed immense, the bogeyman of all their nocturnal dreams, a creature from uneasy dimday sleeps. He was clad in shaggy white fur, stained by mud and battle. He stood challengingly before his human captors, giving off a resonant smell, his boney head with its two long horns thrust forward between his shoulders. His thick white milt appeared foraging up the slits of his nostrils, first one, then the other.

This brute wore strange accoutrements. A broad stomacher fashioned from hide was strapped round his girth; spurs at ankle and wrist supported protruding spikes. The elegant razored horns were capped with metal. It fitted his gigantic skull like a harness, coming to a two-pronged point in the centre of the forehead between the eyes, curving behind the ears, and fastening elaborately under the jaw so as to encompass the long boney chops.

Baruin stepped forward and said, "See what our concerted action has achieved. We have captured a chief. By his headgear, this beast leads a component. Look at him well, you young men who have never before seen a fuggie close, for they are our traditional enemy, in darkness and light."

Many young hunters stepped forward and tugged the creature's matted hair. He stood unmoving and let forth a fart like a small thunderclap. They fell back, alarmed.

"Fuggies organise their herds into components," Dresyl explained. "Most can speak Olonets. They take humans as slaves, and are beastly enough to eat their captives. As a chief, this brute understands all we say. Don't you?" He clouted its rough shoulder. The monster stared coldly at him.

The old lord, standing beside Dresyl, spoke.

"The male phagors are called stalluns and the females gillots or fillocks, that I know. Males and females alike go on raids and fight together. They are creatures of ice and darkness. Your great ancestor Yuli warned against them. They are bringers of illness and death."

Then the phagor spoke, using the Olonets in a hoarse churring voice.

"You worthless Sons of Freyr will all blow away before the final storm! This world, this town, belong to us, the ancipitals."

The women in the crowd were frightened. They threw stones at the evil thing that spoke in their midst, and shouted, "Kill him, kill him!"

Dresyl raised an arm, pointing.

"Drag him up to the top of the herb tower, friends! Drag him to the top and throw him off."

"Yes, yes," they roared, and at once the bolder hunters ran forward, seized the great stubborn bulk and, by sheer force, thrust it towards the nearby building. Great cheering and commotion reigned, children ran screaming round their elders.

Among those urchins were the two sons of Dresyl, Nahkri and Klils, both scarcely out of toddling stage. Because they were so small, they were able to stagger through the legs of the milling adults, and so came up against the right leg of the phagor, rising like a shaggy column before their eyes.

"You touch it."

"No, you."

"You daren't, coward!"

"You're a coward too!"

Putting forth chubby fingers, they touched the leg together.

Heavy musculature moved below a rug of hair. The limb lifted, the three-toed foot stamped down in the mud.

Though these monstrous creatures could master the Olonets tongue, they were far from human. The thoughts in the harneys of their heads ran aslant. Old hunters knew that inside their barrel bodies they carried their intestines above their lungs. From their machinelike walk, it could be seen how their limbs were jointed in a different way from a man's; at what should have been elbow and knee, phagors could bend lower arms and legs in impossible attitudes. That distinction alone was enough to strike terror into small boys' hearts.

For a moment they were in contact with the unknown. Pulling back their hands as if they had been burnt—in truth, the ancipital body temperature was cooler than man's—the two urchins looked at each other with wild eyes.

Then they burst into howls of fear. Dly Hoin swept the boys into her arms. By then, Dresyl and others had shifted the monster on.

Although the great animal struggled in its bonds, it was hammered through the entrance and into the tower. The crowd, restless in the square, listened to the noise within, which worked its way up the building. A cheer rose in the thick air as the first hunter emerged on the roof. Behind everybody, the kaidaw carcass roasted, untended; its flavours mingled with wood smoke to fill the bowl of the square, full of upturned faces. A second cheer, louder than the first, arose when the phagor chief was dragged into view, black against the sky.

"Throw it down!" screamed the crowd, united in hate.

The monstrous chief fought with his jostling captors. He roared as they prodded him with daggers. Then, as if realising that the game was up, he jumped up onto the parapet and stood there, glaring down at the jostling mob below.

With a last burst of rage, he snapped his bonds. He jumped forward, arms outstretched, with a massive spring that carried him away from the tower. The crowd tried too late to scatter. The great body hurtled down, crushing three people beneath it, a man, a woman, a child. The child was killed outright. A groan of terror and dismay rose from the rest there assembled.

Even then, the great animal was not killed. He raised himself up on his shattered legs to confront the avenging blades of the hunters. Every-

one pierced him through, through the thick coat, through the dense
flesh. He struggled on until his curdled yellow blood streamed across
the trampled ground.

While these terrible events took place, Little Yuli remained in his
chamber with Loil Bry and their infant daughter. When he made to
dress and join the fight, Loil Bry cried that she felt unwell and needed
his company. She clung to him, kissing his lips with her pale mouth, and
would not let him go.

After this, Dresyl felt contempt for his cousin-brother. But he did not
go and kill him, as he had a mind to, although these were savage times.
For he remembered a lesson and recognised that killing divided tribes.
When his sons ruled, this was forgotten.

This forbearance of Dresyl's—based on a friendship begun in his boyhood, before Dresyl had a beard or grey in it—stood the community in
good stead, and earned him new respect. And the things Little Yuli
learned at the expense of his fighting spirit were fruitful in the days to
come.

Immediately after the shock caused by the appearance of the phagor
chief in its midst, the community underwent another ordeal. A mysterious illness, accompanied by fever, cramps, and body rash, seized half
the population of Oldorando. The first to go down were the hunters
who had pushed the phagor to the top of the herb tower. For some days,
little hunting was done. The domesticated pigs and geese had to be eaten
instead. A woman with child died of fever, and the whole hamlet sor-
rowed to lose two precious lives to the world below. Yuli and Loil Bry,
together with their daughter, escaped the illness.

Soon the communal bloodstream was purged of its malady, and life
went on as usual. But the news of the slaying of the phagor spread forth
from the community.

And for a while the climate continued harsh towards mankind. The
cold winds picked out the seams of any badly stitched garment.

The two sentinels of light, Freyr and Batalix, went about their duties
as appointed, and the Hour-Whistler continued to blow.

For half of the year, the sentinels shone together in the skies. Then
the hours of their setting slipped further apart, until gradually Freyr
ruled the sky by day and Batalix the sky by night; then night scarcely
seemed night, day scarcely light enough to be called day. Then the sentinels again became reconciled: days became bright with both lights,
nights became pitch.

One quarter, when there were only shrill stars looking down on
Oldorando, when cold and dark were intense, the old lord, Wall Ein

Den, died; he descended to the world below, to become himself a gossie and sink down to the original boulder.

Another year was finished, and another. A generation grew up, another grew old. Slowly numbers increased under Dresyl's peaceful rule, while the suns performed their sentry duties overhead.

Although Batalix showed the larger disc, Freyr always gave out more light and more warmth. Batalix was an old sentinel, Freyr young and lusty. From one generation to the next, no man could positively swear that Freyr grew towards manhood, but so said the legends. Humanity endured—suffering or rejoicing—from generation to generation, and lived in the hope that Wutra would be victorious in the world above, and ever sustain Freyr.

These legends carried reality within them, as a flower bulb carries the flower within its flesh. So humans knew without knowing they knew.

As for the animals and birds, still many in numbers though few in species, their senses were more closely bound by the magnetic fluctuations of the globe than were mankind's. They also knew without knowing they knew. Their comprehensions told them that ineluctable change was already at hand—was indeed rising under the earth, in the bloodstream, in the air, in the stratosphere, and in all that was in the biosphere.

Above the stratosphere rode a small self-contained world built from the elements of metals gathered in the rich fields among the stars. From the surface of Helliconia, this world appeared in the night sky as a star itself, travelling swiftly overhead.

It was the Earth Observation Station Avernus.

The binary system of Freyr and its companion, Batalix, was closely watched by the Avernus. In particular, the families on the station studied Helliconia, and had done so for more than one of its slow Great Years about Freyr—or Star A, as it was known on the station.

Helliconia was of unique interest of the people of Earth, and never more so than at this period. Helliconia revolved about Batalix—Star B, as it was known on the station. Both sun and planet were beginning to accelerate in their orbit. They were still almost six hundred times as distant from Freyr as Earth is from its primary. But the distance was diminishing, week by week.

The planet was now several centuries past apastron, the coldest part of its orbit. There was new purpose in the corridors of the Observation Station; everyone could read the message in the increasingly favourable temperature gradients.

IV

FAVOURABLE TEMPERATURE GRADIENTS

Children follow their parents or they do not. Laintal Ay grew up knowing his mother as a quiet woman, given to the same kind of studious seclusion as her mother and father. But Loilanun had not always behaved like that, before life defeated her.

In adolescence, she rejected the gentle tutelage of Loil Bry and Little Yuli. She screamed at them that she hated the cloistered atmosphere of their room—which, as they grew older, they were increasingly reluctant to leave. After a violent quarrel, she left them, went to live in another tower with relations.

There was plenty of work. Loilanun became useful at grinding and tanning. While making a pair of hunting boots, she met their future wearer and fell in love with him. She was scarcely at the age of puberty. She ran out with the hunter on bright nights, when no one could sleep. There was the world in all its appalling beauty about her for the first time. She became his woman. She would have died for him.

Manners were changing in Oldorando. He took Loilanun out with him on a deer hunt. Once Dresyl would never have permitted women running with them; but his command had become less certain as he grew older. The deer hunters met with a stungebag in a narrow defile.

Before Loilanun's eyes, her man was run down and pierced through by one of the creature's horns. He died before he could be carried home.

Brokenhearted, Loilanun returned to her parents. They received her back, placidly absorbing her, comforting her. As she lay in the scented shadows, life stirred in her womb. She had conceived. She remembered the joy of that occasion when her time came and she gave birth to a son. She called him Laintal Ay, and him too her parents placidly accepted. It was spring of the Year After Union 13, or 31 by the old calendar of Lordly Years.

"He will grow into a better world," said Loil Bry to her daughter, regarding the baby with her lustrous eyes. "Histories tell that a time will come when the rajabarals will be thrown open, and the air will be heated with the heat of the earth. Food will be plentiful, snow will disappear, people will be naked to each other. How I longed for that time when I was young. Laintal Ay may see it. How I wish he had been a girl—girls feel and see more than boys."

The child liked to watch his grandmother's porcelain window. It was unique in Oldorando, though Little Yuli maintained that there had once been many more, all now broken. Year after year, Laintal Ay's grandparents had lifted their eyes from their ancient documents to watch the window turn pink, orange, and crimson with sunset, as Freyr or Batalix descended into a bath of fire. The colours would die. Night would stain the porcelain black.

In the old days, childrims had come, fluttering about the towers of Oldorando, those selfsame apparitions the first Yuli had seen when struggling across the white wilderness with his father.

Childrims came only at night. Sparks like feathers would flare behind the porcelain window, and the childrims would be there, slowly circling, a single wing flapping. Or was it a wing? When the people ran out to look at them, their outlines were confusing, never clear.

The childrims caused strange thoughts in human minds. Yuli and Loil Bry would lie upon their rugs and skins and feel that all the thoughts in their heads were coming alive at the same time. They saw scenes they had forgotten, and scenes they had never known. Loil Bry often cried and covered her eyes. She said it was like communing with a dozen fessups at once. Afterwards, she longed to experience some of the unexpected scenes once more, but once they had gone they could never more be recalled; their confusing beauty vanished like a fragrance.

The childrims sailed on. No man could fathom their going or their coming.

Their rightful habitat was the upper troposhere. Occasionally, electric pressures forced them to descend close to the surface of the planet. Neural currents in the brains of men and animals held a brief attraction for them, causing them to pause and circle as if they too were creatures of intelligence. Then they rose again and were gone. Depending on local whims of the great magnetic storm sweeping across the Helliconian system, the childrims might sail in any direction, onwards, upwards, swept along with the magnetic tides, circulating without perception or need of rest.

Yet not circulating for ever. Because the electric entities that human beings called childrims could not change. So nothing was more vulnerable to change than they.

Temperatures across the tropical continent of Campannlat varied greatly at any one time. On a mild day in the summer, while Loilanun sat playing listlessly with her young son, the ground temperature in Oldorando climbed several degrees above zero. Only a comparatively few miles north, by Lake Dorzin, there might be ten degrees of frost. In summer, when the sentinels worked day and night, there was no frost at all in sheltered parts, and cereal crops grew.

Three thousand miles from Oldorando, in the Nktryhk, daily temperatures showed wide variation, from minus twelve degrees centigrade to minus one hundred and fifty degrees, about the temperature at which krypton turns to liquid.

Change accumulated, at first as what may be termed latent change. Then its effects were rapid, as temperature gradients in the upper atmosphere responded to increased radiations from Freyr. The process was steady but quantal. On one occasion, Earth Observation Station Avernus recorded a twelve-degree rise in temperature at a 16.6-mile equatorial altitude within the course of an hour.

With this warming up, stratospheric circulation increased strongly, and the planet was swept by storms. Jet streams were observed over Nktryhk travelling at speeds in excess of two hundred seventy-five miles per hour.

Suddenly, the childrims were no more.

The beginnings of what was to spell a renascence for mankind and animals brought disaster for the childrims. The conditions that created them dispersed between one year and the next. Their vortices of piezo-electric dusts and charged particles were too fragile to survive a more dynamic system. They were gone, leaving behind them evanescent trails of sparks in the rarefied upper air. The sparks soon died.

Yuli and Loil Bry looked in vain for the childrims. Laintal Ay soon forgot he had ever seen them.

Groups of phagors were emerging under the greenish sky common at that altitude, where the sentinels—when not buried in cloud—directed their rays through multitudinous ice crystals. The phagors, stalluns and gillots alike, moved into position with their inhuman gait. Many had birds perched on their shoulders or flying just above them. The birds and the phagors were white, the terrain white or brown and exsiccated black, the sky beyond livid green. The living things were outlined against the Hhryggt Glacier.

The course of the glacier was divided at one point by a massif of plutonic rock which, like an infernal castle, had withstood centuries of siege. The ice had scoured its walls, yet it survived, rearing its bunched towers towards the sky. Where the ice river fell away was a firn-covered plateau. Here stood the ancipital leader, immobile, while the cohorts of his crusade assembled.

It was the components belonging to the kzahhns of Hrastyprt who first decided to bring destruction upon the Sons of Freyr who lived in the remote plains. The young kzahhn was Hrr-Brahl Yprt. He would lead the crusade. It was his grandstallun, the great Kzahhn Hrr-Tryhk Hrast, who had been destroyed by those distant Sons. Under Hrr-Brahl Yprt would the legions ride forth in revenge.

For under Hrr-Brahl Yprt the component had prospered, regaining strength lost since Freyr last burned the world. Force of numbers as much as conscious decision urged it from its altitudinous fastnesses to begin this migration of irresistible scale.

Vengeance moved in their harneys, but action was triggered by favourable temperature gradients in the stratosphere. A heat message thrilled along the five-hundred-mile length of the glacier, as it spilled down from the airless plateau of High Nktryhk to the excoriated valleys east of the Oldorandan plain, drawing out ancipitals from its eaves and crevices.

Hrr-Brahl Yprt waited, motionless. He too heard the heat message across his air-octave.

The precursor of major climatic change activated other forms of life in the region, forms on which the phagors were in part dependent for protein. Protognostic tribes called Madis also occupied the boulder-strewn land of the glaciers. Gaunt, perpetually undernourished, they too began to resume a nomadic habit. They drove before them goat and arang, the quadruped that lived on lichens or rocklice. The Madis sought lower pastures. But they would not travel before the phagor crusade left the way clear.

The young Hrr-Brahl Yprt growled an order to mount. Only the highest among his officers had kaidaws to ride. These rusty red steeds were mounted as soon as the order came, the officers seating themselves behind their animals' humps.

That order came late in the Year 13, according to Loil Bry's modest calendar. According to the ancipital calendar, it was the Air-Turn or Year 353 After Small Apotheosis of Great Year 5,634,000 Since Catastrophe. By a more modern reckoning, it was late in the year 433.

Laintal Ay was then an infant, dandled on the knee of his widowed mother.

The time would come when he would have to confront the whole might of Hrr-Brahl Yprt's crusade.

Beside the kzahhn's kaidaw stood a creaght, or young male phagor, bearing a towering standard.

Hrr-Brahl Yprt was as tall as a well-built man and weighed almost half as much again. His keratinous three-toed feet formed a base for thick flanks, massive thews, and a chest broader than any man's.

His head, wedged between sturdy shoulders, was remarkable. It was long, narrow, boney, with prominent ridges above the eyes, giving those eyes, sheltered by long sweeping lashes on which frost glittered, a marked stare. His horns, set back behind his ears, curved forward before turning upwards, in the manner of his line. They were veined grey, as if made of marble, and their edges were deadly sharp. These weapons were used only in combat with other phagors, never against other species; their tips could never be sullied by the red blood of a Son of Freyr.

Hrr-Brahl Yprt's prominent muzzle was black behind the arches of his nostrils, just as his grandstallun's had been. It accentuated the command of his gaze. An air of ferocious authority was reinforced by his every movement.

An elaborate face crown had been wrought by his weapon makers for this crusade. The crown formed almost a fleur-de-lys pattern down the young kzahhn's long nose. It curved about the base of his horns and sprouted two sharp iron horns of its own, which protruded laterally.

When threatening a subordinate, the kzahhn wrinkled up his lip to show two lines of blunt longitudinally ridged teeth, flanked by long incisors.

His body was accoutred with armour: chiefly, a sleeveless jacket of stiff kaidaw skin with three capes and a belt, which latter broadened over his girth into a sort of sporran serving to conceal his genitals swinging under the coarse matted hair of his pelvis.

The name of his kaidaw was Rukk-Ggrl. After mounting Rukk-Ggrl, the young kzahhn raised his hand. An immense curled musical instrument, reamed from a stungebag horn, was sounded by a human slave. Its diaphony echoed across the grey wastes.

Following this mournful call, other slaves appeared from a cave in the plutonian massif, carrying between them the figures of Hrr-Brahl Yprt's father and great-grandstallun.

These illustrious forebears were in a state of tether, slowly sinking towards the final vortices of nonbeing. This marked diminution of the life process had caused them to shrink in size. The great-grandstallun was now almost entirely transformed into keratin.

At the appearance of the totem objects, a stir went through the hosts of the component assembled, male and female. They stretched over the frozen ground, many standing out against the sky on nearby ridges or banks of shattered stone, where their outlines were confused by the brilliant cloud piling up. Some leaned on spears, their huge birds above them. All, when stationary, assumed the daunting immobility of their kind. Only an occasional flicking ear indicated that they were alive. They shifted their positions so as to direct their regard on their young leader and the leaders of the past.

The totem figures were presented to the kzahhn. The human slaves knelt in abasement before him.

Hrr-Brahl Yprt dismounted, to stand between his ancestors and his kaidaw. After making a bow, he humbly buried his face in the rufous hair of the flank of Rukk-Ggrl. His comprehension left his harneys. In a kind of trance, he summoned the spirits of his father and great-grandstallun back to the living present.

The spirits came before him. They were little whiskery figures, no higher than snow rabbits. They uttered squeaks of greeting. As they had never done in real life, they ran on all fours.

"O my sacred forebears, now integrating with earth," cried the young kzahhn, in the thick tongue of his kind, "at last I go to avenge him who should be standing now between you, my valorous grand-stallun, Great Kzahhn Hrr-Tryhk Hrast, who was killed by the peltless Sons of Freyr. Years of trial lie ahead. Strengthen my arm, warn us of danger, hold horns high."

His great-grandstallun appeared to be standing deep inside Rukk-Ggrl. The keratinous image said, "Go, hold horns high, remember enmities. Beware friendship with the Sons of Freyr."

This remark was useless to Hrr-Brahl Yprt. He scarcely thought himself likely to feel other than hatred for the traditional enemy. Those in tether were not always wiser than those in air.

The keratinous image of his father was larger than that of the great-grandstallun since he had entered tether more recently. The image bowed to his son and spoke, sketching a series of pictures in his son's harneys.

Hrr-Anggl Hhrot showed his son an image which the young kzahhn understood only in part. To a human, it would have been incomprehensible. Yet it was a view of the known universe, as pictured by the ancipital race, a view that largely conditioned their approach to life.

A busy organ pumped lustily, expanding and contracting. It consisted of three parts, each somewhat resembling a human fist clenched tight. The parts were interdependent, and of different colours. The grey third was the known world, the dazzling white third Batalix, the mottled black third Freyr. When Freyr puffed itself large, the other parts shrank; when Batalix grew, so did the known world.

This busy organ was surrounded by steam. Through the steam ran yellow threads, the air-octaves. The air-octaves wavered as if in flight from Freyr, yet nevertheless curled about it in some instances. The Freyr-third put forth black exopodites which tugged at the air-octaves, drawing it closer to the known world. It frothed. It grew.

These images were familiar to the young kzahhn and intended to reassure him before he set forth. He understood also the warning that the pictures conveyed: that the air-octaves the crusade would have to follow were becoming more chaotic, and that the perfect sense of direction he and all his kind possessed would be disturbed. The crusade would make slow progress, taking many air-turns, or years.

He thanked the keratinous image with deep churring in his throat.

Hrr-Anggl Hhrot revealed more pictures. These had the scent of ancient things. They were drawn from a well of remembered wisdom, from the heroic ages when Freyr was negligible. An angellike army of keratinous predecessors could be seen, confirming the images.

Hrr-Anggl Hhrot showed what would happen when air-turns to near a stallun's number of toes and fingers had lapsed across the triple organ. Slowly, mottled black Freyr would drag itself into concealment behind Batalix. Twenty times in successive air-turns would it behave so. This was the terrifying paradox: that though the Freyr-part grew larger, it would hide itself behind the shrinking Batalix-part.

The twenty concealments marked the beginning of Freyr's period of cruel dominance. From the twentieth concealment onwards, the ancipital component nations would fall under the power of the Sons of Freyr.

Such was the warning—but it contained hope.

The poor ignorant Sons would become terrified by the concealments of Freyr, who whelped them. The *third* concealment would demoralise them most. *That* was the time to strike against them, that was the time to arrive outside the town where the great kzahhn, Hrr-Tryhk Hrast, had been destroyed. That was the time of revenge. The time to burn and kill.

Remember. Be valiant. Hold horns high. War has begun!

Hrr-Brahl Yprt behaved as if he had received the flow of wisdom for the first time. He had received it many times. It was unalterable. It served him for thought. All of his component with ancestors in tether had received the same images many times over previous quarters. The images came from the known world, from the air, from the long dead. They were incontrovertible.

All component decisions were the result of such flows of wisdom from keratinous ancestors. Those who made the past outnumbered the living. The old heroes lived in an heroic age when Freyr waxed puny.

The young kzahhn emerged from his moment of tether. The host about him stirred, flicked ears. The birds above them were stationary. Again the discordant horn was blown, and the doll-like images were carried away to their cave in the natural fortress.

It was time to move forward.

Hrr-Brahl Yprt swung himself up into Rukk-Ggrl's high saddle. The movement dislodged Zzhrrk, his white cowbird. It wheeled up into the air, and then settled again on Hrr-Brahl Yprt's shoulder. Many of the host had their own cowbirds. The harsh croak of the cowbird was sweet to a phagor ear. The birds played a useful role in ridding the phagors of the ticks that infested their bodies.

This tick, an unconsidered creature, formed a vital link in the complex ecological structure of the world—and an undisclosed bond between deadly enemies.

While the young kzahhn was in tetherlike communication with his ancestors, livid clouds had drawn over the snowscape. Light was reflected back and forth between overcast and ground. In the diffused, nonpolarized illumination, where no shadows were cast and living things became spectres, human beings would have been lost. There was no horizon. Everything was pearly grey.

Whiteout meant little to the ancipital army, with its air-octaves to follow. Now that the communication ceremony was finished, foot servants led four kaidaw ponies forward through the whiteout. The single humps of the animals were scarcely fleshed out; their rough coats were still dapple. Astride each pony was one of the kzahhn's four fillocks. Each fillock wore eagle feathers or pallid papilionaceous rock flowers woven into her head-hair. This quartet of young beauties had been selected by the component to keep the Kzahhn Hrr-Brahl Yprt company during the years of the crusade.

A cool breeze, forty degrees below zero, blew from the glacial heights to the east, to ruffle the delicate filaments of the coats of the ancipital damsels. Beneath those filaments lay the thickly matted phagor coat, almost impenetrable to cold except when soaked with water.

The breeze stirred the cloud cover. As though a shutter had been opened at a window, the shapes of the known world returned. The host of creatures was revealed, and the sheer walls of Hhryggt behind them, and the four fillocks, ghostly pale at first. The whiteout thinned. Ahead, bleak defiles became visible which would lead to a place of destiny twelve thousand metres nearer sea level.

The Hrastyprt standard was raised.

The young kzahhn raised a hand as signal, pointed forward.

He dug his horned toes into Rukk-Ggrl's flank. The beast lifted its horned head and moved forward over the brittle firn. The host got slowly under way with its unnatural shambling movements. Slate grated, ice rang. Cowbirds floated high on updraughts. The crusade had begun.

Its consummation would come as the ancestral images predicted, when Freyr concealed itself behind Batalix for the third time. Then the kzahhn's army would strike the Sons of Freyr who lived in that accursed town where Hrr-Brahl Yprt's noble grandstallun had been killed. That great old kzahhn had been forced to jump from the top of a tower to his death below. Vengeance was on its way: the town would be obliterated.

Perhaps it was no wonder that the infant Laintal Ay cried at his mother's knee.

Year by year, the crusade progressed. The inhabitants of Oldorando remained in ignorance of that distant nemesis. They laboured in the toils of their own history.

Dresyl was no longer as energetic a leader as he had been. He stayed more and more in town, fussing with details of organisations which had gone smoothly before he interfered. His sons hunted in his stead.

The scent of change made everyone restless. Young men in the makers corps wanted to leave and take up hunting and trapping. The young hunters themselves would not behave. Dresyl already had a hunter under his command who had a natural daughter by an older man's wife. Such behaviour was becoming common, and fights with it.

"We behaved better than that when I was a lad," Dresyl complained to Aoz Roon, forgetting the pranks of his own youth. "We'll be murdering each other next, like the savages of the Quzint."

Dresyl could not decide whether to try and crush Aoz Roon or make the man conform by praising him. He inclined to the latter, for Aoz Roon was becoming famed as a cunning hunter, but such moves angered Dresyl's son Nahkri, who felt enmity for Aoz Roon, for the sort of reasons known only to the young.

Dly Hoin, Dresyl's unsatisfactory wife, fell ill and died, even as the Year 17 After Union died away. Father Bondorlonganon came and buried her on her side in her land-octave. When she had gone, a gap opened in Dresyl's life, and he felt he loved her for the first time. Sorrow ruled his heart thereafter.

Despite his years, he learned the arts of father-communing and achieved pauk in order to speak again with his departed Dly Hoin. He met her gossie drifting in the world below. She upbraided him for lack of love, for wasting their life, for being cold of temperament, and many other things that made his heart grieve. He fled from her vituperation, her snapping jaws, and ever after was a more silent man.

Sometimes he spoke to Laintal Ay. The boy was brighter of mind than Nahkri or Klils. But Dresyl stayed away from his old cousin-brother, Little Yuli; whereas before he had felt contempt for Yuli, now he felt envy. Yuli had a living woman to love and make happy.

Yuli and Loil Bry continued in their tower, and tried not to take note of their grey hairs. Loilanun kept an eye on Laintal Ay, and watched as he entered more fully into the rude pleasures of a new generation.

Remote under the Quzints lived a religious sect called the Takers. The first Yuli had once had a glimpse of them. Secure in a gigantic cavern heated by interior warmth, the sect was virtually impervious to temperature gradients in the upper atmosphere. But they maintained a clandestine liaison with Pannoval; from that warren came a perception that, in its way, induced as important a change as any temperature gradient.

Although the perception was wrongheaded, it held beauty for the rigid minds of the Takers, and seemed to possess the truth that goes with beauty.

Takers, male and female, wore an elaborate garment which enveloped them from the chin to the ground. In profile they presented the look of a half-open flower turned upside down. Only this external garment, the charfral, was worn.

The charfral could be seen as emblematic of Taker thinking. Their understandings had become codified through many generations, the ramifications of their theology manifold. They were at once lascivious and puritanical. Even the repressive stratification of their religion contained its paradoxes, and had led to a neurotic form of hedonism.

Belief in the Great Akha was not incompatible with organised lechery, for one basic reason: Great Akha paid no attention to mankind. He fought against the destructive light of Wutra, and this served mankind's interest; but it was not for mankind but himself that Akha fought. It did not matter what mankind did. The ethics of eudemonism sprang from man's powerlessness.

Long after his death, the prophet Naba changed all that. Naba's words eventually filtered down from Pannoval to the cavern. The prophet promised that if men and women forswore concupiscence, and lying so indiscriminately one with another that no one knew his own father, then the Great Father, Akha himself, would have regard for them. He would allow them to participate as warriors in the war against Wutra. The war would be brought to an early close. Mankind—this was the essence of Naba's message—was not powerless unless it chose to be so.

Mankind was not powerless. For the buried Takers, the message was persuasive. It could never be so persuasive in the Holies of Pannoval; there, people had always taken it for granted that mankind could act. But down in the cavern, the charfrals began to burn. Chastity set in.

Within a year, the Takers changed their temperament. The old rigid codification was directed to a restrictive virtue, in the name of the stone god. Those who could not conform to the new morality were executed by the sword, or fled before the sword fell.

In the heat and dialectic of the revolution, it was not enough for the Takers to convert themselves. It never is. Revolutionaries must go forth and convert others. The Faith-Trip of Akha's Naba was undertaken. Through a hundred miles of underground passages, the Faith-Trip went to spread the message. And the first stop on the way was Pannoval.

Pannoval was indifferent to the returning word of its own prophet, who had been executed and forgotten long ago. It was actively against an invasion of fanatics.

The militia turned out in strength, and battle was joined. The fanatics were prepared to fight. They wanted nothing better than to die for the cause. If others died too, so much the better. Their gossies, howling down the land-octaves, urged them to conquer. They flung themselves forward. The militia did its best throughout a long, bloody day. Then it turned and ran.

So Pannoval bowed to the message of potency and to the new regime. Charfrals were hastily made up especially to be burnt. Those who did not conform fled or were killed.

Those who fled made their way to the open world of Wutra, to the everlasting plains of the north. They went at a time when the snow was in retreat. Grasses grew. The two sentinels kept better watch over the skies, and Wutra himself seemed less savage. They survived.

Year by year, they spread northwards in search of food and a sheltered corner of land. They spread along the Lasvalt River to the east of the great plains. They raided the migratory herds of yelk and gunnadu. And they moved towards the isthmus of Chalce.

At the same time, those ameliorating temperatures were causing a stir among the peoples of the frigid continent of Sibornal. Wave after wave of rugged colonisers moved southwards, down the isthmus of Chalce into Campannlat.

One day, when Freyr ruled alone in the sky, the northernmost tribe from Pannoval met the southernmost part of the exodus from Sibornal. What happened then had happened many times before—and was fated to happen again.

Wutra and Akha would see to that.

Such was the state of the world when Little Yuli left it. Salt traders from the Quzints arrived in Oldorando with news of avalanches and freak happenings. Yuli—now quite ancient—hastened down to see them when they arrived, slipped on some steps, broke his leg. Within a week, the holy man from Borlien was calling, and Laintal Ay was delighting in his carved dog with the moveable jaw.

An epoch was over. The reign of Nahkri and Klils was about to begin.

V

DOUBLE SUNSET

Nahkri and Klils were in one of the rooms of the herb tower supposedly sorting deer skins. Instead they were looking out of the window and shaking their heads at what they saw.

"I don't believe it," Nahkri said.

"I don't believe it, either," Klils said. "I just don't believe it at all." He laughed until his brother slapped him on the back.

They watched a tall aged figure running crazily along the banks of the Voral. Nearby towers obscured the figure, then they saw it again, skinny arms and legs flying. It stopped once, scooping up mud to plaster over its head and face, then ran on with its tottering gait.

"She's gone mad," Nahkri said, smoothing his whiskers pleasureably.

"Worse than that, if you ask me. Crazy, high in the harneys."

Behind the running figure went a more sober one, a boy on the verge of manhood. Laintal Ay was following his grandmother to see that no harm came to her. She ran ahead of him, crying aloud. He followed, glum, silent, dutiful.

After shaking their heads, Nahkri and Klils put them together. "I can't see why Loil Bry's behaving like that," Klils said. "You remember what Father told us?"

"No."

"He told us that Loil Bry only pretended to love Uncle Yuli. He said she didn't love him at all."

"Ah, I remember. So why's she keeping up the pretence now that he's dead? It doesn't make sense."

"She's got some clever scheme, with all that learning, you see. It's a trick."

Nahkri went over to the open trap. Women were working below. He kicked the door shut and turned to face his younger brother.

"Whatever Loil Bry does, that's not important. Nobody understands what women do. The important thing is that Uncle Yuli's dead and now you and I are going to rule Embruddock."

Klils looked frightened. "Loilanun? Laintal Ay—what about him?"

"He's still a kid."

"Not for long. He'll be seven, and a full hunter, in two more quarters."

"For long enough. It's our chance. We're powerful—at least, I am. People will accept us. They don't want a kid ruling them, and they had a secret contempt for his grandfather, lying about all the while with that madwoman. We must think of something to tell everyone, to promise them. Times are changing."

"That's it, Nahkri. Tell them times are changing."

"We need the support of the masters. I'll go and speak to them now —you'd better keep away, because I happen to know that the council think you're a trouble-making fool. Then we win round a few leading hunters like Aoz Roon and the others, and everything will work out."

"What about Laintal Ay?"

Nahkri hit his brother. "Don't keep saying that. We'll get rid of him, if he's any trouble."

Nahkri summoned a meeting that evening, when the first sentinel had left the sky and Freyr was moving towards a monochromatic dusk. The hunting party was home, most of the trappers were back. He ordered the gates closed.

As the crowd assembled in the square, Nahkri appeared on the base of the big tower. Over his deerskins he had thrown a stammel, a coarse woollen garment of red and yellow, without sleeves, to lend himself dignity. He was of medium height, with thick legs. His face was plain, his ears large. Characteristically, he jutted his lower jaw forward, giving his features an ominous, top-heavy quality.

He addressed the crowd in a serious way, reminding them of the great qualities of the old triumvirate, of Wall Ein, of his father, Dresyl, and of his uncle, Yuli. They had combined bravery and wisdom. Now the tribe was united; bravery and wisdom were common qualities. He would carry on the tradition, but with new emphasis for a new age. He and his brother would rule with the council, and would always give ear to what any man had to say.

He reminded them all that phagor raids were a continual threat, and that the salt traders from the Quzint had spoken of religious wars in Pannoval. Oldorando must stay united and continue to grow in strength. Fresh efforts were needed. Everyone must work harder. The women must work harder.

A woman's voice interrupted him.

"Get down off that platform and do some work yourself!"

Nahkri lost his presence of mind. He gaped at the crowd below him, unable to think of a reply.

Loilanun spoke from the crowd. Laintal Ay stood beside her, looking down at the ground. Fear and anger shook her frame.

"You've no right to be up there, you and your drunken brother!" she called. "I am Yuli's issue, I am his daughter. Here stands my son, Laintal Ay, whom you all know, who will be a man in two quarters. I have as much wisdom and knowledge as a man—gleaned from my parents. Maintain the triumvirate, as you were intended to do by your father, Dresyl, whom all respected. I demand to rule with you—women should have a voice—I love our family. Speak up for me, everyone, see that I get my rights. Then when Laintal Ay is of age, he will rule in my stead. I'll train him properly."

Feeling his cheeks burn, Laintal Ay looked about under his lowered brow. Oyre was gazing at him sympathetically and made a sign.

Several women and a few men started to shout, but Nahkri had recovered his poise. He outshouted them.

"No one is going to be ruled by a woman while I have anything to do with it. Who ever heard of such a thing? Loilanun, you must be as soft in your head as your mother to think of it. We all know you had bad luck with your man being killed, and everyone's sorry, but what you say is all nonsense."

The people all turned and looked at Loilanun's flushed worn face. She returned the gaze unflinchingly and said, "Times are changing, Nahkri. Brains are needed as well as brawn. To be honest, a lot of us don't trust you and your blockhead brother."

Many murmured in Loilanun's favour, but one of the hunters, Faralin Ferd, said roughly, "She's not going to rule me—she's only a woman. I'd rather put up with those two rogues."

At this there was much good-hearted laughter, and Nahkri carried the day. As the crowd cheered, Loilanun pushed her way through it and went somewhere to weep. Laintal Ay followed her reluctantly. He felt sorry for his mother, he admired her; he also thought in his harneys that it was absurd for a woman to expect to rule over Oldorando. Nobody had ever heard of such a thing, as Uncle Nahkri said.

As he paused on the edge of the crowd, a woman called Shay Tal came to him and touched his sleeve. She was a young friend of his mother's, with a fine complexion and a keen, hawklike look. He knew her as strange and sympathetic, for she occasionally visited his grandmother, bringing bread.

"I'll come with you to comfort your mother, if you don't mind," Shay Tal said. "She embarrassed you, I know—but when people speak from the heart it often embarrasses us. I admire your mother as I admired your wise grandparents."

"Yes, she's brave. But still people laughed."

Shay Tal looked scrutinisingly at him. "Still people laughed, yes. But many of those who laughed admire her nevertheless. They are scared. Most people are always scared. Remember that. We must try to change their minds."

Laintal Ay went along with her, suddenly elated, smiling into her severe face.

Fortune favoured Nahkri and Klils. That night, a furious wind blew from the south, shrieking continuously among the towers like the Hour-Whistler itself. Next day, the fish trappers reported a glut of fish in the river. The women went down with baskets and scooped up the gleaming bodies. This unexpected plenty was taken as a sign. Much of the fish was salted, but enough was left over to provide a feast that night, a feast at which barley wine was drunk to celebrate the new rule of Nahkri and Klils.

But Klils had no sense and Nahkri no wisdom. Worse, neither had much feeling for their fellow men. In the hunt, they performed no better than average. They often quarrelled with each other over what was to be done. And because they were aware in a shadowy fashion of these defects, they drank too much, and so quarrelled the more.

Yet luck remained with them. The weather continued to improve, deer were sometimes more plentiful, and no diseases struck. Phagor raids ceased, though the monsters were sighted occasionally a few miles away.

Fruitful monotony attended the lives in Oldorando.

The rule of the brothers did not please everyone. It did not please some of the hunters; it did not please some of the women; and it did not please Laintal Ay.

Among the hunters was a party of young bloods who formed a company together, and resisted Nahkri's attempts to break them up. Of these, the leader was Aoz Roon Den, now in the full flower of manhood. He was large of frame, with a frank expression on his face, and could run on his two legs as fast as a hog on four. His figure was distinctive;

he wore the skin of a black bear, and the fur enabled him to be picked out at a distance.

That bear was one he had wrestled with and killed. In pride at the feat, he carried the animal back from the hills unaided, and threw it down before his admiring friends in the tower where they lived. After a rathel party, he had summoned in Master Datnil Skar to skin the animal.

And there had been a touch of distinction in the way Aoz Roon had arrived in this tower. He was descended from an uncle of Wall Ein's who had been Lord of the Brassimips. The brassimips were an area and a vegetable vital to the local economy; from the brassimips came the feed for the sows that yielded milk for rathel. But Aoz Roon found his family tyrannical, revolted against it early in life, and established his niche in a distant tower, along with bright sparks of his own age, the mirthful Eline Tal, the lecherous Faralin Ferd, the steady Tanth Ein. They drank to the stupidity of Nahkri and his brother. Their drinking parties were widely regarded as distinguished.

In other ways also, Aoz Roon was distinguished. He was a man noted for courage in a society where courage was common coin. During the tribal dances, he could turn a cartwheel in the air without touching the ground. And he believed strongly in the unity of the tribe.

Nor did the presence of his natural daughter, Oyre, stop women admiring him. He had caught the eye of Loilanun's friend, Shay Tal, and responded warmly to her unique beauty; but he gave his heart to no one. He saw that one day Nahkri and Klils would meet with trouble and fall before it. Since he understood—or thought he did—what was good for the tribe, he wished himself to rule, and could not allow any woman to rule his heart.

To this end, Aoz Roon cultivated his comrades with good fellowship and also paid attention to Laintal Ay, encouraging the boy to come by his side on the chase when he officially reached the years of a hunter.

Out on a deer hunt to the southwest of Oldorando, he and Laintal Ay became separated by flooded ground from the rest of the company. They had to detour through difficult country studded with the great cylinders of rajabarals. There they came on a party of ten traders lying round a grass campfire, torpid after drink. Aoz Roon despatched two of the number as they slept, without any of the others rousing. He and Laintal Ay then rushed from cover holding animal skulls before their faces and screaming. The remaining eight traders surrendered in superstitious fear. This story was told in Oldorando as a great joke for many years.

The eight had traded in weapons, grain, furs, and anything else that came to hand. They came from Borlien, where the people were traditionally regarded as cowards, and travelled from the seas of the south to the Quzints in the north. Most of them were known in Oldorando—and known as cheats and swindlers. Aoz Roon and Laintal Ay brought them back to serve as slaves, and shared their goods among the people. For his personal slave, Aoz Roon kept a young man called Calary, scarcely older than Laintal Ay.

This episode brought Aoz Roon more prestige. He was soon in a position to challenge Nahkri and Klils. Yet he held back, as was his way, and consorted with his fellow bloods.

Unrest was growing among the makers corps. In particular, a young man by the name of Dathka was attempting to break away from the metal-makers corps, refusing to service his long term as apprentice. He was taken before the brothers. They could get no submission from him. Dathka disappeared from everyone's ken for two days. One of the women reported that he was lying bound in an infrequently used cell, with bruises on his face.

At this, Aoz Roon went before Nahkri and asked that Dathka might be allowed to join the hunters. He said, "Hunting is no easy life. There is still plenty of game, but the grazing grounds have altered with this freak weather the last few years have sent us. We're hard pressed, as you know. So let Dathka join us if he wishes. Why not? If he's no good, then we'll kick him out and think again. He's about Laintal Ay's age, and can team up with him."

The light was dim where Nahkri stood, supervising slaves who were milking the rathel sows. Dust filled the air. The ceiling was low, so that Nahkri stooped slightly. He appeared to cringe before the challenge of Aoz Roon.

"Dathka should obey the laws," said Nahkri, offended by Aoz Roon's unnecessary reference to Laintal Ay.

"Permit him to hunt and he'll obey the laws. We'll have him earning his keep before those welts you set on his face can heal."

Nahkri spat. "He's not trained as a hunter. He's a maker. You have to be trained to these things." Nahkri feared that various secrets belonging to the metal makers might be given away; the crafts of the corps were closely guarded and reinforced the rulers' power to rule.

"If he won't work, then let's subject him to our hard life and see how he survives," Aoz Roon argued.

"He's a silent, surly fellow."

"Silence is an aid on the open plains."

Finally Nahkri released Dathka. Dathka teamed up with Laintal Ay as Aoz Roon said. He developed into a good hunter, delighting in the chase.

Silent though he was, Dathka was accepted by Laintal Ay as a brother. There was not an inch to choose between them in height, and less than a year in age. Whereas Laintal Ay's face was broad and humorous,

Dathka's was long, and his glance perpetually cast downward. Their expertise as a team became legendary during the chase.

Because they were so much together, old women said of them that they would one day meet the same fate, as had been predicted in an earlier age of Dresyl and Little Yuli. As then, so now: their fates were to differ greatly. In these young days, they merely seemed alike, and Dathka excelled to such an extent that the vain Nahkri grew proud of him, patronising him, and sometimes making reference to his own far-sightedness in releasing the youth from his bondage with the corps. Dathka kept silent and stared at the ground when Nahkri went by, never forgetting who had beaten him. Some men never forgive.

Loil Bry was not the same after the death of her man. Whereas she had formerly clung to her scented chamber, now, old and vulnerable, she chose to wander in the wilderness of green springing up about Oldorando, talking or singing to herself. Many feared for her, but none dared approach, except Laintal Ay and Shay Tal.

One day, she was attacked by a bear driven down from the hills by fresh avalanches. Dragging herself along, wounded, she was set on by wild dogs, who killed and half ate her. When her mangled body was found, women gathered it up and carried it home weeping.

Then was the extravagant Loil Bry buried in traditional fashion. Many women wailed their grief: they had respected the remoteness of this person, born in the time of snows, who had managed to remain in the midst of them and yet live a life completely apart. There was a kind of inspiration in such remoteness: it was as if they could not sustain it for themselves, and so lived it through her.

Everyone recognised the learning of Loil Bry. Nahkri and Klils came to pay their respects to their ancient auntie, though they did not bother to order Father Bondorlonganon over to supervise her burial. They stood about on the edge of the mourning crowd, whispering together. Shay Tal went with Laintal Ay to support Loilanun, who neither wept nor spoke as her mother was lowered into the sodden ground.

As they left the place afterwards, Shay Tal heard Klils snigger and say to his brother, "Still, brother, she was only another woman . . ."

Shay Tal flushed, stumbled, and would have fallen if Laintal Ay had not grasped her round the waist. She went straight to the draughty room where she lived with her aged mother, and stood with her forehead to the wall.

She was of good build, though she had not what was termed a child-bearing figure. Her outward merits lay in her rich black hair, her fine features, and the way she carried herself. That proud carriage attracted some men, but repelled many more. Shay Tal had rejected an advance by her genial kinsman, Eline Tal. That had been long enough ago for her to notice that no other suitors approached—except Aoz Roon. Even with him, she could not subdue her spirit.

Now, as she stood against the moist wall, where grey lichens scrawled their skeletal flowers, she resolved that Loil Bry's independence should serve as an example to her. She would not be *only another woman*, whatever else they said of her over her grave.

Every morning at dawn, the women gathered in what was known as the women's house. It was a kind of factory. By first light, figures would steal forth from ruinous towers, huddled in their furs and often with additional swathings against the cold, and make their way to this place of work.

A saturating mist filled these mornings, divided into blocks by the shadowing towers. Heavy white birds passed through it like clouds. The stones ran moisture, and mud oozed underfoot. The women's house stood at one end of the main street, near to the big tower. Some way behind it, down a slope, flowed the Voral, with its worn stone embankment. As the women straggled to work, geese—the fowl of Embruddock—came up to be fed, honking and clattering. Every woman had a titbit to throw them.

Inside the house, when its heavy creaking door was closed, the eternal women's tasks were performed: the grinding of grain for flour, boiling and baking, the stitching of garments and boots, and the tanning of hides. The work of tanning was particularly difficult, and was overseen by a man—Datnil Skar, master of the tawyers and tanners corps. Salt was involved in the tanning process, and the tanners traditionally had charge of it. Also involved was the soaking of the hides in goose scumble, work too degrading for men to undertake. The toil was enlivened by gossip, as mothers and daughters discussed the shortcomings of men and neighbours.

Loilanun was forced to work here with the other women. She had become very thin and her face held a yellowy hue. Her bitterness against Nahkri and Klils ate at her vitals so much that she scarcely spoke even to Laintal Ay, who was now allowed to go his own way. She befriended no one but Shay Tal. Shay Tal had a certain fey quality, and a way of thought far removed from the dumb endurance that was a marked characteristic of the women of Embruddock.

One chill dawn, Shay Tal had just climbed from her bed, when a knocking sounded on the door below. The mists had penetrated the tower, beading everything in the room where she slept with her mother. She was sitting in the pearly darkness pulling on her boots when the knock came a second time. Loilanun pushed open the downstairs door and ascended through the stable and the room above it to Shay Tal's room. The family pigs shuffled and snorted warmly in the dark as Loilanun felt her way up the creaking steps. Shay Tal met her as she climbed into the room, and clutched her cold hand. She made a gesture of silence towards the darkest corner of the room, where her mother lay sleeping. Her father was away with the other hunters.

In the dung-scented confinement of the room, they were little more than grey outlines, but Shay Tal detected something amiss in Loilanun's hunched appearance. Her unexpected arrival suggested trouble.

"Loilanun, are you ill?" She whispered the words.

"Weary, just weary. Shay Tal, throughout this night, I spoke with my mother's gossie."

"You spoke with Loil Bry! She's there already. . . . What did she say?"

"They're all there, even now, thousands of them, below our feet, waiting for us. . . . It's frightening to think of them." Loilanun was shivering. Shay Tal put an arm round the older woman and led her over to the bed on the floor, where they sat huddled together. Outside, geese honked. The two women turned their faces to each other, seeking signs of comfort.

"It's not the first time I've been in pauk since she died," Loilanun said. "I never found her before—just a blank down there where she should be—scratched emptiness. . . . My grandmother's fessup was wailing for attention. It's so lonely down there. . . ."

"Where's Laintal Ay?"

"Oh, he's out on the hunt," she said dismissively, immediately returning to her theme. "So many of them, drifting, and I don't believe they talk to each other. Why should the dead hate each other, Shay Tal? We don't hate each other—do we?"

"You're upset. Come on, we'll go to work and get something to eat."

In the grey light filtering in, Loilanun looked quite like her mother. "Maybe they have nothing to say to each other. They're always so desperate to talk to the living. So was my poor mother."

She began to weep. Shay Tal hugged her, while looking round to see if the sleeper stirred.

"We ought to go, Loilanun. We'll be late."

"Mother was so different when she appeared . . . so different, poor shade. All that lovely dignity she had in life was gone. She has started to . . . curl up. Oh, Shay Tal, I dread to think what it will be like to be down there permanently. . . ."

This last remark was forced from her in a loud voice. Shay Tal's mother rolled over and grunted. The pigs below grunted.

The Hour-Whistler blew. It was time to be at work. Arm in arm, they shuffled downstairs. Shay Tal called the pigs softly by name to quiet them. The air was frosty as they leaned on the door to close it, feeling the rime on its panels powder under their fingers. In the greys and sludges of early morning, other figures made for the women's house, armless as they clutched blankets about their shoulders.

As they moved among the anonymous shapes, Loilanun said to her companion, "Loil Bry's gossie told me of her long love for my father. She said many things about men and women and their relationships I don't understand. She said cruel things about my man, now dead."

"You never spoke to him?"

Loilanun evaded the question. "Mother would scarcely let me get in a word. How can the dead be so emotional? Isn't it terrible? She hates me. Everything gone but emotion, like a disease. She said a man and a woman together made one whole person—I don't understand. I told her I didn't understand. I had to stop her talking."

"You told your mother's gossie to stop talking?"

"Don't look so shocked. My man used to beat me. I was scared of him. . . ."

She was panting and lost her voice. They crowded thankfully into the warmth of the house. The soak pit of the tannery steamed. In niches, thick candles made from goose fat burned with a sound like hair being ripped from hide. Twenty-odd women were gathered there, yawning and scratching themselves.

Shay Tal and Loilanun ate lumps of bread together, and took their ration of rathel, or pig's counsel, before moving over to one of the pestles. The older woman, now her face could be seen more clearly, looked ghastly, with hollows under her eyes and her hair matted.

"Did the gossie tell you anything useful? Anything to help? Did she say anything about Laintal Ay?"

"She said we must collect knowledge. Respect knowledge. She scorned me." Talking through her face full of bread, she added, "She said knowledge was more important than food. Well, she said it was food. Probably she was confused—not being used to it down there. It's hard to understand all they say. . . ."

As the supervisor appeared, they moved over to the grain.

Shay Tal looked sideways at her friend, the hollows of whose face were now filled with an ashen light from the eastern window. "Knowledge can't be food. However much we knew, we'd still have to grind the corn for the village."

"When Mother was alive, she showed me a drawing of a machine powered by the wind. It ground the grain and women didn't lift a finger, she said. The wind did the women's work."

"The men wouldn't care for that," Shay Tal said, with a laugh.

Despite her caution, Shay Tal's resolution hardened; she became the most extreme of the women in defying what was unthinkingly accepted.

Her special work was in the boilery. Here, the flour was kneaded with animal fat and salt, and steamed over troughs of rapid-flowing water from the hot underground springs. When the dark brown loaves were ready, they were cooled, and a lean girl named Vry distributed them to everyone in Oldorando. Shay Tal was the expert of this process; her loaves had the reputation of tasting better than those of any other cook.

Now she saw mysterious perspectives beyond the loaves of bread. Routine no longer contented her, and her manner became more remote. When Loilanun fell ill of a wasting disease, Shay Tal took her and Laintal Ay into her house, despite her father's protests, and patiently tended the older woman. They talked together for hours. Sometimes Laintal Ay listened; more often, he grew bored and went off on his own.

Shay Tal began to pass ideas to the other women in the boilery. She talked in particular to Vry, who was at a malleable age. She talked about the human preference for truth over lies as resembling the need for light above dark. The women listened, muttering uneasily.

And not only the women. In her dark furs, Shay Tal had a majesty felt by the men, too—Laintal Ay, among others. With her proud bearing went proud talk. Both the looks and the talk attracted Aoz Roon. He would listen and argue. He released a vein of flirtatiousness in Shay Tal, who responded to his air of authority. She approved of his support of Dathka against Nahkri; but she allowed him no liberties. Her own liberty depended on allowing him none.

The weeks passed, and great storms roared over the towers of Embruddock. Loilanun's voice grew weaker, and one afternoon she passed away. In her illness, she had transmitted some of Loil Bry's knowledge to Shay Tal and to other women who came to see her. She made the past real to them, and all that she said was filtered through Shay Tal's dark imagination.

Loilanun, as she faded, helped Shay Tal to found what they called the academy. The academy was intended for women; there they would seek together to be something other than drudges. Many of the drudges stood wailing by her deathbed until Shay Tal, in a fit of impatience, threw them out.

"We can observe the stars," Vry said, raising her waiflike face. "Have you ever studied how they move on regular paths? I would like to understand the stars better."

"Everything valuable is buried in the past," Shay Tal said, looking down at the countenance of her dead friend. "This place cheated Loilanun, and cheats us. The gossies wait for us. Our lives are so circumscribed! We need to make better people just as we need to bake better loaves."

She jumped up and flung open the worn window shutter.

Her shrewd intellect saw immediately that the academy would be mistrusted by the men of Embruddock, and by Nahkri and Klils above all. Only the callow Laintal Ay would support her, though she hoped to win over Aoz Roon and Eline Tal. She saw that whatever opposition the academy met with, she would have to fight—and that fight was necessary to give new spirit to all. She would defy the general lethargy; time had come for progress.

Inspiration moved Shay Tal. As her poor friend was buried and she stood with a hand on Laintal Ay's shoulder, she caught the eye of Aoz Roon. She burst into speech. Her words carried wild and loud among the geysers.

"This woman was forced to be independent. What she knew helped her. Some of us are not to be owned like slaves. We have a vision of better things. Hear what I say. Things will be different." They gaped at her, pleased at the novelty of her outburst.

"You think we live at the centre of the universe. I say we live in the centre of a farmyard. Our position is so obscure that you cannot realise how obscure.

"This I tell you all. Some disaster happened in the past, in the long past. So complete was it that no one now can explain to you what it was or how it came about. We know only that it brought darkness and cold.

"You try to live the best you can. Good, good, live well, love one another, be kind. But don't pretend that the disaster has nothing to do with you. It may have happened long ago, yet it infects every day of our lives. It ages us, it wears us out, it devours us, it tears our children from us, as it has torn Loilanun. It makes us not only ignorant but in love with ignorance. We're infested with ignorance.

"I'm going to propose a treasure hunt—a quest, if you like. A quest in which every one of us can join. I want you to be aware of our fallen state, and to maintain constant vigilance for evidence as to its nature. We have to piece together what has happened to reduce us to this chilly farmyard; then we can improve our lot, and see to it that the disaster does not befall us and our children again.

"That's the treasure I offer you. Knowledge. Truth. You fear it, yes. But you must seek it. You must grow to love it.

"Seek the light!"

As children, Oyre and Laintal Ay had often explored beyond the barricades. Dotted about the wilderness were stone pillars, the insignia of old tracks, which served as perches for the large birds doing sentry duty over their domain. Together, they scrambled across forlorn ruins, skull-like remains of habitations, backbones of ancient walls, where rime scoured gate towers and age under-ate everything. Little the kids had cared. Their laughter echoed against these stranded anatomies.

Now the laughter was subdued, the expeditions more strained. Laintal Ay had reached puberty; he underwent the blood-drinking ceremony, and was initiated into the chase. Oyre had developed a mischievous will, and walked with a more springy tread. Their play became tentative; old charades were abandoned as carelessly as the structures they haunted, never to be reenacted.

The truce of innocence between them was ended finally when Oyre insisted that her father's slave, Calary, come on one of their excursions. This development marked their last expedition together, though neither realised it at the time; they pretended to hunt for treasure as before.

They came on a pile of masonry from which all trace of timber had been filched. Leaves of brassimips thrust up among the remains of a monument where old skilled work sank to loam crust. Once, as children, they made this their castle: here they had been a host defying charge on charge of phagors, and had imitated the cheerful imaginary sounds of battle.

Laintal Ay was preoccupied with a more troubling panorama which unfolded in his mind. In that panorama—slightly resembling a cloud, but also seeming to be a declaration by Shay Tal, or perhaps some ancient proclamation carved on rock—he and Oyre and their reluctant slave, and Oldorando, and even the phagors and unknown creatures inhabiting the wilderness, were whirled about in a great process . . . but there the light of his intellect went out, to leave him wondering on the edge of a precipice at once dangerous and glamorous. He knew not what he did not know.

He stood on an eminence of the ruin, looking down at Oyre below him. She was doubled up, investigating something far removed from his concern.

"Is it possible there was once a great city here? Could anyone re-build it in times to come? People like us, with wealth?"

Getting no answer, he squatted on the wall, staring down at her back, and added more questions. "What did all the people eat? Do you think Shay Tal knows about such things? Is her treasure here?"

She, sewn into her furs, stooping, looked from above more like an animal than a girl. She was prying into an alcove among the stones, not really attending to him.

"The priest who comes from Borlien says that Borlien was once a huge country that ruled all Oldorando farther than hawk can fly."

He set his keen gaze across the countryside, which a thick cloud layer made tenebrous. "That's nonsense."

He knew as perhaps Oyre did not that the territory of hawks was circumscribed even more severely than that of men. Shay Tal's address had brought to his notice other circumscriptions in life, which he now chewed over fruitlessly while scowling down at the figure below. He

was vexed with Oyre, he could not say why, longing to probe her in
some way, to find tongue for what lay beyond silence.

"Come and see what I've found, Laintal Ay!" Her bright dark face
looked up at him. Her features had recently fined towards womanhood.
He forgot his vexation and slithered down the declivitous wall to land
beside her.

She had fetched from the alcove a small naked living thing, its pink
rat face distorted with alarm as it wriggled in her grasp.

His hair brushed hers as he looked down at this new arrival in the
world. He cupped his rougher hands round hers till their fingers were
interlocked round the struggling centre.

She raised her gaze to regard him direct, her lips apart, smiling
slightly. He smelt her scent. He grasped her about her waist.

But beside them stood the slave, his face showing sullen comprehension of the flame of new intuition which flew between them. Oyre
moved a pace away, then pushed the baby mammal carelessly back
into its nook. She scowled down at the ground.

"Your precious Shay Tal doesn't know everything. Father told me
in confidence that *he* thinks she is definitely strange. Let's go home
now."

Laintal Ay lived with Shay Tal for a while. With his parents and
grandparents dead, he was severed from his childhood; but he and
Dathka were now fully fledged hunters. Disinherited by his uncles, he
determined to prove himself their equal. He thrived and matured early,
growing up with a genial expression on his countenance. His jaw was
firm, his features clear-cut. His strength and speed soon became generally noticed. Many girls cast a smiling glance on him, but he had
eyes only for Aoz Roon's daughter.

Although he was popular, something about him made people keep
their distance. He had taken to heart Shay Tal's brave words. Some
said he was too conscious of his descent from the Great Yuli. He remained apart, even in company. His one close friend was Dathka Den,
corpsman turned hunter, and Dathka rarely spoke, even to Laintal Ay.
As someone said, Dathka was the next best thing to no-one.

Laintal Ay eventually took up residence with some of the other
hunters in the big tower, above Nahkri's and Klils' chamber. There he
heard the old tales re-told, and learned to sing ancient hunters' songs.
But what he preferred was to take supplies and snow shoes, and rove the
countryside newly emerging into green. He no longer sought Oyre's
company on such expeditions.

At this period, nobody else ventured out alone. The hunters hunted
together, the swineherds and gozzards had their fixed paths near the
settlement, those who tended the brassimips worked in groups. Danger

and death so often accompanied solitude. Laintal Ay acquired a reputation for eccentricity, although his good-standing was not damaged,
because he added considerably to the number of animal skulls which
adorned the stockades of Oldorando.

The storm winds howled. He travelled far, untroubled by the in-
hospitality of nature. He found his way to unfrequented valleys, and
to broken old remains of towns from which the inhabitants had long
since fled, leaving their homes to wolves and weather.

At the time of the festival of Double Sunset, Laintal Ay made his
name in the tribe with a feat that rivalled his and Aoz Roon's achievement of capturing the Borlienian traders. He was travelling alone in
high country to the northeast of Oldorando, over deep snow, when a
hole opened under his feet, and he fell in. At the bottom of the drift
sat a stungebag, waiting for its next meal.

Stungebags resemble nothing so much as collapsed wooden huts,
covered by makeshift thatch. They grew to great lengths, having few
enemies but man, feeding rarely, being inordinately slow. All that
Laintal Ay saw of this one, curled at the bottom of its trap, was its
asymmetrical horned head and gaping mouth, in which the teeth appeared to be made of wooden pegs. As the jaws closed on his leg, he
kicked out and rolled to one side.

Fighting against the encompassing snow, he brought up his spear
and wedged it far back in the hinges of the stungebag's mouth. The
animal's rhythmic struggles were slow but powerful. It knocked Laintal
Ay down again, but was unable to close its mouth. Jumping away from
the probing horns, he flung himself on the back of the beast, clinging
to stiff tufts of hair which burst from between octagonal armour
plates. He pulled his knife from his belt. Clutching the hair with one
hand, he hacked away at the fibrous tendons that held one of the plates
in place.

The stungebag screamed with rage. It too was impeded by the snow
and could not roll over sufficiently to crush Laintal Ay. He managed
to sever the plate from its back. The plate was splintery, and in texture
woodlike. He jammed it down the beast's throat, and then commenced
to cut the clumsy head off.

It fell. No blood ran, only a slight whitish ichor. This stungebag
had four eyes—there was a lesser breed with two. One pair stared forward in the skull; the other looked backward and was set in hornlike
protrusions at the back of the skull. Both pairs rolled over into the
snow, still blinking in disbelief.

The decapitated body began to burrow backwards through the snow
at its fastest rate. Laintal Ay followed, struggling through chunks of
falling snow until it and he emerged into daylight.

Stungebags were proverbially difficult to kill. This one would keep
travelling for a long while before falling to pieces.

Laintal Ay let out a whoop of exhilaration. Bringing out his flints, he jumped up on the neck of the creature and set light to the coarse fur, which burnt with a furious sizzling noise. Evil-smelling smoke billowed into the sky. By burning one side or the other, he was able to do a rough job of steering. The creature shunted backwards towards Oldorando.

Horns sounded from high towers. He saw the spray of geysers. The stockade loomed, decorated with skulls painted in bright colours. Women and hunters ran out to greet him.

He waved his fur cap in return. Seated at the hot end of a blazing wooden caterpillar, he rode it backwards in triumph through the lanes of Embruddock.

Everyone laughed. But it was several days before the stink died from rooms along his triumphal route.

The unburnt remains of Laintal Ay's stungebag were used up during the festival of Double Sunset. Even slaves were involved with this event—one of them was offered as a sacrifice to Wutra.

Double Sunset coincided in Oldorando with New Year's Day. It was to be Year 21 by the new calendar, and celebrations were in order. Despite everything that nature could do, life was good and had to be secured by sacrifice.

For weeks, Batalix had been overtaking its slower fellow sentry in the sky. In midwinter, they came close, and days and nights were of equal length, with no dimday intervening.

"Why should they move as they do?" Vry asked Shay Tal.

"That's how they have always moved," Shay Tal said.

"You don't answer my question, ma'am," said Vry.

The prospect of a sacrifice first, with a feast succeeding, lent excitement to the ceremony of the sunsets. Before the ceremonies began, there was dancing round a mighty fire in the square; the music was of tabor and pipe and fluggel—which latter instrument some claimed was invented by Great Yuli himself. Rathel was provided for the dancers, after which all, in a glow of sweat beneath their hides, moved beyond the stockades.

A sacrificial stone lay to the east of the old pyramid. The citizens gathered about it, standing at a respectful distance, as one of the masters commanded.

Lots had been drawn among the slaves. The honour of being victim fell to Calary, the young Borlienian slave belonging to Aoz Roon. He was led forth, hands lashed behind his back, and the crowd followed expectantly. A cold stillness filled the air. Overhead was barred grey cloud. To the west, the two sentinels sank towards the horizon.

Everyone carried torches fashioned from stungebag hide. Laintal Ay led his silent friend Dathka to walk along with Aoz Roon, because Aoz Roon's beautiful daughter was there.

"You must feel sorry to lose Calary, Aoz Roon," Laintal Ay said to the older man, making eyes at Oyre.

Aoz Roon clapped him over the shoulder. "My principle in life is never to feel regret. Regret's death to a hunter, as it was to Dresyl. Next year, we will capture plenty more slaves. Never mind Calary." There were times when Laintal Ay mistrusted his friend's heartiness. Aoz Roon looked at Eline Tal, and both laughed together, emitting rathel fumes.

Everyone was jostling along and laughing, except for Calary. Taking advantage of the crowd, Laintal Ay seized Oyre's hand and squeezed it. She gave him an answering pressure and smiled, not daring to look at him directly. He swelled with exhilaration. Life was truly wonderful.

He could not stop grinning as the ceremony proceeded more seriously. Batalix and Freyr would disappear simultaneously from Wutra's realm and sink into the earth like gossies. Tomorrow, if the sacrifice proved acceptable, they would rise together, and for a while their parades across the sky would coincide. Both would shine by day, and night be left to darkness. By spring, they would be out of step again, and Batalix commencing dimday.

Everyone said the weather was milder. Signs of improvement abounded. Geese were fatter. Nevertheless, a solemn silence fell over the crowd as they faced towards the west and their shadows lengthened. Both sentinels were leaving the realm of light. Illness and ill things were presaged. A life must be offered lest the sentinels depart forever.

As the double shadows extended, the crowd grew still, though it shuffled its feet like a great beast. Its cheerful mood evaporated. It became faceless in the smoke from the raised torches. The shadows spread. A greyness which was not to be dispersed by the torches blanketted the scene. People were submerged in evening and the massed psyche of the crowd.

Elders of the council, all grey and bent, came forth in line, and called out a prayer in shaky singsong. Four slaves brought Calary forward. He staggered between them with his head hanging, saliva flecking his jaw. A flight of birds wheeled overhead, the sound of its wings like rainfall, and was gone towards the western gold.

Upon a sacrificial stone, lozenge-shaped, the sacrificial victim was laid, his head set in a depression carved in its leprous upper surface, directed to the west. His feet were secured in a wooden brace, pointing to the direction—now slatey with oncoming night—where the sentinels would next appear if they completed their perilous journey. Thus, in his body, with its vents and passages, the victim represented the mystic union between the two immense mysteries of human and cosmic life: as above, so, with an effort of massed will, below.

The victim had already shed its individuality. Although its eyes rolled, it made no sound, stilled as if awed by the presence of Wutra.

As the four slaves stepped back, Nahkri and Klils appeared. Over their furs they had assumed cloaks of stammel, dyed red. Their women accompanied them to the edge of the crowd, then left them to proceed alone. Their straggling rat beards for once lent solemnity to their visages; indeed their pallor matched that of the victim on whom Nahkri bent his regard as he picked up the axe. He hefted this formidable instrument. A gong was struck.

Nahkri stood there, balancing the axe in both hands, the slighter figure of his brother just behind him. As the pause lengthened, a murmur came from the crowd. There was a time for the sundering stroke: miss that time, and who knew what might befall the sentinels. The murmur expressed an almost unspoken mistrust of the two ruling brothers.

"Strike!" cried a voice from the massed ranks. The Hour-Whistler sounded.

"I can't do it," Nahkri said, lowering the axe. "I won't do it. A fuggie, yes. Not a human, not even a Borlienian. I can't."

His younger brother lurched forward and grasped the instrument. "You coward—making us look fools before everyone. I'll do it myself and shame you. I'll show you who's the better man, you queme!"

With teeth bared, he swung the axe up on his shoulder. He glared down into the stark face of the victim, which stared up from its depression as from a grave.

Klils' muscles twitched, appearing to disobey him. The blade of the instrument signalled back the rays of sunset. Then it was lowered, and rested against the stone, while Klils leaned over the shaft, groaning.

"I should have drunk more rathel. . . ."

An answering groan came from the crowd. The sentinels now had their discs entangled with the unkempt horizon.

Individual voices made themselves heard.

"They're a couple of clowns. . . ."

"They listened too much to Loil Bry, I say."

"It was their father stuffing them full of head learning—the muscles are weakened."

"Have you been on the nest too much, Klils?" That coarse shouted question drew laughter, and the sullen mood was broken. The mob closed in as Klils let the axe slip into the trampled mud.

Aoz Roon ran forward, breaking away from his fellows, and seized up the instrument. He growled like a hound, and the two brothers fell away from him, protesting feebly. They stumbled back farther, arms raised protectively, as Aoz Roon swung the axe above his head.

The suns were going down, half sunk with glory in a sea of dark. Their light was spilled like yolk from two goose eggs, drab gold, as if phagor and human blood were mingled over the stagnant waste. Bats flittered. The hunters raised their fists and cheered Aoz Roon.

Sun rays converged on the pyramid, and were split into bars of shadow by its peak. The divided lights ran precisely along the flanks of the worn stone on which the victim lay, defining its shape. The victim himself was in shadow.

The blade of the instrument of execution swung in sunlight, bit in shade.

After the clean clop of the stroke came a united sound from the crowd, a kind of echoing stroke from lungs exhaling in unison, as though all present also gave up the ghost.

The victim's head fell severed to one side, as if kissing the confining stone. It began to drown in blood, which gushed up from the wound and spread, trickling down into the earth. It was running still as the last segment of the sentinels drowned below the horizon.

Ceremonial blood was the thing, the magic fluid that fought non-life, precious human blood. It would continue to drip throughout the night, lighting the two sentinels among the vents and passages of the original boulder, seeing them safe to another morning.

The crowd was satisfied. Bearing their torches aloft, they made their way back through the stockade to the ancient towers, which were now smoulderingly black against the cloudscape, or mottled with phantom light as the torches grew nearer.

Dathka walked by Aoz Roon, who was given respectful clearance by the crowd. "How could you bear to lop your own slave?" he asked.

The older man shot him a contemptuous look. "There are moments of decision."

"But Calary . . ." Oyre protested. "It was so frightening."

Aoz Roon brushed his daughter's objection aside. "Girls can't understand. I filled Calary full of rungebel and rathel before the ceremony. He felt nothing. He probably still thinks he's in the arms of some Borlienian maid." He laughed.

The solemnities were over. Few doubted now that Freyr and Batalix would arise on the morrow. They moved in to celebrate, to drink with extra cheer, for they had a scandal to whisper about, the scandal of the feebleheartedness of their rulers. There was no more delightful subject over mugs of pig's counsel, before the Great Tale was retold.

But Laintal Ay was whispering to Oyre as he clutched her in the dark. "Did you fall in love with me when you saw me ride in on my captured stungebag?"

She put out a tongue at him. "Conceited! I thought you looked silly."

He saw that the celebrations were going to have their more serious side.

VI

"WHEN I WERE ALL
BEFUDDOCK..."

All he could see before him was the land rearing up, making a clear bow of horizon close at hand. The tiny springy plants underfoot stretched to that horizon and, away below him, to the valley. Laintal Ay stopped, resting with his hands on one knee, breathing heavily, and looked back. Oldorando was six days' walk away.

The other side of the valley was bathed in a clear blue light which picked out every detail with lucidity. The sky above was slatey purple with future snowstorms. Where he stood, all was in shadow.

He resumed his upward trudge. More land emerged over the curved near horizon, black, black, unassailable. He had never been there. Farther, the top of a tower rose as the near horizon sank beneath his progress. Stone, ruined, built long ago to an Oldorando mould, with the same inward-sloping walls, and windows placed at each of the four corners on each of the floors. Only four floors stood.

At last Laintal Ay surmounted the slope. Large grey birds cropped outside the tower, which was surrounded by its own debris. Behind, the unassailable hill, enormous, its blackness lit by the slate sky. A line of rajabarals interposed themselves between him and infinity. Chill wind rattled against his teeth, so that he drew his lips together.

What was the tower doing, so far from Oldorando?

Not so far if you were a bird, not so far at all. Not so far if you were a phagor mounted on a kaidaw. No distance if you were a god.

As if to emphasize the point, the birds took off, wings clattering, flying low over the moor. He watched them until they were out of sight and he alone in the great landscape.

Oh, Shay Tal must be right. The world had once been different. When he had talked about her speech to Aoz Roon, Aoz Roon had said that such matters were not important; they could not be changed; what was important was the survival of the tribe, its unity; if Shay Tal had her way, the unity would be lost. Shay Tal said that unity was unimportant beside the truth.

His head occupied by thoughts that moved across his consciousness like cloud shadows over the landscape, he went into the tower and looked up. It was a hollow ruin. The wooden flooring had been pulled out for fuel. He set his pack and spear down in a corner and climbed up the rough stonework, taking advantage of every foothold, until he stood perched on the top of one of the walls. He looked about him. First he looked for phagors—this was phagor country—but only barren and in-animate shapes met his survey.

Shay Tal never left the village. Perhaps she had to invent mysteries. Yet there was a mystery. Looking over the gigantic landforms, he asked himself in awe, *Who made them? What for?*

High on the great round hill behind him—not even a foothill to the foothills of the Nktryhk—he saw bushes moving. They were small, a sickly green under the dense light. Watching intently, he recognised them as protognostics, clad in shaggy coats, bent double as they climbed. They drove before them a herd of goat or arang.

He deliberately let the time go by, experienced the drag of it across the world, to watch the distant beings, as if they held the answer to his questions, or to Shay Tal's. The people were probably Nondads, itin-erant tribesmen speaking a language unrelated to Olonets. As long as he watched, they toiled through their allotted landscape and seemed to make no progress.

Closer to Oldorando were the herds of deer that supplied the villages with much of their food. There were several ways of killing deer. This was the method preferred by Nahkri and Klils.

Five tame hinds were kept as decoys. The hunters led these beasts on leather reins to where the herd grazed. By walking in a crouched posi-tion behind the deer, the men could manoeuvre their mobile cover close to the herd. Then the hunters would rush forth and hurl their spears with the aid of spear throwers, killing as many animals as possible.

Later, they dragged the carcasses home, and the decoys had to carry their dead fellows on their backs.

On this hunt, snow was falling. A slight thaw about midday made the going heavy. Deer were scarcer than usual. The hunters walked eastwards steadily for three days over difficult ground, leading their decoy deer, before they caught sight of a small herd.

The hunters were twenty in number. Nahkri and his brother had restored themselves to favour after the night of the Double Sunset by a liberal distribution of rathel. Laintal Ay and Dathka travelled beside Aoz Roon. They spoke little during the hunt, but words were scarcely necessary when trust had been established. Aoz Roon, in his black furs, stood out as a figure of courage against the surrounding desolation, and the two younger men kept to his side as faithfully as his huge dog, Curd.

The herd was cropping on the crest of a slight rise some way ahead, and to windward of the men. It was necessary to work round to the right, where there was higher ground and their scent would not carry.

Two men were left behind holding the dogs. The rest of the party moved up the slope, over two inches of slushy snow. The crest of the rise was marked by a broken line of tree stumps, and a heap or two of shattered masonry, well-rounded by the force of centuries of weather. They were in dead ground, and the herd was visible only when—on hands and knees now, trailing their spears and spear throwers—they came to the top of the rise and surveyed the field.

The herd comprised twenty-two hinds and three stags. The latter had divided the hinds between them, and occasionally roared defiance at each other. They were shaggy and ill-conditioned beasts, their ribs showing, their reddish manes trailing. The hinds foraged complacently, heads down most of the time, nuzzling the snow aside. They grazed into the wind, which blew into the faces of the hunters as they crouched. Large black birds strutted under their hoofs.

Nahkri gave the sign.

He and his brother led out two of the tame deer, walking them round to the left flank of the herd, keeping the animals between them and the grazing hinds, who ceased foraging to see what was going on. Aoz Roon, Dathka, and Laintal Ay led out the other three decoys, working round to the right flank.

Aoz Roon walked his hind, keeping its head steady. Conditions were not absolutely as he liked them. When the herd fled, they would run away from the line of hunters, instead of towards them; the hunters would be deprived of excitement and practice. Had he been in charge, he would have spent more time on preliminaries—but Nahkri was too unsure of himself to wait. The grazing was to his left; a straggling grove of denniss trees separated the grazing from broken and rocky ground on the right. In the distance stood harsh cliffs, backed by hills, on and on, with mountains in the far distance, thunderous under plumes of purple cloud.

The denniss trees provided some cover for the hunters' approach. Their silvered, shattered trunks were denuded of bark. Their upper branches had been stripped away in earlier storms. Most of them sprawled horizontally, pointing their tusks away from the wind. Some lay entangled, as if locked in eon-long battle; all, so abraded were they by age and elements, resembled cordilleras in miniature, riven by chthonic upheaval.

Every detail of the scene was checked by Aoz Roon as he advanced under cover of his deer. He had been here often before, when the going was easier and the snow reliable; the place was sheltered and afforded the wide visibility the herds preferred. He noted now that the dennisses, for all their appearance of death, even of fossilization, were putting out green shoots, which curled from their boles to hug the ground on their leeward side.

Movement ahead. A renegade stag came into view, emerging suddenly from among the trees. Aoz Roon caught a whiff of the beast—with a sourer smell he did not immediately identify.

The new stag thrust itself rather awkwardly on the herd, and was challenged by the nearest of the three resident stags. The resident advanced, pawing the ground, roaring, tossing its head to make the most of its antler display. The newcomer stood its ground without adopting the usual defensive posture.

The resident stag charged and locked antlers with the intruder. As the points came together, Aoz Roon observed a leather strap stretched across the antlers of the newcomer. He immediately passed his hind back to Laintal Ay and faded behind the nearest tree stump. Leaving the cordage of its grounded trunk, he ran to the next tree in line.

This denniss was blackened and dead. Through its broken ribs, Aoz Roon sighted a yellowish lump of hair, protruding between farther trees. Grasping his spear in his right hand, drawing back his arm for a blow, he began to run as only he could run. He felt the sharp stones under the snow beneath his boots, heard the bellowing entangled animals, watched as the great dead wood bole loomed—and all the while he sped as silently as he could. Some noise was inevitable.

The hair moved, became the shoulder of a phagor. The monster turned. Its great eyes flashed red. It lowered its long horns and spread wide its arms to meet the attack. Aoz Roon plunged his spear in under its ribs.

With a churring cry, the great ancipital fell backwards, borne over by Aoz Roon's charge. Aoz Roon was carried down too. The phagor wrapped its arms about Aoz Roon, digging its horned hands into his back. They rolled in the slush.

The black and the white creatures became one animal, an animal that fought with itself in the midst of an elemental landscape, struggling to tear itself apart. It struck against a silvered root and again became two component parts, black half below.

The phagor pulled back its head, opening its jaws ready for a strike. Rows of yellow teeth, spadelike, set in grey-white gums, confronted Aoz Roon. He managed to drag an arm free, grasp a stone, and thrust it between the heavy lips, the teeth, as they closed upon his head. Aoz Roon stood, found the shaft of the spear still in the monster's body, and bore his weight upon it. With a harsh exhalation of breath, the phagor gave up the ghost. Yellow blood spurted up from the wound. Its arms fell open, and Aoz Roon climbed panting to his feet. A cowbird rose from the ground nearby and flapped heavily towards the east.

He was in time to see Laintal Ay despatch another phagor. Two more ran from the shelter of a horizontal denniss. Both galloped away on one kaidaw, heading for the cliff. White birds followed with sweeping wings, screeching towards the echoes that returned to them from the wilderness.

Dathka came over and clutched Aoz Roon's shoulder without speaking. They regarded each other and then smiled. Aoz Roon revealed his white teeth, despite his pain. Dathka kept his lips together.

Laintal Ay came up, exulting. "I killed it. It died!" he said. "Their bowels are in their chest, their lungs in their bellies. . . ."

Kicking the phagor body aside, Aoz Roon went to lean against a tree stump. He breathed out strongly through mouth and nostrils to rid himself of the sick milky stench of the enemy. His hands trembled.

"Call Eline Tal," he said.

"I killed it, Aoz Roon!" Laintal Ay repeated, pointing back at the body lying in the snow.

"Fetch Eline Tal," Aoz Roon ordered.

Dathka went over to where the two stags still struggled, heads down, antlers locked, scuffling the snow to mud with their hoofs. He took out his knife and cut their throats like an old hand. The animals stood and bled yellow blood until they could stand no longer, whereupon they collapsed and died, still locked together.

"The strap between the antlers—that's an old fuggie trick to catch game," Aoz Roon said. "When I saw it, I knew they were about. . . ."

Eline Tal ran up with Faralin Ferd and Tanth Ein. They pushed the younger men away and supported Aoz Roon. "You're meant to kill these vermin, not cuddle them," Eline Tal said.

The rest of the herd had long since fled. The brothers had killed three hinds between them and were triumphant. The other hunters arrived to see what had gone wrong. Five carcasses was not a bad kill; Oldorando could eat when they got home. The phagor carcasses would be left where they were to rot. Nobody wanted their skins.

Laintal Ay and Dathka held the decoy hinds while Eline Tal and the others examined Aoz Roon. The latter threw off their detaining hands with a curse.

"Let's scumb off," he said, clutching his side with a look of pain. "Where there were four of the vermin there may be others."

Lumping the dead hinds onto the backs of the decoys, dragging the stags, they commenced the trek home.

But Nahkri was angry with Aoz Roon.

"Those rotten stags are starved. Their meat will taste like leather."

Aoz Roon said nothing.

"Only vultures eat stag in preference to hind," Klils said.

"Keep quiet, Klils," Laintal Ay shouted. "Can't you see that Aoz Roon is hurt? Go and practise swinging an axe."

Aoz Roon kept his gaze down at the ground, saying nothing—which angered the elder brother still more. The eternal landscape stood silent about them.

When at last they got within sight of Oldorando and its sheltering hot springs, the tower lookouts blew their horns. The lookouts were men too old or sick to hunt. Nahkri had given them an easier task—but if their horns did not sound the moment the hunting party appeared in the distance, he stopped their ration of rathel. The horns were a signal for the young women to stop work and come out beyond the barricades to meet their men. Many were fearful lest there had been a death—widowhood would entail menial jobs, bare subsistence, early death. This time, they counted heads and rejoiced. All the hunters were returning. This night, there would be celebrations. Some of them might conceive.

Eline Tal, Tanth Ein, and Faralin Ferd called out to their own women, employing endearments and abuse in equal measure. Aoz Roon limped on alone, saying no word, though he looked up under his dark brows to see if Shay Tal was there. She was not.

No women greeted Dathka either. He made his youthful face long and hard as he pressed through the welcoming gaggle, for he had hoped Shay Tal's unobtrusive friend Vry might have shown herself. Aoz Roon secretly despised Dathka because no women ran up to clasp his arm, although he was himself in the same situation.

Under those dark brows, he watched a hunter catch the hand of Dol Sakil, the midwife's daughter. He watched his own daughter, Oyre, run to grasp the hand of Laintal Ay; he reckoned to himself that they would suit each other well enough, and that there might be advantage from the match.

Of course the girl was headstrong, whereas Laintal Ay was rather soft. She would lead him a dance before consenting to be his woman. Oyre was like the precious Shay Tal in that respect—difficult, pretty, and with a mind of her own.

He limped through the wide gates, head down, still nursing his side. Nahkri and Klils were walking nearby, fending off their screeching women. They both threw him a threatening look. "Keep your place, Aoz Roon," Nahkri said.

He looked away, hunching a shoulder against them.

"I wielded the axe once and, by Wutra, I'll wield it again," he growled.

The world trembled before his sight. He gulped down a mug of rathel and water, but still sickness rose in him. He climbed to the lair he shared with his companions, indifferent for once how the game he had helped kill was stripped. Once in his room, he collapsed. But he would not suffer the slave woman to cut open his clothes or examine his wounds. He rested and hugged his ribs. After an hour, he went out alone and sought Shay Tal.

Since it was near a sunset, she was taking crusts of bread down to the Voral to feed the geese. The river was wide. It had unfrozen during the day, revealing black water fringed by shelves of white ice across which geese came honking. When they were both young, it was always frozen from bank to bank.

She said, "You hunters go so far away, yet I saw game on the other side of the river this morning. Hoxneys and wild horses, I believe."

Dark and moody, Aoz Roon looked down upon her and grasped her arm. "You've always a contrary idea, Shay Tal. Do you think you know better than the hunters? Why didn't you come out at the sound of the horn?"

"I was busy." She took her arm away and started to crumble the barley crusts as the geese surrounded her. Aoz Roon kicked out at them and grasped her arm again.

"I killed a fuggy today. I'm strong. It hurt me but I killed the dirty thing. All hunters look up to me, and all maidens. But it's you I want, Shay Tal. Why don't you want me?"

She turned a face with stabbing eyes up to his, not angry, but containedly angry. "I do want you, but you would break my arm if I went against you—and we should always be arguing. You never speak softly to me. You can laugh and you can scowl, but you can't coo. There!"

"I'm not the sort to coo. Nor would I break your lovely arm. I would give you real things to think about."

She answered nothing, but fed the birds. Batalix buried itself in snow, casting gold into strands of her hair which were loose. In the crisp dead scene, all that moved was the black rift of water.

After standing awkwardly regarding her, shifting his weight from one foot to another, he said, "What were you so busy at earlier?"

Not returning his gaze, she said intensely, "You heard my words on the doleful day when we buried Loilanun. I was speaking mainly to you. Here we live in this farmyard. I want to know what goes on in the world beyond it. I want to learn things. I need your assistance, but you are not quite the man to give it. So I teach the other women when there's time, because that's a way of teaching myself."

"What good's that going to do? You're only stirring up trouble."

She said nothing, staring across at the river, on which was cast the last of the day's beggarly gold.

"I ought to put you over my knee and spank you." He was standing below her on the bank, gazing up at her.

She looked angrily at him. Almost immediately, a change came over her face. She laughed, revealing her teeth and the ribbed pink roof of her mouth, before covering them with her hand. "You really don't understand!"

Using the moment, he took her strongly into his arms. "I'd try to coo for you, and more besides, Shay Tal. Because of your lovely spirit, and your eyes as bright as those waters. Forget this learning which all can do without, and become my woman."

He whirled her around, her feet off the ground, and the geese scattered indignantly, stretching their necks towards the horizon.

When she was standing again, she said, "Speak in an ordinary way to me, Aoz Roon, I beg. My life is twice precious, and I can give myself away once only. Knowledge is important to me—to everyone. Don't make me choose between you and learning."

"I've loved you a long while, Shay Tal. I know you're vexed about Oyre, but you should not say no to me. Be my woman at once, or I'll find another, I warn you. I'm a hot-blooded man. Live with me, and you'll forget all about this academy."

"Oh, you just repeat yourself. If you love me, try to hear what I'm saying." She turned and started to walk up the slope towards her tower. But Aoz Roon ran forward and caught up with her.

"Are you going to leave me with no satisfaction, Shay Tal, after making me say all those silly things?" His manner was meek again, almost sly, as he added, "And what would you do if I were ruler here, Lord of Embruddock? It's not impossible. You'd have to be my woman then."

In the way she looked at him, he saw why he pursued her; just momentarily, he felt to the essence of her as she said softly, "So that's how you dream, Aoz Roon? Well, knowledge and wisdom are another kind of dream, and we are fated each to pursue his own dream separately. I love you too, but no more than you do I want anyone to have power over me."

He was silent. She knew he found her remark hard to accept—or thought he did; but he was pursuing another line of reasoning, and said, with a hard glance, "But you hate Nahkri, don't you?"

"He doesn't interfere with me."

"Ah, but he does with me."

As usual when the hunt returned, a feast was held, with drinking and eating into the night. In addition to the customary rathel, newly fermented by the brewers corps, there was dark barley wine. Songs were sung, jigs danced, as the liquors took hold. When the intoxication was at its height, most men were drinking in the big tower, which commanded a view down the main street. The ground floor had been cleared, and a fire burned there, sending its smoke curling against the metal-lined rafters. Aoz Roon remained moody, and broke away from the singing. Laintal Ay watched him go, but was too busy pursuing Oyre to pursue her father. Aoz Roon climbed the stairs, through the various levels, to emerge on the roof and gulp the cool of the air.

Dathka, who had no talent for music, followed him into the darkness. As usual, Dathka did not speak. He stood with his hands in his armpits, staring out at the vague looming shapes of night. A curtain of dull green fire hung in the sky overhead, its folds shading into the stratosphere.

Aoz Roon fell back with a great roar. Dathka grasped him and steadied him, but the older man fought him away.

"What ails you? Drunk, are you?"

"There!" Aoz Roon pointed into the vacant dark. "She's gone now, damn her. A woman with the head of a pig. Eddre, the look in her eyes!"

"Ah, you're seeing things. You're drunk."

Aoz Roon turned angrily. "Don't you call me drunk, you shrimp! I saw her, I tell you. Naked, tall, thin-shanked, hair from slit to chin, fourteen dugs—coming towards me." He ran about the roof, waving his arms.

Klils appeared through the trapdoor, staggering slightly, holding a femur of deer on which he was gnawing. "You two have no business up here. This is the Big Tower. Those who rule Oldorando come here."

"You scumble," Aoz Roon said approaching. "You dropped the axe."

Klils coshed him savagely on the side of the neck with the deer bone. With a roar, Aoz Roon grasped Klils by the throat and tried to throttle him. But Klils kicked his ankle, pummelled him under the heart, and drove him back against the parapet surrounding the roof, part of which crumbled and fell away. Aoz Roon sprawled with his head hanging over into space.

"Dathka!" he called. "Help me!"

Silently, Dathka came up behind Klils, took him with a firm grasp about the knees, and lifted his legs. He swung the man's body, angling it across the wall, and over the seven-floor drop.

"No, no!" cried Klils, fighting furiously, locking his arms about Aoz

Roon's neck. The three men struggled in the green dark, accompanied by the sound of singing from below, two of them—both befuddled by rathel—against the willowy Klils. Eventually they had him, prizing away his grip on life. With a last cry, he fell free. They heard his body strike the ground below.

Aoz Roon and Dathka sat gasping on the parapet. "We got rid of him," Aoz Roon said finally. He hugged his ribs in pain. "I'm grateful, Dathka."

Dathka answered nothing.

At last, Aoz Roon said, "They'll kill us for this, the scumble. Nahkri will see to it they kill us. People hate me already." After another wait, he burst out angrily, "It was all that fool Klils' fault. He attacked me. It was his fault."

Unable to endure the silence, Aoz Roon jumped up and paced about the roof, muttering to himself. He snatched up the gnawed femur and flung it far out into the gloom.

Turning on the impassive Dathka, he said, "Look, go down and speak to Oyre. She'll do what I say. Get her to lead Nahkri up here. He'd wear a pig's nose if she suggested it—I've been watching the way that scumb's eyes go to her."

Shrugging his shoulders, saying nothing, Dathka left. Oyre was currently working in Nahkri's household, much to Laintal Ay's disgust; being well-favoured, she had an easier time of it than other women.

After Aoz Roon had hugged himself and shivered and paced the roof and projected oaths into the darkness, Dathka returned.

"She's bringing him," he said shortly. "But it's ill-advised, whatever you have in mind. I'll have no part in it."

"Keep quiet." It was the first time anyone had ever given Dathka that order. He slouched back in deepest shadow when figures started climbing through the trapdoor—three figures, the first of them being Oyre. After her came Nahkri, mug of drink in hand, then Laintal Ay, who had decided to stay close to Oyre. He looked angry, and his expression did not soften when he looked at Aoz Roon. The latter scowled back.

"You stay downstairs, Laintal Ay. You need not be involved in this," said Aoz Roon harshly.

"Oyre's here," replied Laintal Ay, as if that was sufficient, not budging.

"He's looking after me, Father," said Oyre. Aoz Roon brushed her aside and confronted Nahkri, saying, "Now, you and I have always had a quarrel, Nahkri. Prepare to fight it out with me directly, man to man."

"Get off my roof," ordered Nahkri. "I will not have you here. Below's where you belong."

"Prepare to fight."

"You were ever insolent, Aoz Roon, and you dare to speak up again after your failure in the hunt. You've drunk too much pig's counsel." Nahkri's voice was thick from wine and rathel.

"I dare and I dare and I do," cried Aoz Roon, and he flung himself at Nahkri.

Nahkri threw the mug in his face. Both Oyre and Laintal Ay took Aoz Roon by the arms, but he shook himself free, and hit Nahkri across the face.

Nahkri fell, rolled over, and brought a dagger from his belt. The only light to be had was a glow coming up from a fat wick burning on the floor below. It glinted on the blade. The green folds in the sky lent nothing more than a tincture to human affairs. Aoz Roon kicked at the knife, missed, and fell heavily on Nahkri, winding him. Groaning, Nahkri began to vomit, making Aoz Roon roll away from him. Both men picked themselves up, panting.

"Give it up, both of you!" cried Oyre, clinging to her father again.

"What's the quarrel?" Laintal Ay asked. "You provoked him over nothing, Aoz Roon. The right's on his side, fool though he is."

"You keep quiet if you want my daughter," roared Aoz Roon, and charged. Nahkri, still gasping for breath, had no defence. He had lost the dagger. Under a rain of blows, he was carried to the edge of the parapet. Oyre screamed. He tottered there for a moment, then his knees buckled. Then he was gone.

They all heard him strike the ground at the foot of the tower. They stood frozen, guiltily regarding one another. Drunken singing came up to them from inside the building.

> "When I were all befuddock
> A-going to Embruddock,
> I saw a pig a-doing a jig,
> And fell down on me buddock . . ."

Aoz Roon hung over the edge of the parapet. "That's done for you, I imagine, Lord Nahkri," he said in a sober voice. He clutched his ribs and panted. He turned to survey them, marking each with his wild eye.

Laintal Ay and Oyre clung silently together. Oyre sobbed.

Dathka came forward and said to them in a hollow voice, "You'll keep silent about this, Laintal Ay, and you, Oyre, if you care for your lives—you've seen how easily life's lost. I shall give out that I witnessed Nahkri and Klils arguing. They fought, and went over the edge together. We could not stop them. Remember my words, see the scene. Keep silent. Aoz Roon will be Lord of Embruddock and Oldorando."

"I will, and I'll rule better than those fools did," said Aoz Roon, staggering.

"You see you do," said Dathka quietly, "for we three here know the truth about this double murder. Remember we had no part in it: this was your doing, all of it. Treat us accordingly."

The years in Oldorando under the lordship of Aoz Roon were to pass much as they had under previous leaders; life has a quality rulers cannot touch. Only the weather became more freakish. But that, like many other things, was beyond the control of any lord.

The temperature gradients in the stratosphere altered, the troposphere warmed, ground temperatures began to climb. Lashing rains fell for weeks at a time. Snow disappeared from lowlands in tropical zones. Glaciers withdrew to higher ground. The earth turned green. Tall plants sprang up. Birds and animals never seen before came bounding over or past the stockades of the ancient hamlet. All patterns of life were reforming themselves. Nothing was as it had been.

To many older people, these changes were unwelcome. They recalled untrammelled vistas of snow from their youth. The middle-aged welcomed the changes, but shook their heads and said that it was too good to last. The young had never known anything different. Life burned in them as in the air. They had a greater variety of things to eat; they produced more children, and fewer of those children died.

As for the two sentinels, Batalix appeared the same as ever. But every week, every day, every hour, Freyr was growing brighter, hotter.

Set amid this drama of climate was the human drama, which every living soul must play out, to his own satisfaction or disappointment. To most people, this weaving of minute circumstance was of the utmost importance, each seeing himself the centre of the stage. All over the great globe Helliconia, wherever small groups of men and women struggled to live, this was so.

And the Earth Observation Station recorded everything.

When he became Lord of Oldorando, Aoz Roon lost his lighthearted manner. He grew morose, for a while shunning even the witnesses and accomplices to his crime. Even those who maintained some access to him did not perceive how much his self-imposed isolation owed to ceaseless fermentation of guilt; people do not trouble to understand one another. Tabus against murder were strong; in a small community where all were related, even if distantly, and where the loss of even one able-bodied person was felt, consciousness was so precious that the dead themselves were not allowed to depart utterly from their fellows.

It happened that neither Klils nor Nahkri had children by their women, so that only their women were left to communicate with their men's gossies. Both reported from the spirit world only raging anger. The anger of gossies is painful to endure, for it can never be relieved. The anger was attributed to a fury the brothers would naturally feel at an outburst of drunken fratricidal madness; the women were excused further communication. The brothers and their hideous end ceased to be a common topic of conversation. The secret of the murder was kept for the present.

But Aoz Roon never forgot. On the dawn of the day after the killing, he had risen wearily and rinsed his face in icy water. The chill merely reinforced a fever he had been suppressing. His whole body raged with a pain that seemed to lumber from organ to organ.

Shivering with an anguish he dared not communicate to his companions, he hurried from his tower, his hound Curd by his side. He got himself into the lane where, in the phantasmal mists of first light, only swathed bodies of women were to be seen, moving slowly to work. Avoiding them, Aoz Roon stumbled towards the north gate. He had to pass by the big tower. Before he knew it, he was confronting the broken body of Nahkri, sprawled at his feet, its eyes still open in terror. He found the ugly corpse of Klils, lying on the opposite side of the tower base. The bodies had not yet been discovered or the alarm given. Curd whimpered and jumped back and forth over Klils' sodden body.

A thought pierced his daze. Nobody would believe that the brothers had killed each other if they were found lying on different sides of the tower. He grasped Klils' arm and tried to move the body. The corpse was stiff, and immobile as if it had rooted itself in the ground. He was forced to bend down, thrusting his face almost in the wet rotted hair, to pick up the body under its arms. He heaved again. Something had happened to his great careless strength. Klils would not move. Gasping, whimpering, he went to the other end and tugged at the legs. Geese honked distantly, mocking his efforts.

At last he shifted the corpse. Klils had fallen face downwards, and his hands and one side of his face had frozen to the mud. Now they broke away, and the body bumped over the dead ground. He dumped it by its brother, an unmoving, meaningless thing which he tried to wipe from his mental vision. Then he ran for the north gate.

A number of ruinous towers stood beyond the barricades, often surrounded by—or indeed ruined by—the rajabarals that loomed above their remains. In one of these monuments to time, overlooking an icy stretch of the Voral, he found refuge. A littered room on the second floor was intact. Although the wooden stairs had disappeared long ago, he was able to scramble up a pile of rubble and pull himself through into the stone chamber. He stood panting, resting one hand against the wall for support. Then he took his dagger and commenced frantically to cut himself free from his skins.

A bear had died in the mountains to clothe Aoz Roon. No one else wore a similar black fur. He ripped it off heedlessly.

At last he stood naked. Even to himself, the sight was shaming.

Nudity had no part in the culture. The hound sat and panted, and watched, and whimpered.

His body, with its hollow belly and marked muscle, was consumed with the flamelike pattern of a rash. The tongues lapped him all over. From his knees to his throat, he burned.

Clutching his penis in misery, he ran about the room, crying in many kinds of pain.

To Aoz Roon, the fire on his body was an imprimatur of guilt. Murder! Here was the effect; his dark mind leaped to the cause. Never for one moment did he cast his memory back to the incidents of the hunt, when he had been in close contact with the great white phagor. Never could he reflect that the lice which afflicted that shaggy species had transferred themselves to his body. He was without the knowledge to make such connections.

The Earth Observation Station rode overhead, observing.

Aboard it were instruments that enabled the observers to learn things about the planet beneath them that the inhabitants did not know. They comprehended the life cycle of the tick that had adapted itself to parasitism on both phagor and humanity. They had analysed the composition of the andesitic crust of Helliconia. From the smallest to the greatest, all facts were there to be collected, analysed, and signalled back to earth. It was as if Helliconia could be dismantled, atom by atom, and despatched to an alien destination across the galaxy. Certainly, it was in a sense being recreated on Earth, in encyclopaedias and Eductainment media.

When, from the Avernus, the two suns were seen to rise in the east above the shoulders of the Nktryhk Range, some of whose peaks towered into the stratosphere, and glory and shadow burst from them, penetrating the depths of the atmosphere with mystery, there were romantics aboard the station who forgot their facts and longed to be part of the rude activities taking place down on the bed of the ocean of air.

Grumbling and cursing, wrapped figures made their way through the murk to the big tower. A chill wind raged from the east, whistling between the ancient towers, slamming into their faces and conjuring rime on their bearded lips. Seven o'clock of a spring evening, and blackest night.

Once they got inside the tower, they jammed the rickety wooden door behind them, straightened up, and exclaimed. Then they mounted the stone steps that led to Aoz Roon's room. This room was warmed by the hot water flowing through the stone pipes in the basement. Upper rooms towards the top of the tower, where Aoz Roon's slaves and some of his hunters slept, were farther from the heat source, and consequently colder. But tonight the wind, squirrelling in through a thousand cracks, made everything icy.

Aoz Roon was holding his first council as Lord of Oldorando.

Last to arrive was old Master Datnil Skar, head of the tawyers and tanners corps. He was also the oldest person present. He came slowly up into the light, looking cautiously, half wary of a trap. The old are always suspicious of changes in government. Two candles burned in pots in the centre of a floor luxuriously covered with skins. Their ragged flames slanted towards the west, in which direction two pennants of smoke trailed.

By the uncertain light of the candles, Master Datnil saw Aoz Roon, seated on a wooden chair, and nine other people, squatting on the skins. Six of them were the masters of the other six makers corps, and to them he bowed individually after a courtesy towards Aoz Roon. The other two men were the hunters Dathka and Laintal Ay, sitting together rather defensively. Datnil Skar disliked Dathka for the simple reason that the lad had quit his corps for the feckless life of a hunter; such was Datnil Skar's opinion; and he also disliked Dathka's habit of silence.

The only female present was Oyre, who kept her dark gaze fixed uneasily on the floor. She sat partly behind her father's chair, so as to remain in the shadows that danced against the wall.

All these faces were familiar to the old master, as were the more spectral ones ranged on the walls below the beams—the skulls of phagors and other enemies of the hamlet.

Master Datnil seated himself on a rug on the floor next to his fellow corpsmen. Aoz Roon clapped his hands, and a slave woman came down from the floor above, carrying a tray on which were a jug and eleven carved wooden cups; Master Datnil realised when a measure of rathel was handed to him that the cups had once belonged to Wall Ein.

"You are welcome," Aoz Roon said loudly, lifting his cup. All drank the sweet cloudy liquid.

Aoz Roon spoke. He said that he intended to rule with more firmness than his predecessors. He would tolerate no lawlessness. He would consult the council as before, the council to consist as before of the masters of the seven makers corps. He would defend Oldorando against all enemies. He would not let women or slaves interfere with decent life. He would guarantee that nobody would starve. He would permit people to consult their gossies when they wished. He thought the academy a waste of time when the women had work to do.

Most of what he said was meaningless, or meant only that he intended to rule. He spoke, it could not but be noted, in a peculiar way, as if he wrestled with demons. His eyes often stared, he clutched the arms of his chair as if he was struggling with an inward torment. So that although his remarks were themselves inconsequential, the manner of delivery was horrifyingly original. The wind whistled and his voice rose and fell.

"Laintal Ay and Dathka will be my chief officers, and see my orders are carried out. They're young and sensible. All right, damn it, that's enough talk."

But the master of the brewers' corps interrupted in a firm voice, saying, "My Lord, you move too fast for those of us with slow wits. Some of us might like to ponder on why you appoint as your lieutenants two saplings, when we have men of oak about us who would serve better."

"I've made my choice," said Aoz Roon, rubbing his trunk to and fro against the back of his chair.

"But perhaps you have made it too fast, sire. Consider how many good men we have . . . what of your own generation, such as Eline Tal and Tanth Ein?"

Aoz Roon brought his fist down on the chair arm. "We need youth, action. That's my choice. Now you may go, all of you."

Datnil Skar rose slowly, and said, "My Lord, forgive me, but such hasty dismissal damages your merit, not ours. Are you ill, are you in pain?"

"Eddre, man, go, can't you, when asked? Oyre—"

"The custom is for your council of masters to drink to you, to toast your reign, sire."

The gaze of the Lord of Embruddock rolled up to the beams and down again.

"Master Datnil, I know you old men are short of breath and long on words. Spare me. Go, will you, before I have you replaced too. Away, all of you, my thanks, but go, away into this beastly weather."

"But—"

"Go!" He groaned and clutched himself.

A surly dismissal, and the old men of the council departed muttering, blowing out their toothless cheeks in indignation. Not a good omen. . . . Laintal Ay and Dathka left, shaking their heads.

As soon as he was alone with his daughter, Aoz Roon fell on the floor and rolled about, groaning, kicking, and scratching himself.

"Did you bring that medicated goose fat from Mistress Datnil, girl?" he asked his daughter.

"Yes, Father." Oyre produced a leather box containing a soft hunk of grease.

"You're going to have to rub it on my body."

"I can't do that, Father."

"Of course you can, and you will."

Her eyes flashed. "I will not do it. You heard what I said. Get your slave woman to do it. That's what she's for, isn't it? Or else I'll get Rol Sakil."

He jumped up, snarling, and took hold of her. "You'll do it. I can't afford to let anyone else see my state, or word will spread. *They'll find out, don't you see?* You'll do it, damn you, or I'll break your eddring neck. You're as difficult as Shay Tal."

When she whimpered, he said, with fresh anger, "Close your eyes if you're so squeamish, do it with your eyes shut. You don't have to look. But do it fast, before I go out of my harneys."

As he began to strip himself of his skins, still with madness in his look, he said, "And you will be spliced to Laintal Ay, to keep you both quiet. I want no argument. I've seen the looks he gives you. It'll be your turn one day to rule Oldorando."

Off came his trousers, and he stood there naked in front of her. She closed her eyes tightly, turning away her face, sick with disgust at this humiliation. Yet she could not shut out the sight of that hard, spare hairless body, which seemed to writhe under its skin. Her father was covered to his throat with scarlet flames.

"Get on with it, you great silly fillock! I'm in agony, damn you, I'm dying."

She reached out a hand and began to plaster the sticky lard across his chest and stomach.

Afterwards, Oyre fled from him, spitting curses, and ran from the building, to stand with her face turned to the chill wind, retching with disgust.

Such were the early days of her father's reign.

A group of Madis lay in their shapeless clothes, sleeping uneasily. They rested in a broken valley trackless miles from Oldorando. Their sentry dozed.

Walls of schist surrounded them. Under the onslaughts of frost, the rock broke into thin layers which crunched underfoot. There was no vegetation, except for an occasional stunted holly bush, the leaves of which were too bitter even for the omnivorous arang to eat.

The Madis had been caught in a thick mist which frequently descended on these uplands. Night had come and they had remained dispiritedly where they were. Batalix-rise had already visited the world, but dark and mist still reigned in the cold cleft of the canyon, and the protognostics still slumbered uneasily.

The young kzahhn's crusade commander, Yohl-Gharr Wyrrijk, stood on an eminence some feet above them, watching as a mixed party of warrior gillots and creaghts under his orders crept up on the defenceless group.

Ten adult Madis made up the company crouched in the obscurity.

They had with them a baby and three children. Beside them were seventeen arangs, sturdy goatlike animals with thick coats which provided most of the humble needs of the nomads.

This family of Madis was institutionally promiscuous. The exigencies of their existence were such that mating took place indiscriminately; nor were there any tabus against incest. Their bodies lay pressed together to conserve heat, while their horned animals crawled in close against them, forming a kind of outer ring of defence against the bone-numbing cold. Only the sentry was outside this circle, and he lay innocently with his head resting on the pelage of one of the arangs. The protognostics had no weapons. Their one defence was flight.

They had relied on the mist for protection. But the sharp eyes of the phagors had found them out. The extreme difficulty of the terrain had cut Yohl-Gharr Wyrrijk off temporarily from the main body of Hrr-Brahl Yprt's command. His warriors were almost as starved as the prehumans upon whom they were descending.

They bore clubs or spears. The crunch of their approach over the beds of schist was covered by the snores and snuffles of the Madis. A few more steps. The sentry woke from a dream and sat up, full of terror. Through the dank mist, ugly figures emerged like ghosts. He gave a cry. His companions stirred. Too late. With savage cries, the phagors attacked, striking without mercy.

In almost no time, all the protognostics were dead, and their little flock with them. They had become protein for the crusade of the young kzahhn. Yohl-Gharr Wyrrijk climbed down from his rock to give orders for its distribution.

Through the mist, Batalix arose, a dull red ball, and peered into the desolate canyon.

It was the Year 361 After Small Apotheosis of Great Year 5,634,000 Since Catastrophe. The crusade had now been eight years on its way. In five more years, it would arrive at the city of the Sons of Freyr which was its destination. But as yet no human eye could see the connection between the fate of Oldorando and what happened in a remote and leafless canyon.

VII

A COLD WELCOME
FOR PHAGORS

Lord or not, *he'll* have to come to *me*," Shay Tal said to Vry proudly, when in a still dimday they could not sleep.

But the new Lord of Embruddock also had his pride, and did not come.

His rule proved neither better nor worse than the previous one. He remained at odds with his council for one reason and with his young lieutenants for another.

Council and lord agreed where they could for the sake of a peaceful life and one matter on which they could agree without inconvenience to themselves was on the subject of the troublesome academy. Discontent must not be allowed to breed. Needing the women to work communally, they could not forbid them to gather together, and so the prohibition was useless. Yet they did not revoke it—and that vexed the women.

Shay Tal and Vry met privately with Laintal Ay and Dathka.

"You understand what we're trying to do," Shay Tal said. "*You* persuade that stubborn man to change his mind. You are closer to him than I can manage."

All that came of this meeting was that Dathka started making eyes at the reticent Vry. And Shay Tal became slightly more haughty.

Laintal Ay returned later from one of his solitary expeditions and sought Shay Tal out. Covered with mud, he squatted outside the women's house until she emerged from the boilery.

When she appeared, she had with her two slaves bearing trays of fresh loaves. Vry walked in a docile way behind the slaves. Once more, Oldorando's bread was ready, and Vry set off to supervise its distribution —though not before Shay Tal had snatched a spare loaf for Laintal Ay. She gave it to him, smiling and throwing back her unruly hair.

He munched gratefully, stamping his feet to warm them.

Milder weather, like the new lord, had proved more a convulsion than an actual progression. Now it was cold again, and the moisture beading Shay Tal's dark eyelashes froze. All about, white stillness prevailed. The river still flowed, broad and dark, but its banks were fanged by icicles.

"How's my young lieutenant? I see less of you these days."

He swallowed down the last of the loaf, his first food in three days.

"Hunting has been difficult. We've had to travel far afield. Now that it's colder again, the deer may move nearer home."

He stood alertly, surveying her as she stood before him in her ill-fitting furs. In her coiled quietness was the quality that made people admire and stand back from her. He perceived before she spoke that she saw through his excuse.

"I think much of you, Laintal Ay, as I did of your mother. Remember your mother's wisdom. Remember her example, and don't turn against the academy, like some of your friends."

"You know how Aoz Roon admires you," he blurted out.

"I know the way he has of showing it."

Seeing that he was disconcerted, she was more kind, and took his arm, walking with him, asking him where he had been. He glanced now and again at her sharp profile as he told her of a ruined village he had visited in the wilds. It lay half buried among boulders, its deserted streets like dried streambeds, fringed with roofless houses. All its wooden parts had been taken or had rotted away. Stone staircases ascended to floors that had long since disappeared, windows opened on prospects of tumbled rock. Toadstools grew in the doorsteps, driven snow accumulated in the fireplaces, birds made their nests in flaking alcoves.

"It's part of the disaster," said Shay Tal.

"It's what happens," he said innocently, and went on to tell of a small party of phagors he had stumbled across—not military ones, but humble fungusmongers, who had been as scared of him as he of them.

"You risk your life so needlessly."

"I need to . . . I need to get away."

"I have never left Oldorando. I must, I must—I want to get away as you do. I'm imprisoned. But I tell myself we are all prisoners."

"I don't see that, Shay Tal."

"You will see. First, fate moulds our character; then character moulds our fate. Enough of that—you're too young."

"I'm not too young to help you. You know why the academy is feared. It may upset the smooth running of life. But you tell us that knowledge will contribute to a general good, isn't that right?"

He regarded her half-smilingly, half-mockingly, and she thought, gazing back into his eyes, Yes, I understand how Oyre feels about you. She assented with an inclination of her head, smiling in return.

"Then you need to prove your case."

She raised a fine eyebrow and said nothing. He lifted his hand and uncurled his dirty fingers before her eyes. In his palm lay the ears of two grasses, one with seeds arranged in delicate bells, the other shaped like a miniature teazle.

"Well, ma'am, can the academy pronounce upon these, and name them?"

After a moment's hesitation, she said, "They are oats and rye, aren't they?" She searched in her mental store of folk wisdom. "They were once a part of—farming."

"I picked them beside the broken village, growing wild. There may have been fields of them once—before your catastrophe. . . . There are other strange plants, too, climbing against the ruins in sheltered spots. You can make good bread with these grains. Deer like them— when the grazing's good, the does will choose the oats and leave the rye."

As he transferred the green things to her hands, she felt the rasp of the rye's beard against her skin. "So why did you bring them to me?"

"Make us better bread. You have a way with loaves. Improve the bread. Prove to everyone that knowledge contributes to the general good. Then the ban on the academy will be lifted."

"You are very thoughtful," she said. "A special person."

The praise embarrassed him. "Oh, many plants are springing up in the wilderness which can be used to benefit us."

As he made to go, she said, "Oyre is very moody nowadays. What is troubling her?"

"You are wise—I thought you would know."

Clutching the green seeds, she hitched her skins about her body and said warmly, "Come and talk to me more often. Don't disregard my love for you."

He smiled awkwardly and turned away. He was unable to express to Shay Tal or anyone else how witnessing the murder of Nahkri had clouded his life. Fools though they were, Nahkri and Klils were his uncles and had enjoyed life. The horror would not go away, though two years had passed. He also guessed that the difficulties he experienced with Oyre were part of the same involvement. Towards Aoz Roon, his feelings were now intensely ambivalent. The murder estranged his powerful protector even from his own daughter.

His silence since the deaths implicated him in Aoz Roon's guilt. He had become almost as speechless as Dathka. Once he had fared forth on his solitary expeditions out of high spirits and a sense of adventure; now sorrow and unease drove him forth.

"Laintal Ay!" He turned at Shay Tal's call.

"Come along and sit with me until Vry returns."

The summons pleased and shamed him. He went quickly with her into her old rough refuge above the pigs, hoping none of his hunter friends saw him go. After the cold outside, its fug made him sleepy. Shay Tal's furfuraceous old mother sat in a corner against the garde-robe, droppings from which fell immediately to the animals below. The Hour-Whistler sounded the hour; darkness was already gathering in the room.

Laintal Ay greeted the old woman and sat himself down on skins beside Shay Tal.

"We'll collect more seed and plant little fields of rye and oats," she said. He knew by her tone she was pleased.

After a while, Vry returned with another woman, Amin Lim, a plump, motherly young woman who had appointed herself Shay Tal's chief follower. Amin Lim went straight to the rear wall of the room, sitting cross-legged with her back to the stonework; she wished only to listen, and to be within sight of Shay Tal.

Vry was also self-effacing. She was of comparatively slight build. Her breasts scarcely made more show under her silver-grey furs than two onions would have done. Her face was narrow, but not without its good looks, because her eyes were deep-set and brilliant against the pale skin. Not for the first time, Laintal Ay thought that Vry bore a resemblance to Dathka; perhaps that accounted for Dathka's attraction to her.

The one feature that marked Vry out was her hair. It was rich and dark. When seen in sunshine, it disclosed itself as dark brown, rather than the bluey black of Oldorandan hair. Her hair was the only indica-tion that Vry was of mixed extraction; her mother had been a slave woman from the south of Borlien, light of hair and complexion, who had died when she entered into captivity.

Too young to feel resentment against her captors, Vry had been fascinated by everything in Oldorando. The stone towers and the hot water pipes had particularly excited her childish admiration. She poured out questions and gave her heart to Shay Tal, who answered them. Shay Tal appreciated the child's lively mind, and took care of her as she grew up.

Under Shay Tal's tuition, Vry learned to read and write. She was one of the most ardent members of the academy. Of recent years, more children were born; in her turn, Vry was now teaching some of them the letters of the Olonets alphabet.

Vry and Shay Tal began to give Laintal Ay an account of how they had discovered a system of passageways under the town. With a grid of passages running north–south and east–west, the system connected all the towers, or had once done so; earthquakes, floods, and other natural disasters had blocked some passages. Shay Tal had hoped to reach the pyramid that stood half-buried by the sacrifice grounds, since she believed that structure to contain treasures of all kinds, but sludge had buried the necessary passages up to the roof.

"Many things connect of which we have no understanding, Laintal Ay," she said. "We live on the surface of the earth, yet I have heard that in Pannoval people live comfortably beneath it, and in Ottassol to the south, according to some traders. Perhaps the passages connect with the world below, where live the gossies and fessups. If we could find a way to them, in the flesh and not just in the spirit, then we should possess much buried knowledge. That would please Aoz Roon."

Overcome by the warmth, Laintal Ay merely nodded in drowsy fashion.

"Knowledge is not just a buried thing like a brassimip," Vry said. "Knowledge can be generated by observation. I believe there are passages through the air similar to the passages beneath us. When it is night, I watch the stars as they rise and set in progression across the sky. Some go by different passages—"

"They're too far away to influence us," said Shay Tal.

"Not so. All are Wutra's. What he does there will influence us."

"You were afraid underground," said Shay Tal.

"And I believe the stars scare you, ma'am," retorted Vry promptly.

Laintal Ay was amazed to hear this shy young woman, no older than he, drop her usual deferential manner and speak out to Shay Tal in this way; she had changed as much as the weather of late. Shay Tal appeared not to mind.

"Of what use are the underground passages?" he asked. "What do they signify?"

"They're just a relic of some old forgotten past," Vry said. "The future lies in the heavens."

But Shay Tal said firmly, "They demonstrate what Aoz Roon denies, that this farmyard in which we live was once a grand place, filled with arts and sciences, and people that were better than we. There were more people, there must have been—all now transformed to fessups—dressed grandly, as Loil Bry used to dress. And they had many thoughts like brilliant birds in their heads. We are all that remains, us, with mud in our heads."

Throughout the conversation, Shay Tal referred ever and again to Aoz Roon, gazing intensely into the dark corner of the room as she spoke.

The cold went, and rains came, then cold again, as if the weather at this period was specially designed to plague the people of Embruddock. The women did their work and dreamed of other places.

The plain was striped by folds which ran roughly in an east–west direction. Remains of snowdrifts still lay cupped in the synclines on northern sides of crests—tattered reminders of the snow desert that had once swathed the whole land. Now green stalks poked through the stippled snow, each stalk creating its own miniature rounded valley over which it was sole ruler.

Against the snow lay gigantic puddles, the most remarkable feature of the new landscape. They barred the entire landscape with parallel fish-shaped lakes, each reflecting fragments of the cloudy sky overhead.

This area had once formed rich hunting grounds. The game had gone with the snows, heading for drier grazing in the hills. In their place were flocks of black birds, wading phlegmatically on the margin of the transient lakes.

Dathka and Laintal Ay sprawled on a ridge, watching some moving figures. Both young hunters were soaked to the skin and in a bad humour. Dathka's long hard face was creased into a scowl which hid his eyes. Where their fingers pressed into the mud, half-moons of water appeared. All about them were the sipping sounds of hydropic earth. Some way behind, six disappointed hunters squatted on their haunches, concealed behind a ridge; as they waited indifferently for a command from their leaders, their eyes followed birds winging overhead, and they blew softly on their damp thumbs.

The figures being observed were walking eastwards in single file along the top of a ridge, heads low before a fine drizzle. Behind the file lay a broad curve of the Voral. Moored against the Voral's banks were three boats which had brought the hunters to invade traditional Oldorandan hunting grounds.

The invaders wore heavy leather boots and scoop-shaped hats which betrayed their origins.

"They're from Borlien," Laintal Ay said. "They've driven off what game there was. We'll have to drive them off."

"How? They're too many." Dathka spoke without taking his gaze from the moving figures in the distance. "This is our land, not theirs. But there are more than four handsful of them. . . ."

"There's one thing we can do: burn their boats. The fools have left only two men behind to guard them. We can deal with them."

With no game to hunt, they might as well hunt Borlienians.

From one of the southerners they had recently captured, they knew the state of unrest that prevailed in Borlien. The people there lived in mud buildings, generally two stories high, with the animals below and their owners above. Recent unprecedented rains had washed the huts out of existence; whole populations were homeless.

As Laintal Ay's party made its way towards the Voral, keeping from view of the boats, the rain increased. It came from the south. This was the beginning of the winter period. The rain fell capriciously in gusts, sprinkling the moving figures, then settling in more sullenly, until it beat a tattoo on their backs and moisture ran down their faces. They blew it from the ends of their blunt noses. Rain was something none of them had experienced until a few years ago; not a man in the party but wished for the crisp days of his childhood, with snow underfoot and deer stretching to the horizon. Now the horizon was hidden by dirty grey curtains, and the ground leaked.

The murk worked in their favour when they reached the riverbank. Here thick succulent grasses had sprung up as high as a man's knee, despite recent frosts, grasses that bowed and shimmered under the pressure of the downpour. There was nothing to be seen as they ran forward except wavering grass, the overburdened clouds, and muddy water the colour of cloud. A fish plopped heavily in the river, sensing an extension of its universe.

The two Borlienian guards, crouching for shelter in their boats, were killed without a struggle; perhaps they thought it better to die than get any wetter. Their bodies were cast into the water. They floated against the boats, and blood spread from their corpses, while the firemaker of the party tried vainly to make fire; the river was shallow at this point, and the bodies would not go away even when struck at by oars. With air trapped under their skins, they drifted just below the rain-pocked surface of the water.

"All right, all right," Dathka said impatiently. "Leave the firemaking. Break up the boats instead, men."

"We can use the boats ourselves," Laintal Ay suggested. "Let's row them to Oldorando."

The others stood and watched impassively as the two youths argued.

"What will Aoz Roon say when we return home without meat?"

"We'll have the boats to show him."

"Even Aoz Roon doesn't eat boats." Laughter greeted the remark.

They climbed into the boats and juggled with the oars. The dead men were left behind. They managed to row themselves slowly back to Oldorando, the rain beating continually in their faces.

Aoz Roon's reception of his subjects was morose. He glared at Laintal

Ay and the other hunters with a silence they found more daunting than words, since he offered them nothing to refute. At last, he turned from them and stood staring out of his open window at the rain.

"We can go hungry. We have gone hungry before. But we have other troubles. Faralin Ferd's party have returned from foraging in the north. They sighted a party of fuggies in the distance, riding kaidaws and heading this way. They say it looks like a war party."

The hunters looked at each other.

"How many fuggies?" one asked.

Aoz Roon shrugged his shoulders.

"Were they coming from Dorzin Lake?" Laintal Ay asked.

Aoz Roon merely shrugged his shoulders again, as if he found the question irrelevant.

He swung round on his audience, fixing them with his heavy gaze. "What do you think is the best strategy in the circumstances?"

When there was no reply, he answered his own question. "We're not cowards. We go out and attack them before they arrive here and try to burn Oldorando down, or whatever is in their thick harneys to do."

"They won't attack in this weather," an older hunter said. "The fuggies hate water. Only extreme madness can drive them into water. It ruins their coats."

"The times are extreme," Aoz Roon said, striding restlessly about. "The world will drown under this rain. When's the eddring snow coming back?"

He dismissed them, and paddled through the mud to see Shay Tal. Vry and her other close friend, Amin Lim, were sitting with her, copying out a design. He sent them packing.

He and Shay Tal looked warily at each other, she at his wet face and his air of having more to say that he could express, he at the wrinkles under her eyes, the first white hairs glinting in her dark locks.

"When will this rain stop?"

"The weather's getting worse again. I want to plant rye and oats."

"You're suppose to be so wise, you and your women—you tell me what will happen."

"I don't know. Winter's setting in. Perhaps it will get colder."

"Snow? How I'd love the damned snow back, and the rain gone." He made an angry gesture, raising his fists, then dropping them again.

"If it gets colder, the rain will turn into snow."

"Wutra's scumble, what a female answer! Have you no certainty for me, Shay Tal? No certainty in this damned uncertain world?"

"No more than you have for me."

He turned on his heel, to pause at her door. "If your women don't work, they won't eat. We can't have people idle—you understand that."

He left her without a word more. She followed him to the door and stood there, frowning. She was vexed that he had not given her a chance to say no to him again; it would have renewed her sense of purpose. But his mind, she realised, had not really been on her at all, but on more important questions.

She hunched her rough garments about her and went to sit on her bed. When Vry returned, she was still in that attitude, but jumped up guiltily at the sight of her young friend.

"We must always be positive," she said. "If I were a sorceress, I would bring back the snows, for Aoz Roon's sake."

"You are a sorceress," Vry said loyally.

News of the approaching phagors travelled fast. Those who remembered the last raid on the town spoke of nothing else. They talked of it at night as they tumbled, rathel-rich, into their beds; they talked of it at dawn, grinding grain by goose light.

"We can contribute more than talk," Shay Tal told them. "You have brave hearts, women, as well as quick tongues. We'll show Aoz Roon what we can do. I want you to listen to my idea."

They decided that the academy, which must always justify its existence in the eyes of the men, should propose a plan of attack that would spare Oldorando. Choosing suitable ground, the women would reveal themselves at a safe place where the phagors would see them. When the phagors approached, they would be ambushed by the hunters, waiting concealed on either flank to cut them down. The women screamed and cried for blood as they discussed the idea.

When the plan had been discussed to their satisfaction, they chose one of their prettiest girls to act as emissary to Aoz Roon. The girl was almost of an age with Vry; she was Dol Sakil, daughter of the old midwife, Rol Sakil. Oyre escorted Dol to her father's tower, where the girl was to present Shay Tal's compliments and to request him to come to the women's house: there a defensive proposal would be presented to him.

"He won't take much notice of me, will he?" Dol said. Oyre smiled and pushed her ahead.

The women waited while the rain poured down outside.

It was midmorning when Oyre returned. She was alone, and looking furious. Finally she burst out with the truth. Her father had rejected the invitation—and kept Dol Sakil. He regarded her as a present from the academy. Dol would live with him from now on.

At this news, a high anger overcame Shay Tal. She fell to the floor. She danced with rage. She screamed and tore her hair. She gestured and swore vengeance on all imbecile men. She prophesied that they would all be eaten alive by phagors, while their supposed leader lay in bed copulating with an imbecile child. Many other terrible things she said. Her companions could not calm her and went in fear of her. Vry and Oyre were driven away.

"It is a vexation," said Rol Sakil, "but it will be nice for Dol."

Then Shay Tal gathered her clothes about her body and stormed down into the lane, to stand before the big tower where Aoz Roon lived. The rain poured on her face as she cried aloud the scandal of his conduct, daring him to show himself.

Her noise was so great that men of the makers corps and some hunters ran out to listen. They stood against the ruinous buildings for shelter, grinning, with folded arms, while the downpour beat the steam from the geysers close to the ground, and mud bubbled between their boots.

Aoz Roon came to the window of his tower. He looked down and shouted to Shay Tal to go away. She shook her fist at him. She screamed that he was abominable, and his behaviour such that all Embruddock would meet with disaster.

At this juncture, Laintal Ay arrived and took Shay Tal by the arm. He spoke lovingly. She stopped screaming a moment to listen. He said that she must not despair. The hunters knew how to handle phagors. Aoz Roon knew. They would go out and fight when the weather improved.

"When! If! Who are you to make conditions, Laintal Ay? You men are so weak!" She raised her fists to the clouds. "You will follow my plan or else disaster will strike you down—and you, Aoz Roon, you hear? I see it all clearly with an inner eye."

"Yes, yes." Laintal Ay tried to hush her.

"Don't touch me! Just follow the plan. The plan or death! And if that fool leader, so called, hopes to remain leader, he must give up Dol Sakil from his couch. Raper of children! Doom! Doom!"

These prophecies were uttered with wild assurance. Shay Tal continued her harangue with variations, damning all ignorant and brutal men. Everyone was impressed. The downpour increased. The towers dripped. The hunters grinned mirthlessly at each other. More onlookers arrived in the lane, eager for drama.

Laintal Ay called up to Aoz Roon that he was convinced of the truth of what Shay Tal said. He advised Aoz Roon to fall in with the prophecies. The women's plan sounded a good one.

Again Aoz Roon appeared at his window. His face was as black as his furs. Despite his anger, he was subdued. He agreed to follow the women's plan when the weather improved. Not before. Certanly not before. Also, he was going to keep Dol Sakil. She was in love with him and needed his protection.

"Barbarian! Ignorant barbarian! You're all barbarians, fit only for this stinking farmyard. Wickedness and ignorance have brought us low!"

Shay Tal marched up and down the lane in the mud, screaming. The prize barbarian was the uncouth rapist whose name she refused to speak. They lived only in a farmyard, a pool of mud, and they had forgotten the grandeur that once was Embruddock. All the ruins lying outside their miserable barricades had once been fine towers, clad in gold, all that was now mud and filth had once been paved with fine marble. The town had been four times its present size, and everything had been beautiful—clean and beautiful. The sanctity of women had been respected. She clutched her wet furs to herself and sobbed.

She would no longer live in such a filthy place. She was going to live at a distance, beyond the barricades. If the phagors came by night, or the wily Borlienians, and caught her, why should she care? What had she to live for? They were disaster's children, all of them.

"Peace, peace, woman," said Laintal Ay, splashing along beside her.

She rejected him contemptuously. She was only an ageing woman whom nobody loved. She alone saw truth. They would regret it when she was gone.

Thereupon, Shay Tal suited deeds to words, and commenced moving her few goods to one of the ruinous towers standing among the rajabarals, outside the fortifications to the northeast. Vry and others assisted her, splashing back and forth through the rain with her poor possessions.

The rain stopped next day. Two remarkable events occurred. A flock of small birds of a kind unknown flew over Oldorando and wheeled about its towers. The air was full of their twittering. The flock would not settle in the village proper. It alighted on the isolated towers beyond, especially on the ruin to which Shay Tal had exiled herself. Here the birds set up a remarkable noise. They had small beaks and red heads, with feathers of red and white on their wings, and a darting flight. Some hunters ran forth with nets and tried to catch the birds, without success.

The event was considered an omen.

The second event was even more alarming.

The Voral flooded.

Rain had caused the river to rise. As the Hour-Whistler sounded noon, a great swell approached from upstream and the direction of distant Dorzin Lake. An old woman, Molas Ferd, was down by the riverbank collecting geese scumble when she sighted the swell. She straightened as much as she was able and stared in amazement as a wall of water bore down on her. Geese and ducks took fright, clattering up to perch on the barricades. But old Molas Ferd stood where she was, shovel in hand, staring openmouthed at the waters. They rushed upon her and hurled her against the side of the women's house.

The flood filled the village before subsiding, washing away grain, invading people's homes, drowning sows. Molas Ferd was battered to death.

The hamlet was turned into a swamp. Only the tower where Shay Tal had taken up residence was spared the onslaught of muddy waters.

This period marked the true beginning of Shay Tal's reputation as a sorceress. All who had heard her cry out against Aoz Roon sat inside and muttered.

That evening, as first Batalix, then Freyr set in the west, turning the flood waters to blood, the temperature dropped dramatically. The village was filled with thin crackling ice.

Next Freyr-dawn, the town was aroused by Aoz Roon's angry shouting. The women, scuffling into their boots to go to work, listened in dismay, and woke their menfolk. Aoz Roon was taking a leaf from Shay Tal's book.

"Out you come, damn you all! You're going to fight the phagors today, every one of you! I set my resolve against your idleness. Rise, rise, all of you, get up and fight. If phagors are to be found, then phagors you will fight. I fought them single-handed, you scum can fight them together. This will be a great day in history, you hear me, a great day, even if you all die!"

As the dawn clouds scudded bleakly overhead, his great figure in its black furs stood on top of the tower, fist waving. With his other hand, Aoz Roon clutched a struggling Dol Sakil, who fought and yelled to get out of the cold. Eline Tal loomed behind them, grinning feebly.

"Yes, we'll slay the milk-struck phagors according to the women's plan—you hear that, you idle quemes of the academy?—we'll fight according to the women's plan, for good or ill—carry it out to the letter. By the original boulder, we'll see what happens today, we'll see whether or not Shay Tal talks sense, we'll see what her prophecies are worth!"

A few figures were emerging in the lane, clattering through the thin ice, staring up at their lord. Many clutched each other timidly, but old Rol Sakil, mother of Dol, cackled and said, "He must be well developed, yelling like that—that's what our Dol said he was. Bawls like a bull!"

He came to the edge of the parapet and glared down at them, dragging Dol with him, still shouting.

"Yes, we'll see what her words are worth, we'll test her. We'll test Shay Tal in battle, since you all seem to think so much of her. Do you hear me, Shay Tal? We'll make or break today, and blood shall flow, red or yellow."

He spat down at them, then withdrew. The trapdoor slammed after him as he climbed back into his tower.

When they had eaten some black bread, everyone set forth, urged on by the hunters. All were subdued, even Aoz Roon. His storm of words had blown itself out. They proceeded in a southeasterly direction. The weather remained below freezing. The day was still, the suns were lost in cloud. The ground was hard and ice crackled underfoot.

Shay Tal went with them, keeping in with the women, her mouth pursed, her skins swinging about her thin body.

Progress was slow, for the women were unaccustomed to walking distances that meant nothing to the men. They came at length to the broken plain from which Laintal Ay's hunting party had sighted the Borlienians only two days before the Voral flooded. Here lay the series of ridges with shallow flood lakes between, glinting like stranded fish. Here the ambush could be set up. The cold would bring out phagors, if there were any. Batalix had set, unseen.

They went down into the plain, men first, the women following, in confused groups. All were apprehensive under the hard sky.

By the edge of the first flood lake, the women halted, looking at Shay Tal in none too friendly a fashion. They realised the danger of their position, should any phagors arrive—particularly if they came mounted. No amount of anxious glancing about could reassure them on that score, for the ridges restricted their view.

They were exposed to danger and the elements. The temperature remained two or three degrees below freezing. Quiet reigned; the air was hard. The shallow lake lay silent before them. It was some forty metres wide by one hundred metres long, occupying the hollow between two ridges with its unwelcoming expanse. Its waters were motionless but still unfrozen, reflecting the sky without a ripple. Its sullen appearance increased a certain supernatural fear which fell upon the women as they watched the hunters disappear over the ridge. Even the grass at their feet, crisped by frost, seemed under a curse, and no birds cried.

The men were unhappy about having their womenfolk nearby. They stood in a neighbouring depression, by another lake, and complained about their leader.

"We've seen no sign of phagors," Tanth Ein said, blowing on his nails. "Let's turn back. Supposing they destroyed Oldorando while we were away? A fine thing that would be."

The cloud of breath about their heads united them as they leaned on their spears and looked accusingly at Aoz Roon. The latter paced about, keeping himself separate from them, his expression black.

"Turn back? You talk like women. We came to fight, and fight we will, even if we throw our lives to Wutra while we do so. If there are phagors near, I'll summon them. Stand where you are."

He went at a run to the top of the ridge behind him, so that the women were again within his view, intending to shout at the top of his voice and awaken all the echoes in the wilderness.

But the enemy was already in view. Now, too late, he understood why they had seen no more wandering Borlienians; they had been driven off. Like old Molas Ferd before the flood, he stood paralysed before the sight of humanity's ancient enemy.

The women straggled at one end of the fish-shaped lake, the ancipitals grouped at the other. The women made frightened and uncertain movements; the ancipitals were motionless. Even in their surprise, the women responded individually; the phagors could be seen only as a group.

It was impossible to make out the number of the enemy. They merged together with the late afternoon mists filling the hollow, and with the scarred greys and blues of the scene. One of them gave a thick protracted cough; otherwise they might have been lifeless.

Their white birds had settled on a ridge behind them, at first with some jostling, now spaced out regularly, with heads submissively on one side, like the souls of those departed.

From their frosty outline, it could be determined that three of the phagors—presumably the leaders—were mounted on kaidaws. They sat, as was their habit, leaning forward with their heads close to their mounts' heads, as if communion was in progress. The foot phagors clustered against the flanks of the kaidaws, shoulders hunched. Nearby boulders were not more still.

The cougher coughed again. Aoz Roon threw off his spell and called to his men.

They climbed along the crest of the ridge, to stare at the enemy in dismay.

In response, the phagors made a sudden move. Their strangely jointed limbs geared themselves from immobility to action with no intermediate stage. The shallow lake had checked their advance. They had a well-known aversion to water, but times were changing; their harneys said "Forward." The sight of thirty human gillots at their mercy decided them. They charged.

One of the three mounted brutes swung a sword above his head. With a churring cry, he kicked his kaidaw, and mount and rider burst forward. The other brutes followed as one, whether mounted or running. Forward they dashed—into the waters of the shallow lake.

Panic scattered the women. Now that their adversary was almost on them, they ran hither and thither between the ridges. Some climbed one side, some the other, making small sharp noises of despair, like birds in distress.

Only Shay Tal remained where she was, facing the charge, and Vry and Amin Lim clung to her in terror, hiding their faces.

"Run, you fool woman!" bellowed Aoz Roon, coming down the ridge at a run.

Shay Tal did not hear his voice above the shrieks and the furious splashing. She stood firm at the end of the fish lake and flung out her arms, as if gesturing to the phagor horde to halt.

Then the transformation. Then the moment that ever after in the annals of Oldorando would be referred to as the miracle of Fish Lake.

Some claimed later that a shrilling note rang through the frosty air, some said a high voice spoke, some vowed Wutra struck.

The whole group of marauders, sixteen in number, had entered the lake, led by the three mounted stalluns. Their rage drove them into the alien element, they were thigh deep in it, churning it up with the fury of their charge, when the entire lake froze.

One moment, it was an absolutely still liquid, lying, because undisturbed, unfrozen at three degrees below freezing point. The next moment, disturbed, it became solid. Kaidaws and phagors all were locked in its embrace. One kaidaw fell, never to rise again. The others froze where they were, and their riders froze with them, hemmed in ice. The stalluns behind, brandishing their arms—all were trapped, held in the grip of the element they had invaded. None took as much as one further step. None could fight free to gain the safety of the shore. Soon, their veins froze within their bodies, despite the ancient biochemistries that coloured their bloodstream and protected it from the cold. Their coarse white coats became further sheathed in rime, their glaring eyes frosted over.

What was organic became one with the great inorganic world that ruled.

The tableau of furious death was absolute, carved from ice.

Above it, white birds wheeled and dipped, crying with gaping beaks, finally making off to the east in desolate flight.

Next morning, three people rose up early from a skin bivouac. Powdery snow had fallen during the night, giving the wilderness a peppery appearance. Freyr ascended from the horizon, casting watery purple shadows over the plain. Several minutes later, the second faithful sentinel also struggled free into Wutra's realm.

By then, Aoz Roon, Laintal Ay, and Oyre were on their feet, beating and stamping circulation into their limbs. They coughed, but were otherwise silent. After looking at each other without speaking, they moved forward. Aoz Roon stepped out onto the lake of ice, which rang beneath his tread.

The three of them walked across to the frozen tableau.

They stared at it almost in disbelief. Before them was a monumental piece of statuary, fine in detail, wild in imagining. One kaidaw lay almost under the hoofs of the other two, the greater part of its bulk submerged by brittle waves, its head rearing up in fear, its nostrils distended. Its rider struggled for control, half fallen from its back, terrible in immobility.

All the figures were caught in mid-action, many with weapons raised, eyes staring ahead to the shore they would never reach. All were encased in rime. They formed a monument to brutality.

Finally, Aoz Roon nodded and spoke. His voice was subdued.

"It did happen. Now I believe. Let's get back."

The miracle of Year 24 was confirmed.

He had sent the rest of the party back to Oldorando the previous evening, under Dathka's leadership. Only after he had slept could he believe he did not dream the incident.

Nobody else said anything. They had been saved by a miracle; the thought dazed their minds, silenced their tongues. They trudged away from the alarming sculpture without another word.

Once they were back in Oldorando, Aoz Roon ordered one of his slaves to be taken by two hunters to Fish Lake, to the site of the miracle. When the slave had seen the tableau with his own eyes, his hands were lashed behind his back, he was faced towards the south, and booted on his way. Back in Borlien, he would tell his fellows that a powerful sorceress watched over Oldorando.

VIII

IN OBSIDIAN

The room in which Shay Tal stood erect was ancient beyond her computation. She had furnished it with what she could: an old tapestry, once Loil Bry's, once Loilanun's—that illustrious line of dead women; her humble bed in the corner, built of woven bracken imported from Borlien (bracken kept out rats); her writing materials set on a small stone table; some skins on the floor, on which thirteen women sat or squatted. The academy was in session.

The walls of the room were leprous with yellow and white lichen which, starting from the single narrow window, had, over uncounted years, colonised all the adjacent stonework. In the corners were spiders' webs; most of their incumbents had starved to death long ago.

Behind the thirteen women sat Laintal Ay, legs folded under him, resting his chin on his fist and his elbow on his knee. He looked down at the floor. Most of the women gazed vacantly at Shay Tal. Vry, Amin Lim, were listening; of the others, she could not be sure.

"The effects in our world are complex. We can pretend they are all a product of the mind of Wutra in that eternal war in Heaven, but that is too easy. We would do better to work things out for ourselves.

We need some other key to understanding. Does Wutra care? Perhaps we have sole charge of our own actions. . . ."

She ceased to listen to what she was saying. She had posed the eternal question. Surely every human being who had ever lived had had to face up to that question, and answer it in her own way: have we sole charge of our own actions? She could not tell the answer in her own case. In consequence, she felt herself totally unfit to teach.

Yet they listened. She knew why they listened, even if they listened without understanding. They listened because she was accepted as a great sorceress. Since the miracle at Fish Lake, she was isolated by their reverence. Aoz Roon himself was more distant than before.

She looked out through the ruinous window at the ecrhythmous world, now freeing itself from the recent cold, its slimes and snows spatch-cocked with green, its river streaked with muds from remote places she would never visit. There were miracles. The miraculous lay beyond her window. Yet—had she performed a miracle, as everyone assumed?

Shay Tal broke off her talk in mid-sentence. She perceived that there way a way of testing her own holiness.

The phagors charging at Fish Lake had turned to ice. Because of something in her—or something in them? She recalled tales about phagors dreading water; perhaps the reason was that they turned to ice in it. That could be tested: there were one or two old phagor slaves in Oldorando. She would try one out in the Voral and see what happened. One way or the other, she would know.

The thirteen were staring at her, waiting for her to go on. Laintal Ay looked puzzled. She had no idea what she had been saying. She perceived that she had to conduct an experiment for her own peace of mind.

"We have to do what we're told . . ." one of the women said from the floor, in a slow puzzled voice, as if repeating a lesson.

Shay Tal stood listening to someone tramping up the steps from the floor below. There was no way in which she could answer politely a statement she had been contradicting since the Hour-Whistler last blew; any interruption was welcome at this point. Some of the women were irredeemably stupid.

The hatch was flung open. Aoz Roon appeared, looking rather like a great black bear, followed by his dog. Behind him came Dathka, to stand poker-faced in the rear, not even casting a glance at Laintal Ay. The latter stood rather awkwardly, and waited with his back to the cold wall. The women gaped at the intruders, some giggling nervously.

Aoz Roon's stature seemed to fill the low room. Though the women craned their necks at him uneasily, he ignored them and addressed Shay Tal. She had moved back to the window, but stood facing him, framed against a background of muddy village, fumaroles, and the parti-coloured landscape stretching to the horizon.

"What do you want here?" she asked. Her heart beat as she beheld him. For this above all she cursed her new reputation, that he no longer bullied her, or held her arms, or even pursued her. His whole manner suggested this was a formal and unfriendly visit.

"I wish you to come back into the protection of the barricades, ma'am," he said. "You are not safe, living in this ruin. I cannot protect you here in the event of a raid."

"Vry and I prefer living here."

"You're under my control, for all your reputation, you and Vry, and I must do my best to protect you. All you other women—you should not be here. It is too dangerous outside the barricades. If there was a sudden attack—well, you can guess what would happen to you. Shay Tal, as our powerful sorceress, must please herself. The rest of you must please me. I forbid you to come here. It's too dangerous. You understand?"

All evaded his gaze except the old midwife, Rol Sakil. "That's all nonsense, Aoz Roon. This tower is safe enough. Shay Tal's scared off the fuggies, we all know that. Besides, even you have been here on occasions, haven't you now?"

This last was said with a leer. Aoz Roon dismissed it.

"I'm talking about the present. Nothing's safe now the weather's changing. None of you enter here again or there will be trouble."

He turned, raising a beckoning finger to Laintal Ay.

"You come with me." He marched down the steps without a farewell, and Laintal Ay and Dathka followed.

Outside, he paused, pulling at his beard. He looked up at her window. "I'm still Lord of Embruddock, and you had better not forget it."

She heard his shout from within, but would not go to the window. Instead, she stood where she was—alone despite the company—and said in a voice loud enough for him to hear, "Lord of a rotten little farmyard."

Only when she heard the squelch of three pairs of boots retreating did she deign to glance out the window. She watched his broad back as he trudged with his young lieutenants towards the north gate, Curd trotting at his heel. She understood his loneliness. None better.

As his woman, she would surely not have lost stature, or whatever it was she valued so highly. Too late to think of that now. The rift was between them, and an empty-headed doll kept his bed warm.

"You'd better all go home," she said, afraid to look directly at the women.

When they got back to the muddy main square, Aoz Roon ordered Laintal Ay to stay away from the academy.

Laintal Ay flushed. "Isn't it time that you and the council gave up your prejudice against the academy? I hoped you'd think better of it since the miracle of Fish Lake. Why upset the women? They'll hate you for it. The worst the academy can do is keep the women content."

"It makes the women idle. It causes division."

Laintal Ay looked at Dathka for support, but Dathka was gazing at his boots. "It's more likely to be your attitude that causes division, Aoz Roon. Knowledge never hurt anyone; we need knowledge."

"Knowledge is slow poison—you're too young to understand. We need discipline. That's how we survive and how we always have survived. You stay away from Shay Tal—she exerts an unnatural power over people. Those who don't work in Oldorando get no food. That's always been the rule. Shay Tal and Vry have ceased working the boilery, so in future they will have nothing to eat. We'll see how they like that."

"They'll starve."

Aoz Roon drew his brows together and glared at Laintal Ay, "We will all starve if we do not cooperate. Those women have to be brought to heel, and I will not tolerate you siding with them. Argue with me any more and I'll knock you down."

When Aoz Roon had gone, Laintal Ay gripped Dathka's shoulder. "He is getting worse. It's his personal battle with Shay Tal. What do you think?"

Dathka shook his head. "I don't think. I do what I'm told."

Laintal Ay regarded his friend sarcastically. "And what are you told to do now?"

"I'm going up by the brassimips patch. We've killed a stungebag." He exhibited a bleeding hand.

"I'll be there in a while."

He walked by the Voral, idly watching the geese swimming and parading, before following his friend. He thought to himself that he understood both Aoz Roon's and Shay Tal's points of view. To live, all had to cooperate, yet was it worth living if they merely cooperated? The conflict oppressed him and made him long to leave the hamlet—as he would do if only Oyre were to agree to come with him. He felt that he was too young to understand how the argument, the growing division, would resolve itself. Slyly, seeing nobody was looking, he brought out from his pocket a carved dog given him long ago by the old priest from Borlien. He held it forward and worked its tail. The dog began to bark furiously at nearby geese.

Someone else was wending her way towards the brassimips and heard the imitation dog bark. Vry saw Laintal Ay's back between two towers. She did not intrude on him, for that was not her way.

She skirted the hot springs and the Hour-Whistler. An easterly breeze took the steam from the waters as it emerged from the ground, to blow it hissing across wet rock. Vry's furs were pearled with a bead of moisture at every hair end.

The waters ran gargling, yellow and chalky in their crevices, full of an infectious fury to be somewhere. She squatted down on a rock and absentmindedly dipped her hand in a spring. Hot water ran up her fingers and explored her palm.

Vry licked the liquid off her fingers. She knew the sulphurous flavour from childhood. Children were playing here now, calling to each other, running across slippery rock without falling, agile as arangs.

The more adventurous children ran naked, despite the stiff breeze, inserting their androgynous bodies into clefts between rocks. Spuming waters cascaded up their stomachs and over their shoulders.

"Here comes the Whistler," they called to Vry. "Look out, missus, or you'll get a soaking." They laughed heartily at the thought.

Taking the warning, Vry moved away. She thought that a stranger here would credit the children with a sixth sense, able to predict exactly when the Hour-Whistler blew.

Up it went, a solid column of water, muddy for a moment then brilliant pure. Ascending, it whistled on an ascending note—its unvarying note, sustained for an unvarying duration. The water sailed upwards to about three times the height of a man before falling back. The wind curved the jet towards the west, hammering the rocks where Vry had squatted a moment earlier.

The whistle stopped. The column died back into the black lips of earth from which it had sprung.

Vry waved to the children and continued up the brassimip track. She knew how they knew when the geyser was about to blow. She still remembered the thrill of wriggling naked between ochre rocks, plugging one's body into the streaming earth, toes among hot slimes, flesh tickled by bursting bubbles. When the hour was near, a tremor shook the ground. One wedged oneself into the rock and felt in every fibre the strength of the earth gods as they tensed themselves to deliver their triumphant ejaculation of hot liquids.

The path she followed was trodden mainly by women and pigs. It wandered hither and thither, unlike straighter paths created by hunters, since its course had been dictated largely by that wayward creature, the hairy black sow of Embruddock. To follow the direction in which the track tended was to arrive eventually at Lake Dorzin; but the path ceased long before that, at the brassimip patch. The rest of the way was still a wilderness of marsh and frost.

As she moved up the path, Vry wondered if all things aspired to a highest level, and if there was a competing force trying to drag them to the lowest. One looked up to the stars, one ended as a gossie, a fessup. The Hour-Whistler was an embodiment of the two opposed forces. Its spouting waters always fell back to earth. In her unobtrusive way, she willed her spirit to soar to the sky, the region she studied without Shay

Tal's aid, the place of sublime movement, the riddling place of stars and suns, of as many secret passages as the body.

Two men came towards her. She could see little of them but legs, elbows, and the tops of their heads, as they staggered downhill under heavy loads. She could identify Sparat Lim by his spindly legs. The men were carrying slabs of stungebag. After them came Dathka, carrying only a spear.

Dathka gave her a grin of welcome and stood to one side of the path, surveying her with his dark eyes. His right hand was bloody, and a thin trail of blood ran down the spear shaft.

"We killed a stunge," he said, and that was all. As usual, Vry was both embarrassed and comforted by his lack of words. It was pleasant that he never boasted, unlike many of the young hunters, less pleasant that he never revealed his thoughts. She tried to feel something for him.

She halted. "It must have been a big one."

"I'll show you." He added, "If you'll let me."

He turned back along the track and she followed, unsure whether she ought to speak or not. But that was silly, she told herself; she understood perfectly that Dathka desired to communicate with her.

She blurted out the first thing that came into her head.

"How do you account for human beings in the world, Dathka?"

Without a backward glance, he said, "We came up from the original boulder." He spoke without the consideration she would have wished him to give to such an important matter, and there the conversation languished.

She regretted that there were no priests in Oldorando; she could have talked to them. Legends and songs related that Embruddock had once had its fair share of priests, administering an elaborate religion which united Wutra with the living of this world and the fessups of the world below. One dark season before Wall Ein Den ruled, when breath froze to people's lips as it issued forth, the population rose and slew the priesthood. Sacrifices had ceased from then on, except on festival days. The old god, Akha, was no longer worshipped. No doubt a body of learning had also been lost. The temple had been stripped. Now pigs were housed in it. Perhaps other enemies of knowledge had been about, when pigs were preferred to priests.

She risked another question of the ascending back.

"Do you wish you understood the world?"

"I do," it said.

She was left wrestling with the brevity of the reply; did he understand or did he wish he understood, she asked herself.

The forces that had thrown up the Quzint Mountains had folded the earth in all directions, causing attendant deformations like buttresses, like the roots of trees, to extend outwards for many miles from the mountains themselves. Between two such rocky extrusions grew a line of brassimips which had long been essential to the local economy. Today, the plot was a scene of mild excitement, and several women were clustered round the open tops of the brassimips, warming themselves and herding their pigs while watching the work in progress.

Dathka indicated that this was where the stungebag was killed.

His gesture was scarcely necessary. The carcass lay about in piles, sprawling up the desolate hillside. Towards its tail, Aoz Roon himself was investigating it, his yellow hound about his heels. The stubby legs of the immense corpse pointed into the air, fringed by stiff black hairs and spines.

A group of men waited about the body, laughing and talking. Goija Hin supervised the slaves, human and phagorian, who wielded axes. They were splitting the fibrous carcass into slabs that could be carried down to the hamlet. They stood up to their knees in coir and woody sections of the stungebag's flesh. Great splinters flew as they dismembered the remains.

Two older women dodged about with buckets, gathering up spongey white entrails. They would boil the mess down later to distill a coarse sugar from it. The coir would be used for ropes and mats, the flesh for fuel for the various corps.

From the paddlelike digging paws of the stungebag, oils would be extracted to form a narcotic called rungebel.

The older women were exchanging impolite remarks with the men, who grinned and stood in nonchalant poses about the hillside. It was unusual for stungebags to venture near human habitation. The beasts were easy to kill, and every part of them was useful to the fragile economy. The present kill was thirty metres long, and would benefit the community for days to come.

Pigs ran squealing round Vry's feet as they rooted among the fibrous debris. Their swineherds were working below in the brassimips. Nothing of the giant trees was visible above ground except heavy fungoid leaves, cossetting the earth with their twisted growth pattern. The leaves stirred like elephant ears, not from the prevailing breeze but from draughts of warm air blowing out of the crowns of the trees.

A dozen brassimips formed the patch. The tree rarely grew singly. The soil about each tree bulged upwards and was starred with cracks, suggesting the considerable bulk of vegetation below. The heat that the trees syphoned up to their leaf system enabled the plants to thaw frozen ground, so that they continued to grow even in permafrost conditions.

Jassiklas lived under the leathery leaves. They took advantage of the sheltering warmth to put forth timid brown-blue flowers. As Vry stooped to pick one, Dathka returned to her side and spoke.

"I'm going into the tree."

She construed this as an invitation to join him, and followed. A slave was pulling up leather buckets full of chips from the interior and throwing them to the pigs. Pulped brassimip chips had fed Embruddock's pigs through the dark centuries.

"That's what attracted the stungebag," Vry said. The monstrous animals were as fond of brassimip as the pigs.

A wood ladder led into the tree. As she followed Dathka down, her eyes came for a moment level with the ground. As if drowning in earth, she saw the leather leaves waving about her. Beyond the backs of the pigs were the men, fur-clad, standing among the wreckage of the giant stungebag. There was snowy high ground and a sky of slate over all. She climbed down into the tree.

Warm air assailed her cheeks, making her blink, carrying with it a perfumed rotting smell that both repelled and attracted her. The air had come from a long way down; brassimip roots bored far into the crust. With age, the core of the tree commenced a fermenting process which released a hardening substance resembling keratin. A tube formed through the centre of the tree. A heat pump was established, warming leaves and underground branches with heat trapped at lower levels.

This favourable environment created a refuge for several sorts of animal, some decidedly nasty.

Dathka reached out a hand to steady Vry. She climbed off the ladder beside him and stood in a bulb-shaped natural chamber. Three dirty-looking women were working there. They greeted Vry, then went on scraping chips of brassimip flesh from the walls of the trees, loading them into the bucket.

Brassimip had a flavour rather like parsnip or turnip, but was bitter. Humans ate it only in times of starvation. Normally, it made pig feed— in particular, feed for the sows whose milk went to the making of rathel, Oldorando's staple winter drink.

A narrow gallery opened to one side. It led into the topmost branch of the tree, the leaves of which would surface in a bunch some distance away. Mature brassimips had six branches. The topmost branches were generally left to grow without interference; being nearest to the surface, they harboured a variety of sheltering nasties.

Dathka indicated the central tube going down into the darkness. He climbed down. After a moment's hesitation, Vry followed, and the women paused in their labours to watch her go, smiling part in sympathy, part in mockery. Directly she got into the tube, it was completely dark. Below was only the eternal night of earth. She thought that she, like Shay Tal, was having to descend into the world of fessups to gather knowledge, despite her protests.

The tube was marked by growth rings which formed ridges. The ridges were used as steps. The tube was narrow enough for anyone ascending or descending to plant her back securely against the opposite side of the tube.

Rising air whispered in their ears. A cobwebby thing, a living ghost, brushed Vry's cheek. She resisted an impulse to scream.

They climbed down to a point where the second branches left the main trunk. Here the bulb-shaped chamber was even smaller than the one above; they stood close, heads together. Vry could smell Dathka and feel his body against hers. Something stirred in her.

"See the lights?" Dathka said.

There was tension in his voice. She fought with herself, terrified by the lust that flooded her. Should he lay a finger on her, this silent man, she would fall into his arms, would rip away her furs, strip herself naked, fall copulating with him in the dark subterranean bed. Obscenely delightful images filled her.

"I want to go up again," she said, forcing the words from her throat.

"Don't be scared. Look at the lights."

In a daze, she looked about, still catching his scent. She was staring into the second branch down from the surface. There spots of light, starlike—galaxies of red stars, imprisoned in the tree.

He shuffled in front of her, eclipsing constellations with his shoulder. He thrust something pillowlike into her arms. It was light, covered with what she took for coir, as stiff as the hairs of a stungebag. Its star eyes looked unwinkingly up at her. In her confused state she did not identify it.

"What is it?"

For answer—perhaps he felt her desire after all; but could he make no stronger response, if so?—Dathka stroked her face with a clumsy tenderness.

"Oh, Dathka," she sighed. Trembling took her, beginning from the viscera and spreading through her eddre. She could not control herself.

"We'll take it up. Don't be scared."

The black-haired pigs were scuttling among the brassimip leaves as they emerged into daylight. The world seemed blindingly bright, the ring of axes intolerably loud, the scent of jassiklas unduly strong.

Vry sank down and listlessly regarded the small crystalline animal she held. It was in a state like the phagor's tether, curled into a ball with its nose tucked into its tail, its four legs folded neatly into its stomach. It was immobile, and felt as if made of glass. She could not uncurl it. Its eyes fixed her with a remote gaze, unwinking between immobile lids. Through its dusty grey coat, striations of faded colour showed.

In some way, she hated it, as she hated him—so insensitive to a woman's feelings that he had mistaken her trembling for the vibrations of fear. Yet she was grateful that his stupidity had prevented her from certain disgrace, grateful and resentful.

"It's a glossy," Dathka said, squatting by her, looking aslant into her face as if puzzled.

"A gossie?" For a moment she wondered if he was trying to be uncharacteristically funny.

"A *glossy*. They hibernate in the brassimips, where it's warm. Take it home."

"Shay Tal and I have seen them west of the river. Hoxneys. That's what they're called when they emerge from hibernation." And what would Shay Tal have thought if . . .

"Take it," he repeated. "A present from me."

"Thank you," she said, with contempt. She rose, emotions in place again.

She found she had blood on her cheek, where he had stroked her with his cut hand.

The slaves were still hacking away at the monstrous carcass. Laintal Ay had arrived, and was talking to Tanth Ein and Aoz Roon. The latter summoned Dathka vigorously, waving his hand over his head in command. With a resigned look of farewell to Vry, Dathka made off towards the Lord of Embruddock.

The busy things men did were nothing to her. She tucked the glossy between her arm and her shallow bosom and turned downhill towards the distant towers.

When she heard the sound of someone running to catch her up, she said to herself, Well, he's too late now, but it was Laintal Ay.

"I'll walk down with you, Vry," he said. As she remarked, he seemed in a carefree mood.

"I thought you were having trouble with Aoz Roon."

"Oh, he's always a bit touchy after a brush with Shay Tal. He's a great man, really. I'm pleased about the stungebag, too. Now that the weather is warming up, they're harder to find."

The children were still romping by the geysers. Laintal Ay admired her glossy, and burst into a snatch of hunter's song:

> "*The glossies that sleep*
> *When the snowdrifts are deep*
> *Will wake up to eddre-filling rain,*
> *And then hoxneys will spread*
> *With their high-stepping tread*
> *Across the plain, across the flower-thrilling plain.*"

"You are in a good humour! Is Oyre being nice to you?"

"Oyre's always nice."

They went their different ways, Vry heading for her ruined tower, where she showed her present to Shay Tal. Shay Tal examined the little crystalline animal.

"It's not good to eat at this stage of its life. The flesh may be poisonous."

"I don't plan to eat it. I want to guard it till it wakes."

"Life is serious, my dear. We may have to go hungry if Aoz Roon sets himself firmly against us." She contemplated Vry for a while without speaking, as was increasingly her habit. "I shall fast and defy him. I need no material things. I can be as ruthless with myself as he can be with me."

"But really he . . ." Words failed Vry. She could utter no reassurance to the older woman, who continued determinedly.

"As I told you, I have two immediate intentions. First, I shall conduct a scientific experiment to determine my powers. Then I shall descend into the world of the gossies, to hold concourse with Loilanun. She must now know much that I don't. Depending on what I learn from these things, I may decide to leave Oldorando entirely."

"Oh, don't leave, please, ma'am. Are you sure that's the right thing to do? I'll go with you if you go, I swear!"

"We'll see about that. Leave me now, please."

Feeling deflated, Vry climbed the ladder to her ruinous room. She flung herself down on her couch.

"I want a lover, that's what I want. A lover . . . Life's so empty. . . ."

But after a while, she roused herself and looked out of the window at the sky, where clouds and birds sailed. At least it was better to be here than in the world below, where Shay Tal planned to go.

She recalled Laintal Ay's song. The woman who had written the song—if it was a woman—had known that the snow would eventually disappear and that flowers and animals would emerge. Perhaps it would happen.

From her nighttime observations, she knew that there were changes in the sky. The stars were not fessups but fires, fires burning not in rock but air. Imagine a great fire burning in outer darkness. As it came nearer, its warmth would be felt. Perhaps the two sentinels would draw nearer, and warm the world.

Then the glossies would come back to life, turning into hoxneys with high-stepping tread, just as the song had it.

She determined to concentrate on her astronomy. The stars knew more than the gossies, for all that Shay Tal said, though it was shocking to find that one disagreed with such a majestic person.

She tucked the glossy into a warm corner by her couch, wrapping the pathetic little thing in fur so that only its face showed. Day by day, she willed it to come alive. She whispered to it and encouraged it. She longed to see it grow and skip about her room. But after a few days, the gleam in the glossy's eyes dimmed and went out; the creature had expired with never a blink.

Despairingly, Vry took it to the crumbling top of the tower and flung the bundle away. It was still wrapped in furs, as if it were a dead baby.

A passion of restlessness seized Shay Tal. More and more, her statements became preachments. Though the other women brought her food, she preferred to starve herself, preparing to go into deep pauk to confer with the illustrious dead. If wisdom was not found there, then she would look farther afield, beyond the farmyard.

First, she determined to test out her own powers of sorcery. A few miles away to the east lay Fish Lake, scene of her "miracle." While she teased herself as to the true nature of what had happened there, the citizens of Oldorando were in no doubt. Throughout that cold spring, they made pilgrimages to gaze upon the spectacle in the ice, and to tremble with fear not unmixed with pride. The pilgrims encountered numbers of Borlienians who also came to marvel. Once, two phagors were seen, cowbirds perched with folded wings upon their shoulders, standing mute upon the far shore, regarding their crystalline dead.

As warmth returned to the world, the tableau began to slip. What was awesome turned grotesque. One morning, the ice was gone, the statuary became a heap of decomposing flesh. Visitors encountered nothing more impressive than a floating eyeball or a mop of hide. Fish Lake itself drained and disappeared almost as rapidly as it had formed. All that remained to mark the miracle was a pile of bones and curving kaidaw horns. But the memory remained, enlarging through the lenses of reminiscence. And Shay Tal's doubts remained.

She went down into the square in the afternoon, at an hour when milder weather tempted people to walk out and talk in a way once foreign to them. Women and daughters, men and sons, hunters and corpsmen, young and old, strolled forth to pass the time of day. Almost anyone would put himself or herself at Shay Tal's beck and call; almost no one wanted to talk to her.

Laintal Ay and Dathka were standing with their friends, laughing. Laintal Ay caught Shay Tal's glance, and came over to her reluctantly when she beckoned.

"I'm about to conduct an experiment, Laintal Ay. I want you with me as a reliable witness. I won't get you into further trouble with Aoz Roon."

"I'm on good terms with him."

She explained that the experiment was taking place by the Voral; first, she had a mind to explore the old temple. They walked together through the crowd, Laintal Ay saying nothing.

"Are you embarrassed to be with me?"

"I always take pleasure in your company, Shay Tal."

"You need not be polite. Do you think I am a sorceress?"

"You are an unusual woman. I revere you for that."

"Do you love me?"

At that, he was embarrassed. Instead of answering directly, he cast his gaze down to the mud, muttering, "You are like a mother to me, since my mother died. Why ask such questions?"

"I wish I were your mother. Then I could be proud. Laintal Ay, you also have an inwardness to your nature. I feel it. That inwardness will distress you, yet it gives you life, it is life. Don't ignore it, cultivate it. Most of these people jostling us have no inwardness."

"Is inwardness the same as conflict?"

She gave a sharp laugh, gripping her body with her forearms.

"Listen, we are trapped in this wretched hamlet among meagre personalities. A whole series of greater realities can be happening elsewhere. So much must be done. I may leave Oldorando."

"Where will you go?"

She shook her head. "Sometimes I feel that the mere crush of dull people will cause us to explode, and we'll all scatter from here across the world. You note how many babies have been born of recent years."

He looked round at all the friendly familiar faces in the lane, and suspected that she was talking for effect, though there were more children.

He put his shoulder to the door of the old temple and heaved it open. They entered and stood silent. A bird was trapped inside. It flew round and round, darting close to them as if scrutinizing them, then soared upward and escaped through a hole in the roof.

Light filtered down through the gaps, creating shafts through the twilight in which particles of dust whirled. The pigs had recently been moved to outside sties, but their smell still lingered. Shay Tal walked restlessly about, while Laintal Ay stood by the door, looking out into the street, remembering how he used to play here as a child.

The walls had been decorated with paintings executed in a stiff manner. Many had been spoiled. She looked up at the tall alcove above where the sacrificial altar stood, its stone dark still with something that could have been blood. Too high for vandals easily to deface hung a representation of Wutra. Shay Tal stood staring up at it, fists on hips.

Wutra was depicted, head and shoulders, in a furry cloak. His eyes glared down from a long animallike face with an expression which could be interpreted as compassion. His face was blue, representing an ideal colour of sky, where he dwelt. Rough white hair, almost manelike, surmounted the head; but the most startling departure from the human norm was a pair of horns thrusting upwards from his skull and terminating in silver bells.

Behind Wutra crowded other figures of a forgotten mythology, mainly horrendous, teeming through the sky. On his left and right shoulder perched his two sentinels. Batalix was depicted as oxlike, bearded, grey and old, with rays of light streaming from his spear. Freyr was larger, a virile green monkey with an hourglass suspended round his neck. His spear was bigger than that of Batalix, and also radiated rays of light.

She turned away, saying briskly, "Now my experiment, if Goija Hin is ready."

"Did you see what you wanted?" He was puzzled by her abruptness.

"I don't know. Later, I may know. I plan to go into pauk. I would have liked to ask one of the old priests whether Wutra was supposed to preside over the world below as he does over the earth and sky. . . . So many discontinuities."

Meanwhile, Goija Hin was bringing Myk out of the stable under the big tower. Goija Hin was the slave master, a man who exhibited all the stigmata of his calling. He was short but immensely solid, with bulging arms and legs. His features fitted clumsily on his low-browed face, which was adorned with wisps of whisker, randomly sited. His garments were leather and, waking or sleeping, he was accompanied by a leather knout. Everyone knew Goija Hin, a man impervious to blows or thought.

"Come on, Myk, you brute, time to make yourself useful," he said, speaking in his customary low snarl.

Myk ambled forth promptly, having grown up in slavery. He was the phagor longest in servitude in Oldorando, and could remember Goija Hin's predecessor, a man of far more terrible aspect. Black hairs grew in his patchy coat. His face was wrinkled, and the sacks under his eyes were messy with rheum.

He was always docile. On this occasion, Oyre was nearby to soothe him. While Oyre patted his bent shoulders, Goija Hin prodded him with a stick.

Oyre had acted as intermediary for Shay Tal and asked her father for permission to use a phagor in Shay Tal's experiment. Aoz Roon had carelessly told her to take Myk, since he was old.

The two humans led Myk to a curve of the Voral where the river flowed deep. Shay Tal's ruined tower stood not far away. Shay Tal and Laintal Ay were already waiting when the trio arrived. Shay Tal stood peering into the depths of the stream as if trying to decipher its secrets, her cheeks hollow, her expression bleak.

"Well, then, Myk," she said challengingly, as the beast approached. She regarded him calculatingly. Scrawny sacks of flesh hung down from his chest and stomach. Goija Hin had already strapped his hands behind his back. His head rolled apprehensively between his hunched shoulders. When he saw the Voral, he ran his milt anxiously up his nostril slits several times in quick succession, uttering a low cry of fear. Could it be that water would turn him into a statue?

Goija Hin gave Shay Tal a rough salute.

"Tie his legs together," Shay Tal ordered.

"Don't hurt him too much," Oyre said. "I've known Myk since I was a small girl and he's entirely docile. He used to give us rides, didn't he, Laintal Ay?"

Thus appealed to, Laintal Ay came forward. "Shay Tal won't hurt him," he said, smiling at Oyre. She regarded him questioningly.

Attracted by possible excitement, several women and boys came up to see what was going on, and stood in knots on the bank.

The river ran deep in the curve, cutting into the near bank only a few inches below the ground on which they stood. On the opposite side of the river, where it was shallower, a thin shelf of ice remained, preserved from direct sun by an overhang. This wafer jutted out towards deeper water, elaborately marked in glassy whorls, as if the water itself had taken a knife to carve it.

When Goija Hin had bound the legs of the unfortunate Myk, he pushed him to the edge of the river. Myk stuck his long head in the air, curled back his lower lips onto his stubbly chin, and let out a trumpet of fear.

Oyre clutched at his coat, begging Shay Tal not to harm him.

"Stand back," Shay Tal said. She gave the signal to Goija Hin to push the phagor in.

Goija Hin set his thick shoulders to Myk's ribs. The phagor tottered then plunged into the river with a splash. Shay Tal raised her arms in imperious gesture.

The watching women gave a shout and rushed forward. Rol Sakil was among them. Shay Tal motioned them back.

She stared down into the water and could see Myk struggling below the surface. Swathes of his coat came roiling upward with the disturbed water, brushing the surface like yellow weed.

The water remained water. The phagor remained alive.

"Pull him up," she ordered.

Goija Hin had Myk by two straps. He tugged and Laintal Ay helped. The old phagor's head and shoulders broke the surface and Myk gave a pathetic cry.

"Don't killydrown poor me!"

They dragged him ashore and he lay panting at Shay Tal's feet. She chewed her underlip, frowning at the Voral. The magic was not working.

"Throw him in again," one of the onlookers called.

"No more water or I finish," Myk said, thickly.

"Push him in again," Shay Tal ordered.

Myk went in a second time, and a third. But the water remained water. No miracle happened, and Shay Tal had to conceal her disappointment.

"That's enough," she said. "Goija Hin, take Myk away and feed him extra."

Oyre knelt compassionately by Myk's throat, crying and patting him. Dark water flowed from the phagor's lips and he began coughing. Laintal Ay knelt and put his arm round Oyre's shoulder.

Disdainfully, Shay Tal turned away. The experiment showed that phagors plus water did not make ice. The process was not inevitable. So what had happened at Fish Lake? Equally, she had not managed to turn the Voral to ice, as she had wished to do. So the experiment did not prove she was a sorceress. It did not prove she was not a sorceress; it seemed to prove that she had turned the phagors at Fish Lake to ice—unless there were other factors involved she had not considered.

She paused with her hand on the rough stone of the doorway to her tower, feeling the rasp of lichen against her palm. Until she found another explanation, she would have to treat herself as others treated her, as a sorceress. The more she starved, the more she respected herself. Of course, as a sorceress, she was destined to remain a virgin; sexual intercourse would destroy her magical powers. She gathered her furs against her lanky form and climbed the worn stairs.

The women on the bank looked from Myk's half-drowned body, surrounded by a growing puddle, to Shay Tal's retreating figure.

"Now what did she want to go and do that for?" old Rol Sakil asked the company. "How come she didn't drown the stupid thing properly while she was about it?"

The next time the council met, Laintal Ay rose and addressed them. He said that he had heard Shay Tal lecture. All knew of her miracle at Fish Lake, which had saved many lives. Nothing she did was directed to the ill of the community. He proposed that her academy should be recognised and supported.

Aoz Roon looked furious while Laintal Ay spoke. Dathka sat rigid in silence. The old men of the council peered at each other under their eyebrows and muttered uneasily. Eline Tal laughed.

"What do you wish us to do to aid this academy?" Aoz Roon asked.

"The temple is empty. Give it to Shay Tal. Let her hold meetings there every afternoon at promenade time. Use it as a forum, where anyone can speak. The cold has gone, people are freer. Open the temple as an academy for all, for men, women, and children."

His resounding words died into silence. Then Aoz Roon spoke.

"She cannot use the temple. We don't want a new lot of priests. We keep pigs in the temple."

"The temple is empty."

"From now on, pigs are kept in the temple."

"It's a bad day when we put pigs above the community."

The meeting eventually broke up in some disorder, as Aoz Roon marched out. Laintal Ay turned to Dathka, his cheeks flushed.

"Why didn't you support me?"

Dathka grinned sheepishly, tugged his narrow beard, stared down at the table. "You could not win if all Oldorando supported you. He has already banned the academy. You waste your breath, my friend."

As Laintal Ay was leaving the building, feeling disgusted with the world, Datnil Skar, master of the tawyers and tanners corps, called to him and grasped his sleeve.

"You spoke well, young Laintal Ay, yet Aoz Roon was right in what he said. Or, if not right, not unreasonable. If Shay Tal spoke in the temple, she would become a priestess and be worshipped. We don't want that—our ancestors got rid of the priests some generations ago."

Laintal Ay knew Master Datnil for a kindly and modest man. Restraining his anger, he looked down at the worn face and asked, "Why tell me this?"

Master Datnil looked about to see that no one was listening.

"Worship arises from ignorance. Believing in one fixed thing is a mark of ignorance. I respect attempts to drum facts into people's heads. I wanted to say that I am sorry you were defeated, though I don't agree with your proposition. I would be willing to address Shay Tal's academy if she will have me."

He removed his fur hat and set it on the lichenous sill. He smoothed his sparse grey hair and cleared his dry throat. He looked about him and smiled nervously. Although he had known everyone in the room since he was born, he was unaccustomed to the role of speaker. His stiff clothes creaked as he shifted from one foot to another.

"Don't be afraid of us, Master Datnil," Shay Tal said.

He caught the note of impatience in her voice. "It's only of your intolerance I'm afraid, ma'am," he replied, and some of the women squatting on the floor hid smiles behind their hands.

"You know what we do in our corps, because some of you work for me," Datnil Skar said. "Membership in the corps is for men only, of course, for the secrets of our profession are handed down from generation to generation. In particular, a master teaches all he knows to his personal novice or chief boy. When a master dies or retires, then the chief boy becomes master in his turn, as Raynil Layan will soon take over my position. . . ."

"A woman could do that just as well as any man," said one of the women, Cheme Phar. "I've worked for you long enough, Datnil Skar.

I know all the secrets of the brine pits. I could pickle myself, if need arose."

"Ah, but we have to have order and continuity, Cheme Phar," said the Master mildly.

"I could give the orders all right," said Cheme Phar, and everyone laughed, then looked at Shay Tal.

"Tell us about the continuity," the latter said. "We know, as Loila-nun taught us, that some of us are descended from Yuli the Priest, who came from the north, from Pannoval and Lake Dorzin. That's one continuity. What about continuity within the corps, Master Datnil?"

"All members of our corps were born and bred in Embruddock, even before it was Oldorando. To many generations."

"How many generations?"

"Ah, a good many . . ."

"Tell us how you know this."

He wiped his hands on his trousers.

"We have a record. Each master keeps a record."

"In writing?"

"That's correct. Writing in a book. The art is passed on. But the records are not to be disclosed to others."

"Why do you think that is?"

"They don't want the women taking over their jobs and doing it better," someone called, and again there was laughter. Datnil Skar smiled with embarrassment, and said no more.

"I believe that secrecy served a protective purpose at one time," Shay Tal said. "Certain arts, like metal forging and tannery, had to be kept alive in bad times, despite starvation or phagor raids. Probably there were very bad times in the past, and some arts were lost. We cannot make paper any longer. Perhaps there was once a paper-makers corps. Glass. We cannot make glass. Yet there are pieces of glass about —you all know what glass is. How is it that we are more stupid than our ancestors? Are we living, working, under some disadvantage we don't fully understand? That's one of the big questions we must keep in mind."

She paused. No one said anything, which always vexed her. She longed for any comment that would push the argument forward.

Datnil Skar said, "Mother Shay, you speak true, to the best of my belief. You understand that as master I am under oath to disclose secrets of my art to nobody; it's an oath I take to Wutra and to Embruddock. But I know that there were once bad times, of which I am not supposed to speak. . . ."

When he fell silent, she helped him with a smile. "Do you believe that Oldorando was once bigger than it is now?"

He looked at her with his head on one side. "I know you call this town a farmyard. But it survives. . . . It's the centre of the cosmos.

Well, that's not answering your question. My friends, you found rye and oats growing north of here, so let's speak of them. To the best of my belief, that place was once carefully tended fields, enclosed against wild beasts. The fields belonged to Embruddock. Many other cereals grew there and were cultivated. Now you cultivate them again, which is wise.

"You know we need bark for our tanning. We have a job to get hold of it. I do believe—well, I know . . ." He fell silent, then he said quietly, "Great forests of tall trees, which yield bark and wood, grew to the west and north. The region was called Kace. It was hot then, and there was no cold."

Someone said, "The time of heat—that's a legend left over from the priesthood. The sort of tale we're supposed to get out of our minds in the academy. We do know that it was once *colder* than it is now. Ask my grandma."

"What I'm saying is that, to the best of my belief, it was hot before it was cold," Datnil Skar said, slowly scratching the back of his grey head. "You should try to understand these things. Many lives go by, many years. There's a lot of history vanished. I know you women think that men are against you learning, and it may be so; but I speak sincerely when I say that you should support Shay Tal, despite various difficulties. As a master, I know how precious knowledge is. It seems to run out of the bottom of a community like water out of a sock."

They stood and clapped him politely when he left.

At Freyr-set, two days later, Shay Tal was pacing restlessly in her room in the isolated tower. A shout came from below. Immediately she thought of Aoz Roon, though the voice was not his.

She wondered who would venture beyond the barricades when light was growing dim. Putting her head out of the window, she saw Datnil Skar, his figure insubstantial in the dusk.

"Oh, come up, my friend," she cried. She went down to meet him. He appeared clutching a box, smiling nervously. They sat down facing each other on her stone floor, and she poured him a measure of rathel.

After some idle conversation, he said, "I think you know that I am due to retire soon as master of the tawyers and tanners corps? My chief boy will take my place. I'm getting old and he long ago knew all I have to teach."

"You come here because of that?"

He smiled and shook his head. "I come here, Mother Shay, because I—I experience an old man's admiration for you, for your person and your worth. . . . No, let me say it. I have always served and loved this community, and I believe you do the same, though you have the opposition of many men. So I wanted to do you a good turn while I was able to."

"You're a good man, Datnil Skar. Oldorando knows it. The community needs good people."

Sighing, he nodded. "I have served Embruddock—or Oldorando as we should call it—every day of my life, and have never left it. Yet scarcely a day's gone by . . ." He broke off in his shy way, smiled, and said, "I believe I am speaking to a kindred spirit when I say that scarcely a day has gone by since I was a lad when I haven't wondered . . . wondered what was happening in other places, far away from here."

He paused, cleared his throat, then said more briskly, "I'll tell you a tale. It's only brief. I remember one terrible winter when I was a lad when the phagors attacked, and disease and famine followed. Many people died. And the phagors were dying too, although we didn't know it at the time. It was so dark, I swear days are brighter now. . . . Anyhow, the phagors left behind a human boy during the slaughter. His name was—I'm ashamed to say I've forgotten it, but to the best of my belief it was something like Krindlesheddy. A long name. Once I knew it clearly. The years have made me forget.

"Krindlesheddy had come from a country a long way to the north, Sibornal. He said that Sibornal was a land of perpetual glaciers. I was selected to be chief boy in my corps, and in Sibornal he was to be a priest, so we were both dedicated to our calling. He—Krindlesheddy or whatever his name was—thought our life was easy. The geysers kept Oldorando warm.

"As a young member of the priesthood, my friend had belonged with some colonists who moved south to escape the cold. They came to a better land by a river. There they had to fight with the local inhabitants of a realm called—well, the name has gone after these many years. A great battle raged, in which Krindlesheddy—if that was his name—was injured. The survivors fled, only to be caught by raiding phagors. It was mere fortune that he escaped them here. Or perhaps they left him because he was wounded.

"We did what we could to help the lad, but he died after a month. I cried for him. I was only young. Yet even then I envied him because he'd seen something of the world. He told me that in Sibornal the ice came in many colours and was beautiful."

As Master Datnil finished his story, sitting meekly beside Shay Tal, Vry entered the room, on her way to the floor above.

He smiled kindly at her, saying to Shay Tal, "Don't send Vry away. I know she's your chief boy and you trust her, as I wish I could trust my chief boy. Let her hear what I have to say." He laid his wooden box on the floor in front of him. "I have brought the Master Book of our corps for you to see."

Shay Tal looked as if she would faint. She knew that if this borrowing was discovered, the makers corps would kill the master without hesitation. . . . She could guess at the inner struggle the old man had gone through before bringing it. She wrapped her thin arms about him and kissed him on his wrinkled forehead.

Vry came and knelt down by him, excitement on her face.

"Let's have a look!" she exclaimed, reaching out a hand, forgetting her diffidence.

He put his hand over hers, detainingly.

"Notice first the wood of which the box is made. It's not from a rajabaral; the grain is too beautiful. Notice how it's carved. Notice the delicate metal chasing that binds the corners. Could our metal-makers corps do such fine work today?"

When they had examined the details, he opened the box. He brought out a large tome bound in heavy leather, tooled with an elaborate design.

"This I did myself, Mother. I rebound the book. It's the inside that's old."

The pages inside were carefully, often elaborately, written by a number of different hands. Datnil Skar turned the pages rapidly, even now reluctant to reveal too much. But the women clearly saw dates, names, lists, and various entries and figures.

He looked up into their faces, smiling a grave smile. "In its way, this volume gives a history of Embruddock over the years. And each surviving corps has a similar volume, of that I am certain."

"The past is gone. We're trying now to look outward to the future," said Vry. "We don't want to be stuck in the past. We want to go out . . ."

Indecisively, she let the sentence die, regretting that in her excitement she had brought herself to their attention. Looking at the faces of the other two, she saw they were older and would never agree with her. Although their aims were in general agreement, a difference existed that could never be bridged.

"The clue to the future lies in the past," Shay Tal said, comfortingly but dismissively, for she had made such remarks to Vry before. Turning to the old man, she said, "Master Datnil, we greatly appreciate your brave gesture in letting us look at the secret book. Perhaps some day we may examine it more thoroughly. Would you tell us how many masters there have been in your corps since records commenced?"

He closed the book and began packing it in its box. Saliva trickled from his old mouth, and his hands shook badly.

"The rats know the secrets of Oldorando . . . I'm in danger, bringing this book here. Just an old fool . . . Listen, my dears, there was a great king who ruled over all Campannlat in the old days, called King Denniss. He foresaw that the world—this world which the ancipitals call Hrrm-Bhhrd Ydohk—would lose its warmth, as a bucket slops water when you carry it down a lane. So he set about founding our corps, with iron rules to be enforced. All the makers corps were to preserve wisdom through dark times, until warmth returned."

He spoke chantingly, as from memory.

"Our corps has survived since the good king's time, though in some periods it had no wherewithal to tan leather. According to the record here, its numbers once sank to a master and an apprentice, who lived below ground a distance away. . . . Dreadful times. But we survived."

As he was wiping his mouth, Shay Tal asked what period of time they were discussing.

Datnil Skar gazed at the darkening rectangle of window as if contemplating flight from the question.

"I don't understand all the notations in our book. You know our confusions with the calendar. As we can understand from our own day, new calendars represent considerable dislocations. . . . Embruddock—forgive me, I fear telling you too much—it didn't always belong to . . . our sort of people."

He shook his head, darting his gaze nervously round the room. The women waited, motionless as phagors in the old dull room. He spoke again.

"Many people have died. There was a great plague, the Fat Death. Invasions . . . the Seven Blindnesses . . . tales of woe. We hope our present Lord—" again a glance round the room—"will prove as wise as King Denniss. The good king founded our corps in a year called 249 Before Nadir. We do not know who Nadir was. What we do know is that I—allowing for a break in the record—am the sixty-eighth master of the tanners and tawyers corps. The sixty-eighth . . ." He peered shortsightedly at Shay Tal.

"Sixty-eight . . ." Trying to hide her dismayed astonishment, she gathered her furs about her with a characteristic gesture. "That's many generations, stretching back to antiquity."

"Yes, yes, stretching right back." Master Datnil nodded complacently, as if personally acquainted with vast stretches of time. "It's nearly seven centuries since our corps was founded. Seven centuries, and still it freezes of nights."

Embruddock in its surrounding wilderness was a beached ship. It still gave the crew shelter, though it would never sail again.

So greatly had time dismantled a once proud city that its inhabitants did not realise that what they regarded as a town was nothing more than the remains of a palace, which had stood in the middle of a civilisation obliterated by climate, madness, and the ages.

As the weather improved, the hunters were forced to go in increasingly long expeditions in search of game. The slaves planted fields and dreamed of impossible liberty. The women stayed at home and grew neurotic.

While Shay Tal fasted and became more solitary, Vry became full of a repressed energy and developed her friendship with Oyre. With Oyre, she talked over all that Master Datnil had said, and found a sympathetic listener. They agreed that there were puzzling riddles in history, yet Oyre was lightly sceptical.

"Datnil Skar is old and a bit gaga—Father always says so," she said, and limped round the room in parody of the Master's gait, exclaiming in a piping voice, " 'Our corps is so exclusive we didn't even let King Denniss join. . . .' "

When Vry laughed, Oyre said, more seriously, "Master Datnil could be executed for showing his corps Master Book about—that's proof he's gaga."

"And even then he wouldn't let us look at it properly." Vry was silent, and then burst out, "If only we could put all the facts together. Shay Tal just collects them, writes them down. There must be a way of making a—a structure from them. So much has been lost—Master Datnil is right there. The cold was so bitter, once on a time, that almost everything inflammable was burnt—wood, paper, all records. You realise *we don't even know what year it is?*—Though the stars might tell us. Loil Bry's calendar is stupid, calendars should be based on years, not people. People are so fallible . . . and so am I. Oh, I'll go mad, I swear!"

Oyre burst out laughing and hugged Vry.

"You're the sanest person I know, you idiot." They fell to discussing the stars again, sitting on the bare floor close together. Oyre had been with Laintal Ay to look at the fresco in the old temple. "The sentinels are clearly depicted, with Batalix above Freyr as usual, but almost touching, above Wutra's head."

"Every year, the two suns get closer," Vry said, decisively. "Last month, they virtually touched as Batalix overtook Freyr, and no one paid any notice. Next year, they will collide. What then? . . . Or maybe one passes behind the other."

"Perhaps that's what Master Datnil meant by a Blindness? It would suddenly be dimday, wouldn't it, if one sentinel disappeared? Perhaps there will be Seven Blindnesses, as once before." She looked frightened, and moved nearer her friend. "It will be the end of the world. Wutra will appear, looking furious, of course."

Vry laughed and jumped to her feet. "The world didn't end last time and won't do so this time. No, perhaps it will mark a new beginning." Her face became radiant. "That's why the seasons are growing warmer. Once Shay Tal has done her ghastly pauk, we will tackle the question anew. I shall work at my mathematics. Let the Blindnesses come—I embrace them!"

They danced round the room, laughing wildly.

"How I long for some great experience!" Vry cried.

Shay Tal, meanwhile, showed more clearly than before the little bird bones below her flesh, and her dark skins hung more loosely about her body. Food was brought her by the women, but she would not eat.

"Fasting suits my ravenous soul," she said, pacing about her chilly room, when Vry and Oyre remonstrated with her, and Amin Lim stood meekly by. "Tomorrow I will go into pauk. You three and Rol Sakil can be with me. I will dredge up ancient knowledge from the well of the past. Through the fessups I will reach to that generation which built our towers and corridors. I will descend centuries if necessary, and confront King Denniss himself."

"How wonderful!" Amin Lim exclaimed.

Birds came to perch on her crumbling window sill and be fed the bread Shay Tal would not touch.

"Don't sink into the past, ma'am," Vry counselled her. "That's the way of old men. Look ahead, look outward. There's no profit in interrogating the dead."

So unused to argument had Shay Tal grown that she had difficulty in refraining from scolding her chief disciple. She looked and saw, almost with startlement, that the diffident young thing was now a woman. Her face was pallid, with shadows under her eyes, and Oyre's the same.

"Why are you two so pale? Are you ill?"

Vry shook her head.

"Tonight there's an hour of darkness before dimday. I'll show you then what Oyre and I are doing. While the rest of the world was sleeping, we have been working."

The evening was clear at Freyr-set. Warmth departed from the world as the younger women escorted Shay Tal up to the roof of the ruinous tower. A lens of ghost light stretched upwards from the horizon where Freyr had set, reaching halfway to zenith. There was little cloud to conceal the heavens; as their eyes became accustomed to the darkness, the stars overhead flashed out in brilliance. In some quarters of the sky, the stars were relatively sparse, in others they hung in clusters. Overhead, trailing from one horizon to the other, was a broad, irregular band of light, where the stars were as thick as mist, and there occasional brilliances burned.

"It's the most magnificent sight in the world," Oyre said. "Don't you think so, ma'am?"

Shay Tal said, "In the world below hang fessups like stars. They are the souls of the dead. Here you see the souls of the unborn. As above, so below."

"I think we have to look to an entirely different principle to explain the sky," Vry said firmly. "All motions here are regular. The stars advance about that bright star there, which we call the polar star." She pointed to a star high above their heads. "In the twenty-five hours of the day, the stars rotate once, rising in the east and setting in the west like the two sentinels. Doesn't that prove they are similar to the two sentinels, only much farther from us?"

The young women showed Shay Tal the star map they were making, with the relative positions of stars marked on a vellum sheet. She evinced little interest, and said, "The stars cannot affect us as the gossies do. How does this hobby of yours advance knowledge? You'd do better to sleep at night."

Vry sighed. "The sky is alive. It's not a tomb, like the world below. Oyre and I have stood here and seen comets flaring, landing on the earth. And there are four bright stars that move differently from all the others, the wanderers, of which the old songs sing. Those wanderers sometimes double back in their passage across the sky. And one comes over very fast. We'll see it presently. We think it's close to us, and we call it Kaidaw, because of its speed."

Shay Tal rubbed her hands together, looking apprehensively about. "Well, it's cold up here."

"It's colder still down below, where the gossies lie," Oyre retorted.

"You keep a watch on your tongue, young woman. You're no friend of the academy if you distract Vry from her proper work."

Her face became cold and hawklike; she turned away quickly, as if to shield Oyre and Vry from its sight, and climbed back downstairs without further words.

"Oh, I shall pay for this," Vry said. "I shall have to be extra humble to make up for this."

"You're too humble, Vry, and she's too haughty. Scumb her academy. She's scared of the sky, like most people. That's her trouble, sorceress or no sorceress. She puts up with stupid people like Amin Lim because they pander to her haughtiness."

She clutched Vry with a sort of angry passion and began to list the stupidities of everyone she knew.

"What upsets me is that we did not get the chance to make her look through our telescope," Vry said.

It was the telescope that had made the greatest difference to Vry's astronomical interest. When Aoz Roon had become lord, and had gone to live in the big tower, Oyre had been free to grub through all kinds of decaying possessions stored there in trunks. The telescope had come to light tucked among moth-riddled clothes which fell to pieces at the touch. It was simply made—perhaps by the long-defunct glass-makers corps—being no more than a leather tube which held two lenses in place; but when turned upon the wandering stars, the telescope had the power to change Vry's perceptions. For the wanderers showed distinct discs. In that, they resembled the sentinels, though they did not emit light.

From this discovery, Vry and Oyre had concluded that the wanderers were near to the earth, and the stars far away—some very far. From trappers who worked by starlight they had the names of the wanderers: Ipocrene, Aganip, and Copaise. And there was the fast one they had named themselves, Kaidaw. Now they sought to prove that these were worlds like their own, possibly even with people in them.

Gazing at her friend, Vry saw only the general outlines of that beautiful face and powerful head, and recognised how much Oyre resembled Aoz Roon. Both Oyre and her father seemed so full of spirit— and Oyre had been born outside agreements. Vry wondered if by chance—by any remote chance—Oyre had been with a man, in the dark of a brassimip or elsewhere. Then she shut the naughty thought away and turned her gaze to the sky.

They stayed rather soberly on the top of their tower until Hour-Whistler sounded again. A few minutes later Kaidaw rose and sailed up to the zenith.

Earth Observation Station Avernus—Vry's Kaidaw—hung high over Helliconia, while the continent of Campannlat turned beneath it. The station's crew devoted most of their attention to the world below; but the other three planets of the binary system were also under constant surveillance by automatic instrumentation.

On all four planets, temperatures were rising. Improvement overall was steady; only on the ground did anomalies register on tender flesh.

Helliconia's drama of generations in travail was set upon a stage sparsely structured by a few overriding circumstances. The planet's year about Batalix—Star B to the scholars of the Avernus—took 480 days (the "small" year). But Helliconia also had a Great Year, of which the people of Embruddock knew nothing in their present state. The Great Year was the time Star B, and its planets with it, took to make an orbit round Freyr, the Star A of the scholars.

That Great Year took 1825 Helliconian "small" years. Since one Helliconian small year was the equivalent of 1.42 terrestrial years, this meant a Great Year of 2592 terrestrial years—a period during which many generations flourished and departed from the scene.

The Great Year represented an enormous elliptical journey. Helliconia was slightly larger than Earth, with a mass 1.28 times Earth's; in many respects, it was Earth's sister planet. Yet on that elliptical journey across thousands of years, it became almost two planets—a frozen one at apastron, when farthest from Freyr, an overheated one at periastron, when nearest Freyr.

Every small year, Helliconia drew nearer to Freyr. Spring was about to signify its arrival in spectacular fashion.

Midway between the high stars in their courses and the fessups sinking slowly towards the original boulder, two women squatted one on either side of a bracken bed. The light in the shuttered room was dim enough to render them anonymous, giving them the aspect of two mourning figures set on either side of the prostrate figure on the couch. It could be determined only that one was plump and no longer youthful, and the other gripped by the desiccating processes of age.

Rol Sakil Den shook her grizzled head and looked down with lugubrious compassion on the figure before her.

"Poor dear thing, she used to be so nice as a girl, she's no right to torture herself as she does."

"She should have kept to her loaves, I say," said the other woman, to make herself agreeable.

"Feel how thin she is. Feel her loins. No wonder she's gone weird."

Rol Sakil was herself as thin as a mummy, her frame eroded by arthritis. She had been midwife to the community before growing too old for such exertions. She still tended those in pauk. Now that Dol was off her hands, she hung on the fringes of the academy, always ready to criticise, rarely prepared to think.

"She's got so narrow she couldn't bring forth a stick from that womb of hers, never mind a baby. Wombs have to be tended—they are the central part of a woman."

"She has much to look to beside babies," said Amin Lim.

"Oh, I've as much respect for knowledge as the next person, but when knowledge gets in the way of the natural facilities of copulation, then knowledge should move over."

"As for that," Amin Lim said with some asperity, from the other side of the bed, "her natural facilities were set aback when your Dol settled herself in Aoz Roon's bed. She feels deeply for him, as who doesn't? A presentable man, Aoz Roon, besides being Lord of Embruddock."

Rol Sakil sniffed. "That's no reason why she should go off intercourse entirely. She could always fill in time elsewhere, to keep herself in training. Besides, *he* won't come round knocking at *her* door again, you mark my words. He's got his hands full with our Dol."

The old woman beckoned Amin Lim nearer to bestow a confidence and they put their heads together over the supine body of Shay Tal. "Dol always keeps him at it—both by inclination and policy. A course I'd recommend to any woman, you included, Amin Lim. I hazard you enjoy a length now and again—it ain't human not to, at your age. You ask your man."

"Oh, I daresay there isn't a woman as hasn't fancied Aoz Roon, for all his tempers."

Shay Tal sighed in her pauk. Rol Sakil took her hand in her own withered one and said, still using a confidential mode, "My Dol tells me as he mutters terribly in his sleep. I tell her that's the sign of a guilty conscience."

"What's he got to be guilty about, then?" Amin Lim asked.

"Now, then—there I could tell you a tale. . . . That morning, after all the drinking and carrying on, I was about early, as of old. And as I went out, well wrapped against the cold of morning, I come on a body in the dark and I says to myself, 'Why here's some fool drunk out of his wits, lying asleep on the ground.' There he was, at the base of the big tower."

She paused to observe the effect of her story on Amin Lim, who, having nothing else to do, was listening intently. Rol Sakil's little eyes became almost hidden in wrinkles as she continued.

"I'd never have thought a mite more of it—I likes a drop of pig's counsel myself. But round the other side of the tower, what do I find but another body lying there. 'That's two fools drunk out of their wits, lying asleep on the ground,' says I to myself. And I'd never have thought a mite more of it, but when it's given out that young Klils and his brother Nahkri were found dead together, lying at the bottom of their tower, why, that's another matter. . . ." She sniffed.

"Everyone said that's where they were found."

"Ah, but I found them first, and they weren't together. So they didn't fight together, did they? That's fishy, Amin Lim, isn't it? So I says to myself, 'Someone went and pushed them two brothers off the top of the tower.' Who might it be, who stood most to gain by their deaths? Well, girl, that's something I leave to others to judge. All I says is, I says to our Dol, 'You cultivate your fear of heights, Dol. Don't you go near no edges of towers while you're with Aoz Roon,' I says. 'Don't you go near no edges of towers and you'll be all right. . . .' That's what I says."

Amin Lim shook her head. "Shay Tal wouldn't love Aoz Roon if he did that kind of thing. And she'd know. She's wise, she'd know for sure."

Rol Sakil rose and hobbled nervously about the stone room, shaking her head in doubt. "Where men's concerned, Shay Tal is the same as the rest of us. She doesn't always think with her harneys—sometimes she uses the thing between her legs instead."

"Oh, hush with you." Amin Lim looked sorrowfully down at her friend and mentor. Privately, she wished that Shay Tal's life were ruled more in the way Rol Sakil indicated: she might then be happier.

Shay Tal lay stretched out stiffly on her left side, in the pauk attitude. Her eyes seemed barely closed. Her breathing was scarcely audible, punctuated by long-drawn-out sighs. Looking at the austere contours of that loved face, Amin Lim thought she was watching someone facing death with composure. Only the mouth, growing tighter occasionally, indicated the terror it was impossible to suppress in the presence of the denizens of the world below.

Although Amin Lim had once gone into pauk herself, under guidance, the fright of seeing her father again had been enough for her. The extra dimension was now closed; she would never again visit that world until her final call came.

"Poor thing, poor little thing," she said as she stroked her friend's head, lovingly regarding its grey hairs, hoping to ease her passage through the black realm lying below life.

Though the soul had no eyes, yet it could see in a medium where terror replaced vision.

It looked down, as it began to fall, into a space more enormous than the night sky. Into that space, Wutra could never come. This was a region of which Wutra the Undying had no cognisance. With his blue face, his undaunted gaze, his slender horns, he belonged to the great frosty battle taking place elsewhere. This region was hell because he was not. Every star that gleamed was a death.

There was no smell except terror. Every death had its immutable position. No comets flared down here; this was the realm of entropy absolute, without change, the event death of the universe, to which life could respond only with terror.

As the soul did now.

The land-octaves wound over real territory. They could be likened to paths, except that they more resembled winding walls, endlessly dividing the world, only their tops showing above the surfaces. Their real substance went down deep into the seamless ground, penetrating to the original boulder on which the disc of the world rested.

In the original boulder, at the bottom of their appropriate land-octaves, the gossies and fessups were stacked, like thousands of ill-preserved flies.

The gaunt soul of Shay Tal sank down on its predestined land-octave, negotiating a course between the fessups. They resembled mummies; their stomachs and eye sockets were hollow, their boney feet dangled; their skins were coarse as old sacking, yet transparent, allowing a glimpse of luminescent organs beneath. Their mouths were open like fish, as if they still recalled the days when they breathed air. Less ancient gossies had their mouths stuffed with things like fireflies which issued forth in smokey dust. All these old put-away things were without motion, yet the wandering soul could sense their fury—a fury more intense than any of them could have experienced before obsidian claimed them.

As the soul settled between their ranks, it saw them suspended in irregular rows which stretched to places she could not travel, to Borlien, to the seas, to Pannoval, to far Sibornal, and even to the icy wildernesses of the east. All were relegated here to being units of one great collection, filed under their appropriate land-octaves.

To living senses, there were no directions. Yet there was a direction. The soul had its own sail. It had to be alert. A fessup had little more volition than dust, yet fury pent in its eddre gave it strength. A fessup could swallow any soul sailing too close, thus freeing itself to walk upon the earth again, causing terror and disease wherever it went.

Well aware of danger, the soul sank through the obsidian world, through what Loilanun had called scratched emptiness. It arrived finally before the gossie of Shay Tal's mother. The drab thing appeared made of wires and twigs, which formed patterns like dried halters of breasts and thrusting hipbones. It glared at its daughter-soul. It showed its old brown teeth in its slack lower jaw. It was itself a brown stain. Yet all its details could be viewed, as a pattern of lichen on a wall can perfectly depict a man or a necropolis.

The gossie emitted a noise of unceasing complaint. Gossies are negatives of human lives and believe nothing good of life in consequence. No gossie considers that its life on earth was long enough, or that its tenure there achieved the happiness it deserved. Nor can it believe that it has earned such oblivion. It craves living souls. Only living souls can give ear to its endless grievances.

"Mother, I come dutifully before you again and will listen to your complaints."

"You faithless child, when did you last come, how long, and reluctant, oh, always reluctant, evermore reluctant, as in those thankless days—I should have known, I should have known—when I bore you not wishing another offspring squeezed from my poor sore loins—"

"I will listen to your complaints—"

"Pah, yes, reluctantly, just as your father cared nothing, nothing for my pain, knew nothing, did nothing, just like all men but who's to say children are any better sucking your life from you—oh, I should have known—I tell you I despised that clod of a man always demanding, demanding everything, more than I had to give, never never satisfied, the nights of grief, the days, caught in that trap, that's what it was, and you come here, a trap designed to swindle me out of my youth, pretty, yes, yes, I was pretty, that damned disease—I see you laughing at me now, little you care—"

"I care, I care, Mother, it's agony to behold you!"

"Yes, but you and he you cheated me out of it, out of all I had and all I hoped for, he with his lust, the filthy pig, if men only knew the hatreds they stir when they overpower us, override us in the dim unendurable dark, and you with that piddling feebleness, that ever sucking mouth forever with that mouth like his prod demanding too much, too much by far in patience and your scumble ever needing wiping, witless, wailing, wanting something all the while, the days, the years, those years, draining my strength, ah my strength, my sweet strength and I once so lovely, all stolen, no pleasure left for life, I should have known, no life my mother promised me at her breast and then she too no better than the rest dying damn her dying curse the stinking milkless bitch that bore me dying when I needed her. . . ."

The little thing's voice scratched against the pane of obsidian, trying to get at the soul.

"I do sorrow for you, Mother. I am now going to ask you a question to help take your mind off your sorrows. I will ask you to pass that question on to your mother, and to her mother and her mother's mother, and so down to remote depths. You must find me an answer to the question, and then I shall be so proud of you. I wish to discover if Wutra really exists. Does Wutra exist, and who or what is he? You must send the question back and back until some far fessup returns an answer. The answer must be full. I wish to understand how the world works. The answer must come back to me. Do you understand?"

A reply was screamed at her before she had finished speaking.

"Why should I do anything for you after the way you spoilt my life and why and why and why and what care I down here for any of your stupid problems you mean little piddling fool, it lasts for ever being down here, you hear, for ever and my sorrow too—"

The soul broke into the monologue.

"You have heard my demand, Mother. If you do not carry it out to the letter, I shall never visit you again in the world below. No one will address you ever again."

The gossie made a quick gulp at the soul. The soul remained just out of harm's reach, watching dusty sparks issue from the unbreathing mouth.

Without another word, the gossie began to pass on Shay Tal's question, and the fessups below snapped in fury at it.

All hung suspended in obsidian.

The soul was aware of other fessups nearby, hanging like shabby jackets on pegs in a midnight hall. Loilanun was there, and Loil Bry, and Little Yuli. Even Great Yuli was hanging here somewhere, reduced to a furious shade. The soul's father's gossie was nearby, more feared even than its mother's gossie, its wrath surging at her like a tide.

And the voice of the father's gossie was like the scratching of the nails of a hand on a windowpane.

". . . and another thing, ungrateful girl, why weren't you a boy, you wretched failure you knew I needed a boy wanted a boy a good son to carry on the miserable suffering of our line, so I'm regarded as a laughingstock by all my friends not that I thought aught of that gang of miserable cowards, ran from danger they did, ran when the wolves howled and I ran with them not knowing if I could have my time again —my time again oh yes my damned time again—and the wind blowing fresh in the lungs and every joint on the move down the trail where the deer flickered free with their white scuts bobbing—oh, the time again— and no involvements with that sexless breastless hag you call your mother here in the clutches of this unbreathing stone I hate her hate her hate you too you prattling scumble you'll be here one day soon yourself yes here for ever in the tomb you'll see. . . ."

And there were other messages from other dried mouths, tail ends of grunts, sticking into her fabric like old animal bones protruding from soil, verdigrised over with earth, age, eddre, envy, and poisonous to the touch.

The soul of Shay Tal waited amid the venoms, sail aquiver, waited for her answer. And eventually a message travelled up from dry insensate mouth to dry insensate mouth through the obsidian, passing something like a response to the question through the crystallized centuries.

". . . all our festering secrets why should you share them you prying slut with slime for harneys why should you presume to share that little that we have here in our destitution far from sun? What once was knowledge is lost, leaked from the bottom of the bucket despite all that was promised, and what remains you would not understand you would not understand whore nothing you'll ever understand except the final throes of heart giving in for all your pretensions and Wutra what of him he did not aid our distant fessups when they lived. In the days of the old iron cold came the white phagors out of the murk and took the town by storm making the humans their slaves who worshipped their new masters by the name Wutra because the gods of ice winds ruled. . . ."

"Stop, stop, I wish to hear no more—" cried the soul, overwhelmed.

But the malicious gale blew over her. "You asked you asked you could not stand the truth you mortal soul, you'll see when you get here. To find your wish of useless wisdom you should journey far to far Sibornal there to seek the great wheel where all is done and known and all things understood as pertains to existence on your side of the bitter bitter grave, yet good none good will it do you you prying dry-quemed failure of the dead's daughter for what is real or true or tested or a testament to time even Wutra himself except this prison where we find ourselves all undeserving . . ."

The soul, quailing, hoisted sail and floated upwards through the bleak mansions, through rank after rank of screaming mouths.

The word, the poisonous word, had come from the far fessups. Sibornal had to be her goal, and a great wheel. Fessups were deceivers, their endless rages led them to limitless malice, but their powers in that respect were limited. It seemed true that Wutra had deserted not merely the living but the dead as well.

The soul fled upward in anguish, scenting far above it a bed on which lay a pallid body without movement.

Above ground, processes of change, endless periods of upheaval, expressed themselves through such biological beings as animals, men, and phagors.

From the northern continent, Sibornalans still moved southwards across the treacherous isthmus of Chalce, propelled by a sporadically improving climate to seek more hospitable lands. The inhabitants of Pannoval expanded northwards across the great plains. Elsewhere, too, from a thousand favoured habitats, people began to emerge. On the south of the continent of Campannlat, in such coastal fortresses as Ottassol, numbers multiplied, growing fat on the abundance of the seas.

In that haven of life, the sea, many things moved. Faceless beings shaped like men climbed to the shore, or were washed by storms far inland.

And the phagors, too. Lovers of cold, they also were propelled by change, seeking new habitats along benign air-octaves. Over all the three measureless continents of Helliconia, their components stirred and reproduced and fought the war against the Sons of Freyr.

The crusade of the young kzahhn of Hrastyprt, Hrr-Brahl Yprt, came slowly down from the high shoulders of Nktryhk, proceeding through the mountains, always obeying the air-octaves. The kzahhn and his advisers knew that Freyr was slowly gaining the ascendancy over Batalix, and so moving against them; but that knowledge could not speed the pace of their advance. Often they stopped to make raids, on the protognostic peoples humbly traversing the snowfields barefoot, or on components of their own kind towards whom they smelled hostility. No sense of urgency burned in their pale harneys, only a sense of destination.

Hrr-Brahl Yprt rode Rukk-Ggrl, and his cowbird rode mainly on his shoulder. Sometimes it took off with a clatter of wings, climbing to soar above the company, whence it could watch with its beady eyes the long procession of stalluns and gillots, most of them on foot, tailing all the way back to the defiles of higher ground. Zzhrrk would ride the updraught so that he maintained a position directly above his master for hours at a time, wings outstretched, only his head moving from side to side, alert for other cowbirds gliding nearby.

There were little knots of the protognostic peoples, generally Madis trying to lead their goats to the next thorn or ice bush, who sighted the white birds from afar. They would cry to each other and point. All knew what the distant cowbirds signified. And they would escape while they had the chance, from death or captivity. Thus the insignificant louse that lived on phagors, burrowing in their coats, a titbit for cowbirds, became an unknowing instrument in saving the lives of many a protognostic.

The Madis themselves were infested with parasites. They feared water, and the yearly application of goat dripping to their lean carcasses increased rather than hampered infestations, but their insects played no accountable role in history.

Proud Hrr-Brahl Yprt, his long skull adorned with face crown, looked up at his mascot soaring high above, before glaring ahead again, alert for possible danger. He saw the three fists of the world in the harneys of his head, and the place at which they would eventually arrive, where lived the Sons of Freyr who had killed his grandfather, Great Kzahhn Hrr-Tryhk Hrast, who had dedicated his life to despatching the enemy in uncounted numbers. The Great Kzahhn had been killed by the Sons in Embruddock, and so had lost his chance of sinking into tether; thus was he destroyed for ever. The young kzahhn admitted to himself that his nations had been less active in killing Sons than they should have been, indulgently seeking instead the majestic ice storms of High Nktryhk, for which their yellow blood was brewed.

Now amends were being made. Before Freyr grew too strong, the Sons of Freyr in Embruddock would be eliminated. Then he would himself fade into the eternal peace of tether with no stain on his conscience.

As soon as she was strong enough, Shay Tal leaned on Vry's shoulder and took herself down the lane to the old temple.

The doors of the temple had been removed and a fence substituted. In the dim interior, pigs squealed and rooted. Aoz Roon had been true to his word.

The women picked their way among the animals and stood in the middle of the muddied space, while Shay Tal stared up at the great ikon of Wutra, with his white hair, animal face, and long horns.

"Then it's true," she said in a low voice. "The fessups spoke true, Vry. Wutra is a phagor. Humanity has been worshipping a phagor. Our darkness is much greater than we guessed."

But Vry was looking up hopefully at the painted stars.

IX

IN AND OUT OF A
HOXNEY SKIN

The enchanted wildernesses began to chart their riverbanks with succulent-stemmed trees. Mists and fogs were syphoned from reviving bournes.

The great continent of Campannlat was some fourteen thousand miles long by five thousand miles wide. It occupied most of the tropical zone in one entire hemisphere of the planet of Helliconia. It contained staggering extremes of temperature, of height and depth, of calm and storm. And now it was reawakening to life.

A process of ages was bringing the continent, grain by grain, mountain by mountain, down into the turbid seas that fringed its coastline. A similar trend, as remorseless, as far-reaching, was increasing its energy levels. Climatic change triggered an acceleration in metabolism, and the ferment of the two suns brought forth eructations from the veins of the world: tremors, volcanic eruptions, subsidences, fumaroles, immense suppurations of lava. The bed of the giant creaked.

These hypogean stresses had their parallels on the planetary surface, where carpets of colour sprang from the old icefields, green spears thrusting up before the last dregs of snow rotted into the soil, so urgently did Freyr call them forth. But the seeds had packaged themselves against precisely that advantageous moment. The flower responded to the star.

After the flower, again the seed. And those seeds provided the energy requirements for new animals that streamed across the new veldts. The animals too were packaged to the moment. Where few species had been, proliferation was. Crystalline states of cataplexy were exercised away under cantering hoofs. Moulting, they left haystacks of discarded winter hair behind them, which was seized upon immediately for nesting material by birds, while their dung provided foodstuffs for insects.

The long fogs were alive with darting birds.

Multitudinous winged life flashed like jewels across what had been sterile icefields only a moment before. In a torment of life, the mammals stretched their legs in full gallop towards summer.

All the manifold terrestrial changes following the one inexorable astronomical change were so complex that no man or woman could comprehend them. But the human spirit responded to them. Eyes opened and saw afresh. All across Campannlat, the human embrace had new passion in its sap.

People were healthier, yet disease spread. Things were better, yet things were worse. More people died, yet more people lived. There was more to eat, yet more people went hungry. For all these contradictions, the prompting was ever outward. Freyer called, and even the deaf responded.

The eclipse that Vry and Oyre had anticipated occurred. The fact that they alone in Embruddock had expected it was a source of satisfaction, although otherwise the effects of the eclipse were alarming. They perceived how terrifying the event was to the uninitiated. Even Shay Tal dropped on her bed and hid her eyes. Bold hunters stayed indoors. Old men had heart attacks.

Yet the eclipse was not total.

The slow erosion of Freyr's disc began early in the afternoon. Perhaps it was the sloth of the whole thing which was so disturbing, and its duration. Hour by hour, the erosion of Freyr increased. When the suns set, they were still locked together. There was no guarantee that they would appear again, or appear again whole. Most of the population ran out into the open to watch this unprecedented sunset. In ashen silence, the maimed sentinels slid from view.

"It's the death of the world!" cried a trader. "Tomorrow the ice will be back!"

As darkness descended, rioting broke out. People ran madly with torches. A new wooden building was set on fire.

Only the immediate intervention of Aoz Roon, Eline Tal, and some of their strong-armed friends saved a more general madness. A man died in the fire and the building was lost, but the rest of the night remained quiet. Next morning, Batalix rose as usual, then Freyr, entire. All was well—except that the geese of Embruddock stopped laying for a week.

"What happens next year?" Oyre and Vry asked each other. Independently of Shay Tal, they began serious work on the problem.

On the Earth Observation Station, the eclipses were merely a part of a pattern predicated by the two intersecting ecliptics of Star A and Star B, which were inclined to each other at an angle of ten degrees. The ecliptics intersected 644 and 1428 terrestrial years after apastron or, in Helliconian terms, 453 and 1005 years after apastron. On either side of the intersections were ranged annual eclipses; in the case of Year 453, an imposing array of twenty eclipses.

The partial eclipse of 632, heralding the series of twenty, was viewed by the scholars on the Observation Station with correct scientific detachment. The ragged fellows barging through the lanes of Embruddock were treated to compassionate smiles by the gods who rode high overhead.

After the mists, after the eclipse, floods. What was cause, what effect? Nobody wading through the residual mud could tell. The land to the east of Oldorando, as far as Fish Lake and beyond, lost its herds of deer, and food became scarce. The swollen Voral acted as a barrier to the west, where abundant animal life was frequently sighted.

Aoz Roon showed his gift for leadership. He made his peace with Laintal Ay and Dathka and, with their aid, drove the citizens to build a bridge across the river.

Such a project had never been attempted in living memory. Timber was scarce, and a rajabaral had to be cut into suitable lengths. The metal-makers corps produced two long saws with which an appropriate tree was sawn up. A temporary workshop was established between the women's house and the river. The two boats stolen from Borlienian marauders were carefully broken up and reassembled to form parts of the superstructure. The rajabaral was turned into a thicket of chocks, wedges, planks, bars, struts, and posts. For weeks, the whole place was a timberyard; curls of shavings floated away downstream among the geese; Oldorando was full of sawdust and the fingers of its labourers of splinters. Thick piles were hauled and driven with difficulty into the bed of the river. Slaves stood up to their necks in the flood, tied to one another for safety; amazingly, no lives were lost.

Slowly, the bridge grew, and Aoz Roon stood there, calling them on. The first row of piers was washed away in a storm. Work began again. Wood was driven against wood. The thuggish heads of sledgehammers took their arcs from the air to land with a thwack on great wooden wedges, the tops of which turned to fur under repeated blows. A narrow platform crept out across the waters and proved secure. Dominating the operation stood the bear-wrapped figure of Aoz Roon, swinging his arms, wielding a mallet or a whip, encouraging or cursing, ever active. They remembered him long afterwards over their rathel, saying, with admiration, "What a devil he was!"

The work prospered. The workers cheered. A bridge four planks wide with a handrail along one side spanned the dark Voral. Many of the women refused to cross it, disliking the glimpse of fast water through the gaps between the planks, and the everlasting *splap-flub* of current against the piles. But access to the western plains had been won. Game was plentiful there, and starvation was averted. Aoz Roon had reason to be pleased.

With the arrival of summer, Freyr and Batalix parted company, rising and setting at different times. Day was rarely so bright, night rarely entire. In the increased hours of daylight, everything grew.

For a while, the academy also grew. During the heroic period of the bridge building, everyone worked together. The shortage of meat meant for the first time an increased awareness of the importance of grain. The handful of seeds that Laintal Ay had pressed on Shay Tal became a clutch of fields, where barley, oats, and rye grew in profusion and were guarded from marauders as being among the precious possessions of the Den tribe.

Now that several women could reckon and write, the grain that was harvested was weighed and stored and fairly rationed; any carcasses brought in were tallied; fish yields were noted. Every pig and goose in the town was entered on a balance sheet. Agriculture and accountancy brought their own rewards. Everyone was busy.

Vry and Oyre had charge of the cereal fields, and of the slaves working there. From the nearer acres, they could see the big tower in the distance, over the waving ears of grain, with a sentry standing there on watch. They still studied the constellations; their star chart was as complete as they could make it. Stars were in their conversation often as they prowled among the grasses.

"The stars are always on the move, like fish in a clear lake," Vry said. "All the fish turn together at the same moment. But the stars aren't fish. I wonder what they are, and what they swim in."

Oyre held a grass stalk up to the nose that Laintal Ay admired so much and closed first one eye and then the other.

"The stalk seems to move back and forth across my vision, yet I know it's still all the while. Perhaps the stars are still and it's we who move. . . ."

Vry received this and was silent. Then she said in a small voice, "Oyre, my beauty, perhaps it's so. Perhaps it's the earth that moves all the while. But then . . ."

"What about the sentinels?"

"Why, they don't move either. . . . That's right, we move, we go round and round like an eddy in the river. And they're far away, like the stars. . . ."

". . . But coming nearer, Vry, because it's getting warmer. . . ."

They gazed at each other, mouths open, eyebrows slightly raised, breathing lightly. Beauty and intelligence flowed in them.

The hunters, released by the bridge into the west, gave little thought to the revolving sky. The plains were open for their despoliation. Green rose up everywhere, crushed under their running feet, their sprawling bodies. Flowers burst. Insects that flew no more than a man's height above the ground blundered among pale petals. Game in plenty was near at hand, to be brought down and dragged back to the town, spotting the new bridge with its dull blood.

With the growth of Aoz Roon's reputation, Shay Tal's went into eclipse. The diversion of women into labour connected either with the bridge or with agriculture weakened her hold on the intellectual life of the community. It hardly appeared to bother Shay Tal; since her return from the world below, she increasingly shunned companionship. She avoided Aoz Roon, and her gaunt figure was seen less often about the lanes. Only her friendship with old Master Datnil prospered.

Although Master Datnil had never again allowed her as much as a glimpse of the secret book of his corps, his mind wandered frequently to the past. She was content to listen to him unwinding the skein of his reminiscence, peopled with bygone names; it was not unlike, she thought, a visit to the fessups. What seemed dark to her held luminance for him.

"To the best of my belief, Embruddock was once more complicated that it is now. Then it suffered a catastrophe, as you know. . . . There was a mason-makers corps but it was destroyed some centuries ago. The master of the corps was particularly well thought of."

Shay Tal had observed before his endearing habit of speaking as if he were present during the events he described. She guessed he was recalling something he had read in his secret book.

"How was so much building achieved in stone?" she asked him. "We know the labour of working in wood."

They were sitting in the master's dim room. Shay Tal squatted before him on the floor. Because of his age, Master Datnil sat on a stone set against the wall, so that he could rise easily. Both his old woman and Raynil Layan, his chief boy—a mature man with a forked beard and unctuous manners—came and went in the room; the master kept his talk guarded in consequence.

He answered Shay Tal's question by saying, "Let us go down and walk in the sun for a few paces, Mother Shay. The warmth is good for my bones, I find."

Outside, he put his arm through hers and they walked down the lane where curly-haired pigs foraged. Nobody was about, for the hunters were away in the west veldt and many of the women were in the fields, keeping company with the slaves. Mangy dogs slept in the light of Freyr.

"The hunters are now away so much," Master Datnil said, "that the women misbehave in their absence. Our male Borlienian slaves harvest the women as well as the crops. I don't know what the world's coming to."

"People copulate like animals. The cold for intellect, the warmth for sensuality." She looked above their heads, where little wanton birds swooped into holes in the stonework of the towers, bearing insects for their young.

He patted her arm and looked into her pinched face. "Don't you fret. Your dream of going to Sibornal is your kind of satisfaction. We all must have something."

"Something? What?" She frowned at him.

"Something to hang on to. A vision, a hope, a dream. We don't live only by bread, even the basest of us. There's always some kind of inner life—that's what survives when we become gossies."

"Oh, the inner life . . . It can be starved to death, can't it?"

He stopped by the herb tower and she paused with him. They regarded the blocks of stone forming the tower. Despite the ages, the tower stood well. The blocks fitting neatly one into the other raised unanswered questions. How was stone quarried and cut? How was it built up so that it formed a tower which could stand for nine centuries?

Bees droned round their feet. A flight of large birds moved across the sky and disappeared behind one of the towers. She felt the day going by in her ears, and longed to be seized up in something great and all-embracing.

"Perhaps we could make a small tower out of mud. Mud dries good and solid. A small mud tower first. Stone later. Aoz Roon should build mud walls round Oldorando. At present the village is virtually unguarded. Everyone's away. Who will blow the warning horn? We are open to raiders, human and inhuman."

"I read once that a learned man of my corps made a model of this world in the form of a globe which could be rotated to show the lands on it—where was once Embruddock, where Sibornal, and so on. It was stored in the pyramid with much else."

"King Denniss feared more than the cold. He feared invaders. Master Datnil, I have kept silent for a while with respect to many of my secret thoughts. But they torment me and I must speak. . . . I have learnt from my fessups that Embruddock . . ." She paused, aware of the burden of what she was going to say, before completing her sentence. ". . . Embruddock was once ruled by phagors."

After a moment, the old man said, in a light conversational tone, "That's enough sunlight. We can go in again."

On the way up to his room, he stopped on the third floor of the tower. This was the assembly room of his corps, smelling strongly of leather. He stood listening. All was silent.

"I wanted to make sure that my chief boy was out. Come in here."

Off the landing was a small room. Master Datnil pulled a key from his pocket and unlocked the door, looking round once more, anxiously. Catching Shay Tal's eye, he said, "I don't want anyone butting in. What I'm about to do in sharing the secrets of our corps carries the death penalty, as you understand. Ancient though I may be, I want the last few years of my life out."

She looked round as she stepped into the small cubbyhole off the assembly room with him. For all their caution, neither of them saw Raynil Layan—as chief boy of the corps, due to inherit Master Datnil's mantle when the old man retired. He stood in the shadows, behind a post supporting the wooden stair. Raynil Layan was a cautious, precise man, whose manner was always circumspect; he stood at this moment absolutely rigid, without breathing, showing no more movement than the post that partly protected him from view.

When the master and Shay Tal had entered the cubbyhole and closed the door behind them, Raynil Layan moved with some alacrity, his step light for so large a man. He applied his eye to a crack between two boards which he had engineered himself some while ago, the better to observe the movements of the man he would supplant.

Distorting his face by tugging considerably on his forked beard—a nervous habit imitated by his enemies—he watched Datnil Skar remove from its box the secret record of the tawyers and tanner corps. The ancient spread it open before the gaze of the woman. When that information was laid before Aoz Roon, it would mark the end of the old master—and the beginning of the rule of the new. Raynil Layan descended the stairs one step at a time, moving with quiet deliberation.

With trembling finger, Master Datnil pointed to a blank in the pages of his musty tome. "This is a secret which has weighed heavy on me for many years, Mother, and I trust your shoulders are not too frail for it. At the darkest, coldest time of an earlier epoch, Embruddock was overrun by the accursed phagors. Its very name is a corruption of an ancipital name: Hrrm-Bhhrd Ydohk. . . . Our corps was then driven out into caves in the wild. But both men and women were kept here. Our kind was then in servitude, and the phagors ruled. . . . Isn't that a disgrace?"

She thought of the phagor god Wutra, worshipped in the temple.

"A disgrace not yet past. They ruled us," she said, "and are worshipped still. Doesn't that make us a race of slaves to this day?"

A fly with viridian plates on its body, of a kind only recently seen in the settlement, buzzed from a dusty corner and alighted on the book.

Master Datnil looked up at Shay Tal in sudden fear. "I should have resisted the temptation to show you this. It's nothing you should know." His face was haggard. "Wutra will punish me for this."

"You believe in Wutra despite the evidence?"

The old man was trembling, as if he heard a step outside that spelt his doom. "He's all about us. . . . We are his slaves. . . ."

He struck out at the fly, but it eluded him as it set off in a spiral for a distant target of its own.

The hunters watched the hoxneys in professional amazement. Of all the life that invaded the western plains, it was the hoxney that, in its sportiveness, most embodied the new spirit. Beyond the settlement was the bridge, and beyond the bridge the hoxneys.

Freyr had called forth the glossies from their long hibernation. The signal had gone from sun to gland; life filled their eddres, they unrolled and lived again, crawling out of their dark comfortable places to stretch, to abound in movement—to rejoice and be hoxneys. To be herds and herds of hoxneys, to be careless as a breeze, to be striped and hornless, to resemble asses or small kaidaws, to gallop and gambol and graze and plunge hock-deep into delicious grasses. To be able to outstrip almost anything else that ran.

Every hoxney bore stripes of two colours, running horizontally from nose to tail. The stripes might be vermilion and black, or vermilion and yellow, or black and yellow, or green and yellow, or green and sky blue, or sky blue and white, or white and cerise, or cerise and vermilion. When the herds threw themselves down to rest, sprawling like cats, their legs carelessly stretched, they faded into the landscape, which also had put on new shows for the new seasons. Just as the hoxneys had broken from the glossy state, so "the flower-thrilling plain" transformed itself back from song into reality.

At first, the hoxneys had no fear of the hunters.

They galloped among the men, snorting with glee, tossing their manes, throwing up their heads, showing wide teeth made crimson by chomping veronika, raige, and the scarlet dogthrush. The hunters stood perplexed, caught between delight and the lust of the hunt, laughing back at the sportive beasts, whose rumps zithered with fire where the light of the sentinels touched them. These were the beasts that drew the dawn across the plains. In the first enchantments of meeting, they seemed impossible to kill.

Then they'd fart and be off like volted zephyrs, thundering between the pointless brown steeples that ants were raising everywhere, wheeling about, gazing mischievously back, shaking manes, whinneying, often charging back again to prolong the game. Or, when they tired of that, and of grazing with their soft muzzles to the floor, the stallions would set upon their fillies, rolling them in delight among the tall white orling flowers. Calling with shrill dove notes like laughter, they plunged their striped prods into the willing quemes of the mares, then pranced off, dripping still, to the applause of the hunters.

The mood of ease had its effect on the men. No longer were they so keen to return to their stone rooms. After they had brought down a capering animal, they delighted in lying by the fire that roasted it, talking of women, bragging, singing, sniffing the sage, dogthrush, and scantiom that blossomed about them and, crushed by their bodies, gave out pleasing aromas.

Generally speaking, they were harmonious. When Raynil Layan appeared—it was unusual to see a man of the corps in the hunting grounds —the mood was broken for a while. Aoz Roon went apart from the others and talked to Raynil Layan with his face to the far horizon. When he returned, his expression was grim, and he would not tell Laintal Ay and Dathka what had been said.

When false evening came to Oldorando, and one or other of the two sentinels scattered its ashes over the western sky, the hoxney herds scented a familiar challenge. Lifting their nostrils to the flushed air, they watched for sabre-tongues.

Their enemies also sported bright colours. Sabre-tongues were striped like their prey, always black and one other colour, a blood colour, generally scarlet or a rich maroon. Sabre-tongues bore a close resemblance to hoxneys, although their legs were shorter and thicker, and their heads rounder, the rotundity emphasised by lack of visible ears. The head, set on a sturdy neck, housed the sabre-tongue's chief weapon: fast in pursuit over short distances, the sabre-tongue could project a sword-sharp tongue from its throat and sever the leg of a hoxney as it fled.

Having once seen this predator in action, the hunters held it in respect. The sabre-tongue, for its part, showed the men neither fear nor aggression; mankind had never appeared on its menu nor, as far as it knew, was it on mankind's.

Fire seemed to attract the animal. Sabre-tongues developed a habit of slouching up to the campfire in twos, male and female, to sit or sprawl there. They licked each other with their white sword tongues and would devour pieces of meat the men threw them. Yet they would never allow themselves to be touched, drawing away snarling from a cautiously proffered hand. The snarl was sufficient warning for the hunters; they had seen what damage that terrible tongue could do, used in anger.

Brakes of thorn tree and dogthrush were in blossom about the land-scape. Beneath their heavy boughs the men slept. They dwelt among blossom and its cloying scents, with flowers never seen or smelt before, except by long-gone fessups. In the dogthrush thickets they found the hives of wild bees, some brimming with honey. The honey fermented easily to make beethel. On the glutinous beethel the men got drunk and pursued one another through the grasses, laughing, shouting, wrestling, until the curious hoxneys came to see what all the fun was about. The hoxneys too would not permit a man to touch them, although many a man tried when caught up by the beethel, running across the veldt after the frolicking animals until he fell over and slept where he lay.

In the old days, the return home had been the crowning pleasure of the hunt. The challenge of the chill snowfields had been exchanged for warmth and sleep. That was altered. The hunt had become play. Their muscles were no longer stretched, and there was warmth on the flowering veldt.

Also, Oldorando held less attraction for the hunters. The hamlet was growing crowded as more children survived the hazards of their first year on earth. The men preferred convivial beethel binges on the plain to the complaints that often attended their return.

So they no longer came back boastfully in the old tight-knit bunch, straggling home instead in ones and twos, in a less obtrusive way.

These new-style returns held one excitement previously absent, at least as far as the women were concerned; for if the men had their irre-sponsibility, the women had their vanity.

"Let's see what you've brought me!"

That, with variations, was the popular cry, as women dragged their brats out to meet their men. They went as far as the new bridge and waited there, standing on the east bank of the Voral while the kids threw stones at the ducks and geese, waiting impatiently for the men to arrive with meat—and skins.

The meat was their due, their necessity, and it was no good a hunter coming back without meat.

But what aroused frenzies of delight in the hearts of the women were the skins, the brilliant hoxney skins. Never before in their impoverished lives had they visualised a change of garb. Never before had the tanners been in such demand. Never before had the men been driven out to kill for the sake of killing. Every woman wished to possess a hoxney skin—preferably more than one—and to dress her offspring in one.

They competed with each other for brighter skins. Blue, magenta, aquamarine, cherry. They blackmailed the men in ways men enjoyed. They preened themselves, they stained their lips. They paraded. They dressed their hair. They even took to washing themselves.

Correctly worn, with those electric stripes running vertically up the body, hoxney skins could make even a dumpy woman look elegant. The skins had to be properly cut. A new trade prospered in Oldorando: tailor. As flowers put forth bells and spikes and faces along the lanes between the ancient worn towers, and flowering ivies climbed the towers themselves, so the women began more to resemble flowers. They decked themselves in bright colours their mothers had never set eyes on.

It was not long before the men, in self-defence, also cut off their old heavy furs and took to hoxney skins.

The weather became still and threatening, and the rajabarals steamed from their flat lids.

Oldorando was silent under towering cumulus. The hunters were away. Shay Tal sat alone in her room writing. She no longer cared about her appearance, and still went round in her old ill-fitting skins. In her head she still heard the creaking voices of fessups and her parents' gossies. She still tried to dream of perfection and travel.

When Vry and Amin Lim came down from the room above, Shay Tal looked up sharply and said, "Vry, what would you think of a globe as a model of the world?"

Vry said, "It would make sense. A globe rotates most smoothly of all figures, and the other wanderers are round. So we must be too."

"A disc, a wheel? We've been brought up to believe that the original boulder rests on a disc."

"Much we were brought up to believe is incorrect. You taught us that, Mother," Vry said. "I believe our world revolves round the sentinels."

Shay Tal sat where she was, contemplating them, and they fidgeted under her inspection. Both of the younger women had shed their old skins and wore bright hoxney suits. Stripes of cerise and grey ran up Vry's body. The ears of the dead animal adorned her shoulders. Despite all Aoz Roon's threatened restrictions on the academy, the skins had been presented to her by Dathka. She walked more confidently. She had acquired glamour.

Suddenly, Shay Tal's temper flared up. "You stupid wenches, you silly gillies, you are defying me. Don't pretend you aren't. I know what goes on under that air of meekness. Look at the way you dress nowadays! We get nowhere with our understanding, nowhere. Everything seems to lead us to fresh complexities. I shall have to go to Sibornal, to find this great wheel the gossies speak of. Perhaps real freedom, clear truth, lives there. Here is only the curse of ignorance. . . . Where are you two going, in any case?"

Amin Lim spread her hands to demonstrate their innocence. "Nowhere, ma'am, only to the fields, to see if we've cured the mildew on the oats."

She was a big girl, even bigger at this time with the seed her man had planted within her. She stood there pleadingly, released by a slight flicker of assent in Shay Tal's eye, whereon she and Vry almost scuttled from the oppressive room.

As they retreated down the dirty stone steps, Vry said resignedly, "There she goes again, blowing up, as regular as the Hour-Whistler. Poor thing, something is really worrying her."

"Where's this pool you mentioned? I don't feel like walking far in my condition."

"You'll love it, Amin Lim. It's only a little way beyond the northern fields, and we can walk slowly. I expect Oyre's there."

The air had thickened to an extent where it no longer carried the scent of flowers, but emanated a metallic trace of its own. Colour appeared dazzling in the actinic light; the geese looked supernaturally white.

They passed between the columns of great rajabarals. The stark cylinders with their concave curve were better suited to the geometries of a winter landscape; with the growing lushness they formed a forbidding contrast.

"Even the rajabarals are changing," Amin Lim said. "How long has steam been coming out of their tops?"

Vry did not know and was not particularly interested. She and Oyre had discovered a warm pool, knowledge of which they had so far kept to themselves. In a narrow valley, the mouth of which pointed away from Oldorando, fresh springs had burst forth from the ground, some at a temperature near boiling, some rushing down to meet the Voral in a cloud of vapour. One spring, damned by rock, flowed a different way and formed a secluded pool, fringed by verdure but open to the sky. It was to this pool that Vry led Amin Lim.

As they parted the bushes and saw the figure standing by the pool, Amin Lim shrieked and threw her hand to her mouth.

Oyre stood on the bank. She was naked. Her skin shone with moisture and water dripped from her ample breasts. With no sign of shyness, she turned and waved excitedly to her friends. Behind her lay her discarded hoxney skins.

"Come on, where you have been? The water's glorious today."

Amin Lim stood where she was, blushing, still covering her mouth. She had never seen anyone naked before.

"It's all right," Vry said, laughing at her friend's expression. "It's lovely in the water. I'm going to strip off and go in. Watch me—if you dare."

She ran forward to where Oyre stood and began unlacing the cerise and grey suit. Hoxneys were tailored to be climbed in and out of. In another minute, the suit was thrown aside and Vry stood there naked, her more slender lines contrasting with Oyre's sturdy beauty. She laughed in delight.

"Come on, Amin Lim, don't be stuffy. A swim will be good for your baby."

She and Oyre jumped into the water together. As it swallowed up their limbs, they squealed with delight.

Amin Lim stood where she was and squealed with horror.

They had gorged down an enormous feast, with bitter fruits to follow the slabs of meat. Their faces still shone with fat.

The hunters were heavier than they had been last season. Food was all too plentiful. The hoxneys could be slaughtered without anyone's having to run. The animals continued to come close, capering among the hunters and rolling their parti-coloured bodies against the hides of their dead fellows.

Still wearing his old black furs, Aoz Roon had been talking apart to Goija Hin, the slave master, whose broad back was still visible as he trudged towards the distant towers of Oldorando. Aoz Roon returned to the company. He grabbed up a chunk of rib still sizzling on a stone and rolled over in the grass with it. Curd, his great hound, frisked playfully with him, growling, until Aoz Roon brought a branch of fragrant dogthrush down to keep the brute from his meat.

He kicked out at Dathka in a friendly way.

"This is the life, friend. Take it easy, eat as much as you can before the ice returns. By the original boulder, I'll never forget this season as long as I live."

"Splendid." That was all Dathka said. He had finished eating, and sat with his arms wrapped round his knees, watching the hoxneys, a herd of which was wheeling fast through the grass not a quarter of a mile away.

"Damn you, you never say anything," Aoz Roon exclaimed good-humouredly, pulling at his meat with his strong teeth. "Talk to me."

Dathka turned his head so that his cheek rested on his knee and gave Aoz Roon a knowing look. "What's going on between you and Goija Hin then?"

Aoz Roon's mouth went hard. "That's private between the pair of us."

"So you won't talk either." Dathka turned away and regarded the cantering hoxneys once more, where they wheeled below the high cumulus piling up on the western horizon. The air was full of green light, robbing the hoxneys of their brilliant colour.

Finally, as if he could feel the black regard of Aoz Roon through his shoulder blades, he said, without shifting his gaze, "I was thinking."

Aoz Roon flung his chewed bone to Curd and lay flat under the blossoming bough. "All right, then, out with it. What have you been saving up all your lifetime to think?"

"How to catch a live hoxney."

"Ha! What good would that do you?"

"I wasn't thinking of good, any more than you were when you called Nahkri to the top of the tower."

A heavy silence followed, in which Aoz Roon said no word. Eventually, as distant thunder sounded, Eline Tal brought round some beethel. Aoz Roon demanded angrily of the company in general, "Where's Laintal Ay? Wandering again, I suppose. Why is he not with us? You men are getting too lazy and disobedient. Some of you are in for a surprise."

He got up and walked heavily away, followed at a respectful distance by his hound.

Laintal Ay was not studying hoxneys like his silent friend. He was after other game.

Since that night, four long years ago, when he was witness to the murder of his uncle Nahkri, the incident had haunted him. He had ceased to blame Aoz Roon for the murder, for he now understood better that the Lord of Embruddock was a tormented man.

"I'm sure he thinks himself under a curse," Oyre had once told Laintal Ay.

"He can be forgiven a lot for the western bridge," Laintal Ay replied, in a practical way. But he felt himself spoiled by his involvement in the murder, and increasingly kept his own counsel.

The bond between him and the beautiful Oyre had been both strengthened and distorted by that night when too much rathel had been drunk. He had even become wary with her.

He had spelt out the difficulty to himself. "If I am to rule in Oldorando, as my lineage decrees, then I must kill the father of the girl I wish to make mine. It's impossible."

No doubt Oyre also understood his dilemma. Yet she was marked out as his and no one else's. He would have fought to the death any other man who went near her.

His wild instincts, his sense for the cunning trap, for the unregarding moment that spells disaster, made him see as clearly as did Shay Tal that Oldorando was now left regularly vulnerable to attack. In the present warm spell, nobody was alert. Sentries droused at their posts.

He raised the question of defence with Aoz Roon, who had a reasonable answer.

Aoz Roon said dismissively that nobody, friend or foe, travelled far any more. A mantle of snow had made it easy for men to go wherever they pleased; now everywhere was choked with green things, with thickets growing denser every day. The time for raids was past.

Besides, he added, they had had no phagor raids since the day Mother

Shay Tal performed her miracle at Fish Lake. They were safer than they had ever been. And he passed Laintal Ay a tankard of beethel.

Laintal Ay was not satisfied with the answer. Uncle Nahkri had considered himself perfectly safe that night he had climbed the stairs of the big tower. Within a couple of minutes, he was lying in the lane below with his neck broken.

When the hunters went out today, Laintal Ay had got no further than the bridge. There he turned silently back, determined to make a survey of the village and see how it would fare under an unexpected attack.

As he commenced circling the outskirts, the first thing he observed was a light plume of steam on the Voral. It rode along on a certain line in midstream, never deviating, seeming to advance above the dark rapid glide of the water, yet ever remaining in the identical place. Feathers of vapour shredded back from it along the breast of the river. What it signified he could not determine. He proceeded with a sense of unease.

The atmosphere grew heavier. Saplings were springing up over mounds that had once been buildings. He viewed the remaining towers through their slender bars. Aoz Roon was right in one respect: it had become difficult to get round Oldorando.

Yet warning images formed in his mind. He saw phagors riding kaidaws, leaping obstacles and charging into the heart of the settlement. He saw the hunters straggling home, loaded with bright skins, their heads heavy from too much beethel. They had time to witness their homes burnt, their women and children dead, before they too were trampled under savage hoof.

He forced his way through prickly bushes.

How the phagors rode! What could be more wonderful than to mount a kaidaw and ride it, master it, share its power, be one with its action? Those ferocious beasts submitted to no mount but a phagor: or so the legends said, and he had never heard of the man who had ridden a kaidaw. The very notion made one dizzy. Men went on foot. . . . But a man on a kaidaw would be more than the equal of a phagor on a kaidaw.

Half concealed by bushes, he could see across to the north gate, which stood open and unguarded. Two birds perched on top of the gate, twittering. He wondered if a sentry had been posted that morning, or if the man had deserted his post. The silence, through the heavy air, took on a booming quality.

A shambling figure came into his line of vision. It was immediately recognisable as the slave master, Goija Hin. Behind him went Myk, led by a rope.

"There now, you'll enjoy this afternoon's work," Laintal Ay heard the slave master say. He stopped beyond the gate and tied the phagor to a small tree. The creature's legs were already chained. He patted Myk almost affectionately.

Myk looked at Goija Hin with apprehension. "Myk can sit here in the sunshine some time."

"Not sit, stand. You stand, Myk, you do as you're told, or you know what you'll get. We're going to do exactly as Aoz Roon says, or we'll both be in trouble."

The old phagor made a growling sound. "Trouble is always all round us in the air-octaves. What are you Sons of Freyr but trouble?"

"Any more of that I rip your stinking hide off," Goija Hin said, without malice. "You stay there and do what we were told and you'll have your chance on one of us Sons of Freyr in a minute."

He left the monster where he was concealed from gaze and marched off with his flat-footed walk, back towards the towers. Myk promptly lay down on the ground and was lost to Laintal Ay's view.

Like the trail of vapour riding on the Voral, this incident made Laintal Ay uneasy. He stood waiting, listening, wondering. The twittering stillness was one he would have regarded as unnatural only a few years ago. He shrugged his shoulders and walked on.

Oldorando was unguarded. An undertaking must be made to rouse the hunters to a sense of peril. He observed that steam seeped from the caps of the bare rajabarals. There was another portent he could not interpret. Thunder rumbled, far to the north, yet with intimate menace.

He crossed a brook which bubbled and let forth steam, the vapour snarling itself among teeth of fern growing from the bank. When he bent to dip his hand, he found the water tolerably warm. A dead fish floated past, tail uppermost, just under the surface. He squatted there, looking across it at the tangle of new green through which the tops of the towers showed. No hot spring had existed here before.

The ground trembled. Reed trailed in the water, for ever uncurling; newts flashed in it then were gone. Birds rose crying over the towers, then sank again.

As he waited for the tremor to be repeated, the Hour-Whistler blew nearby, the sound of Oldorando he remembered since the cradle. It lasted a fraction longer than usual. He knew exactly how long it lasted; this time, the note was sustained for an instant more than it should have been.

He rose and continued his perimeter prowl. When moving with difficulty through raige bushes which reached to his thigh, he heard voices. With the prompt response of a hunter, Laintal Ay froze, then moved forward cautiously, bent double. Ahead was a sharp rise in the ground, patched by thyme bushes. He sank down on his hands among the fragrant leaves, to peer forward cautiously. He felt his stomach swing under him—his lean arc of belly had become convex with recent good living.

Voices—female—again. He raised his head and looked over the mound.

Whatever he had expected to see, the reality was far more delightful. He found himself gazing into a hollow, in the centre of which lay a deep pool surrounded by verdure. Wisps of steam rose from the water and drifted into the bushes round about, which dripped moisture back into the pool. On the far side of this pool were two women dressing themselves in their hoxney skins; one was heavy with child; he quickly identified her as Amin Lim and her companion as Vry. Standing near him on the edge of the pool, her beautiful back turned to him, was his adored and self-willed Oyre, naked.

When he realised who it was, he gasped with pleasure, and lay where he was, regarding those shoulders, that sweep of back, those glowing buttocks and legs, with a delight that caught his breath.

Batalix had broken free from one of the giant purple castles of cloud, to flood the land below with gold. The sentinel's rays scattered obliquely over Oyre's cinnamon skin, which was pearled about her shoulders and breasts with water drops. Runnels of water chased themselves down the mazes of her flesh, finally spreading to the stone on which she stood, as if to unite her, naiadlike, to the nearby element they shared. Her pose was relaxed, her feet were slightly apart. One hand was raised, to wipe away water from her eyelashes as she watched her friends preparing to leave. Oyre's was the carelessness of an animal—unconscious at this moment of the hunter's predatory regard, yet poised for escape if need be.

Her dark hair clung wetly to her skull, damp tails of it curling about her shoulders and throat, lending her an otterlike quality.

Laintal Ay could catch only glimpses of her face from where he crouched. He had never seen any naked body before, male or female; custom, reinforcing cold, had banished nudity from Oldorando. Overcome by what he saw, he allowed his face to sink into the fragrant thyme. Pulses beat heavily in his temples.

When he could raise his head and look upon the sight again, the movement of her buttocks as she waved her friends good-bye and turned away worked a strong enchantment in him. He breathed a different air. Oyre now regarded the pool almost drowsily, gazing into its pure depths, her lashes gleaming against her cheeks. At her next movement, he could consider her pudendum, covered with tiny wet pigtails, her superb belly, and the cunning whorl of her navel. All was momentarily revealed as she flung up her arms and jumped into the pool.

He was alone with the heavy sunlight and the steam rolling into the bushes until she surfaced again, laughing.

She climbed out quite near him, her breasts swinging clear of her body, jellying lightly against each other.

"Oyre, golden Oyre!" he called in ecstasy.

He rose.

She stood in a crouch before him, a pulse throbbing by a little hollow on her neck. Her regard was heavy upon him, her dark eyes lustrous, yet with a kind of sensuous dullness induced by the general ripe warmth. He saw anew the beauty of the short oval of her face, framed in otter hair, and the sweetness about her eyebrows and the folds of her eyelids. Those eyebrows were arched at present, but after her first surprise she showed no fear, simply looking at him with parted lips, awaiting his next move as if puzzled as to what it might be. Then, belatedly, she curled one hand down and covered her queme. The gesture was more provocative than protective. Well aware of her beauty, she possessed a natural composure.

Four little lascivious birds fluttered down between them, overcome by the heaviness of the afternoon.

Laintal Ay strode across the grass and clutched her, looking fiercely into her eyes, feeling her body against his furs. He reached forward and grasped her, kissing her passionately on the lips.

Oyre stepped back and licked those lips, smiling slightly, her eyes narrowed.

"Strip yourself. Let Batalix see how you are made," she said.

The words were part invitation, part taunt. He unlaced his neckties, then grasped the opening of his tunic and tugged, so that the stitches tore. With loud ripping sounds, the tunic came away and he flung it down. Then he treated his trousers similarly, and kicked them off. He was aware of how his prod stood out stiff from his body, as he crossed to her.

Oyre grasped his outstretched arm, pulled, kicked at his shin, and stepped back swiftly, propelling him full length into the water.

The moist lips of the pool closed over Laintal Ay. It felt astonishingly hot. He surfaced, yelling for breath.

She leaned down laughing with her hands on her handsome knees.

"You wash yourself before you are fit for me, you flea-bitten warrior!"

He splashed her, smacking the surface of the water between laughter and anger.

When she helped him out, she was considerably softer. She felt slippery in his grasp. As they knelt down in the grass, he slid a hand between her legs, feeling her fine details. Immediately, his seed burst from him across the grass.

"Oh, you fool, you fool!" she cried, and caught him a slap across the chest, her face distorted by disappointment.

"No, no, Oyre, it's all right. Give me a minute, please. I love you, Oyre, with all my eddre. I want you always, always. Come to me, rouse me again."

But Oyre stood up, full of annoyance and inexperience. Despite his coaxing words, he felt enraged with her, with himself. He jumped up beside her.

"Scumb you, you shouldn't be so pretty, you minx!"

He grabbed hold of her arm, swung her brutally round, and thrust her towards the steaming pool. She grabbed his hair, snarling and screeching. Together they tumbled into the water.

He got an arm about her back, caught her underwater, kissed her as they surfaced, grabbing a breast with his left hand. Laughing, they climbed to the muddy bank, rolling over together. He hooked a leg round hers and climbed on top. She kissed him passionately on the lips, thrusting her tongue into his mouth even as he entered her queme.

There they lay in the secret place, serene, ecstatic, making love. The mud beneath them, plastering their sides, emitted comfortable noises, as if full of microbes all copulating to express their joy in life.

She was climbing languorously into her hoxney skins. The soft pelts were distinctively marked with dark blue and light blue stripes, each stripe varying in width as it chased its way down Oyre's body. The afternoon had become stifling, and thunder rumbled near at hand, occasionally breaking into claps like sharp cries of protest.

Laintal Ay sprawled close, watching Oyre's movements, eyes half-closed.

"I've always wanted you," he said. "For years. Your flesh is a hot spring. You'll be my woman. We'll come here every afternoon."

She said nothing. She started singing under her breath.

> *"The stream on its way*
> *Glides like our day . . ."*

"I want you badly, every day, Oyre. You want me too, don't you?"

She looked at him and said, "Yes, yes, Laintal Ay, I wanted you. But I cannot be your woman."

He felt the ground tremble under him.

"What do you mean?"

She seemed to hesitate, then she leaned towards him. When he automatically reached for her, she pulled herself away, tucked her breasts into her tunic, and said, "I love you, Laintal Ay, but I am not going to become your woman.

"I always suspected that the academy was just a diversion—a consolation for silly women like Amin Lim. Now the weather's fine, it has fallen apart. To be honest, only Vry and Shay Tal care about it—and possibly old Master Datnil. Yet I value Shay Tal's example of independence, and imitate it. Shay Tal will not submit to my father—though I expect she desires him madly, as everyone does—and I follow her example: if I become your possession, I become nothing."

He scrambled up on his knees, looking wretched. "Not so, not so. You'll be—everything, Oyre, everything. We're nothing without each other."

"For a few weeks, yes."

"What do you expect?"

"What do I expect. . . ." Her eyes rolled upwards, and she sighed. She smoothed back her still damp hair and looked away, at the young bushes, at the sky, at the birds. "It's not that I have such a high regard for myself. I can do so little. By remaining independent like Shay Tal, perhaps I can achieve something."

"Don't talk that way. You need someone to protect you. Shay Tal, Vry—they're not happy. Shay Tal never laughs, does she? Besides, she's old. I'd look after you and make you happy. I want nothing better."

She was buttoning up her tunic, looking down at the toggles which she herself had designed (to the tailor's amazement), so that the skins could be put on and off without trouble.

"Oh, Laintal Ay, I'm so difficult. I have difficulty with myself. I don't really know what I want. I long to dissolve and flow like this wonderful water. Who knows where it comes from, where it goes to?— from the very eddre of earth, maybe. . . . I do love you, though, in my horrid way. Listen, we'll have an arrangement."

She stopped fiddling with her tunic and came to stand looking down at him, hands on her hips.

"Do something great and astonishing, one thing, one deed, and I'll be your woman for ever. You understand that? A great deed, Laintal Ay —a great deed and I'm yours. I'll do whatever you wish."

He got up and stood away from her, surveying her. "A great deed? What sort of great deed do you mean? By the original boulder, Oyre, you are a strange girl."

She tossed her damp hair. "If I told you, then it would no longer be great. Do you understand that? Besides, I don't know what I mean. Strive, strive . . . You're getting fat already, as if you were pregnant. . . ."

He stood without moving, his face hard. "How is it that when I tell you I love you you insult me in return?"

"You tell me truth—I hope; I tell you truth. But I don't mean to hurt you. Really I'm gentle. You just released things in me, things I've said to no one else. I long for . . . no, I can't say what the longings are for . . . glory. Do something great, Laintal Ay, I beg you, something great, before we grow too old."

"Like killing phagors?"

Suddenly she laughed on rather a harsh note, narrowing her eyes. For a moment, her resemblance to Aoz Roon was marked. "If that's all you can think of. Provided you kill a million of them."

He looked baffled.

"So you imagine you're worth a million phagors?"

Oyre pretended to smite herself hard on the forehead, as if her harneys had come loose. "It's not for *me*, don't you see? It's for yourself. Achieve one great thing for your own sake. Here we're stuck in what Shay Tal says is a farmyard—at least make it a legendary farmyard."

The ground trembled again. "Scumble," he said. "The earth really is moving."

They stood up, shaken out of their argument, ignoring each other. A bronze overcast spread from the aerial castles, which now took on purple hearts and yellow edges. The heat became intense, and they stood in the midst of an oppressive silence, backs to each other, looking about.

A repeated smacking sound made them turn towards the pool. Its surface was marred by yellow bubbles which rose and grew until they burst, to spread filth through the hitherto clear water. The bubbles sailed up from the depths, releasing a stink of rotten eggs, coming faster and blacker. Thick mist filled the hollow.

A jet of mud burst from the pool and sprayed into the air. Gobbets of scalding filth flew, pocking the foliage all about. The humans ran in terror, she in her garb the colour of summer skies.

Within a minute of their leaving, the pool was a mass of black seething liquid.

Before they could get back to Oldorando, the skies opened, and down came the rain, grey, and chilling to the flesh.

As they climbed into the big tower, voices could be heard overhead, Aoz Roon's prominent among them. He had just arrived back with allies of his own generation, Tanth Ein, Faralin Ferd, and Eline Tal, all sturdy warriors and good hunters; with them were their women, exclaiming over new hoxney skins, and Dol Sakil, who sat sulkily apart on the window sill, regardless of the rain beating down. Also in the room was Raynil Layan, his skins perfectly dry; he fingered his forked beard and looked anxiously back and forth, without either speaking or being spoken to.

Aoz Roon spared his natural daughter no more than a look before saying challengingly to Laintal Ay, "You've been missing again."

"For a while, yes. I'm sorry. I was inspecting the defences. I—"

Aoz Roon laughed curtly and looked at his companions as he said, "When you enter in that state, with Oyre with her fancy garb unlaced, I know you have been inspecting something other than the defences. Don't lie to me, you young fighting cock!"

The other men laughed. Laintal Ay went crimson.

"I'm no liar. I went to inspect our defences—but we have no defences. There are no sentries, no guards, while you were lying drinking in the wilderness. Oldorando could fall to one single armed Borlienian. We're taking life too easy, and you set a poor example."

He felt Oyre's steadying hand on his arm.

"He spends little time here now," Dol called, in a teasing voice, but was ignored, for Aoz Roon had turned to his other companions and said, "You see what I have to endure from my lieutenants, so-called. Always impudence. Oldorando is now concealed and protected by green, growing higher every week. When the warlike weather returns, as return it will, that will be time enough for war. You're trying to make trouble, Laintal Ay."

"Not so. I'm trying to prevent it."

Aoz Roon walked forward and confronted him, his immense black figure towering over the youth.

"Then keep quiet. And don't lecture me."

Above the noise of the downpour, cries could be heard outside. Dol turned to stare out of the window and called that someone was in trouble. Oyre ran to join her.

"Stand back," Aoz Roon shouted, but the three older women also jostled to get close to the window. The room became even darker.

"We'll go and see what's happening," Tanth Ein said. He started down the stairs, his great shoulders almost blocking the trap as he descended, with Faralin Ferd and Eline Tal after him. Raynil Layan remained in the shadows, watching them go. Aoz Roon made as if to stop them, then stood indecisively in the middle of the dull room, regarded only by Laintal Ay.

The latter came forward and said, "My temper ran away with me; you shouldn't have called me a liar. Don't let that mean that my warning goes unheeded. Our responsibility is to keep the place guarded as we used to."

Aoz Roon bit his lip and did not listen.

"You get your ideas from that damned woman Shay Tal." He spoke absently, one ear cocked to the noises outside. Masculine shouts were now added to the earlier cries. The women at the window also set up a great noise, running about and clinging to Dol and to each other.

"Come away!" cried Aoz Roon, grabbing Dol angrily. Curd, the great yellow hound, started to howl.

The world danced to drumming rain. The figures below the tower were grey in the downpour. Two of the three burly hunters were lifting a body from the mud, while the third, Faralin Ferd, was endeavouring to put his arms about two old women in rain-soaked furs and direct them towards shelter. The old women, uninterested in comfort, raised their faces in grief, rain pouring into their open mouths. They were recognisable as Datnil Skar's woman and an ancient widow, the aunt of Faralin Ferd.

The women had dragged the body in from the north gate between them, covering it and themselves with mud in the process. As the hunters straightened up with their burden, the body was revealed. Its visage was distorted and masked by blood so caked that the rain did not wash it away. Its head fell back as the hunters heaved it high. Blood still gouted across its face and garments. Its throat had been bitten out, as cleanly as a man bites a great mouthful from an apple.

Dol began to shriek. Aoz Roon pushed past her, thrust his burly shoulders into the window space, and called down at those below, "Don't bring that thing in here."

The men chose to disregard him. They were making for the nearest shelter. Jets of rainwater were spewing down from the parapets above them. They floundered in the muck with their muddy burden.

Aoz Roon cursed and ran from the room, charging downstairs, Curd following. Caught by the drama of the moment, Laintal Ay followed, with Oyre, Dol, and the other women behind him, jostling on the narrow steps. Raynil Layan came more slowly in the rear.

The hunters and the old women dragged or escorted the dead body into the low-ceilinged stable to drop it on scattered straw. The men stood away, wiping their faces with their hands, as a puddle of water in which blood spiralled leaked from the body, to set afloat wisps of straw, which turned uncertainly on the flood like boats seeking an estuary. The old women, grotesque bundles, cried on each other's shoulders monumentally. Although the face of the dead man was plastered with blood and hair there was no doubt of his identity. Master Datnil Skar, with Curd sniffing at his cold ear, lay dead before them.

Tanth Ein's woman was a personable creature, by name Farayl Musk. She broke into a series of long wailing cries, which she was unable to stifle.

Nobody could mistake the deadly neck wound for anything but a phagor bite. The mode of execution common in Pannoval had been passed on, for when need arose, as it rarely did, by Yuli the Priest. Somewhere outside in the pouring rain was Wutra, waiting. Wutra, for ever at war. Laintal Ay thought of Shay Tal's alarming claim that Wutra was a phagor. Perhaps there really was a god, perhaps he really was a phagor. His mind went back to the time earlier in the day, before he had found Oyre naked, when he had seen Goija Hin leading Myk to the north gate. There was no doubt who was responsible for this death; he thought how Shay Tal would have fresh cause for sorrow.

He looked at the stricken faces about him—and Raynil Layan's gloating one—and took courage. In a loud voice, he said, "Aoz Roon, I name you the killer of this good old man." He pointed at Aoz Roon as if imagining that some present did not know whom he designated.

All eyes turned to the Lord of Embruddock, who stood with his head against the rafters, his face pale. He said harshly, "Don't dare speak against me. One word more from you, Laintal Ay, and I will strike you down."

But Laintal Ay could not be stopped. Full of anger, he cried mockingly, "Is this another of your cruel blows against knowledge—against Shay Tal?"

The others murmured, restless in the confined space. Aoz Roon said, "This is justice. I have information that Datnil Skar allowed outsiders to read the secret book of his corps. It's a forbidden act. Its just penalty is now, as it always was, death."

"Justice! Does this look like justice? This blow has all the stealth of murder. You've all seen—it's carried out like the murder of—"

Aoz Roon's attack was hardly unexpected, but its ferocity knocked his guard away. He struck back at Aoz Roon's face, dancing black with rage before him. He heard Oyre shriek. Then a fist caught him squarely on the side of the jaw.

Detachedly, he saw himself stagger backwards, trip over the sodden corpse, and sprawl powerless on the stable floor.

He was aware of screams, shouting, boots trampling round him. He felt the kicks in his ribs. There was confusion as they took him up like the body they had dropped—he attempting to protect his skull from knocking against a wall—and carried him outside into the downpour. He heard thunder like a giant pulse.

From the steps, they flung him bodily into the mud. The rain came flying down into his face. As he sprawled there, he realised that he was no longer Aoz Roon's lieutenant. From now on, their enmity was out in the open, apparent to all.

Rain continued to fall. Belts of dense cloud rolled across the central continent. An atmosphere of stalemate prevailed over the affairs of Oldorando.

The distant army of the young kzahhn, Hrr-Brahl Yprt, was forced to halt its advance, to shelter among the shattered hills of the east. Its components went into a sort of tether rather than face the downpour.

The phagors also experienced earth tremors, which originated from the same source as those afflicting Oldorando. Far to the north, old rift zones in the Chalce region were undergoing violent seismic upheaval. As the burden of ice disappeared, the earth shook and rose up.

By this period, the ocean that girdled Helliconia became free of ice even beyond the wide tropical zones, which stretched from the equator to latitudes thirty-five degrees north and south. The westward circulation of oceanic waters built up in a series of tsunami, which devastated coastal regions all round the globe. The floodings often combined with vulcanism to alter the land area.

All such geological events were monitored by the instruments of the Earth Observation Station, which Vry called Kaidaw. The readings were signalled back to distant Earth. No planet in the galaxy was watched more intensely than Helliconia.

Account was taken of the dwindling herds of yelk and biyelk which inhabited the northern Campannlat plain; their pasturage was threatened. Kaidaws, on the other hand, were multiplying as marginal lands, hitherto barren, provided grazing.

There were two sorts of ancipital community on the tropical continent: static components without kaidaws, which lived close to the land, and mobile or nomadic groups with kaidaws. Not only was the kaidaw a highly mobile animal in its own right; its fodder consumption forced those who domesticated it to move continuously in search of new foraging grounds. The army of the young kzahhn, for example, consisted of numerous small components committed to a nomadic and often warlike existence. Their crusade was only one aspect of a migration, which would take decades to complete, from east to west of the entire continent.

A tremor which brought down avalanches about the kzahhn's army marked the tail end of an upheaval in the planet's crust which deflected a river of meltwater flowing from the Hhryggt Glacier. A new valley opened. The new river coursed through it, and henceforth flowed westwards instead of north, as previously.

This river burst its way down to become a tributary of the river Takissa, streaming southwards to empty into the Sea of Eagles. Its waters ran black for many years; they carried with them dozens of metric tons of demolished mountain every day.

Flooding caused by the new river through its new valley forced one insignificant group of phagors of the nomadic type to disperse in the direction of Oldorando instead of heading east. Their destiny was to encounter Aoz Roon at a later date. Though their deflection at the time was of little seeming importance even to the ancipitals themselves, it was to alter the social history of the sector.

There were, on the Avernus, those who studied the social history of Helliconian cultures; but it was the heliographers who regarded their science as the most valuable. Before all else came the light.

Star B, which the natives below called Batalix, was a modest spectral class G4 sun. In real terms slightly smaller than Sol, its radius being 0.94 Sol's, its apparent size as seen from Helliconia was 76 percent that of Sol seen from Earth. With a photosphere temperature of 5600 Kelvin, its luminosity was only 0.8 that of Sol. It was about five billion years old.

The more distant star, known locally as Freyr, about which Star B revolved, was a much more impressive object as viewed from the Avernus. Star A was a brilliant white spectral class A-type supergiant, with a radius sixty-five times that of Sol's, and a luminosity sixty thousand

times as great. Its mass was 14.8 times Sol's, and its surface tempera-
ture 11,000K, as opposed to Sol's 5780K.

Although Star B had its constant students, Star A was a greater mag-
net for attention, especially now that the Avernus was moving, along
with the rest of Star B's system, nearer to the supergiant.

Freyr was between ten and eleven million years old. It had evolved
away from the main sequence of stars and was already entering its old
age.

Such was the intensity of the energy it poured out that the disc of
Star A was always more intense as viewed from Helliconia than that of
Star B, though it never appeared so large, owing to its much greater
distance. It was a worthy object for ancipital fear—and for Vry's
admiration.

Vry stood alone on the top of her tower, her telescope by her side.
She waited. She watched. She felt the history of private relationships
flowing towards the morrow like a silt-laden river; what had been fresh
was clogged with sediment. Beneath her passivity was an unformulated
longing to be seized up by some larger thing which would provide
wider, purer perspectives than faulty human nature could command.

When darkness fell, she would look again at the stars—provided the
cloud cover parted sufficiently.

Oldorando was now surrounded by palisades of green. Day by day,
new leaves unfurled and mounted higher, as if nature had a plan to bury
the town in forest. Some of the more distant towers had already been
overwhelmed by vegetation.

She saw a large white bird hover above one such mound without paying it particular attention. She watched and admired its effortless hover-
ing above the earth.

Distantly came the sound of men singing. The hunters were back in
Oldorando from a hoxney hunt, and Aoz Roon was holding a feast. The
feast was in honour of his three new lieutenants, Tanth Ein, Faralin
Ferd, and Eline Tal. These friends of his childhood supplanted Dathka
and Laintal Ay, who were now relegated to the chase.

Vry tried to keep her thoughts abstract, but they drifted back continually to the more emotional subject of defeated hope—hers, Dathka's, whose desires she could not find it in herself to encourage, Laintal
Ay's. Her mood was in tune with the long-protracted evening. Batalix
was down, the other sentinel would follow in an hour. This was a time
when men and beasts made preparations against the reign of night. This
was a time to bring out a stub of candle against some undreamed-of
emergency, or to resolve to sleep until the light of dawn.

From her eyrie, Vry saw the common people of Oldorando—whether or not further on with their hopes—coming home. Among them was the thin crooked shape of Shay Tal.

Shay Tal returned to the tower with Amin Lim, looking grimy and tired. Since the murder of Master Datnil, she had become increasingly remote. The curse of silence had fallen on her too. She was currently trying to follow a suggestion made by the dead master, to dig her way into King Denniss's pyramid, out by the sacrificial ground. Despite the aid of slaves, she had no success. People who went to look at the earth-work being thrown up laughed, openly or secretly, for the stepped walls of the pyramid went on down into the earth without feature. For every foot dug, Shay Tal's mouth grew grimmer.

Moved by both pity and her own loneliness, Vry went down to speak to Shay Tal. The sorceress seemed to have precious little that was magi-cal about her; almost alone among the women of Oldorando, she still wore the old clumsy furs, hanging ungracefully about her body, giving her an outdated air. Everyone else was in hoxneys.

Afflicted by the older woman's woebegone air, Vry could not resist giving some advice.

"You make yourself so unhappy, ma'am. The ground is full of the dark and the past—do stop scratching there."

With a flash of humour, Shay Tal said, "We neither of us see happi-ness as our prime duty."

"Your attention's so downcast." She pointed out of the window. "Look at that white bird, circling gracefully in the air. Doesn't the sight lift your spirits? I'd like to be that bird, and fly up to the stars."

Somewhat to Vry's surprise, Shay Tal went to the window and looked in the direction Vry pointed. Then she turned, brushing her hair from her brow, and said calmly, "You observe it's a cowbird you pointed out?"

"I suppose so. What of it?" Shadows were already gathering in the room.

"Do you not recall Fish Lake and other encounters? Those birds are the familiars of phagors."

She spoke placidly, in her detached academy manner. Vry was fright-ened, thinking how self-absorbed she had been to neglect an elementary fact. She put her hand to her mouth, looking from Shay Tal to Amin Lim and back.

"Another attack? What should we do?"

"It appears that I have ceased to communicate with the Lord of Em-bruddock, or he with me. Vry, you must go and inform him that the enemy may be at his gates while he feasts with his cronies. He will know that I can't be relied on to forestall the brutes, as once I did. Go right away."

As Vry hastened down the path, rain started to drip again. She followed the singing. Aoz Roon and his cronies sat in the lowest room in the tower of the metal-makers corps. Their faces were ripe with the food and beethel set before them. A trencher piled with geese stuffed with raige and scantiom formed the chief dish; its aroma made the starved Vry's mouth water. Those present included the three new lieutenants and their women, the newest master of the council, Raynil Layan, and Dol and Oyre. The last two alone looked pleased at Vry's entry. As Vry knew—as Rol Sakil had proudly announced—Dol now carried Aoz Roon's child inside her.

Candles burned already on the tables; dogs milled in the shadows under the tables. Flavours of cooked goose and raw dogs' piss intermingled.

Although the men were red and shining, despite the piped heating the room felt cold. Rain gusted in, causing streamlets to run between the flags. It was a small dirty room, with cobwebs festooning every corner. Vry took it all in as she broke her news nervously to Aoz Roon.

She had once been familiar with every adze mark on the beams overhead. Her mother had served as a slave to the metal makers, and she had lived in this room, or in a corner of it, and witnessed the degradation of her mother every night.

Although he had looked far gone in drink a moment earlier, Aoz Roon jumped up immediately. Curd started to bark furiously, and Dol kicked him into silence. The other feasters stared at each other rather stupidly, reluctant to digest Vry's news.

Aoz Roon marched round the table, clouting their shoulders as he issued an order to each.

"Tanth Ein, alert everyone and turn out the hunters. God's eddre, why aren't we properly guarded? Mount sentries on all towers, report when all's done. Faralin Ferd, fetch in all women and children. Lock them in the women's house for safety. Dol, Oyre, you two remain here, and you other women. Eline Tal, you have the loudest voice—you stay on top of this tower and relay any messages needed. . . . Raynil Layan, you're in charge of all corps men. Have them paraded at once, go."

After this rapid fire of orders, he shouted them into action, himself pacing about furiously. Then he turned to Vry, "All right, woman, I want to see the lie of the land for myself. Yours is the northernmost tower—I'll look from there. Move, everyone, and let's hope this is a false alarm."

He set off rapidly down to the door, his great hound bursting past him. With a last glance at the stuffed geese, Vry followed. Soon, shouts resounded among the leprous old buildings. The rain was tapering off. Yellow flowers, abloom in the lanes, unbent their heads and stood erect again.

Oyre ran after Aoz Roon and fell in by his side, smiling despite his growled dismissal. She sprang along in her dark blue and light blue hoxney with something like glee.

"It's not often I see you unprepared, Father."

He shot her one of his black looks. She thought merely, He has grown older of late.

At Vry's tower, he gestured to his daughter to stay, and entered the pile at a run. As he climbed the crumbling steps, Shay Tal emerged on her landing. He spared her only a nod and continued upwards. She followed him to the top, catching his scent.

He stood by the parapet, scrutinising the darkening land. He set his hands in a platform across his eyebrows, elbows out, legs apart. Freyr was low, its light spilling through rifts of western cloud. The cowbird was still circling, and not far distant. No movement could be observed in the bushes beneath its wings.

Shay Tal said from behind his broad back, "There's only the one bird."

He gave no answer.

"And so perhaps no phagors."

Without turning or changing his attitude, he said, "How the place is altered since we were children."

"Yes. Sometimes I miss all the whiteness."

When he did turn, it was with an expression of bitterness on his face, which he seemed to remove with an effort.

"Well, there's evidently little danger. Come and see, if you wish."

He then went down without hesitation, as if regretting his invitation. Curd stayed close as ever. She followed to where the others waited.

Laintal Ay came up, spear in hand, summoned by the shouting.

He and Aoz Roon glared at each other. Neither spoke. Then Aoz Roon drew out his sword and marched down the path in the direction of the cowbird.

The vegetation was thick. It scattered water over them. The women got the worst of it as the men pressed back boughs which showered in the faces of those who followed.

They turned a bend where young damson trees were growing, trunks thinner than a man's arm. There was a ruined tower, reduced to two floors and swamped by vegetation. Beside it, under the leprous stone, in a tunnel of sullen green gloom, a phagor sat astride a kaidaw.

The cowbird could be seen through branches overhead, croaking a warning.

The humans halted, the women instinctively drawing together. Curd crouched, snarling.

Horny hands resting together on the pommel of its saddle, the phagor sat its tall mount. Its spears trailed behind it in an unprepared way. It widened its cerise eyes and twitched an ear. Otherwise, it made no move.

The rain had soaked the phagor's fur, which clung about it in heavy grey clumps. A bead of water hung and twinkled at the tip of one forward-curving horn. The kaidaw was also immobile, its head outstretched, its furled horns twisting below its jaws and then up. Its ribs showed, and it was spattered with mud and gashes on which its yellow blood had caked.

The unreal tableau was broken, unexpectedly, by Shay Tal. She pushed past Aoz Roon and Laintal Ay, to stand alone on the path in front of them. She raised her right hand above her head in a commanding gesture. No response came from the phagor; it certainly did not turn to ice.

"Come back, ma'am," called Vry, knowing the magic would not work.

As if under compulsion, Shay Tal moved forward, bringing all her attention to bear on the hostile figure of mount and rider. Twilight was encroaching, light dying: that would be to the advantage of the adversary, whose eyes saw in the dark.

Taking pace after pace forward, she had to raise her eyes to watch the phagor for any unexpected movement. The stillness of the creature was uncanny. Drawing nearer, she saw that this was a female. Heavy brownish dugs showed beneath the soaked fur.

"Shay Tal, get back!" As he spoke, Aoz Roon ran forward, passing her, his sword ready.

The gillot moved at last. She raised a weapon with a curved blade and spurred her mount.

The kaidaw came on with extraordinary speed. At one moment it was still, at the next charging towards the humans down the narrow path, horns first. Screaming, the women dived into the dripping undergrowth. Curd, without being told, raced in, dodging under the kaidaw's prognathous jaw to nip it in the fetlock.

Baring her gums and incisors, the gillot leaned from her saddle and struck at Aoz Roon. Ducking backwards, he felt the crescent slice by his nose. Farther back down the path, Laintal Ay stuck the butt of his spear in the ground, fell on one knee, and pointed the weapon at the chest of the kaidaw. He crouched before its charge.

But Aoz Roon reached out for the leather girth that was strapped around the animal's body, clasping it as the brute thundered by. Before the phagor could get in a second swipe, he worked with the momentum of the charge and swung himself up on the kaidaw's back, behind its mount.

For a second it seemed that he would fall over on the far side. But he hooked his left arm about the gillot's throat and stayed in place, head well out of reach of the deadly sharp horns.

She swung her head about. Her skull was as heavy as a club. One blow would have knocked the man senseless, but he ducked under her shoulder and tightened his stranglehold on her neck.

The kaidaw halted as suddenly as it had started into action, missing Laintal Ay's point by inches. Beset by Curd, it sheered about, furiously trying to toss the great hound with its horns. As it plunged, Aoz Roon brought up his sword with all the force he could muster, and thrust it between the ribs of the gillot, into her knotted intestines.

She stood up in her leather stirrups and screamed, a harsh, rending noise. She threw up her arms and her curved sword went flying into the nearest branches. Terrified, the kaidaw pranced on its hind legs. The phagor fell free, and Aoz Roon with her. He twisted as they fell, so that she bore the brunt of the tumble. Her left shoulder struck the ground jarringly.

From the dusky sky, the cowbird came swooping in, screeching, to defend its mistress. It dived at Aoz Roon's face. Curd leapt high and caught it by a leg. It slashed at him with curved beak, it battered his head with furious wings, but he tightened his grip and dragged it to the ground. A quick change of grip and he had its throat. In no time, the great white bird was dead, its pinions sprawled without motion across the muddy path.

The gillot also was dead. Aoz Roon stood over it, panting.

"By the boulder, I'm too fat for this kind of activity," he gasped. Shay Tal stood apart and wept. Vry and Oyre inspected the dead brute, regarding its open mouth, from which a yellow ichor seeped.

They heard Tanth Ein shouting in the distance, and answering shouts coming nearer. Aoz Roon kicked the gillot's corpse so that it rolled on to its back, causing a heavy white milt to flop from the jaws. The face was severely wrinkled, the grey skin wormlike where it stretched over bone. The body hair was moulting; patches of bare skin showed.

"It has some filthy disease perhaps," Oyre said. "That's why it was so feeble. Let's get away from it, Laintal Ay. Slaves will bury its corpse."

But Laintal Ay had dropped to his knees and was uncoiling a rope from the corpse's waist. He looked up to say grimly, "You wanted me to perform some great deed. Perhaps I can."

The rope was fine and silken, finer than any rope woven from stunge-bag fibre in Oldorando. He coiled it about his arm.

Curd was holding the kaidaw at bay. The mount, taller at the shoulder than an average man, stood a-tremble, head high, eyes rolling, making no attempt to escape. Laintal Ay tied a noose in the rope and flung it over the animal's neck. He drew it tight and approached the trembling creature step by step, until he could pat its flank.

Aoz Roon had recovered his composure. He wiped his sword on his leg and sheathed it as Tanth Ein arrived on the scene.

"We'll keep watch, but this was a solitary brute—a renegade near death. We have reason for continuing our celebrations, Tanth Ein."

As they clapped each other's shoulders, Aoz Roon looked about him. Ignoring Laintal Ay, he concentrated his regard on Shay Tal and Vry.

"We have no quarrel, whatever you imagine to the contrary," he told the women. "You did well to sound the alarm. Come with Oyre and me and join the festivities—my lieutenants will welcome you."

Shay Tal shook her head. "Vry and I have other things to do."

But Vry remembered the stuffed geese. She could still smell them. It would be worth enduring even that hated room for a taste of that superb flesh. She looked in torment at Shay Tal, but her stomach won. She yielded to temptation.

"I'll come," she told Aoz Roon, flushing.

Laintal Ay had his hand on the kaidaw's trembling flank. Oyre stood with him. She turned to her father and said coldly, "I shall not come. I'm happier with Laintal Ay."

"You please yourself—as usual," he said, and marched off along the dripping lane with Tanth Ein, leaving the humiliated Vry to follow behind as best she could.

The kaidaw stood tossing its great bracketted head up and down, looking sideways at Laintal Ay.

"I'm going to make a pet of you," he said. "We shall ride you, Oyre and I, ride you over the plains and mountains."

They made their way through a gathering crowd, all pressing to see the body of the vanquished enemy. Together, they went back to Embruddock, whose towers stood like decaying teeth against the last rays of Freyr. They walked hand in hand, differences submerged in this decisive moment, pulling the quivering animal after them.

X

LAINTAL AY'S
ACHIEVEMENT

The veldt was banded with upstart flowers as far as eye could see, and farther, farther than any man on two legs could investigate. White, yellow, orange, blue, viridian, cerise, a storm of petals blew across the unmapped miles to wash against the walls of Oldorando and incorporate the hamlet into its blast of colour.

The rain had brought the flowers and the rain had gone. The flowers remained, stretching to the horizon where they shimmered in hot bands, as if distance itself were stained for spring.

A section of this panorama had been fenced off.

Laintal Ay and Dathka had finished work. They and their friends were inspecting what they had achieved.

With saplings and thorn trees, they had built a fence. They had chopped down new growth till the sap ran from their blades over their wrists. The saplings had been trimmed and secured horizontally to serve as the bars of the fence. The uprights and horizontals were packed branches and whole thorn trees. The result was almost impenetrable, and as high as a man. It enclosed about a hectare of ground.

In the middle of this new enclosure stood the kaidaw, defying all attempts to ride it.

The kaidaw's mistress, the gillot, had been left to rot where she fell, as the custom was. Only after three days were Myk and two other slaves sent to bury the body, which had begun to stink.

Blossom hung neglected like spittle from the kaidaw's lips. It had taken a mouthful of pink flowers. Eaten in captivity, they seemed not to its taste, for the great gaunt animal stood with its head high, staring out over the top of the stockade, forgetting to munch. Occasionally, it moved a few yards, with its high step, and then came back to its original vantage point, eyes showing white.

When one of its downward-sweeping horns became entangled in the thorns, it freed itself with an impatient shake of the head. It was strong enough to break through the fence and gallop to freedom, but the will was lacking. It merely gazed towards freedom, blowing out sighs from distended nostrils.

"If the phagors can ride it, so can we. I rode a stungebag," Laintal Ay said. He brought up a bucket of beethel and set it by the animal. The kaidaw took a sniff and backed away, bridling.

"I'm going to sleep," Dathka said. It was his only comment after many hours. He crawled through the fence, sprawled on the ground, stuck his knees in the air, clasped his hands behind his head, and closed his eyes. Insects buzzed about him. Far from taming the animal, he and Laintal Ay had earned themselves only bruises and scratches.

Laintal Ay wiped his forehead and made another approach to the captive.

It brought its long head down so as to look him levelly in the eye. It was blowing softly. He was aware of the horns pointing at him, and made coaxing noises, poised to jump aside. The great beast shook its ears against the base of its horns and turned away.

Laintal Ay controlled his breathing and moved forward again. Ever since he and Oyre had made love by the pool, her beauty had sung in his eddre. The promise of more loving hung above him like an unreachable bough. He must prove himself by that imaginary great deed she required. He woke every morning to feel himself smothered in dreams of her flesh, as if buried under dogthrush blossom. If he could ride and tame the kaidaw, she would be his.

But the kaidaw continued to resist all human advances. It stood waiting as he approached. Its hamstrings twitched. At the last possible moment, it bucked away from his outstretched hand, to prance off, showing him its horns over one shoulder.

He had slept in the stockade with it on the previous night—or dozed fitfully, afraid of being trampled under its hoofs. Still the beast would not accept food or drink from him, and shied away from every approach. The performance had been repeated a hundred times.

Finally, Laintal Ay gave up. Leaving Dathka to slumber, he returned to Oldorando to try a new approach.

Three hours later, as the Hour-Whistler sounded, a curiously deformed phagor approached the enclosure. It dragged itself through the fence with awkward movements, so that gouts of wet yellow fur were torn out by the thorns, to remain hanging among the twigs like dead birds.

With a dragging gait, the oddity approached the kaidaw.

It was hot inside the skin, and it stank. Laintal Ay had a cloth tied round his face, with a sprig of raige against his nostrils. He had made two Barlienian slaves dig up the three-day-old corpse and skin it. Raynil Layan had soaked the skin in brine to remove some of its unpleasant associations. Oyre accompanied him back to the enclosure and stood with Dathka, waiting to see what happened next.

The kaidaw put its head low and breathed a soft question. Its dead mistress's saddle, complete with flamboyant stirrups, was still strapped about its girth. As soon as Laintal Ay reached the puzzled beast, he set one foot high in the near stirrup and swung himself up into the saddle. He was mounted at last, positioned in front of the animal's single low hump.

Phagors rode without reins, crouching over the necks of their mounts or holding the harsh frizzled hair growing along the ridge of their necks. Laintal Ay clutched the hair tightly, awaiting the next move. From the corner of his eye, he could see other villagers, strolling across the Voral bridge, coming to join Oyre and Dathka and watch the proceedings.

The kaidaw stood in silence, head still low, as if weighing its new burden. Then, slowly, it began an absurd movement, arching its neck inward, bringing its head round until its eyes, from an upside-down position, could look up and regard the rider. Its gaze met Laintal Ay's.

The animal remained in its extraordinary position but began to tremble.

The trembling was an intense vibration, seemingly originating at its heart and working outwards, much like an earthquake on a small planet. Yet still its eyeballs glared fixedly at the being on its back, and it was bereft of voluntary movement. Laintal Ay also stayed motionless, vibrating with the kaidaw. He remained looking down into its twisted face, on which—so he afterwards reflected—he read a look of intense pain.

When it did finally move, the kaidaw shot upwards like a released spring. In one continuous movement, it came erect and jumped high in the air, arching its spine like a cat's and curling its clumsy legs beneath its belly. This was the legendary spring jump of the kaidaw, experienced at first hand. The jump took it clear over the stockade fence. It did not even brush the uppermost sprigs of thorn.

As it fell, it snapped its skull down between its forelegs and thrust its horns upwards, so that it struck the ground neck first. One of the horns was immediately driven through its heart. It fell heavily on its side and kicked twice. Laintal Ay flung himself free and sprawled among the clover.

Even before he climbed shakily to his feet, he knew that the kaidaw was dead.

He pulled the stinking phagor skin from his body. He whirled it round his head and flung it away. It fell into a sapling's branches and dangled there. He cursed in frustration, feeling a terrible heat inside his head. Never had the enmity between man and phagor been more clearly demonstrated than in the self-destruction of this kaidaw.

He took a pace towards Oyre, who was running to him. He saw the villagers behind, and bands of colour. The colours rose, took wing, became the sky. He floated towards them.

For six days, Laintal Ay lay in a fever. His body was lapped in a flamelike rash. Old Rol Sakil came and applied goosegrease to his skin. Oyre sat by him. Aoz Roon came and looked down at him without speaking. Aoz Roon had Dol with him, made heavy with child, and would not let her stay. He departed stroking his beard, as if remembering something.

On the seventh day, Laintal Ay put on his hoxneys again and returned to the veldt, full of new plans.

The fence they had built already looked more natural, dappled all over with green shoots. Beyond the enclosure, herds of hoxneys grazed among the bright-coloured pastures.

"I am not going to be beaten," Laintal Ay said to Dathka. "If we can't ride kaidaws, we can ride hoxneys. They are not adversaries, like kaidaws—their blood is as red as ours. See if we can't capture one between us."

Both of them were wearing hoxney skins. They picked out a white-and-brown-striped animal and approached it on hands and knees. It was resting. At the last moment, it got up and walked away disgustedly.

They tried approaching it from different sides, while the rest of the herd watched the game. Once, Dathka got near enough to touch the animal's coat. It showed its teeth and fled.

They brought up the rope taken from the gillot and tried to lasso the animals. They ran about the plain for several hours, chasing hoxneys.

They climbed young trees, lying in wait in the branches with the lasso ready. The hoxneys came sportingly near, pushing each other and whinneying, but none ventured under the bough.

By dusk, both men were exhausted and short-tempered. The nearby carcass of the kaidaw was being stripped by several scholarly-looking vultures, whose clerical garb contrasted with the gobbets of golden meat they were swallowing. Now sabre-tongues arrived, driving the birds away and quarrelling over the feast among themselves. Soon it would be dark.

The two retired to the comparative safety of their enclosure, ate pancakes and goose eggs with salt, and went to sleep.

Dathka was the first to waken in the morning. He gasped and propped himself on one elbow, hardly able to believe his eyes.

In the cool dawn light, colour had scarcely returned to the world. Grey mist lay in strata, completely screening the old hamlet from their sight. The world lay in a succulent grey-green mist, characteristic of a Batalixian sunrise in these days. Even the four hoxneys now grazing contentedly in the stockade appeared as little more than pewter imitations of hoxneys.

He woke Laintal Ay with a prodding boot. Together, they crawled on their bellies over the wet grass and through the protecting barrier of thorns. When they were beyond the barricade, they stood up quietly, beaming at each other, clasping each other's shoulders in an attempt to keep from laughing.

No doubt the hoxneys had sought shelter from the sabre-tongues. Now they were in deeper trouble.

Drawing their knives, the men cut fresh armfuls of spikey thorn bush, ignoring the tears they gave their own flesh. These sinewy shrubs had grown even in the snows, keeping each cluster of leaf buds protectively rolled into spikes. Now the spikes unfurled into coppery green, revealing the silver curve of true thorns.

The hoxneys had broken a gap in the fence where they had entered. It was not difficult to intertwine the thorns and repair the hole. They soon had the four animals secure.

At which point, Laintal Ay and Dathka fell into an argument. Dathka claimed that the animals should be left without water until they were weakened and would submit to domination. Laintal Ay said that extra feeding and buckets of water would win the day. Eventually his method, being more positive, prevailed.

But they were still a long way from making mounts of the beasts. For ten days they worked concertedly, bedding down in the enclosure every night as the night grew shorter. The capture was a sensation; the whole population flocked across the Voral bridge to watch the fun. Aoz Roon and his lieutenants came every day. Oyre watched at first, but lost interest as the hoxneys spiritedly defied their would-be riders. Vry came frequently, often in the company of Amin Lim, who was carrying her newborn infant in her arms.

The battle for domestication was won only when the young hunters hit on the idea of dividing the enclosure into four with more fences. Once the animals were separated from each other, they became dejected, standing about with their heads low, refusing to eat.

Laintal Ay had been feeding the animals on barley bread. To this diet, he added rathel. Stocks of rathel had been accumulating steadily in Prast's Tower. Even the men now preferred the sweeter beethel or barley wine, and Embruddock's traditional drink was going out of fashion. One result of this was that women were released from the brassimip patch to work in the new fields. There was rathel to spare for four hoxneys.

A small measure mixed with the bread was enough to make the captive animals skip merrily, fall about, and later become slow and heavy-lidded. During their heavy-lidded phase, Laintal Ay slipped a strap round the neck of the hoxney they had named Gold. He mounted. Gold reared up and bucked. Laintal Ay stayed on for about a minute. On a second attempt, he stayed longer. Victory was his.

Dathka was soon astride Dazzler.

"God's eddre, this is better than sitting on burning stungebags," Laintal Ay shouted, as they rode round the enclosure. "We can ride anywhere—to Pannoval, to the end of the lands, to the edge of the seas!"

At last they dismounted and thumped each other, laughing with achievement.

"Wait until Oyre sees me riding into Oldorando. She won't resist me any longer."

"It's surprising what women can resist," Dathka said.

When they were sure enough of their mounts, they rode side by side across the bridge and into town. The inhabitants turned out and cheered, as if aware of the great social change upon them. From this day forth, nothing would be the same.

Aoz Roon appeared with Eline Tal and Faralin Ferd, and claimed one of the other two hoxneys, which was christened Grey. His lieutenants started to quarrel over the remaining animal.

"Sorry, friends, the last one is for Oyre," Laintal Ay said.

"Oyre's not riding a hoxney," Aoz Roon said. "Forget that idea, Laintal Ay. Hoxneys are for men. . . . They present us with immense possibilities. Riding hoxneys, we are on equal terms with phagors, Chalceans, Pannovalians, or any breed you may name."

He sat astride Grey, gazing at the ground. He foresaw a time when he would lead not simply a few hunters but an army—a hundred men, even two hundred, all mounted, striking fear into the enemy. Every conquest made Oldorando richer, more secure. Oldorandan banners flew across the unmapped plains.

He looked down at Laintal Ay and Dathka, who stood in the middle of the lane, reins in their hands. His dark face wrinkled into a grin.

"You've done well. We'll let yesterday rest with yesterday's snows. As Lord of Embruddock, I appoint you both Lords of the Western Veldt."

He leaned forward to clasp Laintal Ay's hand.

"Accept your new title. You and your silent friend are in charge of all hoxneys from now on. They are yours—my gift. I'll see you have help.

You'll have duties and privileges. I'm a just man, you know that. I want all the hunters mounted on broken hoxneys as soon as possible."

"I want your daughter as my woman, Aoz Roon."

Aox Roon scratched his beard. "You get to work on the hoxneys. I'll get to work on my daughter." Something veiled in his look suggested that he had no intention of encouraging the match; if he had a rival to power, it was not his three complaisant lieutenants but young Laintal Ay. To bind him to Oyre was to reinforce that potential threat. Yet he was too cunning actively to discourage his wayward daughter from her interest in Laintal Ay. What he wanted was a contented Laintal Ay, and a stream of armed, mounted warriors.

Although his vision was impossibly grand, yet the epoch would come when all he dreamed of doing was achieved by others a hundred times over. That epoch had its beginnings when he and Dathka and Laintal Ay first sat astride the woolly backs of their hoxney mares.

Powered by the dream, Aoz Roon threw off a state of indolence which had overcome him with better weather, and reverted to the man of action. He had inspired his people to build a bridge: now it was stables and corrals and a shop where harness and saddles were made. The dead gillot's saddle with adjustable stirrups was used as a model for all Oldorandan saddles.

The tamed hoxneys were used as decoys in the manner of captive deer, and more of the wild animals were caught. Despite their protests, all hunters had to learn to ride; soon, each had a hoxney of his own. The age of hunting on foot was dead.

Fodder became an overwhelming problem. The women were driven to plant more fields of oats. Even the old were sent out to do what they could. Fences were built round the fields to exclude hoxneys and other despoilers. Expeditions went out to discover fresh brassimip plants, once it was discovered that hoxneys would eat ground brassimip—the food from the plant where their glossies had sheltered in darker days.

For all these new developments, power was needed. The greatest innovation was the building of a mill; a hoxney, plodding round and round in a circle, ground all the grain required, and the women were released from their immemorial morning chore.

Within a few weeks, days even, the hoxney revolution was well under way. Oldorando became a different kind of town.

Its population had doubled: for every human, there was a hoxney. In the base of every tower, hoxneys were quartered beside pigs and goats. In every lane, hoxneys were tethered, champing down grasses. Along the banks of the Voral, hoxneys were watered and traded. Beyond the town gates, primitive rodeos and circuses were held, with hoxneys in starring roles. Hoxneys were everywhere, in towers, in talk, in dreams.

While auxiliary trades grew up to cater for the new obsession, Aoz Roon furthered his plans for turning his hunters into light cavalry. They drilled incessantly. Old objectives were forgotten. Meat became scarce, promises of more meat more plentiful. In order to stave off complaints, Aoz Roon planned his first mounted foray.

He and his lieutenants chose as their target a small town to the south-east, by name Vanlian, within the province of Borlien. Vanlian was situated on the Voral, where that river broadened into a valley. It was protected on its east side by tall crumbling cliffs honeycombed by caves. The inhabitants had dammed the river to create a series of shallow lakes in which they bred fish, the chief item of their diet. Sometimes traders brought the fish, dried, to Oldorando. Vanlian, with over two hundred inhabitants, was larger than Oldorando, but had no strong-holds equivalent to the stone towers. It could be destroyed by surprise attack.

The marauding cavalry numbered thirty-one. They attacked at Batalix-dawn when the inhabitants of Vanlian were out of their caves and attending to their fish harvest. Although their town was surrounded by ditches backed by steep embankments, the hoxneys climbed this forti-fication with ease, and bore down on the helpless people, their riders uttering wild cries and striking out with their spears.

Within two hours, Vanlian was destroyed. The men were killed, the women raped. Huts were burned down, fires were started in the caves, the dykes regulating the artificial lakes despoiled. A celebratory feast was held among the ruins, with much of the local small ale consumed. Aoz Roon made a speech praising his men and their mounts. None of the cavalry had died, although one hoxney had been mortally wounded by a Vanlianian sword thrust.

The victory against tall numerical odds was achieved so easily be-cause the local people were aghast at seeing brightly clad men riding in on bright steeds. They stood with mouths open to receive their death blow. Only youths and children of both sexes were spared. These were forced to round up their livestock and move off in the direction of Oldorando, driving pigs, goats, and cattle before them. Under the eyes of six cavalry selected as guards, they took a day to make a journey that Aoz Roon and his triumphant lieutenants achieved in an hour.

Vanlian was hailed as a great victory. More conquests were called for. Aoz Roon tightened his grip, and the population learned that con-quests call for sacrifices. The Lord addressed his subjects on this ques-tion when he and his cavalry had returned from another successful raid.

"We shall never want again," he announced. He stood with his arms akimbo and his legs apart. A slave stood behind him, holding Grey's rein. "Oldorando will be a great place, as legends say that Embruddock was in bygone days. We are like phagors now. Everyone will fear us, and we shall grow rich. We will take in more land, and have more slaves to tend it. Soon, we shall raid Borlien itself. We need more people, there are not enough of us. You women must bear your men more children. Babies will soon be born in the saddle as we spread far and wide."

He pointed to a wretched huddle of prisoners, guarded by Goija Hin, Myk, and others. "These people will work for us, just as the hoxneys work for us. But for a while we must all work doubly hard, and eat less, so that these things come about. Don't let me hear you complaining. Only heroes deserve the greatness that will soon be ours."

Dathka scratched his thigh and looked at Laintal Ay with one eyebrow up and one eyebrow down. "See what we've started."

But Laintal Ay was carried away by excitement. Whatever his feelings for Aoz Roon, he believed many of the things the older man said to be true. Certainly, there was no excitement like that of riding on hoxneyback, being at one with the lively creature, and feeling the wind on one's cheek and the ground thundering by below. Nothing so wonderful had ever been invented—with one exception.

He said to Oyre, gathering her to him, "You heard what your father said. I have done a great thing—one of the greatest things in history. I have tamed the hoxneys. That's what you wished, isn't it? Now you must be my woman."

But she pushed him away. "You smell of hoxneys, just as my father does. Ever since you were ill, you have talked of nothing but those stupid creatures, good only for their skins. Father talks only of Grey, you talk only of Gold. Do something that makes life better, not worse. If I was your woman, I'd never see you, because you're out riding all day and night. You men have gone mad over the hoxneys."

The women in the main felt as Oyre did. They experienced the bad effects of hoxney-mania without its excitements. Forced to work in the fields, they no longer enjoyed a sleepy afternoon's visit to the academy.

Only Shay Tal took a close interest in the animals. The wild hoxney herds were no longer as plentiful as they had been. Taking alarm at last, they moved to new grazing grounds to the west and south, in order to avoid captivity or slaughter. It was Shay Tal who had the initiative to breed from a mare and a stallion. She set up a stud by King Denniss's pyramid in which foals were soon being born. The result was a strain of domesticated and mild-mannered animals, easy to train for whatever job was required.

One of the best mares she christened Loyalty. Over all the foals she exercised great care, but her special attention was directed towards Loyalty. She knew that she now held by a halter her means of leaving Oldorando and getting to far Sibornal.

XI

WHEN SHAY TAL WENT

I n sun and rain, Oldorando expanded. Before its industrious inhabitants realised what had happened, it had crossed the river Voral, had
leaped the marshy tributaries to the north, had stretched out to the
corrals on the veldt and the brassimip patches in the low hills.

More bridges were built. None was heroic like the first one. The corps
had relearnt the art of sawing planks, carpenters came forth—among
both the free and the slaves—for whom arches and joints and abut-
ments presented few problems.

Beyond the bridges, fields were planted and fenced, sties were built
for pigs and pens for geese. Food production had to be dramatically
increased, to feed the increasing numbers of domesticated hoxneys, and
to feed the slaves needed to tend the extra fields. Beyond or between the
fields, new towers were built along the old Embruddock lines, to house
the slaves and their keepers. The towers were built according to a
demonstration given by the academy, using mud blocks instead of stone,
and rising only to two stories instead of five. The rains, heavy on
occasion, washed away the walls. The Oldorandans cared little for that,
since only slaves lived in the new blocks. But the slaves themselves cared
—and demonstrated how straw harvested from the cereal fields could

be used as overhanging thatch, to preserve the mud buildings and keep them intact even in heavy rainstorms.

Beyond the fields and new towers were bridle paths, patrolled by Aoz Roon's cavalry. Oldorando was not merely a town but an armed camp as well. Nobody left or entered without permission, except in the traders' quarters—nicknamed the Pauk—developing to the south side.

For every proud warrior mounted on a steed, six backs must bend in the field. But the harvest was good. The ground gave forth abundantly, following its long rest. Prast's Tower had been used in cold times to store first salt, than rathel; now it stored grain. Outside, where the ground had been beaten flat, women and slaves worked to winnow an immense pile of grain. The men turned over the grain with wooden paddles, the women flapped skins tied to square frames, fanning away the chaff. It was hot work. Modesty went by the board. The women, at least the young ones, threw off their smart jackets and worked with naked breasts.

Fine particles of dust rose. The dust stuck to the moist skins of the women, powdering their faces, lending their flesh a furry appearance. It rose in the air, creating a pyramid above the scene, gold in the sunlight, before dispersing to fall elsewhere, deadening footfalls on stairs, staining vegetation.

Tanth Ein and Faralin Ferd rode up, closely followed by Aoz Roon and Eline Tal, with Dathka and younger hunters riding behind. They had returned from a hunt and had brought in several deer.

For a minute, they were content to sit in their saddles, watching the women at work. Among the women were the wives of the three lieutenants; they paid no attention to the jocular remarks of their lords. The frames fanned the grain, the men leaned indulgently forward in their saddles, the chaff and dust flew high, flecking the sunshine.

Dol appeared, walking slowly, heavy with child, and Myk the aged phagor walked by her, driving her geese. With her came Shay Tal, her skinniness emphasised by the plumpness of Dol. When they saw the Lord of Embruddock and his men, both women paused, glancing at each other.

"Say nothing to Aoz Roon," Shay Tal cautioned.

"He's amenable just now," Dol said. "He hopes for a boy."

She strode forward and stood by the side of Grey. Aoz Roon looked at her but said nothing.

She slapped his knee. "Once there were priests to bless the harvest in Wutra's name. Priests used to bless newborn babes. Priests cared for all, men and women, high and low. We need them. Can't you capture some priests for us?"

"Wutra!" Aoz Roon exclaimed. He spat into the dust.

"That's no answer."

His dark eyebrows and eyelashes were dusted with the golden pepper in the air as he switched his heavy glance beyond Dol to where Shay Tal stood, her dark narrow face as blank as an alleyway.

"She's been talking to you, Dol, hasn't she? What do you know or care about Wutra? Great Yuli threw him out, and our forefathers threw out the priests. They're only lazy mouths to feed. Why are we strong while Borlien is weak? Because we have no priests. Forget this nonsense, don't bother me with it."

Dol said, pouting, "Shay Tal says the gossies are angry because we have no priests. Isn't that right, Shay Tal?" She looked appealingly over her shoulder at the older woman, who still made no move.

"Gossies are always angry," Aoz Roon said, turning away.

"They're twitching down there like a bed of fleas," Eline Tal agreed, pointing at the earth and laughing. He was a big, red-cheeked man, and his cheeks wobbled when he laughed. More and more, he had become Aoz Roon's closest companion, with the other two lieutenants playing rather subsidiary roles.

Stepping one pace forward, Shay Tal said, "Aoz Roon, despite our prosperity, we Oldorandans remain divided. Great Yuli would not have wished that. Priests might help us become a more united community."

He looked down at her, and then climbed slowly from his hoxney, to stand confronting her. Dol was pushed to one side.

"If I silence you, I silence Dol. No one wants the priests back. You only want them back because they'll help fortify your craving for learning. Learning's a luxury. It creates idle mouths. You know that, but you're so damned stubborn you won't give up. Starve yourself if you will, but the rest of Oldorando is growing fat—see for yourself. We grow fat without priests, without your learning."

Shay Tal's face crumpled. She said in a small voice, "I do not wish to fight you, Aoz Roon. I'm sick of it. But what you say is not true. We prosper in part because of applied knowledge. The bridges, the houses—those were ideas the academy contributed to the community."

"Don't anger me, woman."

Looking down at the ground, she said, "I know you hate me. I know that's why Master Datnil was killed."

"What I hate is division, constant division," Aoz Roon roared. "We survive by collective effort, and always have done."

"But we can only grow through individuality," Shay Tal said. Her face grew paler as the blood mounted in his cheeks.

He made a violent gesture. "Look about you, for Yuli's sake! Remember what this place was like when you were a child. Try to understand how we have built it to what it is now by united effort. Don't stand in front of me and try to argue differently. Look at my lieutenants' women —tits swinging, working in with everyone else. Why are you never with them? Always on the fringe, mouthing discontent, whining."

"No tit to swing, I'd say," Eline Tal said, chuckling.

His remark had been intended for the delectation of his friends, Tanth Ein and Faralin Ferd. But it also reached the alert ears of the young hunters, who burst into jeering laughter—all except Dathka, who sat silent, hunched in his saddle, alertly surveying the participants in the momentary drama.

Shay Tal also caught Eline Tal's comment. Since he was distant kin to her, the remark stung the more. Her eyes glittered with tears and wrath.

"Enough, then! I'll stand no more abuse from you and your cronies. I'll worry you no more, Aoz Roon, I'll argue never again. You've seen the last of me, you thickheaded, disappointing, treacherous bully—you and your little pregnant cow of a bedmate! At Freyr-dawn tomorrow, I leave Oldorando for good. I shall depart alone, on my mare, Loyalty, and no one will ever see me more."

Aoz Roon flung out his arm. "No one leaves Oldorando without my permission. You're not going from here until you grovel at my feet, begging to leave."

"We'll see about that in the morning," Shay Tal snapped. She turned on her heel, clutched her loose dark furs about her body, and made off towards the north gate.

Dol was red in the face. "Let her go, Aoz Roon, drive her out: Good riddance. Pregnant cow, indeed, the juiceless creature!"

"You keep out of this. I'll settle this my way."

"I suppose you're going to have her killed, like the others."

He struck her across the face, lightly and with contempt, still looking after the retreating figure of Shay Tal.

It was the night period when everyone slept, though Batalix still burned low in the sky. Although slaves twitched in the dreams of dim-day-sleep, some of the free were still about on this occasion. In the room at the top of the big tower, full council was met, consisting of the masters of the seven old corps, plus two new masters, younger men from newly constituted corps, the harness and lorimers, and the outfitters. Also present were Aoz Roon's three lieutenants and one of his Lords of the Western Veldt, Dathka. The Lord of Embruddock presided over the meeting, and serving wenches kept their wooden cups filled with beethel or small beer.

After much argument, Aoz Roon said, "Ingsan Atray, give us your voice on this question."

He was addressing the senior master, a greybeard who ruled over the metal-makers corps, and who had as yet said nothing. The years had curved Ingsan Atray's spine and turned his scanty hair white, so that the great width of his skull was emphasized; for this reason, he was regarded as wise. He had a mannerism of smiling a great deal, though his eyes, barricaded behind wrinkled lids, always looked wary. He smiled now, squatting on the skins piled on the floor for his comfort, and said, "My Lord, Embruddock's corps have traditionally protected the women. Women, after all, are our source of labour when the hunters are in the field, and so on. Of course, times are changing, I grant you that. It was different in the times of Lord Wall Ein. But women also serve as channels of much learning. We have no books, but women memorise and pass on the legends of the tribe, as is seen whenever we tell the Great Tale on feast days—"

"Your point, please, Ingsan Atray . . ."

"Ah, I was coming to it, I was coming to it. Shay Tal may be difficult and so on, but she is a sorceress and learned woman, widely known. She does no harm. If she leaves, she will take other women with her, and so on, and that will be a loss. We masters would venture to say that you were correct in forbidding her to leave."

"Oldorando's not a prison," Faralin Ferd shouted.

Aoz Roon nodded curtly, and looked about. "The meeting was called because my lieutenants disagreed with me. Who agrees with my lieutenants?"

He caught the eye of Raynil Layan, nervously stroking his forked beard.

"Master of the tanners corps, you always like to air your voice—what have you to say?"

"As to that—" Raynil Layan gestured dismissively. "There is always the *difficulty* of preventing Shay Tal leaving. She can easily slip away, if so disposed. And there is the general principle . . . Other women will think . . . Well, we don't want discontented women. But there's Vry, for instance, another thinking woman, yet attractive, and *she* gives no trouble. If you could rethink your order, many would be grateful to you. . . ."

"Speak out and don't mince your words so," Aoz Roon said. "You're a master now, as you wished, and don't have to cringe."

Nobody else spoke. Aoz Roon glared at them. All avoided his gaze, burying their faces in their cups.

Eline Tal said, "Why are we worrying? What's the odds? Let her go."

"Dathka!" the lord snapped. "Are you going to grant us a single word tonight, since your friend Laintal Ay has not put in an appearance?"

Dathka set down his beaker and looked directly at Aoz Roon.

"All this debate, this talk of principle . . . it's rubbish. We all know you and Shay Tal long wage great personal war. So *you* decide what to do, not us. Kick her out now you have your chance. Why bring us into it?"

"Because it concerns you all, that's why!" Aoz Roon pounded his fist on the floor. "By the boulder, why does that woman always have such a grudge against me, against everyone? I don't understand. What rotten maggot chews at her harneys? She keeps on the academy, doesn't she? She sees herself in a long line of female troublemakers—Loilanun, Loil Bry, who became Little Yuli's woman. . . . But where would she go? What would happen to her?"

His sentences seemed wild and disconnected.

No one answered. Dathka had spoken for all of them; all were secretly aghast when he said what he did. Aoz Roon himself had nothing more to say. The meeting broke up.

As Dathka was slipping away, Raynil Layan grasped Dathka's arm and said softly, "A cunning speech you made. With Shay Tal out of the way, the one you fancy will head the academy, won't she? Then she'll need your support. . . ."

"I leave the cunning to you, Raynil Layan," Dathka said, pulling away. "Just keep out of my path."

He had no trouble in finding Laintal Ay. Despite the lateness of the hour, Dathka knew where to go. In Shay Tal's ruined tower, Shay Tal was packing, and many friends had come to bid her farewell. Amin Lim was there with her child, and Vry, and Laintal Ay with Oyre, and several other women beside.

"What was the verdict?" Laintal Ay asked Dathka immediately, coming to his side.

"Open."

"He won't stop her leaving if she's bent on it?"

"Depends how much he drinks during the night, he and Eline Tal and that crew—and that wretched hanger-on, Raynil Layan."

"She's getting old, Dathka; should we allow her to go?"

He shrugged, using one of his favourite gestures, and looked at Vry and Oyre, who were standing close and listening. "Let's leave with Shay Tal before Aoz Roon has us killed—I'm game if these two ladies will come too. We'll head for Sibornal, the group of us."

Oyre said, "My father would never kill you and Laintal Ay. That's wild talk, whatever happened in the past."

Another shrug from Dathka. "Are you prepared to vouch for his behaviour when Shay Tal's gone? Can we trust him?"

"That's all over long ago," Oyre said. "Father's settled happily with Dol now, and they don't quarrel as much as they used, now a baby's coming."

Laintal Ay said, "Oyre, the world's wide. Let's leave with Shay Tal, as Dathka suggests, and make a new start. Vry, we'll take you with us —you'll be in danger here without Shay Tal's support."

Vry had not spoken. In her usual unobtrusive way, she merely formed part of the group; but she said now, firmly, "I can't leave here. Dathka, I am complimented by your kind suggestion, but I must stay, whatever Shay Tal does. My work is yielding results at last, as I hope soon to announce."

"You still can't bear my presence, can you?" he said, looking grim.

"Oh, I almost forgot something," she said sweetly.

She turned, evading Dathka's brooding gaze, and pushed through the women to Shay Tal's side.

"You must measure all distances, Shay Tal. Don't forget. Have a slave count the number of hoxney strides every day, with the direction taken. Write down details every night. Find out how far away the country of Sibornal is. Be as precise as you can."

Shay Tal was majestic in the midst of the weeping and chattering that filled her chamber. Her hawk face preserved a closed look whenever addressed, as if already her spirit was remote from them. She said little, and that little was uttered in unemotional tones.

Dathka, after staring blankly at the walls, with their elaborate patterning of lichen, looked at Laintal Ay with his head on one side and gestured to the door. When Laintal Ay shook his head, Dathka made a characteristic moue and slipped out. "Pity you can't train women like hoxneys," he said, as he disappeared.

"At least he is consistently revolting," Oyre said disdainfully. She and Vry took Laintal Ay into a corner and began whispering to him. It was essential that Shay Tal should not leave on the morrow; he must help persuade her to wait for the following day.

"That's absurd. If she wants to go, she must go. We've been over all this. First you will not leave, now you don't want her to leave. There's a world out beyond the barricades you know nothing about."

She coolly picked a sliver of straw from his hoxneys. "Yes, the world of conquest. I know—I hear enough of it from Father. The point is, there will be an eclipse tomorrow."

"That's general knowledge. It's a year since the last one."

"Tomorrow will be rather different, Laintal Ay," Vry said, warningly. "We simply wish Shay Tal to postpone her departure. If she leaves here on the day of the eclipse, people will associate the two events. Whereas we know there is no connection."

Laintal Ay frowned. "What of it?"

The two women looked uneasily at each other.

"We think that if she leaves tomorrow, ill things may follow."

"Ha! So you do believe there is a connection. . . . The workings of the female mind! If the connection exists, then there's no way we can evade it, is there?"

Oyre clutched her face in exaggerated disgust. "The male mind . . . Any excuse not to do anything, eh?"

"You witches will meddle with what is no concern of ours."

In disgust, they left him standing in the corner and pressed back into the crowd round Shay Tal.

The old women still chattered away, speaking of the miracle at Fish Lake, speaking obliquely, looking obliquely, to see if their reminiscences registered on the preoccupied Shay Tal. But Shay Tal gave no sign that she heard or saw them.

"You look proper fed up with life," Rol Sakil commented. "Maybe when you reach this Sibornal, you'll marry and settle down happily—if men are made there as they're made here."

"Perhaps they're made better there," another old woman responded, amid laughter. Various suggestions as to improvements were bandied about.

Shay Tal continued to pack, without smiling.

Her belongings were few. When she had finally assembled them in two skin bags, she turned to the crowd in her room and requested them to leave, as she desired to rest before her journey. She thanked them all for coming, blessed them, and said she would never forget them. She kissed Vry on the forehead. Then she summoned Oyre and Laintal Ay to her side.

She clutched one of Laintal Ay's hands in her two thin ones, looking with unusual tenderness into his eyes. She spoke only when all but Oyre had left her room.

"Be wary in all you do, for you are not self-seeking enough, you do not take enough care for yourself. You understand, Laintal Ay? I'm glad you have not struggled for the power that you may feel is your birthright, for it would only bring you sorrow."

She turned to Oyre, her face lined with seriousness.

"You are dear to me, for I know how dear you are to Laintal Ay. My council to you as we part in this: become his woman with all speed. Don't put conditions on your heart, as I did, as your father once did—that leads to inevitable wretchedness, as I understand too late. I was too proud when young."

Oyre said, "You are not wretched. You are still proud."

"One may be both wretched and proud. Heed what I say, I who understand your difficulties. Laintal Ay is the nearest thing I shall ever have to a son. He loves you. Love him—not just emotionally, also physically. Bodies are for roasting, not smoking."

She looked down at her own dried flesh, and nodded them farewell.

Batalix was setting, true night descending.

Traders came to Oldorando in increasing numbers, and from all points of the compass. The important salt trade was conducted from the north and south, whence it arrived often by goat train. There was now a regular track from Oldorando westwards across the veldt, trodden by traders from Kace, who brought gaudy things such as jewels, stained glass, toys, silvery musical instruments, as well as sugar cane and rare fruits; they preferred money to barter, but Oldorando had no currency, so they accepted herbs, skin, suede, and grain instead. Sometimes the men from Kace used stungebags as beasts of burden, but the animals became rarer as the weather grew warmer.

Traders and priests still called from Borlien, although they had learned long ago to fear their treacherous northern neighbour. They sold pamphlets and broadsheets that told lurid tales in rhyme, and fine metal pots and pans.

From the east, by divergent ways, came many traders, and sometimes caravans. Dark little men with enslaved populations of Madis or phagors plied regular routes, on which Oldorando was merely one port of call. They brought delicately wrought ornaments and decorations which the women of Oldorando loved. Rumour had it that some of those women fared onwards with the dark men; certain it was that the easterners traded in young Madi women, who looked wild and lovely, but pined away when shut in a tower. Bad though their reputation was, the traders were tolerated for their wares—not decorations only, but woven rugs, carpets, tapestries, shawls, such as Oldorando had never seen before.

All these travellers needed housing. Their encampments became a nuisance. Oldorando's slaves toiled to erect a separate township just to the south of the towers, known ironically as the Pauk. Here all trade was conducted; in narrow alleys, peltmongers and all other mongers carried on their business, with stables and eating houses nearby, and for a while the traders were forbidden entry to Oldorando proper. But their numbers grew, and some settled in the town, importing their arts and vices.

Oldorandans were also learning the artifices of trade. New merchants approached Aoz Roon and asked for special concessions, including the right to mint coin. This question vexed their minds far more than any problems with the academy, which they regarded as a waste of time.

A party of these Oldorandan traders numbering six, comfortably mounted on hoxneys, was returning to Oldorando from a successful expedition. At Freyr-dawn, they paused on a hill to the north, close by the brassimip patch, from where they could see the outskirts of the town, chill in the grey light. The air was so still that distant voices carried to them.

"Look," exclaimed one of the younger traders, shading his eyes as he gazed. "There's some kind of a hullabaloo by the gate. We'd best go by another way."

"Not fuggies, is it?"

They all stared hard. In the distance, a cluster of persons, men and women, could be observed surging from the town. In a space, some of them halted indecisively, causing the cluster to split in two. The others went forward.

"It isn't anything important," said the young trader, and spurred his hoxney. He had a woman in Embruddock he very much wanted to see, and a new bauble for her in his pocket. The departure of Shay Tal meant nothing to him.

Soon Batalix was rising, overhauling its companion in the sky.

The chill, the etiolated morning in which rain threatened, the sense of adventure, served to make her feel disembodied. She experienced no emotion as she clasped Vry to her in mute farewell. Her servant, Maysa Latra, a willing slave, helped her downstairs with her few things. Beside the tower stood Amin Lim, clutchnig the bridle of her own hoxney and Shay Tal's, and saying a sorrowful farewell to her man and her small child; there, thought Shay Tal, is a sacrifice greater than mine. I'm glad to go. Why Amin Lim comes with me, I shall never know. But her heart warmed to her friend, although she also felt a little contempt.

Four women were leaving with her: Maysa Latra, Amin Lim, and two younger disciples, devout pupils of the academy. All were mounted and were accompanied by a male gelded slave, Hamadranabail, who walked, leading two pack hoxneys and a pair of savage hunting dogs with spiked collars.

More people, women and some older men, followed the procession, calling farewells and sometimes advice, serious or jocular as the fancy took them.

Laintal Ay and Oyre waited at the gate to catch a last glimpse of Shay Tal; they stayed close but avoided looking at each other.

Beyond the gate was Aoz Roon himself, standing there in his black furs, arms folded, chin sunk on chest. Behind him was Grey, in the care of Eline Tal, who for once looked no more cheerful than his lord. Several men stood in a huddle behind their silent ruler, faces sober, hands under armpits.

When Shay Tal appeared, Aoz Roon swung himself into his saddle and began to ride slowly, not towards her but rather almost parallel with her path, so that, continuing on undeflected courses, they would collide some way ahead, where trees began.

Before he reached that point, Aoz Roon struck off the track, picking a course parallel with it among the trees. The women's party, with Amin Lim leading, weeping silently, continued sedately along the path. Neither Aoz Roon nor Shay Tal made any attempt to communicate, or even look at each other.

Freyr was hidden as yet in early cloud, so that the world remained without colour.

The ground rose, the track narrowed, the trees grew closer. They came to a fold in the ground where the trees stopped and the ground was marshy. Frogs splashed to safety as the party approached. The hoxneys picked their way slowly through the wet, flexing their paws in distaste, raising yellow mud that curdled under the water surface.

Trees on the far side of the marsh forced the riders more closely together. As if noticing Aoz Roon for the first time, Shay Tal called in her clear voice, "You do not need to follow."

"I am leading, ma'am, not following. I will see you safely away from Oldorando. It's an honour properly owed you."

No more was said. They proceeded farther, coming at last to rising ground studded with bushes. At the crest, they could pick up a clear traders' path leading northeast, to Chalce and distant Sibornal—how distant, no one knew. Trees began again on the downward slope. Aoz Roon reached the crest first, and positioned himself there, bleak of visage, pointing Grey along the lie of the ridge as the women went by.

Shay Tal turned Loyalty's head and approached him, the lines of her face clear and composed.

"It's good of you to come this far."

"Enjoy a safe journey," he said formally, holding himself upright, pulling in his belly. "You observe that no attempt is made to stop you leaving us."

Her voice softened. "We shall never see each other again; from this date on, we are extinct to each other. Have we ruined each other's lives, Aoz Roon?"

"I don't understand what you're talking about."

"Yes, you do. Since we were children we have been up against each other. Give me a word, friend, as I go away. Don't be proud, as I've always been proud—not now."

He firmed up his mouth and regarded her without saying anything.

"Please, Aoz Roon, a true word on parting. I am well aware I said No to you once too often."

At that he nodded. "There's your true word."

She looked about anxiously, then kicked Loyalty one pace nearer, so that the two hoxneys touched each other.

"Now that I'm leaving for ever, just tell me—that in your heart you still feel for me as once you did, when we were younger."

He gave a snorting laugh. "You're mad. You never understood reality. You were too wrapped up in yourself. I feel nothing for you now—or you for me, if you but knew it."

She reached out to clutch him, but he backed away, showing his teeth like a dog. "Lies, Aoz Roon, all lies! Give me then a gesture as I go—give me a parting kiss, damn you, I who have suffered so much from you. Gestures are better than words."

"Many think not. What's said always remains."

Tears burst from her eyes and were gone, falling aslant her lean cheeks.

"May the fessups feed on you!"

She wrenched round the head of her mare and galloped away, plunging into the trees to catch up with her small procession.

He sat for a moment where he was, drawn up rigid in the saddle, staring ahead with his knuckles white about the reins. Gently, he turned Grey's head and coaxed her among the trees, going away from Oldorando at a tangent, ignoring Eline Tal, who discreetly waited some distance behind.

Grey picked up speed as she moved downhill, encouraged by her master. Soon they were going at full gallop, the ground flying beneath them, and all human beings lost to view. Aoz Roon raised his clenched right fist high in the air.

"Good riddance to the hag-bitch," he cried. Savage laughter was torn from his throat as he rode.

Earth Observation Station Avernus saw everything as it passed overhead. All change was monitored and all data transmitted back to Earth. In the Avernus, members of the eight learned families were at work, synthesising the new knowledge.

They charted not only the movement of human populations but also those of the phagorian populations, both white and black. Every advance or retreat was transformed into an impulse which would eventually make its way across the light-years to the globe and computers back in the Helliconian Centronics Institute on Earth.

From the window of the station, the team could observe the planet below, and the progress of the eclipse, as it spread a grey necrosis over the oceans and the tropical continent.

On one bank of monitor screens, another progress was under survey— the progress of the kzahhn's crusade towards Oldorando. By its own peculiar travelling time, the crusade was now precisely one year away from its anticipated target, the destruction of the old town.

In codified form, these signals were relayed back to Earth. There, many centuries later, Helliconia-watchers assembled to see the final agonies of the drama.

The bleak regions of Mordriat, its echoing canyons, its shattered walls of rock, its moors with their unexpected air of privacy, its drab high valleys through which cloud forever smouldered, as if fire rather than ice had moulded the unyielding contours of its desolation, lay behind.

The straggling crusade, broken into many separate groups, was wending its way over lower country, empty save for Madis with their flocks, and dense flights of birds. Indifferent to their surroundings, the phagors continued towards the southeast.

The kzahhn of Hrastyprt, Hrr-Brahl Yprt, led them onwards. Vengeance was still strong in their harneys, as they made their way through the floods of the east Oldorandan plain; yet many of them had died. Sickness and attacks from merciless Sons of Freyr had cut down their numbers.

Nor had they been well received by small components of phagors through whose land they travelled. Those components without kaidaws pursued a settled way of living, often with large gangs of human or Madi slaves, and fiercely resisted any invasion of their territory.

Hrr-Brahl Yrpt had come victorious through everything. Only sickness was beyond his power to command. As news of his columns preceded him, so living things in his path moved away, causing the ripples of his progress to spread across half a continent.

Now the leaders stood with Hrr-Brahl Yprt before a wide-flowing river. The waters of the river were icy; they plunged down, though the phagor host knew it not, from the same Nktryhk uplands from which the crusade against the Sons of Freyr had started, a thousand miles away.

"Here by these torrents we will stay while Batalix makes her way twice across the sky," Hrr-Brahl Yprt said to his commanders. "Leader scouts will diverge to either side and find us a dry crossing; the airoctaves will guide them."

He whistled down his cowbird, who began to search his pelage for ticks. It was done abstractedly, for the kzahhn had other matters on his harneys; but the minute creatures were suddenly irritating. Perhaps it was the warmth of the valley surrounding them. Green cliffs rose on all sides, trapping the unwelcome heat as cupped hands hold water. The third blindness would soon be upon them. Later, a retreat to colder quarters must commence.

But first came vengeance.

He gestured the graceful Zzhrrk away, and strode off to obtain an understanding of the overall situation, his bird remaining above him with an occasional downthrust of its wings.

They could wait while the rest of the force, which straggled back over several dozen miles, caught up. Banners were hoisted, the kaidaws were released to forage. Minions erected tents for the leadership. Meals and rituals were set in train.

As Batalix and the treacherous Freyr sailed above the encampment, the kzahhn of Hrastyprt strode into his tent, unbuckling his face crown. His long head was thrust forward between burly shoulders, and the barrel of his body—trimmed by the ordeals of travel—also leaned forward in his eagerness.

The sweeping lashes of his eyes came down, slitting his cerise stare, as he glared along the curve of his nose to his four fillocks. They stood within the tent, scratching or jostling each other as they awaited his arrival.

Zzhrrk swooped through the opening of the tent, but Hrr-Brahl Yprt brushed it away. It fluttered, caught off balance, and landed awkwardly, to waddle out of the tent. Hrr-Brahl Yprt pulled down the rug behind him, closing the entrance. He began to divest himself of his armour, his sleeveless jacket, his belt and sporran, all the while looking at his four brides, the imperious gaze switching from one to the other. He snuffed at them, smelling their scents.

The fillocks fretted, scratching at ticks, or adjusting their long white coats so that their plump dugs smacked about in his sight. The eagle feathers in their head hair nodded towards him. They snorted and shot their pale milts neatly into their nostril slits.

"You!" he said, pointing to the one female fully in heat. While her companions banged away and squatted at the rear of the tent, the chosen one turned her back on the young kzahhn and stooped forward. He approached, prodding his three fingers deep into her proffered flesh, then wiping them on the black fur of his muzzle. Without further ado, he hoisted himself upon her, his weight bowing her until she was on all fours. Slowly she sank further as he thrust, until her wide forehead rested on the rug.

When the incursion was over, and the other fillocks trotted forward to nuzzle their sister, Hrr-Brahl Yprt pulled on his armour and strode from the tent. It would be three weeks before his sexual interest reawoke.

His crusade commander, Yohl-Gharr Wyrrijk, was stolidly awaiting him. The two stood foresquare, looking into each other's eyes. Yohl-Gharr Wyrrijk gestured up at the sky.

"The day comes," he said. "The octaves tighten."

His kzahhn swivelled his head, waving a fist to clear the sky overhead of cowbirds. He stared up at the usurper Freyr, perceiving how it dragged itself every day, like a spider across its web, closer to Batalix. Soon, soon, Freyr would hide itself in the belly of its enemy. The hosts would then be at their destination. They would strike then, and kill all the progeny of Freyr who lived where Hrr-Brahl Yprt's noble grandstallun had died; and then they would burn down the town and erase it from memory. Only then could he and his followers attain honourable tether. Those thoughts crawled through his harneys like the slow drip of icicles, which splash as they melt and lose shape and make the ground heavy with their drenchment.

"The two seminals draw together," he growled.

Later, he had a human slave sound the stungebag horn, and the keratinous figures of his father and great-grandstallun were presented before him. The young kzahhn noted how both figures had been damaged by the long journey, despite the care that had been taken of them.

Humbly, and with hosts of the component assembled by the black river, Hrr-Brahl Yprt went into his trance. Everyone became absolutely immobile, according to his nature, as if they were frozen in a sea of air.

No larger than a snow rabbit, the image of the great-grandstallun appeared, running on all fours as once it had been with the phagors in the time long gone, when Batalix had yet to be caught in the web woven by Freyr.

"Hold horns high," said the snow rabbit. "Remember enmities, resent the coming of the green, sprinkle it with the red liquids of the Sons of Freyr, who brought the green and banished the white as it was."

The keratinous father also appeared, scarcely larger, bowing to his son, conjuring a sequence of pictures in his pale harneys.

The world was there before the closed eyes, its three divisions pumping. From the steam of its being blew the yellow strands of the air-octaves, writhing like long ribbons about the clenched fists, and about the clenched fists of other worlds nearby, embracing too beloved Batalix and the spiderous shape of Freyr. Things like lice ran along the ribbons, keening with a shrill note.

Hrr-Brahl Yprt thanked his father for the pictures flickering in his harneys. He had seen them many times before. All present were familiar with them. They must be repeated. They were the lodestones of the crusade. Without repetition, the lights were extinguished, leaving the harney-packed skull like some remote cave, piled with the bodies of dead serpents.

With repetition, it was clearly understood that the needs of one phagor were the needs of the whole world, which those departed for the next world had called Hrl-Ichor Yhar, and the needs of Hrl-Ichor Yhar were the needs of a single phagor. There were pictures now of the Sons of Freyr: when the colours of the air-octaves brightened, the Sons were falling ill on the ground, falling or dying or being transformed into smaller sizes. That time had come before. That time would come soon. Past and future were present. The falling would come also when Freyr hid completely in Batalix. And then would be the time to strike—to strike against all, and especially against those whose forebears had slain the Great Kzahhn Hrr-Tryhk Hrast.

Remember. Be valiant, be implacable. Do not deviate an inch from the programme, transmitted through many ancestors.

There was a scent of ancient days, something far, fusty, and true. An angellike array of predecessors was glimpsed, devouring the primal ice-fields. The air turns marched in millions, never mute.

Remember. Prepare for the next stage. Hold horns high.

The young kzahhn emerged slowly from his trance. His white cow-bird had settled on his left shoulder. It slid its curved beak reassuringly among the hairs and folds of his shoulders, and began to feed on the ticks that clustered there. The horn was sounded again, its mournful note carrying across the ice-cold river.

That melancholy note could be heard some distance away, where a group of phagors had become separated from their main component. They were eight in number, six being gillots and two stalluns. They had with them one old red kaidaw, past riding, on whose back weapons and supplies were lashed. A few days previously, when Batalix prevailed auspiciously in the sky, they had captured six Madi men and women, who, with their animals, were trailing behind a migratory caravan heading for the isthmus of Chalce. The animals had been immediately cooked and eaten, their throats bitten out in the approved way.

The unfortunate Madis were tied together and made to follow on. But the difficulty of making them follow, as well as the delay for the feast, had led to the group's separation from the body of the crusade. They got themselves on the wrong side of a brook which swelled to a torrent. Rainstorms broke over the higher ground, the brook flooded, they were cut off.

That Batalix-night, the phagors made camp in a sombre clearing beneath tall rajabarals; they secured the Madis to a slender tree, where the protognostics were allowed to sleep as best they could, huddled together. The phagors flung themselves down close by, lying flat on their backs; their cowbirds came down and settled on their breasts, with heads and beaks tucked into the warmth of the phagors' necks. The phagors went immediately into their dreamless and motionless sleep, as if preparing for tether.

Squawks of cowbirds and cries of Madis woke them. The Madis in terror had broken loose from their tree and fallen upon their captors—not in anger but hopes of protection, relying on their enemies to defend them against a greater menace.

One of the rajabarals was splitting. The air was brittle with the noise of its destruction.

Seams showed vertically, and thick brown sap like pus spurted from the cracks. Steam from the tree shrouded the writhing thing that was emerging from it.

"Wutra worm! Wutra worm!" cried the protognostics, as the phagors scrambled to their feet. The leading phagor crossed to the hobbled kaidaw, handing out spears in a businesslike manner.

The great drum of the active rajabaral was thirty feet high. Suddenly, its top blew, pieces falling like shattered pottery, and out from the top reared a Wutra's worm. Through the clearing poured the characteristic worm stench, in which scumble, festering fish, and decaying cheese mingled.

The creature's head rose like a snake's, glistening in the sun, poised on the flexing column of its neck. It swung about, and the rajabaral cracked open, revealing more slimy coils unwinding, and the discarded skin of a moult. Boring underground, the creature had entered the rajabaral through its roots, to use the tree as a refuge. Increasing warmth encouraged it to moult and metamorphose. Now it required nourishment as its next stage of development forced it through the imperatives of its life cycle.

By now, the phagors were armed. Their leader, a thick-set gillot with black hairs showing in her pelt, gave the order. Her two best marksmen flung their spears at the Wutra's worm.

The beast twisted, the spears flew harmlessly by. It sighted the figures below it, and immediately snaked its head down in attack. Those on the ground were suddenly aware of its true size, as it confronted them—four banked eyes glaring at them above thick fleshy feelers spreading from its mouth. The feelers waved like fingers as the worm poised itself to strike. The mouth, filled with backward-pointing teeth, was curiously baggy, pursing itself in the middle as well as at the sides.

The head was held sideways, sweeping towards them like a wagging asokin's tail. One moment it loomed above the treetops—the next, it was bearing down on the line of phagors. They flung their spears. The cowbirds scattered.

That oddly working mouth, jawless, seemed infinitely capacious. It snatched up one of the phagors in its fangs and half-lifted her. The gillot was too heavy for the musculature of the supple neck to carry. She was dragged croaking across the swampy ground, one arm striking at the scent pits of the monster.

"Kill it!" cried the gillot leader, dashing forward with her knife raised.

But in the dim slimes of the worm's harneys, a decision had been reached. It bit savagely through the flesh in its mouth and dropped the rest. The head jerked upward, out of harm's way, yellow blood pouring off its whiskers. What remained of the gillot beat its fist on the ground and then lay unmoving.

Even as the worm gobbled its morsel, it began to change, its coils crashing down into the young trees round about. Though not given to fright, the seven surviving phagors fell down in terror. The worm was splitting in twain.

It dragged its bloodied head over the grass, some way distant from them. Membranes tore with protracted noise. Something like a mask peeled from the head, which became, grotesquely, two heads. While these heads lay one on top of each other, they still resembled the old one; then the new upper head lifted and the resemblance was gone.

The jaws of the new heads sprouted fleshy feelers, rapidly growing outstretched and stiff to form a circle of spikes, behind which came a mouth, the cartilage fixed wide without the ability to close. The rest

of the head followed this unseemly opening, with two eyes set horizontally in it. A layer of slime, revealed by the torn membranes, dried,
causing a slight colour change to take place. One head became verdi-
gris-hued green, the other a mottled blue.

The heads rose, rearing away from each other in antagonism,
emitting a low roar.

This action caused more membranes to split all along the old body,
which was revealed as two bodies, one green, one blue, both very slender
and winged. A convulsive struggle, similar to a death paroxysm, shook
the old body. The two new javelin bodies came streaming forth from
it, spreading papery wings as they rose. The heads ascended above the
shattered rajabaral, papery wings thrashed. Eight cowbirds flew round
about them, screeching with open beaks.

The two opposed creatures became more stable. In another moment, their long-whiskered tails had left the ground. They were air-
borne, and the light of Freyr glittered on scales and sutured wings. One
monster, the green one, was male, with a double series of tentacle ap-
pendages dangling from its middle regions, the other, the blue, female,
its scales less bright.

Now their wings had acquired a steady beat, lifting them above the
treetops. The leading aperture, the mouth, gulped in air, expelling it
through rear vents. The creatures circled the clearing in opposite
directions, watched helplessly by the phagor band. Then they were off
on their maiden flight.

The fliers headed away like flying snakes, one towards the distant
north, one towards the far south, obeying mysteriously musical air-
octaves of their own, and suddenly beautiful in their power. Their long
thin bodies undulated through the atmosphere. They gained height,
lifting themselves above the bowl of the valley. Then they were gone,
each to seek mates in the remoteness of the opposed poles.

The imagos had forgotten their previous existences, imprisoned for
centuries in the hibernal earth.

Grunting, the phagors turned to more immediate things. Their
stares swept about the clearing. Their hobbled kaidaw remained,
placidly cropping grass. The Madis had gone. Seizing their opportunity,
the protognostics had beaten it into the forest.

Madis generally mated for life, and it was rare for a widow or wid-
ower to remarry; indeed, a kind of deep melancholia generally carried
off the survivor of the bond-pair. The fugitives comprised three men
and their mates. The senior pair by a few years was called Cathkaarnit,
that being their merged name since marriage; they were distinguished
as Cathkaarnit-he and Cathkaarnit-she.

All six of them were slender and of small stature. All were dark. The transhuman protognostics, of which the Madis formed one tribe, differed little in appearance from true humans. Their pursed lips, caused by the formation of the bones of the skull and the lie of their teeth, gave them a wistful look. They possessed eight fingers on each hand, with four opposed to four, giving them an amazingly strong grip; and their feet also exhibited four toes forward and four aft, behind the heel.

They ran at a steady jog trot from the clearing where the phagors were, a pace they could maintain for hours if necessary. They ran through groves and through bogs, moving in double file, the Cathkaarnits leading, then the next oldest pair, then the next. Several wild animals, chiefly deer, went crashing away from their path. Once they flushed a boar. They hastened on without pause.

Their flight led them mainly westwards; the memory of their eight weeks of captivity lent them strength. Skirting the floods, they climbed out of the great saucer of land in which they had made their escape. The heat grew less. At the same time, the inclination upwards of the land, slight but continuous, wore down their energies. The jog trot relapsed into a fast-walking pace. Their skins burned. They pressed on, heads down, breathing painfully through nose and mouth, occasionally stumbling over the rough ground.

At last the rear pair gave a gasp and fell, to lie panting, clutching their stomachs. Their four companions, looking up, saw that they had almost gained the lip of the rise, after which the land could be relied on to level out. They continued, leaning forward, to drop as soon as they climbed from the slope to the flat. Their lungs laboured.

From here they could look back through the preternaturally clear air. Below them were their two exhausted friends, sprawling at the top of an enormous bowl of land. The sides of the bowl were pitted by gulleys down which water poured. The brooks ran down into two immense coils of a river newly enough formed for half-drowned trees still to be standing in it. Dams were forming where branches and other debris had collected. This flood was lost from view where it curved behind a fold of hillside.

Water noises filled the air. They could see where the massive concave rajabarals stood. Somewhere among those rajabarals was the party of phagors from which they had escaped. Behind the rajabarals, thick young forests grew, covering slopes that formed the opposite side of the great bowl. The trees of the forest were generally of a sombre green, rank after rank, punctuated by a tree bearing brilliant gold foliage, known to the Madis as caspiarn; its bitter buds could be eaten in times of famine.

But the landscape did not end with the forests. Beyond them could be seen cliffs which had collapsed here and there to permit a hazardous downward path for animals or men. The cliffs were part of a mountain which spread its rounded contours from one side of the view to the other. Its soft underlying rocks had split, causing ravines from which vegetation sprouted. Where the vegetation was at its most dense, and the collapsed configuration of the mountain most spectacular, a tributary river glinted, foaming as it burst among its gorges towards the valley.

Beyond and above the spongey mountain, yet other mountains stood, harsher, comprising durable basalts, their flanks excoriated by recent centuries of winter. No green mantle covered them. They remained uncompromised, although here and there they were spread with the yellow and orange and white of tiny upland flowers, their colours pure even when viewed from miles away.

Above the domes of those basalt mountains, other ranges, blue, bleak, dreadful, showed. And as if to demonstrate to every living thing that the world had no end, those ranges too permitted a glimpse of objects beyond—land at great distance and great altitude, showing its teeth in a procession of peaks. These were bastions of matter, standing where the blistering colds of the tropopause commenced.

The keen eyes of the Madis took in this prospect, picking out small touches of white among the nearer trees, between the caspiarns, along the cliffs, between the higher defiles of the mountains, even as far as the flashing tributary in its gorges. Those touches of white the Madis correctly identified as cowbirds. Where the cowbirds were were phagors. For almost as many miles as they could see, the stealthy advance of Hrr-Brahl Yprt's host could be marked by cowbirds. Not one phagor could be viewed; yet the mighty landscape probably concealed ten thousand of them.

As the Madis rested and watched, first one and then the other started to scratch at himself or herself. The scratching began like a tickle, but grew more savage as they cooled down. Soon they were rolling about, scratching and swearing, their bodies stung by sweat which cut into the rash of bites mottling their skin. They curled themselves into balls, scratching with feet as well as hands. This frantic itch had assailed them at intervals, ever since their capture by the phagors.

While raking in their crotches, or groping frantically at their armpits, or dragging their nails through the mops of their hair, they gave no thought to cause and effect, never ascribing their rashes to a tick caught from the matted coats of their captors.

That tick was generally harmless, or at least passed on to humans and protognostics nothing worse than a fever or rash which rarely lasted more than a few days. But heat balances were changing as Helliconia moved nearer to Freyr. Ixodidae multiplied: the female tick paid her tribute to Great Freyr in millions of eggs.

Soon that insignificant tick, so much a part of life as to pass unnoticed, would become the vector of a virus inducing the so-called bone fever, and the world would change because of her.

This virus moved into an active stage of development in the spring of Helliconia's great year, at the time of the eclipses. Every spring, the human population was afflicted with bone fever; only something like half the population could expect to survive. The disaster was so comprehensive, its effects so thoroughgoing, that it could be said to wipe itself from such meagre records as were kept.

As the Madis rolled scratching in the leaves, they paid no heed to the untravelled ground behind them.

There, out of the heat of the valley, lush grasses grew, interspersed with thickets of a rank, warted grass known as shoatapraxi, which had a hollow stem and grew hard in old age. Lightly robed men in high turn-down boots emerged from the shelter of the shoatapraxi clumps, ropes in hand. They pounced on the Madis.

The pair of Madis down the slope took their chance and ran away, though it meant going back towards the phagor columns. Their four friends were made captive, still twitching. Their brief, exhausting spell of liberty was over. This time they were the possessions of human beings, to form an insignificant part of another cyclic event, the southward invasion from Sibornal.

They had involuntarily joined the colonising army of the warrior priest Festibariyatid. Little the Cathkaarnits and their two companions cared about that, bowed down as they were by supplies piled on their backs. Their new masters drove them forward. They staggered southwards, still scratching despite their more novel miseries.

As they made their way, skirting the lip of the great bowl to their left, Freyr rose into the sky. Everything grew a second shadow, which shortened as the sun attained its zenith.

The landscape shimmered. The noonday temperature increased. The unregarded ticks swarmed in a myriad unregarded crannies.

XII

LORD OF THE ISLAND

Eline Tal was a large cheerful man, faithful, dependable, lacking in imagination. He was brave, he hunted well, he rode his hoxney with style. He even had the rudiments of intelligence, although he was suspicious of the academy and could not read. He discouraged his woman and children from reading. He was completely loyal to Aoz Roon, with no ambition but to serve him as best he could.

What he was unable to do was understand Aoz Roon. He dismounted from his bright-striped mount and stood patiently some distance away from the Lord of Embruddock. All he could see was the back of Aoz Roon, as the latter stared stolidly forward with his beard on his chest. The lord wore his old stinking black furs, as always, but had draped a cloak of coarse yellow stammel over his shoulders, presumably intending in some obscure way to do honour to his departing sorceress thereby. The hound, Curd, stayed shivering by Grey's heels.

So Eline Tal remained at a distance, one finger in his mouth, picking idly at a back tooth, and did nothing more. His mind was blank.

After a few more curses, uttered aloud, Aoz Roon set his mount in motion. He looked back once over his shoulder, black brows drawn together, but acknowledged his faithful lieutenant in no way, any more than he paid attention to his dog.

He goaded his hoxney at full tilt up to the brow of escarpment, reining Grey so savagely that she reared upon her hind legs.

"Bitch-hag!" shouted Aoz Roon. His voice echoed back to him.

Liking the sound of his own bitterness, he bellowed in rejoinder to the echoes, indifferent that the mare took him farther from Oldorando, while dog and henchman followed if they would.

He reined Grey suddenly, letting foam drip from the bit between her lips. It was only midmorning. Yet a shade had fallen over the world, quelling its life. He scowled upwards through spiked branches, and observed that a bite was taken from Freyr by the dull globe that had slowly outpaced it through the sky. The blindness was encroaching. Curd whined in apprehension and slunk nearer the hoxney's heels.

A night owl burst from a nearby fallen larch, speeding close to the ground. It had speckled feathers and a wingspan wider than a man's outstretched arms. Screeching, it shot between Grey's legs and rose into the sallow sky.

Grey stood high on her hind legs, then she was up and away, no stopping her, plunging forward at full gallop. Aoz Roon fought to cling on, the hoxney fought to dislodge him.

Alarmed by the heavenly phenomenon, Eline Tal followed, wrestling with Drifter, his stallion, to bring him under control. They went like a southern wind, hot in pursuit of the other animal.

When Aoz Roon at last calmed the frightened steed, his blacker mood had lifted. He laughed without mirth, patting the creature and speaking to it more gently than he did to his fellow human beings. Slowly, stealthily, Batalix was eating more deeply into Freyr. The bite of the phagor; old legends came back to mind; the sentinels were not companions, but enemies, doomed to devour each other throughout eternity.

He hunched his shoulders, letting the quieted animal proceed as it would. Why not? He could return to Oldorando and rule as before. Yet would the place be the same, now that *she* was gone, the bitch? Dol was a poor insipid creature, who cared nothing for what he was. Only danger and disappointment lay at home.

Wrenching at the hoxney's head, he made her proceed through a tangle of dogthrush and thorn bushes, sullenly accepting the lash of branches in his face. The world was in disarray too deep for him to fathom. Among the branches were matted reeds, grasses, and straw. So burdened was his mind, he ignored this evidence of recent flooding.

The lower rim of Batalix was lined with silver fire as it continued to devour Freyr. Then it too was eclipsed by cloud, blowing up black from the east. The rain came in increasing force, seething over the cinereous thickets. Aoz Roon kept his head down and pushed on. The downpour hissed in the bushes. Wutra was showing his hatreds.

He kicked his hoxney out of the thicket, to halt where thick grass squelched underfoot. Eline Tal came slowly up behind him. The rain increased, running off the animals to the ground. Looking up from under dripping brows, the Lord of Embruddock saw how the ground rose to one side, where trees grew over a boulder-strewn slope. At the bottom of the slope, a kind of shelter had been built from split stones. Beyond was marshy land, with waterways winding through it. The view faded into the pallor of rainfall; even the outlines of the shelter were indistinct—but not so vague that he failed to see the figures standing at its entrance.

The figures were immobile. They watched. They must have been aware of his approach long before he saw them. Curd stood his ground and growled.

Without looking back, Aoz Roon motioned Eline Tal up to stand with him.

"Scumbing fuggies," Eline Tal said, cheerfully enough.

"They hate water—the downpour may keep 'em safe where they are. Move steady."

He set the pace, a slow walk forward, called Curd to heel.

He would not turn back or show he was afraid. The marsh might be impassable. Best to go up the hillside. Once at the crest—if the phagors let them get that far—they could ride away hard. He was unarmed, except for a dagger at his belt.

The two men moved forward shoulder to shoulder, the dog continuously snarling behind them. To gain the slope, they had to make an oblique approach to the crude building. Because of the murk, it was difficult to be sure of anything; it looked as if no more than five or six of the monsters crouched in the miserable shelter. Behind it stood two kaidaws, rattling their heads to shake away the rain, occasionally clashing horns; they were held by a slave, either human or protognostic, who stared at Aoz Roon and Eline Tal apathetically.

Perched on the roof of the building were two cowbirds, huddling together. Two more were on the ground, fighting over a pile of kaidaw droppings. A fifth, some way off, perched on a boulder, shredding and eating a small animal it had caught.

The phagors made no move.

The two parties were less than a stone's throw away, and the hoxneys were already changing pace to accommodate the slope of the hillside, when Curd dashed from Grey's side and ran towards the shelter, barking furiously.

Curd's action precipitated the phagors forward. They rushed from shelter and charged to the attack. As so often, they seemed to need a prod before they could act, as if their nervous system was inert below a certain minimum level of stimulus. Seeing them run forward, Aoz

Roon shouted a command, and he and Eline Tal spurred their mounts up the slope.

It was treacherous riding. The trees were young, no higher than a man, their foliage spreading from their crowns like umbrellas. It was necessary to ride with the head low. Underfoot, broken boulders formed a constant hazard for the hoxney's paws. Grey and Drifter needed vigilant guidance to maintain anything like a pace.

Behind them came the sounds of pursuit. A spear flashed near them and embedded itself in the ground, but no others followed. More ominous was the noise of kaidaws coming up, and the throaty shouts of their riders. On level ground, a kaidaw could outrun a hoxney. Among the low trees, the larger animals were disadvantaged. Yet fast as Aoz Roon went, he could not shake off the pursuers. He and Eline Tal were soon cursing, and sweating as freely as their mounts.

They struck a patch where water streamed down the hillside. Aoz Roon took the chance to glance round. Two of the shaggy white monsters on their steeds were plunging up behind, each with an immense forearm raised in front of its skull, warding off the backward lash of branches. In their free hand, they carried spears against the flanks of the kaidaws, controlling the animals with their knees and horned feet. The unmounted phagors were doubling up the slope on foot, a long way behind, and no threat.

"The fuggers never give up," Aoz Roon said. "Move, Grey, rot you!"

They plunged on, but the phagors gained.

The downpour faltered, then came on more heavily. It made no difference. The trees flung water as they rode by. The going underfoot was better, but the boulders became more frequent.

Now the two mounted phagors were within spear throw.

Grasping the reins tightly, Aoz Roon stood in the stirrups. He could see above the umbrella trees. Over to the left, the solid ranks of saplings were broken. With a shout for Eline Tal, Aoz Roon wheeled to the left, and for a while lost the phagors behind piles of boulders, the outlines of which seemed to flicker in the weight of the downpour.

They struck a trail of some kind and took it gratefully, spurring upward again. The trees became sparser on either side. Ahead, the ground fell away, subsiding in sluices of mud.

Even as the men felt a flush of hope and goaded on their animals to greater efforts, the pursuing phagors broke from the umbrella trees. Aoz Roon shook his fist and burst ahead. The great yellow dog rushed along, keeping pace by Grey's side, never faltering.

Then it was downhill, with fine gravel underfoot. Ahead lay an entire melancholy landscape, studded with rajabarals, shuttered with trees, its strong verticals counterbalanced by a broad horizontal of water. All was depicted in subdued greens.

Through the midst of this vista wound a turbulent river, overflowing its limits to push out spurs among the stands of larch, creating a maze of reflection. More distantly, dark lines of trees stretched until curtains of haze obscured the sight. Clouds rolled across the sky, dimming the land, hiding the two interlocked sentinels.

Aoz Roon dashed a hand across his face, wiping away rain and sweat. He saw where greatest safety lay. In the river was an island, covered with stones and black-foliaged trees. If he and Eline Tal could get across to that—and its nearer shores were not too distant from the riverbanks—they would be secure from the monsters.

He pointed ahead, shouting hoarsely.

At the same time, he became aware that he rode alone. He turned in the saddle, bracing himself for what he saw.

The bright horizontal stripes of Drifter flashed some way to his left. The animal was riderless, galloping aimlessly towards the river.

Back at the top of the slope, where the umbrellas trees ended, Eline Tal sprawled on the ground. The two shaggy warriors circled round him. One jumped down from his kaidaw. Eline Tal immediately kicked out at him, but the phagor picked him up with an enormous heave. A stain of red showed on Eline Tal's shoulder—they had brought him out of his saddle with a spear. He struggled feebly; the phagor brought its horns down and prepared to use them in a death thrust.

The other phagor did not wait for the coup de grace. It wheeled its steed with a nimble movement and set off downhill towards Aoz Roon, spear held high.

The lord spurred Grey immediately. There was nothing he could do for his unlucky lieutenant. With all speed, he made for the island, leaning forward encouraging Grey, for he felt the animal flagging.

Advantage lay with the pursuing phagor. The kaidaw made superior time over open ground, however willingly the hoxney ran.

Aoz Roon's yellow cloak flapped in the wind as he goaded himself and his mount towards the riverbank. So near, so near, and ever nearer! The swirling waters, the dank foliage, the blur of distant natural features, a rodent scutting for safety in the grass—all flashed before his eyes. He knew he was too late. The pores of the skin between his shoulder blades seemed to turn to liquid as they awaited the fatal spear strike.

A quick glance back. The brute was almost on him, the sinews of the kaidaw's stretched head and neck standing clear, like strands of creeper entwining a tree. It would draw level now, making sure to kill, the damned thing. Its eyes glared.

Old though he was, Aoz Roon's responses were quicker than any phagor's.

Suddenly he dragged on the reins, forcing Grey's head up with savage strength, breaking its stride so that it slewed about in the path of the pursuer. At the same instant he humped from the saddle, rolling over on the sodden ground, absorbing impetus, then flinging himself quickly into the path of the kaidaw.

Grasping his sodden cloak from his shoulders, he swirled it about him and smartly upwards as the spear stabbed down. The coarse cloth folded itself about the enemy's extended weapon arm. Aoz Roon pulled.

The phagor slid forward. With its free arm, it grasped the kaidaw's mane. Tugging his cloak free, Aoz Roon grasped both ends and slammed it down across the beast's throat. One pull, the phagor was jerked loose and struck the ground, its rust-coloured mount bolting onwards.

Its sickly stale-milk stench assailed Aoz Roon. He stood there, gazing down at it, uncertain. Not so far behind, the other phagors were running to the rescue. Grey galloped off. His plight remained as desperate as ever.

He called Curd, but the hound crouched trembling in the grass and would not come.

As the phagor rose, Aoz Roon started to run for the river, clutching the spear. He could swim to the island—it represented his one hope.

Before he reached the edge of the flood, he saw the danger of that swim. The flood water was black, carrying heavy muds in its progress, and worse than muds. There were also drowned animals and semi-submerged branches against which a swimmer would have to battle.

He hesitated. While he did so, the phagor was upon him.

To Aoz Roon came the memory of wrestling with one of the brutes long ago, before his shaming fever. That adversary had been wounded. But this one—this was no youngster, he felt that instinctively, as he grasped its arm and kicked out with his boot. He could heave this one in the river before the others were on him.

But it was not so easy. The brute had enormous strength still. One of them gave a little ground, then the other. Aoz Roon could not bring up the spear or get at his knife. They struggled, proceeding in hops or small runs, groaning, while the adversary tried to bring its horns into play.

He cried in pain as the phagor managed to wrench one arm. He dropped the spear. As he cried, he got an elbow free. He brought it up, sharp under the other's chin. They staggered backwards a few paces, splashing in floodwater almost to the knees. Desperately he called to the hound, but Curd was rushing back and forth, barking savagely to keep off the three phagors approaching on foot.

A large tree bowled along in the flood, currents rolling it so that it turned as it came. A branch emerged like an arm, dripping, striking phagor and man as they stood interlocked in the shallows. They fell, caught by irresistible forces, and were drawn below the plunging water. Another branch rose from the flood, then it too sank, creating yellowish eddies as it was drawn into the undertow.

For four hours, Batalix worried at the flank of Freyr, as a hound worries a bone. Only then was the brighter light entirely engulfed. All the early afternoon, steely shadow lay on the land. Not an insect stirred.

For three hours, Freyr was gone from the world, stolen from the day sky.

By sunset, it had only partially reappeared. Nobody could guarantee that it would ever be whole again. Thick cloud filled the sky from horizon to horizon. So the day died, and an alarming day it was. Whether child or adult, every human being in Oldorando took to bed in a state of apprehension.

Then a wind rose, dispelling the rain, increasing anxiety.

There had been three deaths in the old town, one a suicide, and some buildings had been burnt, or were still burning. Only the heavy rain had saved worse violence.

Light from one of the fires, woken by the wind, lit a sheet of rain-water outside the big tower. Its reflection cast patterns on the ceiling of the room in which Oyre lay sleepless on her couch. The wind blew, a shutter banged, sparks flew up into the chimney of the night.

Oyre was waiting. Mosquitoes troubled her; they had recently returned to Oldorando. Every week brought something that nobody had experienced before.

The flickering light from outside coalesced with the stains on the ceiling, to give her a glimpse of an old man with long ragged hair, dressed in a gown. She imagined she could not see his face, for his head was hidden by a raised shoulder. He was doing something. His legs moved with the ripples the wind raised on the puddle outside. He was silently walking among the stars.

Tiring of the game, she looked away, wondering about her father. When she looked again, she saw that she had been mistaken; the old man was peering over his shoulder at her. His face was blotched and seamed with age. He was walking faster now, and the shutter banged in time with his steps. He was marching across the world towards her. His body was covered with a poisonous rash.

Oyre roused herself and sat up. A mosquito buzzed by her ear. Scratching her head, she looked across at Dol, who was breathing heavily.

"How goes it with you, girl?"

"The pains are coming faster."

Oyre climbed naked out of bed, put on a long cloak, and padded across to her friend, whose pale face she could dimly discern. "Shall I send for Ma Scantiom?"

"Not yet. Let's talk." Dol reached up a hand, and Oyre took it. "You've become a good friend to me, Oyre. I think of such funny things, lying here. You and Vry . . . I know what you think of me. You're both kind, yet you're so different—Vry so unsure of herself, you so sure always. . . ."

"You've got that quite the wrong way round."

"Well, I never knew much. People do fail each other most dreadfully, don't they? I hope I don't fail the child. I failed your father, I know. Now the scumb has failed me. . . . Fancy not being with me, this night of all nights."

The shutter banged again on the floor below. They crouched together. Oyre put a hand on her friend's swollen belly.

"I'm sure he has not gone off with Shay Tal, if that's what you fear."

Dol eased herself up on her elbows and said, turning her face from Oyre, "I sometimes can't bear my own feelings—this pain's welcome by comparison. I know I'm not half the woman she is. Still I said Yes and she said No, and that counts. I always said Yes, yet he's not here with me. . . . I don't think he ever ever loved me. . . ." She suddenly started to weep so violently that tears sprang from her eyes. Oyre saw them glint in the flickering light as Dol turned and buried her face in Oyre's broad breast.

The shutter slammed again as the wind gave a sullen howl.

"Let me send the slave for Ma Scantiom, love," Oyre said. Ma Scantiom had taken over the duties of midwife since Dol's mother had become too decrepit.

"Not yet, not yet." Gradually, her tears subsided. She sighed deeply. "Time enough. Time enough for everything." Oyre rose, wrapping the cloak round her, and went barefoot to secure the shutter. Damp wind gusted in on her face, blowing tremendously from the south; she breathed it with gratitude. The immemorial Embruddock sound of geese came to her, as the creatures took shelter under a hedge.

"But why do I keep myself alone?" she asked the darkness.

A bitter savour of smoke reached her while she secured the latch. The building was still smouldering nearby, a reminder of the day's public madness.

When she returned to the worn room, Dol was sitting up, wiping her face.

"You'd better get Ma Scantiom, Oyre. The future Lord of Embruddock is waiting to be born."

Oyre kissed her cheek. Both women were pale and wide-eyed. "He'll be back soon. Men are so—unreliable."

She ran from the room to call a slave.

The wind that rapped on Oyre's shutter had travelled a long way, and was destined to blow itself out among the limestone teeth of the Quzints. Its birthplace had been above the fathomless stretches of the sea that future sailors would name Ardent. It moved along the equator westwards, picking up speed and moisture, until encountering the great barrier of the Eastern Shield of Campannlat, the Nktryhk, where it became two winds.

The northern airstream roared up the Gulf of Chalce and exhausted itself melting the spring frosts of Sibornal. The southern airstream curved about the headlands of Vallgos over first the Scimitar Sea and then the northeast region of the Sea of Eagles, to exhale over the lowlands between Keevasien and Ottassol, with fish on its breath. It roared across a wilderness that would one day be the great country of Borlien, sighed over Oldorando, setting Oyre's shutter banging. It continued on its way, not waiting to hear the first cries of Aoz Roon's son.

This warm stream of air carried with it birds, insects, spores, pollen, and microorganisms. It was gone in a few hours, and forgotten almost as soon as gone; nevertheless, it played its part in altering the scheme of things that had been.

As it passed, it brought some comfort to a man sitting uncomfortably in the branches of a tree. The tree grew on an island in the middle of a fast-flowing flood mightily becoming a tributary of the river Takissa. The man had injured one leg and perched in his place of safety in some pain.

Below the tree squatted a large male phagor. Perhaps he waited to make some kind of attack. Whatever he waited for, he remained without movement, beyond occasionally flicking an ear. His cowbird sat on a branch of the tree, as far as it could get from the injured man.

Man and phagor had been washed onto the shores of the island, half-drowned. The former had climbed to the one point of safety he, in his injured state, could find. He clung to the trunk of the tree when the wind blew.

The wind was too warm for the phagor. He moved at last, standing swiftly and turning without a backward look, to pick his way among the boulders that filled most of the narrow island. After watching for a while with its head craned forward, the cowbird extended its wings and flapped after its host.

The man thought to himself, If I could catch and kill that bird, it would be a victory of sorts—and it would be worth eating.

But Aoz Roon had more pressing problems than hunger. First, he had to overcome the phagor. Through the sheltering leaves as dawn came, he could see the riverbanks from which he had been brushed. There, on marshy ground, stood four phagors, each with a cowbird perched on his shoulder or wheeling lazily above him; one held the mane of a kaidaw. They had been standing there for hours, almost without movement, staring towards the island.

Keeping a safe distance from them along the water margin was Curd. The hound sat uneasily, he whined, he paced back and forth, scanning the darkly swirling floods.

Biting his bearded lower lip against the pain, Aoz Roon tried to slide farther along his branch, so as to watch his immediate adversary's retreat. It moved slowly. Since there appeared to be nowhere to go on the island, he imagined that the monster would merely make a circuit and come back; had he been in better fettle, he might have devised some unpleasant surprise for it when it returned.

He squinted out at the sky. Freyr was disentangling itself from a barrier of trees, apparently intact after its experiences of the previous day. Batalix, having risen already, was lost in cloud. Aoz Roon longed to sleep but dared not. The phagor probably felt the same way.

There was neither sight nor sound of the monster. All that could be heard was the perpetual gargle of water in the rush of its progress southwards. It had been icy cold—Aoz Roon remembered that well. His enemy would be suffering from the immersion.

It seemed likely that the phagor would be setting a trap for him. Despite his pain, he felt a compulsion to climb from the tree and investigate. The decision made, he waited a few minutes to gather his strength. He scratched himself.

Movement was difficult. His limbs had stiffened. His great black skins were still heavy with water. The main problem was his left leg; it was painfully swollen and hard; he could not bend his knee. Nevertheless, he managed to slither down the tree, finally falling flat on the ground. He lay there in agony, panting, unable to rise, expecting at any moment to feel the phagor leap out and kill him.

The phagors on the bank had seen his move and were calling, but their voices, which lacked the carrying power of a man's, could scarcely be heard above the rushing water. Curd also set up a howl.

Aoz Roon got to his feet. By the foaming edge of the water, he found a branch stripped to its bark, which served as a crutch. Fear, cold, sickness, swirled in him like floodwater, almost causing him to collapse. He felt his flesh heavy on him—chill yet enflamed. He stared about in desperation, scratching himself, mouth hanging open, watching for attack. The phagor was nowhere to be seen.

"I'll get you, you scumble, if I never manage anything more. . . . I'm Lord of Embruddock yet. . . ."

He moved forward step by step, keeping the piles of boulders that cluttered the spine of the island between him and the nearer bank, so that the phagors standing vigil could not see him. To his right, stones, debris, lank grass, trailed down into the flood, whose smooth treachery whirled away towards a distant bank. Mist allied itself to the water, curling above its marbled surface.

Malnourished saplings and older trees shared his shipwreck, many dismasted by boulders heaved against them by early inundations. This complex area of natural disaster was no more than twelve metres across at its widest; yet its length—like the spine of a great submerged creature—divided the flood for farther than eye could see.

Like a wounded bear, he limped forward, taking care, in his anxious tour of inspection, to lumber on the margins of the water and keep as much space as he could between himself and possible attack.

A stag, head high, eyes aflash, burst from a fern thicket in front of him. He fell in startlement as it plunged into the flood until only its red-brown head bearing three-pointed antlers was above the water. Uttering a plaintive bellow, it yielded its powerful body to the greater power of the waters, which carried it away in a wide arc. The creature appeared unable to gain the farther bank, and was still swimming bravely when Aoz Roon lost sight of it in banks of mist.

Later, clambering over a fallen tree, he sighted the cowbird again.

It was watching him with its lapidary reptile eye, perched on the sod-and-boulder roof of a hut. The hut's walls were of cut stone; piled shingle, ferns, spavined saplings sought to turn the hut into a natural object. Aoz Roon worked his way round to the front of this refuge, concluding that the phagor must be inside.

Where the ground dipped, water swirled within three feet of the door. Here, the island had broken down. It emerged a few metres farther upstream, to continue its circumscribed course, a thin ship bearing a purposeless freight of stones. Its two parts were divided by a stretch of eddying water no more than knee-deep. The bear-man could wade to better safety. The phagor, with that hatred of water which marked its species, would never follow.

The chill of the current bit into his bones like alligator's teeth. He was groaning loudly as he staggered to the continuation of the island. He fell. He remained prone, scrabbling among rock, twisting to look back at the hut. The adversary must be inside—sick, injured, as he himself was.

He dragged himself up and toured the island, casting about stupidly, eventually using his knife to cut two firm stakes. Tucking them under one arm, he thrust himself back into the cruel stream, hobbling across with the aid of his crutch. He kept his gaze fixed on the hut door.

As he reached it, there was movement over his head. The cowbird swooped down and slashed open his temple with the barb of its beak.

Dropping crutch and stakes, he sliced the air with his knife. The next time the bird plunged, he cut its breast. It banked clumsily and landed on a log, shedding feathers speckled with its red blood.

He staggered forward and jammed the two stakes in place, one under the latch, the other under the upper hinge of the door. The door began immediately to shake. Hammering and bellowing followed, as the phagor fought to get out. The stakes held firm.

He picked up his crutch. As he turned to beat his retreat back to the islet, his gaze fell on the cowbird. It was hopping from one foot to the other, blood dripping from its breast. He lifted his crutch above his head and brought it down hard, killing the bird.

Holding it under one arm, he hobbled through the freezing water a third time.

On the other side, he threw himself down to massage some life back into his legs. He cursed the pain in his bones. The hammering on the hut door continued. Sooner or later, one of the stakes would work out of place, but for the present the phagor was out of action and the Lord of Embruddock triumphant.

Dragging the cowbird, Aoz Roon crawled between two trees that leaned together, pulling stones round himself for protection. Weakness flowed over him in waves. He fell asleep with his face buried in the still warm breast feathers of the bird.

Cold and numbness roused him. Freyr was low in the western sky, drowning in golden haze. By wriggling round in his niche, he could observe the nearer bank. The phagors still waited there. Behind them, the ground rose; he could make out the place where Eline Tal had fallen. Behind that, hazy, loomed the greater sentinel. There was no sign of Curd beside the flood.

The leg was less painful. He worked his way backwards out of his hole, dragging the dead bird, and stood up.

The phagor was waiting only a few metres away across the stream. Behind him was the hut, its door still intact. Its roof was broken, its stones rolled aside; that way had the phagor escaped.

Snorting, the phagor turned his head to one side and then the other, his horns catching the sun as he made this enigmatic gesture. He was a doleful specimen, his coat matted from the recent immersion in the river.

He hurled a clumsy spear as Aoz Roon presented him with a full target. Aoz Roon was too stiff, too surprised, to duck, but the missile went wide. He saw it was one of the stakes he had cut to prop against the door. Perhaps the poor throw signified that the phagor had injured his arm.

Aoz Roon shook his fist. It was going to be dark soon, for a short while. Instinct prompted him to light a fire. He busied himself about the task, thanking Wutra that he was feeling stronger, yet puzzled that he felt mysteriously sick. It might be hunger, he told himself; but food was at hand, once he had a fire.

After collecting twigs and rotted wood, and creating a sheltered place among stones, he set to work like a good hunter, rubbing a stick between his palms. The tinder smouldered. The miracle happened, and a small flame burned. The harsh lines of Aoz Roon's face relaxed slightly as he looked down at the glow between his hands. The phagor stood at its distance and watched, unmoving.

"Son of Freyr, you are make warm," he called.

Looking up, Aoz Roon saw his adversary only in outline, silhouetted against the gold of the western sky.

"I make warm, and what's more I'm going to cook and eat your cowbird, fuggie."

"You give me a share cowbird."

"The floods will go down in a day or two. Then we can both go home. You stay where you are for the present."

The phagor's articulation was thick. He said something Aoz Roon did not understand. The latter squatted by his fire, peering across the dark water at the adversary, whose silhouette was now fading into the general silhouette of trees and hills, black against the sunset. Aoz Roon was scratching himself, raking with his nails under his furs, swaying to and fro.

"You, Son of Freyr, are sick and will die in the night." He had difficulty pronouncing the sibilants, rendering them as heavy z's.

"Zick? Yes, I'm zick, but I'm still Lord of Embruddock, scumb you."

Aoz Roon began to call Curd, but no answer came. It was too dark on the ground to see if the phagor group continued to wait by the flood. The whole world was drowning in night, becoming nothing but a shadowy reflection.

Fearful in his weakness, he thought the phagor crouched, as if it was about to attempt to jump the space that intervened between them.

He waved a fist. "You stick to your world, I'll stick to mine."

Merely uttering the words exhausted him. He held his hands over his eyes, panting as Curd had panted after a day's hunting.

The phagor made no reply for a long while, as if trying to digest the man's remark and finally deciding to reject it. This he did without gesture, saying, "We live and die in zame world, zame world. That is why we muzz fight."

The words came to Aoz Roon over the water. He could not understand their meaning. He remembered only that he had shouted to Shay Tal that they would survive by unity. Now he was confused. It was typical of her not to be at hand when he needed her.

Turning to his fire, he fell upon his knees, pushed more branches on the blaze, and began the bloody job of cutting up the bird. He wrenched off one of its legs, from which sinews dangled, and skewered it on a stick. He was preparing to push it into the flames when he realised that the agony of the rash on his skin was echoed throughout his bones; his skeleton felt as if it were on fire. Sickness washed over him. The thought of eating anything was suddenly revolting.

He staggered back to his feet, trod in the fire, blundered forward into the water, went in circles, crying, holding aloft the bloody limb. The water noise was loud. It seemed to him that the river became motionless; the island was a slim boat, moving at speed across the surface of a lake; he could not control its flight; and the lake went on forever, into a great cavern of darkness.

The mouth of the cavern closed, swallowing him.

"You have the bone fever," said the phagor. He was called Yhamm-Whrrmar. He was no warrior. He and his friends were itinerant woodmen and fungusmongers. Their kaidaws were stolen. When two Sons of Freyr had appeared in their midst, they had merely done their bounden duty, with the result that Yhamm-Whrrmar was now in some difficulty.

The fungusmongers had been driven westwards by a combination of factors. They were striking in the opposite direction, following favourable air-octaves, when they met humble dwellers like themselves, who spoke of a great crusade advancing, destroying all before it. Although alarmed, the fungusmongers had continued their quest for cooler ground, but had deflected up a long valley where the air-octaves were tainted. Floods had come. They had been forced to retreat. Unkindness and confusion assailed their very eddres.

He stood motionless on the edge of the flood, awaiting the death of the evil seminal being, Freyr. Its disappearance into darkness brought him relief. He unfroze and massaged his injured arm. Night was welcome.

Some distance away, his enemy lay sprawled across a heap of stones. There would be no further trouble from that quarter. After all, parasitic curse though they were, the Sons of Freyr were to be pitied: they all eventually fell sick in the presence of the Ancipital Race. It was no more than justice. Yhamm-Whrrmar stood motionless, letting hours pass.

"You are zick and will die," he called. But he also felt bad air inside him. He scratched his neck with the hand of his good arm, and surveyed the great dark area in which he stood. Complete blackness was already fading. Somewhere to the east, Batalix, that good soldier, Batalix, father of the ancipital race, was already putting forth pale tidings of his presence. Yhamm-Whrrmar retired to the roofless hut and lay down; his magenta eyes closed; he slept without dream or movement.

Over the great floodwaters stole a glimmer from the east, promise of Batalix-dawn. Batalix would rise many times before the floods died, for those floods were fed by enormous reservoirs of water held in the remote Nktryhk. Time would come when the flood scoured for itself a regular riverbed. Later still, shifts in the land mass would deflect the river elsewhere. By the period—still many centuries distant—when Freyr reached its maximum glory, this land would become parched and form a sector of the Madura Desert, traversed by nations as yet a part of futurity unglimpsed.

As man and phagor slept, neither realised that water would flow past their flimsy strip of island for an age to come. It was a temporary inundation: but that inundation would last for another two hundred Batalix-years.

XIII

VIEW FROM A HALF ROON

O n the Earth Observation Station, the term "bone fever" was
well understood. It was part of a complex disease-mechanism
caused by the virus known to the learned families on the
Avernus as the helico virus, and its workings were better understood by
them than by those who suffered and died from it on the planet below.

Research into Helliconian microbiology was far enough advanced for
the Earthmen to know that the virus manifested itself twice in every
1825 years of the Helliconian great year. However it might appear to
the contrary to the Helliconians, these manifestations were not random.
They occurred invariably during the period of the twenty eclipses which
marked the beginning of true spring, and again during the period of the
six or seven eclipses occurring later in the great year. Climatic changes
coincident with the eclipses acted as triggers to the phases of viral hyper-
activity, which formed, as it were, mirror images of each other, their
effects being equally devastating though entirely different at the different periods.

To the inhabitants of the world below, the two scourges were separate phenomena. They raged more than five Helliconian small centuries

(*that is, slightly over seven Earth centuries*) *apart. So they went by separate names, the bone fever and the fat death.*

The disease stream of the virus, like an irresistible flood, affected the history of all through whose lands it swept its ways. Yet an individual virus, like a single drop of water, was negligible.

A helico virus would have to be magnified ten thousand times before it became visible to the human eye. Its size was ninety-seven millimicrons. It consisted of a bag partly covered in icosahedrons, made up of lipids and proteins, and containing RNA; in many ways, it resembled the pleomorphic helical virus responsible for an extinct terrestrial disease called mumps.

Both the scholars on the Avernus and the Helliconia-watchers back on Earth had deduced the function of this devastating virus. Like the ancient Hindu god Shiva, it represented the ancipital principles of destruction and preservation. It killed, and existence followed in its deadly wake. Without the presence of the helico virus on the planet, neither human nor phagorian life would have been possible.

Because of its presence, no person from Earth could set foot on Helliconia and survive. On Helliconia, the helico virus ruled, and set a cordon sanitaire about the planet.

As yet, the bone fever had not entered Embruddock. It was approaching, as surely as was the crusade of the young kzahhn, Hrr-Brahl Yprt. The question in the minds of the scholars on the Avernus was, which would strike first.

Other questions occupied the minds of those who lived in Embruddock. The question uppermost in the minds of the men within sight of the top of the shaky hierarchy was, how could power be attained and, when attained, how could it be retained.

Fortunately for the run of mankind, no permanent answer to this question has ever been devised. But Tanth Ein and Faralin Ferd, venal and easygoing men, had no interest in the question in the abstract. As time passed, and another year—the fateful year of 26 in the new calendar—dawned, and Aoz Roon's absence grew to over half a year, the two lieutenants ran affairs on a day-to-day basis.

This suited them. It suited Raynil Layan less. He had gained increasing say with both the two regents and the council. Raynil Layan saw that an entirely new system was overdue in Oldorando; by introducing it, he would secure power by the sort of nonviolent means which suited him best.

He would appear to yield to pressure from traders and bring in money to replace the age-old system of barter.

From now on, nothing would be free in Oldorando.

Bread would be paid for in his coin.

Satisfied that they would get their share, Tanth Ein and Faralin Ferd nodded agreement to Raynil Layan's scheme. The city was expanding every day. Trade could no longer be confined to the outskirts; it was becoming the centre of life and so it appeared in the centre. And it could be taxed under Raynil Layan's innovatory thinking.

"Buying food is not right. Food should be free, like the air."

"But we're going to be given money to buy it with."

"I don't like it. Raynil Layan's going to get fat," Dathka said.

He and his fellow Lord of the Western Veldt were strolling towards Oyre's tower, inspecting some of their responsibilities on the way. Those responsibilities grew as Oldorando spread. Everywhere they saw new faces. Learned members of the council estimated—with some wringing of the hands—that little more than a quarter of the present population was born locally. The rest were foreigners, many of them in transit. Oldorando was situated at a continental crossroads which was just beginning to bear traffic.

What had been open land until a few months ago was now a site for huts and tents. Some changes went deeper. The old regime of the hunt, by turns harsh and sybaritic, vanished overnight. Laintal Ay and Dathka kept a slave to feed their hoxneys. Game had become scarce, stungebags had disappeared, and migrants were bringing in cattle which betokened a more settled way of life.

The blandishments of the bazaar had ruined the camaraderie of the hunt. Those who had gloried in riding like the wind over newly discovered grasslands in the days of Aoz Roon were now content to lounge about the streets, serving as stall holders, or ostlers, or strong-arm men, or pimps.

The Lords of the Western Veldt were now responsible for order in the growing quarter of the city that lay to the west of the Voral. They had marshals to assist them. Slaves from the south skilled in masonry were building them a tower in which to live. The quarry was in the brassimips. The new tower imitated the form of the old ones; it would command the tents of those the lords sought to control, and stand all of three stories high.

After inspecting the day's work and exchanging a joke with the overseer, Laintal Ay and Dathka headed towards the old town, pushing through a crowd of pilgrims. Canvas stalls were set up, ready to cater to the needs of such travellers. Each stall was licenced with Laintal Ay's office, and displayed its number on a disc.

The pilgrims surged forward. Laintal Ay stepped out of their way, putting his back against a new wall of canvas. His heel met with air, he slipped and found himself falling into a hole which the canvas had concealed. He drew his sword. Three pale young men, naked to the waist, looked at him in horror as he turned to confront them.

The hole was waist deep, the size of a small room.

The foreheads of the men were painted with central eyes.

Dathka appeared around the corner of the canvas and looked down into the excavation, grinning at his friend's mishap.

"What are you doing?" Laintal Ay demanded of the three men.

Recovering from their astonishment, the three stood firm. One said, "This will be a shrine dedicated to great Naba's Akha, and is therefore sacred ground. We have to ask you to leave at once."

"I own this ground," Laintal Ay said. "Show me your licence to rent a patch here."

While the young men were exchanging looks, more pilgrims gathered round the hole, looking down and muttering. All wore black and white robes.

"We haven't got a licence. We aren't selling anything."

"Where are you from?"

A large man with a black cloth wound about his head stood on the edge of the hole, accompanied by two older women who carried a large object between them. He called down in a pompous voice, "We are followers of the great Naba's Akha and we are proceeding southwards, spreading the word. We plan to erect a small chapel here and we demand you remove your unworthy self immediately."

"I own this ground, every spadeful of it. Why are you digging down if you need to build a chapel up? Don't you foreigners know air from earth?"

One of the young diggers said, apologetically, "Akha is the god of earth and underground, and we live in his veins. We shall spread his good news through all lands. Are we not Takers from Pannoval?"

"You are not taking this hole without permission," Laintal Ay roared. "Get out, all of you."

The large pompous man began to shout, but Dathka drew his sword. He stabbed forward. The object the two older women carried was covered with a cloth. Pricking the cloth with his sword point, Dathka whisked the fabric away. An awkwardly crouching figure was revealed, semihuman, its frog eyes blind but staring. It was carved from a black stone.

"What a beauty!" Dathka exclaimed, laughing. "An ugly mug like that needs to be covered up!"

The pilgrims became furious. Akha had been insulted; sunlight was never allowed to touch Akha. Several men flung themselves at Dathka. Laintal Ay jumped out of the hole shouting, and set about the pilgrims with the flat of his sword. The skirmish brought a marshal and two of his men armed with staves to the scene, and in a short while the pilgrims were battered enough to promise their future good conduct.

Laintal Ay and Dathka continued on to Oyre's new rooms in Vry's tower, which was being rebuilt. Oyre had moved because the square about the big tower had become so noisy, with its wooden stalls and drinking booths. With Oyre had gone Dol and her small son, Rastil Roon Den, together with Dol's ancient mother, Rol Sakil. As Aoz Roon's absence lengthened, Dol had become concerned for her safety in a building that also housed the two increasingly unruly lieutenants, Faralin Ferd and Tanth Ein.

At the entrance to the tower, still referred to as Shay Tal's Tower, four burly young freed Borlienian slaves were on guard. That arrangement was Laintal Ay's doing. He received their salutes as he and Dathka entered.

"How's Oyre?" he asked, already beginning to tramp upstairs.

"Recovering."

He found his beloved lying in a bed, with Vry, Dol, and Rol Sakil beside her. He went to her and she put her arms round him.

"Oh, Laintal Ay—it was so horrible. I felt such fear." She stared into his eyes. He looked upon her face, seeing there weariness, caught in the faint lines under her eyes. All who went father-communing were aged by the experience. "I thought I'd never get back to you, my love," she said. "The world below becomes worse every time you visit it."

Age had bent Rol Sakil double. Her long white hair covered her face, so that all that could be seen was her nose. She squatted by the bed nursing her grandson, and said, "It's only them who are old who fail to return, Oyre."

Oyre sat up and clung more tightly to Laintal Ay. He could feel her shivering.

"It seemed doubly awful this time—a universe without suns. The world below is the opposite of ours, with the original boulder like a sun below everything, black, giving out black light. All the fessups hang there like stars—not in air but rock. All being sucked slowly down into the black hole of the boulder. . . . They're so malign, they hate the living."

"It's true," agreed Dol, soothing her old mother. "They hate us and would eat us up if they could."

"They snap at you as you go by."

"Their eyes are full of evil dusts."

"Their jaws too . . ."

"But your father?" Laintal Ay prompted, bringing her back to the reason for her entering pauk.

"I met my mother in the world below. . . ." Oyre could say no more for a moment. Though she clung to Laintal Ay, the world of air to which he belonged as yet seemed less real to her than the one she had left. Not one kind word had her mother for her, only blame and recrimination, and an intensity of hatred that the living scarcely dared reveal.

"She said how I'd disgraced her name, brought her in shame to her grave. I'd killed her, I was responsible for her death, she had detested me since she first felt me stir in her womb. . . . All the bad things I did as a child . . . my helplessness . . . my scumble. . . . Oh, oh, I can't tell you. . . ."

She began to wail horribly to release her grief.

Vry came forward and helped Laintal Ay hold her. "It's not true, Oyre, it's all imagination." But she was thrust away by her weeping friend.

All had been in pauk at some time. All looked on in gloomy sympathy, locked in their own thoughts.

"But your father," Laintal Ay said again. "Did you meet him?"

She recovered sufficiently to hold him at arm's length, regarding him with red eyes, her face glistening with snot and tears.

"He was not there, thanks be to Wutra, he was not there. The time has not yet arrived when he must fall to the world below."

They gazed round at each other in puzzlement at this news. To cover a dread that Aoz Roon was, after all, with Shay Tal, Oyre went on talking.

"Surely he won't become that kind of evil gossie, surely he has lived a life full enough not to turn into one of those little bundles of malevolence? At least he's spared that fate a while longer. But where is he, all these long weeks?"

Dol began to weep by infection, snatching Rastil Roon from her mother, rocking him, and saying, "Is he still alive? Where is he? He wasn't so bad, to be honest. . . . Are you sure he wasn't down below?"

"I tell you he wasn't. Laintal Ay, Dathka, he's still somewhere in this world, though Wutra knows where, that we can be sure of."

Rol Sakil began to wail, now that her movements were not hampered by the infant.

"We must all go down to that terrible place, sooner or later. Dol, Dol, it will be your poor old mother's turn next. . . . Promise you'll come and see me, promise, and I promise I'll say no word against you. I will never blame you for the way you've become involved with that terrible man who has afflicted all our lives. . . ."

As Dol comforted her mother, Laintal Ay tried to comfort Oyre, but she suddenly pushed him away and climbed from the bed, wiping her face and breathing deep. "Don't touch me—I stink of the world below. Let me wash myself."

During these lamentations, Dathka had stood at the back of the room, his stocky figure against the rough wall, his face wooden. Now he came forward.

"Be silent, all of you, and try to think. We are in danger and must turn this news to our advantage. If Aoz Roon is alive, then we need a plan of action till he gets back—if he can get back. Maybe fuggies have captured him.

"I warn you, Faralin Ferd and Tanth Ein plot to take over control of Oldorando. First, they mean to set up a mint, with that worm Raynil

Layan in command of it." His eyes slid to Vry and then away again. "Raynil Layan already has the metal makers at work, minting a coinage. When they control that and pay their men, they will be all-powerful. They will surely kill Aoz Roon when he returns."

"How do you know this?" Vry asked. "Faralin Ferd and Tanth Ein are his friends of long-standing."

"As for that . . ." Dathka said, and laughed. "Ice is solid till it melts."

He stood alert, looking at each, finally letting his gaze rest on Laintal Ay.

"Now we must prove our real worth. We tell nobody that Aoz Roon is still alive. Nobody. Better that they should be uncertain. Leave everyone in doubt. Oyre's news would prompt the lieutenants to usurp power at once. They would act to forestall him before he got back."

"I don't think—" Laintal Ay began, but Dathka, suddenly in command of his tongue, cut him short.

"Who has the best claim to rule if Aoz Roon is dead? You, Laintal Ay. And you, Oyre. Loilanun's son and Aoz Roon's daughter. This infant of Dol's is a dangerous counterargument that the council could seize on. Laintal Ay, you and Oyre must become united at once. Enough shilly-shallying. We'll command a dozen priests from Borlien for the ceremony, and you will make the announcement that the old Lord is dead, so the two of you will rule in his stead. You'll be accepted."

"And Faralin Ferd and Tanth Ein?"

"We can look after Faralin Ferd and Tanth Ein," said Dathka, grimly. "And Raynil Layan. They have no general support, as you do."

They all regarded each other soberly. Finally, Laintal Ay spoke.

"I am not going to usurp Aoz Roon's title while he is still alive. I appreciate your cunning, Dathka, but I will not carry out your plan."

Dathka put his hands on his hips and sneered. "I see. So you don't care if the lieutenants do take over? They'll kill you if they do—and me."

"I don't believe that."

"Believe what you wish, they'll certainly kill you. And Oyre, and Dol and this kid. Probably Vry too. Come out of your dreams. They are tough men, and they have to act soon. The blindnesses, rumours of bone fever—they'll act while you sit and mope."

"It would be better to get my father back," Oyre said, deliberately looking not at Laintal Ay but Dathka. "Things are in flux—we need a really strong ruler."

Dathka laughed sourly at her remark and watched its effect on Laintal Ay without replying.

A heavy silence fell in the room. Laintal Ay broke it by saying awkwardly, "Whatever the lieutenants may or may not do, I am not going to bid for power. It would only be divisive."

"Divisive?" Dathka said. "The place is divided, it's sliding into chaos with all the foreigners here. You're a fool if you ever believed Aoz Roon's nonsense about unity."

During this argument Vry had remained unobtrusively by the trap-door, and was leaning with arms folded against the wall. She came forward now and said, "You make a mistake by thinking only of earthly things."

Pointing towards the baby, she said, "When Rastil Roon was born, his father had just disappeared. That is three quarters ago. The time of double sunset is past. So it is three quarters since the last eclipse, I will remind you. Or the last blindness, if you prefer the old term.

"I must warn you that another eclipse is approaching. Oyre and I have done our calculations—"

Dol's aged mother set up a wail. "We never had these afflictions in the old days—what have we done to deserve them now? One more will finish everybody off."

"I can't explain the why; I'm only just learning to explain the how," Vry said, casting a sympathetic glance at the old woman. "And if I'm correct, the next eclipse will be of much greater duration than the last, with Freyr totally concealed for over five and a half hours, and most of the day filled with the event, which will have begun when the suns rise. You can imagine the kind of panic that may ensue."

Rol Sakil and Dol started to howl. Dathka ordered them abruptly to be quiet, and said, "A day-long eclipse? In a few years, we'll have nothing but eclipse and no Freyr at all, if you're right. Why do you make such claims, Vry?"

She faced him, looking seekingly at his dark countenance. Fearing what she saw, she answered deliberately in terms she knew he could not accept. "Because the universe is not random. It is a machine. Therefore one can know its movements."

Such a deeply revolutionary statement had not been heard in Oldorando for centuries. It went entirely over Dathka's head.

"If you are sure, we must try to protect ourselves with sacrifices."

Without bothering to argue, Vry turned to the others, saying, "The eclipses will not last for ever. They will go on for twenty years, getting shorter after the first eleven. After number twenty, they will not return."

Her words were meant to reassure. The expression on their faces showed the pain of their inward thought: in twenty years, none of them was likely to be alive.

"How can you know what's going to happen in the future, Vry? Even Shay Tal couldn't do that," Laintal Ay said heavily.

She wanted to touch him, but was too shy. "It's a matter of observation and gathering old facts, putting everything together. It's a matter of understanding what we know, of seeing what we see. Freyr and Batalix are far apart, even when they appear close to us. Each balances on the edge of a great round plate. The plates are tipped at an angle. Where they intersect, there eclipses happen, because our world is in line with Freyr, with Batalix between. Do you understand that?"

Dathka strode up and down. He said impatiently, "Listen, Vry, I forbid you to speak of such mad notions in public. The people will kill you. This is what the academy has led you to. I'm not going to listen to any more."

He gave her a dark look, bitter, yet oddly imploring. She was transfixed. Dathka left the room without further word. Silence was what he left behind.

He had been gone only a couple of minutes when there was a commotion in the street outside. Laintal Ay ran down immediately to see what was happening. He suspected Dathka's intervention, but his friend had disappeared. A man had fallen from his mount and was crying for help— a foreigner by his garb. A crowd gathered round him, among them faces Laintal Ay knew, although none went to help the traveller.

"It's the plague," a man told Laintal Ay. "Anyone who aided this knave would be sick himself by Freyr-fall."

Two slaves were brought up, and the sufferer was dragged towards the hospice.

This was the first public appearance of the bone fever in Oldorando.

When Laintal Ay returned to Oyre's room, she had removed her hoxneys and was washing herself over a bowl, calling out from behind a curtain to Dol and Vry.

Dol's dimpled face was for once registering expression. She uncoupled Rastil Roon from her breast and passed him to her mother, saying, "Listen, my friend, you must act. Call the people together and speak to them. Explain. Never mind Dathka."

"You should do that, Laintal Ay," Oyre called. "Remind everyone of how Aoz Roon built Oldorando, and how you were his faithful lieutenant. Don't follow Dathka's plan. Assure everyone that Aoz Roon is not dead, and will return soon."

"That's right," Dol said. "Remind people how they fear him, and how he built the bridge. They'll listen to you."

"You've sorted out our troubles between you," said Laintal Ay. "But you are mistaken. Aoz Roon has been gone too long. Half the people here scarcely know his name. They're strangers, traders passing through. Go to the Pauk and ask the first man you meet who Aoz Roon is—he won't be able to tell you. That's why the question of power is open." He stood solid before them.

Dol shook her fist at him. "You dare say that! It's lies. If—when he comes back, he'll rule as before. I'll see that he kicks out Faralin Ferd and Tanth Ein, too. Not to forget that reptile, Raynil Layan."

"Maybe so, maybe not, Dol. The point is, he is not here. What about Shay Tal? She's been gone just as long. Who speaks of her nowadays? You may still miss her, Vry, but others don't."

Vry shook her head. She said quietly, "If you want the truth, I miss neither Shay Tal nor Aoz Roon. I think they blighted our lives. I believe she blighted mine—oh, it was my fault, I know, and I owe her much, I being the daughter of a mere slave woman. But I followed Shay Tal too slavishly."

"That's right," old Rol Sakil piped, bouncing the baby. "She was a bad example to you, Vry—too virginal by half, was our Shay Tal. You've gone the same way. You must be fifteen now, near middle age, and still not laid. Get on with it, afore it's too late."

Dol said, "Ma's right, Vry. You saw how Dathka marched out of here, furious because you argued with him. He's in love with you, that's why. Be more submissive, that's a woman's job, isn't it? Throw your arms round him and he'll give you what you want. I should think he'd be quite lusty."

"Throw your legs round him, not your arms, that's my advice," Rol Sakil said, cackling with laughter. "There's pretty women passing through Oldorando now—not like when we was all young, when flesh was in short supply. The things they get up to in the bazaar nowadays! No wonder they want a coinage. I know the slot they'll stuff it in. . . ."

"That's enough," Vry said, her cheeks red. "I'll manage my own life without your crude advice. I respect Dathka but I am not at all fond of him. Change the subject."

Laintal Ay took Vry's arm with a consoling gesture, as Oyre emerged from behind her curtain, her hair piled on the top of her head. She had discarded her hoxney skins, which were now regarded as somewhat outmoded among a younger set in Oldorando. Instead, she wore a green woollen dress which trailed almost to the ground.

"Vry's being advised to take a man soon—just like you," Laintal Ay told her.

"At least Dathka's mature and knows his own mind."

Laintal Ay scowled at this remark. Turning his back on Oyre, he said to Vry, "Explain to me about the twenty eclipses. I didn't understand what you were saying. How is the universe a machine?"

She frowned and then said, "You've heard the elements before, but would not listen. You must be prepared to believe that the world is stranger than you give it credit for. I'll try to explain clearly.

"Imagine that the land-octaves extend into the air high above us, as well as into the ground. Imagine that this world, which the phagors call Hrl-Ichor, follows its own octave regularly. In fact, its octave winds round and round Batalix. Hrl-Ichor goes round Batalix once every four hundred and eighty days—hence our year, as you know. Batalix does not move. It is we that move."

"What when Batalix sets every evening?"

"Batalix is motionless in the sky. It is we that move."

Laintal Ay laughed. "And the festival of Double Sunset? What moves then?"

"The same. We move. Batalix and Freyr remain stationary. Unless you believe that, I can explain no further."

"We have all seen the sentinels move, my dear Vry, every day of our lives. So what follows, supposing I believe both of them to be turned to ice?"

She hesitated, then said, "Well, in fact Batalix and Freyr do move as Freyr grows brighter."

"Come—first you'd have me believe that they didn't move, then that they did. Stop it, Vry—I'll believe your eclipses when they happen, not before."

With a scream of impatience, she raised her scrawny arms above her head. "Oh, you're such fools. Let Embruddock fall, what difference would it make? You can't understand one simple thing."

She left the room even more furiously than Dathka.

"There are some simple matters she don't understand either," Rol Sakil said, cuddling the small boy.

Vry's old room showed the change that had come to Oldorando. No longer was it so bleak. Oddments gathered from here and there decked the room. She had inherited some of Shay Tal's—and hence Loilanun's—possessions. She had traded in the bazaars. A star chart of her making hung near the window, with the paths of the ecliptics of the two suns marked on it.

On one wall hung an ancient map, given her by a new admirer. It was painted in coloured inks upon vellum. This was her Ottaassaal map depicting the whole world, at which she never ceased to wonder. The world was depicted as round, its land masses encircled by ocean. It rested on the original boulder—bigger than the world—from which the world had sprung or been ejected. The simple outlined land masses were labelled Sibornal, with Campannlat below, and Hespagorat separate at the bottom. Some islands were formally indicated. The only town marked was Ottaassaal, set at the centre of the globe.

She wondered how far away one would have to be to see the actual world in such a way. Batalix and Freyr were two other round worlds, as she well understood. But they had no support from original boulders beneath them; why then did the world need one?

In a niche in the wall beside the map stood a little figurine which Dathka had brought her. She lifted it down now, cradling it in her palm rather abstractedly. It depicted a couple enjoying coition in a squatting position. Man and woman were carved out of one stone. The hands through which the object had passed had worn them into anonymity, age had rendered them both featureless. The carving represented the supreme act of being together, and Vry regarded it longingly as it rested in her hand. "That's unity," she murmured, in a low voice.

For all her friends' teasing, she wanted desperately what the stone represented. She also recognised, as Shay Tal had before her, that the path to knowledge was a solitary one.

Did the figurine portray a pair of real lovers whose names had been lost far in the past? It was impossible to tell.

In the past lay the answers to much that was in the future. She looked hopelessly at the astronomical clock she was trying to construct from wood, which lay on the table by her narrow window. Not only was she unused to working in wood, but she still had not grasped the principle that maintained the world, the three wandering worlds, and the two sentinels in their paths.

Suddenly, she perceived that a unity existed among the spheres—they were all of one material, as the lovers were of one stone. And a force as strong as sexual need bound them all mysteriously together, dictating their movements.

She sat down at her table, and commenced wrenching the rods and rings apart, trying to rearrange them in a new order.

She was thus engaged when there was a tap at her door. Raynil Layan sidled in, giving hasty looks about him to see that nobody else was in the room.

He saw her framed in the pale blue rectangle of window, the light brooding on her profile. She held a wooden ball in one hand. At his entrance, she half started up, and he saw—for he watched people closely—that her habitual reserve had left her for once. She smiled nervously, smoothing her hoxney skin over the definitions of her breast. He pushed the door closed behind him.

The master of the tanners had assumed grandeur these days. His forked beard was tied with two ribbons, in a manner he had learned from foreigners, and he wore trousers of silk. Recently, he had been paying Vry attention, presenting her with such items as the Ottaassaal map, acquired in Pauk, and listening closely to her theories. All this she found obscurely exciting. Although she mistrusted his smooth manners, she was flattered by them, and by his interest in all she did.

"You work too hard, Vry," he said, cocking a finger and raising an eyebrow at her. "More time spent outdoors would put colour back into those pretty cheeks."

"You know how busy I am, running the academy now Amin Lim's gone with Shay Tal, as well as doing my own work."

The academy flourished as never before. It had its own building, and was largely run by one of Vry's assistants. They engaged learned men to speak; anyone passing through Oldorando was approached. Many ideas were put into practical operation in the workshops under the lecture room. Raynil Layan himself kept a watch on all that was happening.

His eye missed nothing. Catching sight of the stone figurine among the litter on her table, he scrutinised it closely. She flushed and fidgetted.

"It's very old."

"And still very popular."

She giggled. "I meant the object itself."

"I meant their objective." He set it down, looking archly at her, and settled his body against the edge of the table so that their legs were touching.

Vry bit her lip and looked down. She had her erotic fantasies about this man she did not greatly like, and they came crowding back to her now.

But Raynil Layan, as was his style, had changed tack. After a moment's silence, he moved his leg, cleared his throat, and spoke seriously.

"Vry, among the pilgrims just arrived from Pannoval is a man not as blinded with religion as the rest of his crowd. He makes clocks, working them precisely from metal. Wood is no good for your purpose. Let me bring this craftsman to you, and you can instruct him as you will to build your model expertly."

"Mine's no mere clock, Raynil Layan," she said, looking up at him as he stood against her chair, wondering if she and he could in any way be regarded as being made of the same stone.

"That I understand. You instruct the man about your machine. I'll pay him in coin. I shall soon take up an important post, with power to command as I will."

She stood up, the better to assess his response.

"I hear you are to run an Oldorandan mint."

He narrowed his eyes and surveyed her, half-smiling, half-angry. "Who told you that?"

"You know how news travels."

"Faralin Ferd has been blabbing out of turn again."

"You don't think greatly of him or Tanth Ein, do you?"

He made a dismissive gesture and seized her hands. "I think of *you* all the while. I will have power and, unlike those other fools—unlike Aoz Roon—I believe that knowledge can be wedded to power to reinforce it. . . . Be my woman and you shall have what you wish. You shall live better. We will discover all things. We will split open the pyramid that my predecessor, Datnil Skar, never managed to do, for all his prattle."

She hid her face, wondering if her thin body, her torpid queme, could entice and hold a man.

Pulling her wrists from his grasp, she backed away. Her hands, now free, flew like birds to her face to try to conceal the agitation she felt.

"Don't tempt me, don't play with me."

"You need tempting, my doe."

Narrowing his eyes, he opened the purse at his belt, and brought forth some coins. These he extended towards her, like a man tempting a wild hoxney with food. She came cautiously to inspect them.

"The new currency, Vry. Coins. Take them. They're going to transform Oldorando."

The three coins were improperly rounded and crudely stamped. There was a small bronze coin stamped "Half Roon," a larger copper coin stamped "One Roon," and a small gold coin stamped "Five Roons." In the middle of each coin was the legend:

OLD
ORAN
DO

Vry laughed with excitement as she examined them. Somehow, the money represented power, modernity, knowledge. "Roons!" she exclaimed. "That's rich."

"The very key to riches."

She set them on her worn table. "I'll test your intelligence with them, Raynil Layan."

"What a way you do court a man!" He laughed, but saw by her narrow face that she was serious.

"Let the Half Roon be our world, Hrl-Ichor. The big One Roon is Batalix. This little gold one is Freyr." With her finger, she made the Half Roon circle about the Roon. "This is how we move through the upper air. One circle is one year—in which time, the Half Roon has revolved like a ball four hundred and eighty times. See? When we think we see the Roon move, it is we who move on the Half Roon. Yet the Roon is not still. There's a general principle involved, much like love. As a child's life revolves about its mother, so does the Half Roon's about the Roon—and so also does the Roon, I have decided, about the Five Roons."

"You have decided? A guess?"

"No. Simple observation. But no observation, however simple, can be made except by those predisposed to make it. Between winter and spring solstices, the Half Roon moves its maximum to either side of the Roon." She demonstrated the diameter of its orbit. "Imagine that behind the Five Roons there are a number of tiny sticks standing to represent fixed stars. Then imagine you are standing on the Half Roon. Can you imagine that?"

"More, I can imagine you standing there with me."

She thought how quick he was, and her voice shook as she said, "There we stand, and the Half Roon goes first this side of the Roon, then the other. . . . What do we observe? Why, that the Five Roons appears to move against the fixed stars behind it."

"Only appears?"

"In that respect, yes. The movement shows both that Freyr is close compared to the stars, and that it is we who really move and not the sentinels."

Raynil Layan contemplated the coins.

"But you say that the two small denominations move about the Five Roons?"

"You know that we share a guilty secret. There's the matter of your predecessor illegally presenting Shay Tal with information from your corps book. . . . From King Denniss's dating we know that this is the year he would call 446. That is the number of years after someone—Nadir. . . ."

"I've had a better chance than you to puzzle that dating out, my doe, and other dates to compare it with. The date Zero is a year of maximum cold and dark, according to the Denniss calendar."

"Exactly what I believe. It is now 446 years since Freyr was at its feeblest. Batalix never changes its light intensity. Freyr does—for some reason. Once, I believed that it grew bright or dim at random. But now I think that the universe is no more random than a stream is random. There are causes for things; the universe is a machine, like this astronomical clock which seeks to imitate it. Freyr is getting brighter because it approaches—no, vice versa—we approach Freyr. It's hard to shake off the old ways of thought when they are embedded in the language. In the new language, the Half Roon and the Roon are approaching the Five Roons. . . ."

He fiddled with the little ribbons on his beard. Vry watched him thinking over her statement.

"Why is the approach theory preferable to the dim-bright theory?"

She clapped her hands. "What a clever question to ask. If Batalix doesn't fluctuate from dim to bright, why should Freyr? The Half Roon always approaches the Roon, though the Roon always moves out of the way. So I think the Roon approaches the Five Roons in the same way—taking the Half-Roon with it. Which brings us to the eclipses." She circulated the two lower denomination coins again.

"You see how the Half Roon reaches a point each year where observers on it—you and I—would not see the Five because the One would get in the way? That is an eclipse."

"So why isn't there an eclipse every year? It spoils all your theory if one part of it is wrong, just as a hoxney won't run with only three legs."

You're smart, she thought—much smarter than Dathka or Laintal Ay—and I like clever men, even when they're unscrupulous.

"Oh, there's a reason for it, which I can't properly demonstrate. That's why I am trying to build this model. I'll show you soon."

He smiled and took her slender hand again. She trembled as if she were down the brassimip tree.

"You shall have that craftsman here tomorrow, working in gold to your specifics, if you will agree to be mine and let me publish the news. I want you close—in my bed."

"Oh, you'll have to wait . . . please . . . please . . ." She fell trembling into his arms as he clutched her. His hands moved over her body seeking her narrow contours. He does want me, she thought, in a whirl, he wants me in a way Dathka doesn't dare. He's more mature, far more intelligent. He's not half so bad as they make out. Shay Tal was wrong about him. She was wrong about a lot of things. Besides, manners are different in Oldorando now and, if he wants me, he shall have me. . . .

"The bed," she gasped, tearing at his clothes. "Quick, before I change my mind. I'm so divided. . . . Quick, I'm ready. Open."

"Oh, my trousers, have a care . . ." But he was pleased by her haste. She felt, she saw, his rising excitement, as he lowered his bulk onto her. She groaned as he laughed. She had a vision of the two of them, one flesh, whirling among the stars in the grip of a great universal power, anonymous, eternal. . . .

The hospice was new and not yet complete. It stood near the fringes of the town, extending from what had been called Prast's Tower in the old days. Here came those travellers who had fallen sick on their journeyings. Across the street was the establishment of a veterinary surgeon which received sick animals.

Both hospice and surgery had a bad name—it was claimed that the tools of their respective trades were interchangeable; but the hospice was efficiently run by the first woman member of the apothecary's corps, a midwife and teacher at the academy known to all as Ma Scantiom, after the flowers with which she insisted on decking the wards under her command.

A slave took Laintal Ay to her. She was a tall sturdy person of middle age, with plenty of bosom, and a kindly expression on her face. One of her aunts had been Nahkri's woman. She and Laintal Ay had been on good terms for many years.

"I've two patients in an isolation ward I want you to see," she said, selecting a key from a number that hung at her belt. She had discarded hoxneys in favour of a long saffron apron-dress which hung almost to the floor.

Ma Scantiom unlocked a sturdy door at the rear of her office.

They went through into the old tower and climbed the ramps until they were at the top.

From somewhere below them came the sound of a clow, played by a convalescent patient. Laintal Ay recognised the tune: "Stop, Stop, Voral River." The rhythm was fast, yet with a melancholy which matched the useless exhortation of the chorus. The river ran and would not stop, no, not for love or life itself. . . .

Each floor of the tower had been divided into small wards or cells, each with a door with a grille set in it. Without a word, Ma Scantiom slid back the cover over the grille and indicated that Laintal Ay was to look through.

There were two beds in the cell, each bearing a man. The men were almost naked. They lay in locked positions, nearly rigid but never entirely still. The man nearest the door, who had a thick mane of black hair, lay with his spine arched and his hands clenched together above his head. He was grinding his knuckles against the stone wall so that they seeped blood, which ran down the blue-veined paths of his arms. His head rolled stiffly at awkward angles. He caught sight of Laintal Ay at the grille, and his eyes tried to fix on him, but the head insisted on its continued slow-motion movement. Arteries in his neck stood out like cord.

The second patient, lying below the window, held his arms folded tight into his chest. He was curling himself into a ball and then unrolling, at the same time waggling his feet back and forth so that the little bones cracked. His gaze, distraught, moved between floor and ceiling. Laintal Ay recognized him as the man who had collapsed in the street.

Both men were deathly pale and glistening with sweat, the pungent smell of which filtered out of the cell. They continued to wrestle with invisible assailants as Laintal Ay drew the cover across the grille.

"The bone fever," he said. He stood close to Ma Scantiom, seeking out her expression in the thick shadow.

She merely nodded. He followed down the ramps behind her.

The clow was still wearily playing.

> *Why do you hurry so?*
> *Pray this longing takes me to her*
> *Or else lets me go . . .*

Ma Scantiom said over her shoulder, "The first of them arrived two days ago—I should have called you yesterday. They starve themselves; they can hardly be persuaded to take water. It's like a prolonged muscular spasm. Their minds are affected."

"They'll die?"

"Only about half survive attacks of bone fever. Sometimes, when they have lost a third of their body weight, they simply pull out of it. They then normalise at their new weight. Others go mad and die, as if the fever got in their harneys and killed them."

Laintal Ay swallowed, feeling his throat dry. Back in her office, he took a deep inhalation of a bunch of scantiom and raige on the window sill to cleanse the stench in his nostrils. The room was painted white.

"Who are they? Traders?"

"They have both come from the east, travelling with different groups of Madis. One's a trader, one's a bard. Both have phagor slaves, which are at present in the vet's surgery. You probably know that bone fever can spread fast and become a major plague. I want those patients out of my hospice. We need somewhere away from town where we can isolate them. These won't be the only cases."

"You've spoken to Faralin Ferd about it?"

She frowned. "Worse than useless. First of all, he and Tanth Ein said the sick must not be moved from here. Then they suggested killing them and dumping the bodies in the Voral."

"I'll see what I can do. I know a ruined tower about five miles away. Perhaps that would be suitable."

"I knew you'd help." She put a hand on his sleeve, smiling. "Something brings the disease. Under favourable conditions, it can spread like a fire. Half the population would die—we know of no cure. My belief is that those filthy phagors carry it. Perhaps it is the scent of their pelts. There are two hours of Freyr-dark tonight; in that time, I am going to have the two phagors in the vet's surgery killed and buried. I wanted to tell someone in authority, so I'm telling you. I knew you'd be on my side."

"You think they will spread bone fever further?"

"I don't know. I just don't wish to take any risks. There may be another cause entirely—the blindness may bring it. Wutra may send it."

She tucked her lower lip in. He read the concern in her homely face.

"Bury them deep where the dogs can't scratch them up again. I'll see about the ruined tower for you. Are you expecting"—he hesitated—"more cases soon?"

Without changing her expression, she said, "Of course."

As he left, the clow was still playing its plaintive tune, remote in the depths of the building.

Laintal Ay did not think of complaining to Ma Scantiom, although he had laid other plans for the two hours of Freyr-dark.

Dathka's speech of the morning, when Oyre had returned from her pauk-induced spell of father-communing, troubled him deeply. He saw the strength of the argument which said that he and Oyre together represented invincible claimants to the leadership of Oldorando. In general, he wanted what was rightfully his, as anyone else did. And he certainly wanted Oyre. But did he want to rule Oldorando?

It seemed that Dathka's speech had subtly changed the situation. Perhaps he could now win Oyre only by taking power.

This line of thought occupied his mind as he went about Ma Scantiom's business, which was everyone's business. Bone fever was no more than a legend, yet the fact that nobody had experienced the reality made the legend all the more dark. People died. Plague was like the manic stepping-up of a natural process.

So he worked without complaint, conscripting help from Goija Hin. Together, Laintal Ay and the slave driver collected the two phagors belonging to the bone fever victims and sent them into the isolation cell. There, the phagors were made to roll their sick masters into rush mats and carry them away from the hospice. The innocuous-looking mat rolls would cause no panic.

The small group moved with its burdens out of town towards the ruined tower Laintal Ay knew of. With them shuffled the ancient slave phagor, Myk, to take an occasional turn carrying the diseased men. This was designed to hasten the proceedings, but Myk had become so ancient that progress was slow.

Goija Hin, also bent with age, his hair growing so long and stiff over his shoulders that he resembled one of his miserable captives, lashed Myk savagely. Neither lash nor curses hastened the old burdened slave. He staggered onward without protest, though his calves above his fetters were raw from whipping.

"My trouble is, I neither want to wield the lash nor feel it," Laintal Ay told himself. Another layer of thought arose in his mind, like mist on a still morning. He reflected that he lacked certain qualities. There was little he wished for. He was content with the days as they fled.

I've been too content, I suppose. It was enough to know that Oyre loved me, and to lie in her arms. It was enough that once Aoz Roon was almost like a father to me. It was enough that the climate changed, enough that Wutra ordered his sentinels to keep their place in the sky.

Now Wutra has left his sentinels to stray. Aoz Roon has gone. And what was that cutting thing Oyre said earlier—that Dathka was mature, implying I was not? Oh, that silent friend of mine, is that maturity, to be a mass of cunning plots inside? Wasn't contentment maturity enough?

There was too much of his grandfather, Little Yuli, in him, too little of Yuli the Priest. And for the first time in a long while, he recalled his mild grandfather's enchantment with Loil Bry, and of how they had stayed together happily in the room with the porcelain window. It was another age. Everything had been simpler then. They had been so content then, with so little.

He was not content to die now. Not content to be killed by the lieutenants if they thought him involved with Dathka's plotting. And not content either to die of the bone fever, contracted from these two wretches they were carrying away from the city. It was still three miles to the old tower he had in mind.

He paused. The phagors and Goija Hin trudged on automatically with their vile burdens. Here he was again, once more meekly doing what was asked of him. There was no reason for it. His stupid habit of obedience had to be broken.

He shouted to the phagors. They halted. They stood where they were, without moving. Only the burdens on their shoulders creaked slightly.

The group was standing on a narrow track with thickets of dog-thrush on either side. A child had been eaten near here a few days earlier; evidence suggested a sabre-tongue had been the killer—the predators came in close to settlements now that wild hoxneys were scarce. So there were few people about.

Laintal Ay struck in among the bushes. He got the phagors to carry their sick masters into the thicket and set them down. The monsters did so carelessly, so that the men rolled on the ground, still in locked positions.

Their lips were blue, peeled back to reveal yellow teeth and gums. Their limbs were distorted, their bones creaked. They were in some way aware of their position, yet unable to cease a constant motor movement, making their eyeballs roll horribly in their stretched facial skin.

"You know what's the matter with these men?" Laintal Ay asked.

Goija Hin nodded his head and smiled evilly to demonstrate his mastery over human knowledge. "They're ill," he said.

Nor did Laintal Ay forget the fever he had once caught off a phagor.

"Kill the men. Make the phagors scrape out graves with their hands. As fast as you can."

"I understand." The slave master came heavily forward.

Laintal Ay stood with a branch pressing in his back, watching the fat old man do as he was bid, as Goija Hin had always done. At each step in the proceedings, Laintal Ay gave an order and it was executed. He felt himself fully implicated in everything and would not let himself look away. Goija Hin drew a short sword and stabbed it twice through the hearts of the sick men. The phagors scraped graves with their horny hands—two white phagors, and Myk, as obese as his master, prickled with the black hairs of age and working very slowly.

All the phagors had shackles on their legs. They rolled the corpses into their graves and kicked dirt over them, then stood without movement, as was their fashion, awaiting the next order. They were commanded to scrape three more graves under the bushes. This they did, working like mute animals. Goija Hin ran his sword between the ribs of the two strange phagors, afterwards smearing the yellow ichor on their coats as they lay face down, in order to clean his blade.

Myk was made to push them in their graves and cover them with dirt.

As he stood up, he faced Laintal Ay, sliding his pale milt up the slot of his right nostril.

"Not kill now Myk, master. Strike off my chains and allow me to go away to die."

"What, let you loose, you old scumble, after all these years?" Goija Hin said angrily, raising the sword.

Laintal Ay stopped him, staring at the ancient phagor. The creature had given him rides on his back when he was a boy. It touched him that Myk did not attempt to remind him of the fact. There was no feeble appeal to sentiment. Instead, he stood without movement, awaiting whatever would befall.

"How old are you, Myk?" Sentiment, he thought, my sentiment. You couldn't face giving the necessary order to kill, could you?

"I prisoner, don't count years." The *s*'s were dragged like bees from his throat. "Once, we ancipitals ruled Embruddock, and you Sons of Freyr were our slaves. Ask Mother Shay Tal—she knew."

"She told me. And you killed us as we kill you."

The crimson eyes blinked once. The creature growled, "We kept you alive through the centuries when Freyr was sick. Much foolish. Now you Sons will all die. You strike away my chains, leave me go to die in tether."

Laintal Ay gestured to the open grave. "Kill him," he ordered Goija Hin.

Myk put up no struggle. Goija Hin kicked the huge body into the depression and piled dirt about it with his boot. Then he stood among the tanglewood, facing Laintal Ay, moistening his lips and looking uneasy.

"I knew you when you was a little boy, sir. I was good to you. Myself, I always said you should be Lord of Embruddock—you ask my mates if I didn't."

He made no attempt to defend himself with his sword. It fell from his hands and he went down on his knees, blubbering, bowing his hoary head.

"Myk's probably right," Laintal Ay said. "We've probably got the plague in us. We're probably too late." Without another glance, he left Goija Hin where he was and strode back to the crowded city, angry with himself for not striking the fatal blow.

It was late when he entered his room. He stared round it without relaxing his black expression. Horizontal rays of Freyrlight lit the far corner, flaring up brightly, casting the rest of the room into unlikely shade.

He rinsed his face and hands in the basin, scooping up the cool water, letting it run over his brow, his eyelids, his cheeks, and drip from his jaw. He did it repeatedly, breathing deeply, feeling the heat leave him and the self-anger remain. As he smoothed his face, he noted with satisfaction that his hands had ceased to tremble.

The light in the corner slid to one wall and faded to a smouldering yellow, making a square no bigger than a box in which the world's gold decayed. He went round the room, collecting a few items to take with him, scarcely giving a thought to the task.

There was a knock on the door. Oyre looked in. As if sensing immediately the tension in the room, she paused on the threshold.

"Laintal Ay—where have you been? I've been waiting for you."

"There was something I had to do."

She paused with her hand still on the latch, watching, breathing a sigh. With the light behind him, she could not decipher his expression through the thick dusk gathering in the room, but she caught the abruptness in his voice.

"Is anything the matter, Laintal Ay?"

He stuffed his old hunter's blanket into a pack, punching it down. "I'm leaving Oldorando."

"Leaving . . . ? Where are you going?"

"Oh . . . let's say I'm going to look for Aoz Roon." He spoke bitterly. "I've lost interest in—in everything here."

"Don't be silly." She moved a step forward as she spoke, to see him better, thinking how large he seemed in the low-ceilinged room. "How will you seek him in the wilderness?"

He turned to face her, slinging the pack over one shoulder. "Do you think it's sillier to seek him in the real world or to go down in pauk among the gossies to find him, as you do? You were always telling me I had to do something great. Nothing satisfied you. . . . Well, now I'm off, to do or die. Isn't that something great?"

She laughed feebly, and said, "I don't want you to go. I want—"

"I know what you want. You think Dathka is mature and I'm not. Well, to hell with that. I've had enough. I'm going, as I always longed to do. Try your luck with Dathka."

"I love you, Laintal Ay. Now you're acting like Aoz Roon."

He took hold of her. "Stop comparing me with other people. Perhaps you're not as clever as I thought, or you'd know when you were hurting me. I love you too, but I'm going. . . ."

She screamed. "Why are you so brutal?"

"I've lived with brutes long enough. Stop asking stupid questions."

He put his arms round her, dragging her close, and kissed her hard on the mouth, so that her lips were forced back and their teeth slid together.

"I hope to be back," he said. He laughed sharply at the stupidity of his own remark. With a final glance, he left, slamming the door behind him, leaving her in the empty room. The gold had died to ashes. It was almost dark, though she saw points of fire in the street outside.

"Oh scumb," she exclaimed. "Curse you—and curse me, too."

Then she recovered herself, ran to the door, and flung it open, shouting to him. Laintal Ay was running down the stairs and did not respond. She ran after him, clutching his sleeve.

"Laintal Ay, you idiot, where are you going?"

"I'm going to saddle up Gold."

He said it so angrily, wiping his mouth on the back of his hand, that she remained where she was. Then the thought occurred to her that she must get Dathka at once. Dathka would know how to deal with his friend's madness.

Just recently, Dathka had become elusive. Sometimes he slept in the unfinished building across the Voral, sometimes in one tower or another, sometimes in one of the doubtful new places springing up. All she could think of at this hour was to run to Shay Tal's tower to see if he was with Vry. Fortunately, he was. He and Vry were in the middle of a quarrel; her cheek burned and she cowered almost as if Dathka had struck her. Dathka looked pale with fury, but Oyre broke in on them and poured out her tale, oblivious to their troubles. Dathka gave a choking noise.

"We can't let him leave now, just when everything's falling apart."

With one deadly glance at Vry, he ran from the room.

He ran all the way to the stables, and was in time to catch Laintal Ay walking out, leading Gold. They confronted each other.

"You're plain mad, friend—behave sensibly. No one wants you to go. Come to your senses and look after your own interests."

"I am sick of doing what everyone wants me to do. You want me here because you need me to play a role in your schemes."

"We need you to see that Tanth Ein and his mate, and that slimy toad Raynil Layan, don't take control of everything we've got." His expression was bitter.

"You don't stand a chance. I'm going to find Aoz Roon."

Dathka sneered. "You're mad. Nobody knows where he is."

"I believe he went with Shay Tal to Sibornal."

"You fool! Forget Aoz Roon—his star's set, he's old. Now it's us. You're getting out of Oldorando because you're afraid, aren't you? It so happens I still have a few friends who haven't betrayed me, including one at the hospice."

"What does that mean?"

"I know as much as you know. You're getting out because you're afraid of the plague."

Afterwards, Laintal Ay repeated obsessively the angry words they exchanged, realising that Dathka was not his ordinary rather emotionless self. At the time, he simply acted on reflex. He struck Dathka with all his might, bringing up his open right hand and dealing his friend an upward blow under the nose with the edge of his palm. He heard the bone go.

Dathka fell back immediately, clutching his face. Blood flowed, and dripped from his knuckles. Laintal Ay swung himself up into the saddle, spurred Gold, and edged through the gathering crowd. Chattering with excitement, the crowd swarmed round the injured man, who staggered about, cursing and bent double with pain.

His temper still raging within him, Laintal Ay rode out of town. He had brought few of the things he intended to bring. In his present mood, it felt good to be leaving with little but his sword and a blanket.

As he went, he felt in his pocket and brought out a small carved object. In the twilight, he could scarcely make out its shape—but it was familiar to him since boyhood. It was a dog which moved its jaw when its tail was worked up and down. He had had it since the day his grandfather died.

He pitched it into the nearest bush.

XIV

THROUGH THE EYE
OF A NEEDLE

Humankind feared the bite of the phagor, but the bite of a phagor tick was more to be dreaded.

The bite of a phagor tick causes a phagor no irritation, and scarcely more to a human. Its mouthparts have adapted over the millennia to piercing skin tissue with a minimum of damage, and to sucking up painlessly the fluid food its requires to further its own complex reproductive cycle.

The tick possesses elaborate genital organs and no head. Its mouthparts are divided into two pairs. One pair consists of modified pincers which penetrate and inject a cocktail of local anaesthetic and anti-coagulant into the flesh, the other of sensory organs bearing a complex blade covered with teeth which, projecting backwards, anchor the tick comfortably into position on its host.

There the tick clings, resisting dislodgement, to drop off only when gorged—unless the questing beak of a cowbird discovers it and gobbles it down as a delicacy.

Multitudinous Embruddocks for the helico virus are provided in the cells of the tick. And there the virus tarries, inert, awaiting a certain harmonic which will draw it into the orchestra of life, although it is sparked to quasi-activity if female phagor hosts are on oestrus. Only twice in the cycle of the great Helliconian year does that harmonic trigger the active phase of the virus.

A chain of events then operates that will eventually decide the fate of whole nations. Wutra, the philosophical might claim, is a helical virus.

Obedient to the external signal, the virus streams forth from the cells of the tick, down its mouthparts, and into the body of a human host, where it makes its way along the bloodstream. As if tracing its own air-octaves, the invading force moves through the body until it reaches its new host's brain stem and flows into the hypothalamus, causing severe inflammation of the brain, and frequently death.

Once in the hypothalamus, that ancient sector of awareness, the seat of rage and lust, the virus replicates itself with a reproductive fury which may be likened to a storm over the Nktryhk.

The invasion of the human cell represents an incursion of one genetic system into the precincts of another; the invaded cell capitulates and becomes virtually a new biological unit, complete with its own natural history, much as a city may change hands in a prolonged war, belonging first to one side, then to the other.

Invasion, furious replication: then the outward signs of those events. The victim manifests that manic stiffening and tightening in the sinews witnessed by Laintal Ay at the hospice—and many of his kind before him. On the whole, those who witnessed it left no record, for obvious reasons.

These facts had been established by patient observation and careful deduction. The scholarly families of the Avernus were trained in such matters, and supported by superb instrumentation. The disability of being unable to visit the planetary surface was thus to some extent overcome.

But their imprisonment on the Avernus had drawbacks other than the obvious psychological ones. Firsthand verification of hypotheses was not possible.

Their understanding of the incursions of the so-called bone fever had recently become confused by further knowledge. The situation was again open to debate. For the Pin family had pointed out that it was during the time of the twenty eclipses and the incursions of the virus when—in Oldorando at least—a major change of human diet took place. Rathel had gone out of fashion. The brassimip crop, full of vitamins, which had sustained the community throughout centuries of winter, had fallen from general favour. Was it, the Pins suggested, that this dietary change rendered the humans more susceptible to the bite of the tick, or to the tick's parasite, the virus? The matter was under discussion—often heated. Once more, there were hotheads who voted for an illegal expedition down to the Helliconian surface, despite the dangers.

Not all who contracted bone fever died. It was noticeable that those stricken fell in different ways. Some people were aware of the approach of illness, and had time to suffer apprehension or make their peace with Wutra, according to their disposition; others collapsed in the midst of an activity, unwarned—while talking to friends, when walking in the fields, even when lying in love's embrace. Neither gradual nor sudden succumbing was any warrant for survival. However they sickened, only half recovered. For the rest, it was a lucky corpse—like the patients from Ma Scantiom's hospice—which found a shallow grave; many in the general terror that assailed any stricken community, were left as carrion, while whole populations fled from their homes towards a pestilence that would embrace them on the road.

So it had been as long as there had been human beings on Helliconia. The survivors of the pandemic lost a third of their normal body weight —although "normal" was here a relative term. They never regained the lost weight, nor did their children, nor their children's children. Spring had arrived at last, summer was ahead—when adaptation would lie in ectomorphism. The leaner shape persisted throughout many generations, though gradually with less marked effect as subcutaneous fat again built up, the disease remaining latent, carried in the nerve cells of the survivors.

This status quo continued until late summer of the Great Year. Then the Fat Death struck.

As if in compensation for such extreme seasonal dimorphic contrasts, the two sexes on Helliconia were similar in stature and in body and brain weight. Both sexes when adult weighed on average about twelve staynes, to use the old Oldorandan measure. If they lived through bone fever, they would emerge as a lanky eight staynes or less. The next generation adjusted to its new skeletal appearance. Succeeding generations then slowly increased average body weight—until the ravages of the more obscene Fat Death brought about another dramatic change.

Aoz Roon was one who survived the first onslaught of this cycle of the pandemic. After him, many hundreds of thousands were destined to suffer and die or pull through. Some, hidden in remote corners of the world wilderness, might entirely escape the plague. But their descendants would be disadvantaged in a new world, would be treated as freaks, would stand small chance of continuance. The two great diseases, to which the phagor tick played vector, were in reality one disease: and that one disease, that Shiva of diseases, that destroyer and saviour, carried on its bloodied sword survival for mankind in the extravagant conditions of the planet.

Twice in two and a half thousand Earth years, Helliconian humanity had to go through the eye of the needle plied by the phagor tick. It was the price of their survival, of their continued development. From the carnage, from the apparent disharmony, came an underlying harmony— as if, among the screams of agony, a reassurance rose from the deepest springs of being to murmur that all was ineffably well.

Only those who could believe would believe such reassurance.

When the sound of cracking muscle faded, in floated a strange watery music. A principle of fluidity established itself over the barrens of pain, manifest first of all to Aoz Roon's hearing. All that presented itself to his returning vision was a collection of rounded shapes, speckled, striated, or of dull uniform hue. They had no meaning, nor did he seek for meaning. He simply remained where he was, back arched, mouth open, waiting until his eyeballs ceased jerking and he could focus his sight.

The liquid harmonies helped his return to awareness. Although he was unable to coordinate his body, he became conscious that his arms were in some fashion imprisoned. Random thoughts visited him. He saw deer running, himself running, leaping, striking; a woman laughed, he was astride, sunlight crackled through head-high trees. His muscles gave sympathetic spasms, like those of an old dog dreaming by a camp-fire.

The rounded shapes resolved themselves into boulders. He was wedged among them, as if himself inorganic. A young tree, uprooted far up river and stripped of its bark, was inextricably mingled with boulders and grit; he lay against it, similarly entwined, hands lost somewhere far above his skull.

With painful care, he drew his limbs together. He sat up after a while, arms resting on knees, and looked long at a teeming river. Deep pleasure welled up in him as he listened to its sound. He crawled forward on hands and knees, feeling his skins flap loose about his body, to a strip of beach no wider than his hand. He gazed with vacant gratitude at the ceaseless flood. Night came. He lay with his face on pebbles.

Morning came. The light of two suns struck down upon him. He became warm. He stood up, steadying himself against an upthrust branch.

He turned his shaggy head, delighted by the ease with which the slight movement was accomplished. A few yards away, separated by narrow frothing water, the phagor stood watching him.

"Zo you come alive again," it said.

Back through years and cycles now remote in antiquity, it had been the custom in many parts of Helliconia, and in the continent of Campannlat in particular, to kill the king of any tribe who showed signs of age. Both criteria and mode of despatch had differed with different tribes. Though kings were regarded as set down on earth by Akha or Wutra, their lives were abruptly terminated. Once he showed grey hair, or became unable to sever a man's head from his body with one blow of an axe, or failed to satisfy the sexual desires of his wives, or could no longer jump a certain stream or chasm—or whatever the tribal criterion might be—then the king was strangled, handed a poison cup, or by other methods disposed of.

In the same way, members of tribes who exhibited symptoms of the killer diseases, who began to stretch and groan, were forthwith despatched. In earlier days, no mercy was known. Burning was often their fate, because of a belief in the healing power of flame, and with the sufferer to the pyre went his family and household. This savage propitiatory rite rarely served to ward off the onslaught of an epidemic, so that the screams of the burning often fell on ears that buzzed already with the first intimations of illness.

Through all adversity, the generations of humankind slowly grew more civilised. This was markedly so if we consider that the first token of civilisation—without which men cannot live together and desperate anarchy prevails—is sympathy for one's fellows, imaginative warmth for their failings. Now hospitals had come into existence, and doctors, nurses, and priests—all bent on alleviating suffering rather than terminating it brutally.

Aoz Roon had recovered without such aid. Perhaps his rugged constitution helped him. Ignoring the phagor, he staggered to the margin of the grey flood, bent slowly, and scooped water in his two hands to sip.

Some of the water, escaping between his fingers, ran from his lips to his beard where, caught by a breeze, it blew to one side, splashing back into the greater flood, to be reabsorbed. Those neglected drops were observed in their fall. Millions of eyes caught the tiny splash. Millions of eyes followed every gesture of Aoz Roon as he stood, panting with wet mouth, on his narrow island.

Ranked monitors on the Earth Observation Station kept many things under close surveillance, including the Lord of Embruddock. It was the duty of the Avernus to transmit all signals received from the Helliconian surface back to the Helliconian Institute.

The Helliconian Institute's receiver was situated on Pluto's moon, Charon, on the extreme margins of the solar system. Much of its financial support came from its Eductainment Channel, through which a continuous saga of Helliconian events was beamed to audiences on Earth and the other solar planets. Vast auditoria stood like conch shells upended in sand in every province; each was capable of housing ten thousands of people. Their peaked domes aspired towards the skies from which the Eductainment Channel was beamed.

On occasions, these auditoria remained almost deserted for years at a time. Then, responding to some new development on the distant planet, audiences would again increase. People came like pilgrims. Helliconia was Earth's last great art form. Nobody on Earth, from its rulers to its sweepers, was unfamiliar with aspects of Helliconian life. The names of Aoz Roon, Shay Tal, Vry, and Laintal Ay were on everyone's lips. Since terrestrial gods died, new figures had arrived to take their place.

Audiences received Aoz Roon as a contemporary, removed only to another sphere, like a platonic ideal casting its shadow on the vast cave of the auditorium. Those audiences were again filling the auditoria to capacity. They entered on sandalled feet. Rumours of the forthcoming plague, of the eclipse, spread round Earth almost as they spread round Oldorando, drawing in thousands whose lives were transformed by their wonder and concern for Helliconia.

A few of those pilgrims who watched reflected on the paradox imposed on them by the size of the universe. The eight learned families on the Avernus lived at the same time as the Helliconians. Their lives were contemporaneous in every sense, though the helico virus decreed that they were sundered indefinitely from the Earth-like world they studied.

Yet how much more sundered were the eight families from that distant world they regarded as their native planet! They transmitted signals back to an Earth where not one single auditorium had been constructed, where even the planners of the auditoria were as yet unborn. The signals took a thousand years to cross the compartments of space between the two systems. In that millennium it was not Helliconia alone which changed.

And those who now sat wordless in the auditoria saw the immense figure of Aoz Roon on the holoscreens, saw him sip water which blew from his lips to merge with the flood below, as it was a thousand years ago, a thousand light-years away.

The imprisoned light they watched, even the life they lived, was a technological miracle, a physical construct. And only a metaphysician with omnipresent understanding could say which lived at the moment the drips returned to the river: Aoz Roon or his audiences. Yet it required no great sophistry to deduce that, despite ambiguities imposed by limitations of vision, macrocosm and microcosm were interdependent, laced together by such phenomena as the helico virus, whose effects were ultimately universal, though perceptible only to the phenomenon of consciousness, the eye of the needle through which the macrocosm and microcosm became actual unity. Understanding on a divine scale *might resolve the compartments between the infinite orders of being; it was human understanding which brought past and present into their cheek-by-jowl merging.*

Imagination functioned; the virus was merely a function.

The two yelk trotted at a brisk rate, necks held horizontally. Their nostrils dilated, for they had been trotting for some while. Sweat shone on their flanks.

Their two riders wore high turn-down boots and long cloaks made of a grey cloth. Their faces were keen and grey, tufted with small beards on their chins. Nobody would have mistaken them for anything but Sibornalans.

The pebbly path they rode was shadowed by a shoulder of mountain. The regular *plud-plud-plud* of the yelk's hoofs carried out over an expanse of wilderness threaded with trees and rivers.

The men were scouts belonging to the forces of the warrior-priest, Festibariyatid. They enjoyed their ride, breathing the fresh air, rarely exchanging words, and always keeping a sharp eye for enemies.

Behind them down the trail other Sibornalans followed on foot, leading a group of captured protognostics.

The trail wound down to a river, beyond which the land rose in a rocky promontory. Its sloping cliffs were formed of broken rock strata, displaced almost vertically and studded with stubby trees. Here was the settlement ruled over by Festibariyatid.

The scouts forded the river at a shallow place. Assaying the cliffs, the yelk picked their way cautiously between the strata; they were northern plains animals, and not entirely happy in mountainous ground. They, and others like them, had been brought south with the annual incursion of colonists from the northern continent into Chalce and the regions bordering on Pannoval; hence the presence of yelk so far south.

The rear guard appeared along the trail. Its four members were armed with spears and escorted in their midst some luckless protognostics captured during their patrol. Among the captives, Cathkaarnit-he and Cathkaarnit-she plodded along, still scratching themselves despite weeks as prisoners on the move.

Encouraged by spear point, they waded across the shallow river and were forced to make their way up the cliff path, to the confines of which a scent of yelk still clung, past a sentry, and so to a settlement called New Ashkitosh.

To this ford, and to this perilous point, many weeks later, came Laintal Ay. He was a Laintal Ay that few even of his close friends would have recognised without hesitation. He had lost a third of his body weight, and was lean, skeletal even, with paler skin, with a different expression to his eyes. In particular—the finest of disguises because transparent—he moved his body in a new way. He had suffered and survived bone fever.

On leaving Oldorando, he had struck out to the northeast, across what was later known as Roon's Moor, in the direction that Shay Tal and her cortege had taken. He wandered and lost the trail. The country he had known in his extreme youth, when it was covered in white and showed an open face to the skies, had disappeared under a tangle of green.

What had been a solitude was now populated with danger. He was aware of restless movement, not only of harried animals, but of human, semihuman, and ancipital beings, all stirred up by the tide of the seasons. Hostile young faces peered through the bush at every turn. Every shrub had ears as well as leaves.

Gold was nervous in forest. Hoxneys were creatures of the wide open spaces. She grew more and more stubborn, until Laintal Ay dismounted, grumbling, and led the animal.

He found himself at last by a stone tower, to which he had climbed through a seemingly endless forest of birch and fern. He tied Gold to a tree before reconnoitering. All was quiet. He entered the hollow tower, where he rested, feeling ill. When he climbed to the top, he recognised his surroundings; the tower was one he had visited in his carefree wanderings, looking out to bare horizons.

Full of vexation and fatigue, he left the tower. He sank down wearily, stretched, and found himself unable to bring his arms down. Cramps racked him, a fever took him like a blow, and he arched over backwards in delirium, as if he planned to break his spine.

Small dark men and women emerged from hiding and regarded him, creeping stealthily nearer. They were protognostics of the Nondad tribe, hairy creatures who stood no higher than Laintal Ay's waist. Their hands were eight-fingered, but concealed largely by the thick sandy hair that grew like cuffs from their wrists. Their faces resembled asokins, protruding muzzles giving them the same rather wistful appearance as the Madis.

Their language was a mingling of snorts, whistles, and clicks, in no way resembling Olonets, although a few transfusions from the old language had taken place. They consulted themselves, and finally decided to bear the Freyrian away, since his personal octave was good.

A line of proud rajabarals grew on the ridge behind the tower, their boles concealed by the stands of birch. At the base of one such tree, the Nondads entered their earth, dragging Laintal Ay with them, snorting and chuckling at their own difficulty. Gold snorted and plunged at the rein to no avail—her master disappeared.

Among the roots of the great tree, the Nondads had their safe home. This was the Eighty Darknesses. They slept on beds of bracken, to ward off the rodents who shared the earth with them.

Their activities were dictated by custom. It was a custom to select kings and warriors at birth, to rule over and protect them. These rulers were trained to fierceness, and savage battles to the death took place among the Eighty Darknesses. But the kings served as surrogates for the rest of the tribe, acting out their innate violence, so the rank and file of the Eighty Darknesses were meek and loving, clinging close to each other without much sense of personal identity. Their impulse was always to husband life; Laintal Ay's life was husbanded, although they would have devoured him down to the last phalange had he died. That was custom.

One of the females became snoktruix to Laintal Ay, lying against him, caressing and stroking him, sucking his fevers. His deliriums became choked with animals, small as mice, large as mountains. When he woke into the dark, it was to find he had an alien companion close as life, who would do anything to save him and make him whole. Feeling himself to be a gossie, he yielded ardently to this new mode of being, in which heaven and hell delivered themselves in the same embrace.

As far as he could ever understand the word, snoktruix meant a kind of healer: also stealer, dealer, and, above all, feeler.

He lay in the dark in convulsion, limbs contorted, sweating away his substance. The virus raged uncontrollably, forcing him through the terrible eye of Shiva's needle. He became a landscape of sinew, over which the armies of pain battled. Yet the mysterious snoktruix was there, giving of her presence; he was not entirely in isolation. Her gift was healing.

In time, the armies of pain retreated. The voices in the Eighty Darknesses gradually made themselves intelligible, and he began dimly to comprehend what had happened to him. The extraordinary language of the Nondads had no words for food, drink, love, hunger, cold, warmth, hate, hope, despair, hurt, though it seemed that the kings and warriors, battling in the far dark, did. Instead, the rest of the tribe devoted their spare hours, which were many, in prolonged discussion concerning the Ultimates. The necessities of life remained wordless, because contemptible. It was the Ultimates that mattered.

Laintal Ay, amid the suffocations of his succubus, never mastered the language enough to comprehend the Ultimates. But it appeared that the main thrust of the debate—which also was a custom, carried through many generations—was to decide whether all should merge their identity into a state of being within the great god of darkness, Withram, or whether they should cultivate a different state.

Long was the discourse about that different state, unbroken even when the Nondads ate. That they were eating Gold never occurred to Laintal Ay. His appetite had gone. Meditations concerning the different state flowed through him like water.

That different state was somehow equated with a great many things, some extremely uncomfortable, including light and battle; it was the state thrust upon the kings and warriors, and might be roughly translated as individuality. Individuality opposed Withram's will. But in some way, or so the argument seemed to go, as entangled as the roots among which it was unravelled, opposing Withram's will was also following it.

Everything was very confusing, especially when in one's arms lay a small hairy snoktruix.

She was not the first to die. They all died quietly, crawling off among the Eighty Darknesses. At first, he was aware only that fewer voices joined in the harmonics of argument. Then the snoktruix also became rigid. He clutched her tight, in an anguish of which he had not known himself capable. But the Nondads had no resistance to the disease Laintal Ay had brought down into their earth; disease and recovery was not a custom.

Within a short while, she too was dead. Laintal Ay sat and wept. He had never seen her face, though its little meagre contours, behind which such richness seemed to dwell, were familiar to his fingertips.

The discussion of Ultimates came to an end. The last click, snort, whistle, faded into the Eighty Darknesses. Nothing had been decided. Even death, after all, had shown some indecision on the subject; it had been both individual and corporate. Withram alone could say if he was pleased and, in the manner of gods, Withram maintained silence on the subject.

Overwhelmed by shock, Laintal Ay fought to bring together his scattered wits. On hands and knees, he crawled over the corpses of his rescuers, looking for escape. The full, terrible majesty of the Eighty Darknesses was upon him.

He said to himself, endeavouring to maintain the argument, "I have individuality, whatever problems my dear friends the Nondads had. I know I am myself, I cannot escape being myself. I must therefore be at peace with myself. I do not have to undergo that perennial debate they underwent. That's all settled in my case. Whatever happens to me, I know that at least. I am my own man; whether I live or die, I can conduct myself accordingly. It's vain to seek Aoz Roon. He is not my master; I am. Nor has Oyre so much power over me that I must become an exile. Obligations are not slaveries. . . ."

And similarly, on and on, until the words bore little meaning even to himself. The maze among the roots yielded no exit. Many times, when a narrow tunnel took an upward curve, he would crawl forward hopefully—only to come against a blind end in which a corpse lay curled, with rodents conducting their own kind of debate over the entrails.

Passing through a widening chamber, he stumbled over a king. In the darkness, size had less meaning than in the light. The king felt enormous as he landed claws first, roaring. Laintal Ay rolled over, kicking, yelling, struggling to get out his dagger, and the terrible shapeless thing bit and slashed its way towards his throat. He heaved himself over, trying to flatten it, without effect. An elbow in its eye made the assailant momentarily less enthusiastic. Out came the dagger, to be kicked away as the scrimmage was renewed. His searching fingers found a root. Dragging himself closer to it, he pinned one of the king's arms round the root and battered at the sharp-fanged head. Then the raging thing was loose again, flinging itself down on Laintal Ay with unabated fury. The two figures, made one figure in hatred, knocked down on themselves earth, filth, and scuttling things.

Limp after the ravages of bone fever and his long fast, Laintal Ay felt his will to fight weakening. Claws raked his side. Suddenly, something slammed into their joined bodies. Savage roars and clicks filled the air. So total was his confusion that he took a moment to realise there was a third assailant in the dark—one of the Nondad warriors. The warrior was concentrating most of its venom on the king. It was like being caught between two porcupines.

Rolling and kicking, Laintal Ay fought himself loose from the fray, grasped his dagger, and managed to drag himself bleeding into an obscure corner. Drawing his legs up so that his shins protected his body and face from frontal attack, he found a narrow entryway above his head. Cautiously he pushed his way up into a tunnel scarcely wider than his body. Before the fever struck he would never have squeezed himself through; now, with pythonlike contortions, he managed it, eventually dropping into a small round chamber in the earth. He felt dead leaves under his hands. He lay there, gasping, listening with fear to the sounds of combat nearby.

"Light, by the sentinels!" he gasped. A faint greyness like mist pervaded the nook. He had struggled to the edge of the Eighty Darknesses.

Fear drove him to follow the light. He wormed his way out of the earth, and stood trembling beside the bare concave flank of a rajabaral. The light was a cascade, pouring from the tall lake of the sky.

For a long while he remained breathing deep, wiping blood and earth from his face. He looked down at his feet. A savage ferret face stared up at him, then disappeared. He had quit the realm of the Nondads, and his visitation had left most of them dead.

His mind dwelt poignantly on his snoktruix. Sorrow filled him, and amazement and gratitude.

One of the sentinels was overhead. Near the horizon was the other, Batalix, its rays striking almost horizontally through the great silent forest, creating a sinister beauty of its ocean of leaf.

His skins were in tatters. His flesh was incised by long weals, seeping blood, where the claws of the king had raked him.

Although he looked about and called once for Gold, it was without hope. He did not expect to see his hoxney again. His hunterly instincts warned him against staying where he was; he would become prey to something unless he moved, and he felt too faint to fight another battle.

He listened to the rajabaral. Something inside it rumbled. The Nondads had set great store by the trees under whose roots they lived; Withram was said to live at the top of the rajabaral drum, and occasionally to burst out in fury upon a world that was so unjust to protognostics. What would Withram do, he wondered, when all the Nondads died? Even Withram would be forced to a new individuality.

"Wake up," he said, realising how his mind wandered. He saw no sign of the ruinous tower by which he might have oriented himself. Instead, putting Batalix at his back, he began to move among the speckled trunks of the forest. Body and limbs felt pleasantly insubstantial.

Days passed. He hid from groups of phagors and other foes. He felt no hunger; the disease had left him without appetite and with an unclouded brain. He found his mind filling with things that Vry had said to him, and Shay Tal and his mother and grandmother; how much was owed to women—and to the snoktruix . . . things relating to the world as a place to be understood as one world of many, a place in which it was his extraordinary good fortune to be, with the unexpected happening every day, and the breath filling his lungs like a tide. He knew in his bones he was blessed. Worlds inexhaustible lay hived one within the other.

So, lightly stepping, he came to the ford before the Sibornalan settlement known as New Ashkitosh.

New Ashkitosh was in a constant state of excitement. The colonists liked it that way.

The settlement covered a large area. It was circular, as far as the terrain allowed. Huts and fences were built along the perimeter, interspersed with watchtowers, with farm land inside, divided by paths which radiated from the centre like the spokes of a wheel. In the centre was a cluster of buildings and stores, together with the pens in which captives were contained. All of these were arranged round the centremost hub of the settlement, which consisted of a circular church, the Church of Formidable Peace.

Men and women came and went in a businesslike way. No loitering was allowed. There were enemies—Sibornal always had enemies—enemies within and without.

The outside enemy was anyone or anything not of Sibornal. Not that the Sibornalans were hostile; but their religion taught them to be cautious. And in particular to be cautious of anyone from Pannoval, or of the phagorian kind.

Beyond the settlement, scouts ranged, mounted on yelk. They brought news hourly of the progress towards the settlement of scattered bodies of phagors, followed by a veritable army of the ancipitals, descending from the mountains.

The news caused controlled alarm. Everyone was alert. There was no panic. Although the Sibornalan colonists were hostile to the two-horned invaders, and vice versa, they had developed an uneasy alliance which kept conflict to a minimum. Unlike the people of Embruddock, no Sibornalan ever willingly fought a phagor.

Instead, they traded. The colonists were conscious of their vulnerable position, conscious that no retreat to Sibornal was possible—not that they would be at all welcome if they returned, being rebellious and heretical. What they traded was lives, human or semihuman.

The colonists existed on the edge of starvation, even in good times. This colony was vegetarian; every man was a skilled farmer. Their crops thrived. Yet the bulk of their crop went to feeding the mounts they rode. An enormous number of yelk, hoxney, horses, and kaidaws (the latter goodwill gifts from phagors) had to be kept fed in order for the community to survive at all.

For scouts were always patrolling neighbouring territory, keeping the settlement informed of what was happening elsewhere, and capturing anything that came within their sweep. The central pens were well stocked with a transient population of prisoners.

The prisoners were handed over to phagors as tribute. In exchange, the phagors left the settlement alone. Why not? The warrior-priest Festibariyatid had cunningly founded the settlement on a false octave; no phagor was motivated to invade it.

But there remained the enemy inside the camp. Two protognostics giving their names as Cathkaarnit-he and Cathkaarnit-she had fallen ill on arrival and soon died. The pen master had called a doctor-priest, who had identified bone fever. The fever was spreading, week by week. This morning, a scout was found in the bunkhouse, limbs locked tight, eyeballs rolling, sweat pouring from his flesh.

Inconveniently, the disaster happened at a time when the colonists were trying to build up stocks of captives to present to the approaching phagor crusade. Already, they had informed themselves of the name of the ancipital warrior-priest, who was none less than Kzahhn Hrr-Brahl Yprt. A large number of deaths would spoil the tribute. By order of the High Festibariyatid, extra prayers were sung at each declension.

Laintal Ay heard the prayers as he walked into the settlement and was pleased by the sound. He looked with interest at all about him, ignoring the two armed sentries who escorted him to a central guard-house, outside which prisoners were raking dung into piles.

The guard captain was puzzled by a human who was not from Sibornal and yet walked voluntarily into the camp. After talking to Laintal Ay for a while and trying some bullying, he sent a subordinate to fetch a priest-militant.

By this time, Laintal Ay was having to accustom himself to the fact that anyone who had not suffered the plague looked, to his new eyes, uncomfortably fat. The priest-militant looked uncomfortably fat. He confronted Laintal Ay challengingly, and asked what he thought were shrewd questions.

"I met with some difficulties," Laintal Ay said. "I came here hoping to find refuge. I need clothes. The woods are too populated for my liking. I want a mount of some kind, preferably a hoxney, and am prepared to work for it. Then I'm off home."

"What kind of human are you? Are you from far Hespagorat? Why are you so thin?"

"I have come through the bone fever."

The priest-militant fingered his lip. "Are you a fighter?"

"I recently killed off a whole tribe of Others, the Nondads. . . ."

"So you're not afraid of protognostics?"

"Not at all."

He was given the task of guarding the pens and feeding their miserable inmates. In exchange, he was presented with grey wool clothing. The thinking of the priest-militant was simple. One who had suffered from the fever could look after the prisoners without inconveniently dying or passing on the pandemic.

Yet more of the colonists and the prisoners went down with the scourge. Laintal Ay noticed that the prayers in the Church of Formidable Peace became more fervent. At the same time, people kept more closely to themselves. He went where he would and nobody stopped him. He felt that he somehow lived a charmed life. Each day was a gift.

The scouts kept their mounts in a railed compound. He was in charge of a bunch of prisoners whose job it was to carry in hay and fodder to the animals. Here was where the big fodder problem of the settlement lay. An acre of green grass could feed ten animals for a day. The settlement had fifty mounts, used for scouring an increasingly large area; they consumed an equivalent of 24,000 acres per year, or rather less, since some feeding was done beyond the perimeter. This grave problem meant that the Church of Formidable Peace was generally full of half-starved farmers—a rare phenomenon, even on Helliconia.

Laintal Ay refused to shout at the prisoners; they worked well enough, considering their miserable circumstances. The guards stayed at a distance. A light rain made them keep their heads down. Only Laintal Ay took notice of the mounts as they crowded round, thrusting forward their soft muzzles, breathing gently in expectation of a treat. The time was coming when he would select a mount and escape; in a day or two more, the guard would be disorganised enough for his purposes, judging by the way things were going.

He looked a second time at one of the hoxney mares. Seizing up a handful of cake, he approached her. The animal's stripes ran orangey-yellow from head to tail, with a dark powdery blue between.

"Loyalty!"

The mare came over to him, taking the cake and then plunging her nose under his arm. He clung to her ears and petted them.

"Where's Shay Tal, then?" he asked.

But the answer was obvious. The Sibornalans had caught her and traded her to the phagors. She would never get to Sibornal now. By this time, Shay Tal was a gossie. She and her little party, one with time.

The name of the guard captain was Skitosherill. A wary friendship developed between him and Laintal Ay. Laintal Ay could see that Skitosherill was frightened; he touched nobody, and wore a posy of raige and scantiom at his lapel, to which his long nose frequently resorted, hoping to protect its owner from the plague.

"Do you Oldorandans worship a god?" he asked.

"No. We can look after ourselves. We speak well of Wutra, that's true, but we kicked all his priests out of Embruddock several generations ago. You should do the same in New Ashkitosh—you'd have an easier life."

"Barbarian behaviour! That's why you caught the plague, vexing God."

"Nine prisoners died yesterday, and six of your people. You pray too much, and it does no good."

Skitosherill looked angry. They stood in the open, a breeze rippling their cloaks. The music of prayer drifted over to them from the church.

"Don't you admire our church? We're only a simple farming community, yet we have a fine church. There's nothing like it in Oldorando, I'll gamble."

"It's a prison."

But as he spoke, he heard a solemn melody coming from the church which addressed him with mystery. The instruments were joined by voices, uplifted.

"Don't say that—I could have you beaten. Life's in the Church. The circular Great Wheel of Kharnabhar, the holy centre of our faith. If it was not for the Great Wheel, we'd still be in the grip of snow and ice." He made a circle on his forehead with his index finger as he spoke.

"How's that?"

"It's the Wheel that moves us closer to Freyr all the time. Didn't you know that? I was taken to visit it on pilgrimage as a child, into the Shivenink Mountains. You are not a true Sibornalan unless you've made the pilgrimage."

The following day brought another seven deaths. Skitosherill was in charge of the burial party, which consisted of Madi prisoners, scarcely competent enough to dig graves.

Laintal Ay said, "I had a dear friend who was captured by your people. She wished to make a pilgrimage to Sibornal, to consult the priests of that Great Wheel of yours. She thought they might be the source of all wisdom. Instead, your people made her prisoner and sold her to the stinking phagor. Is that how you treat people?"

Skitosherill shrugged. "Don't blame me. She was probably mistaken for a Pannoval spy."

"How could she be mistaken? She rode a hoxney, as did members of her party. Have the people of Pannoval hoxneys? I never heard so. She was a splendid woman, and you brigands handed her over to the fuggies."

"We're not brigands. We just wish to settle here in peace, moving on when the ground's used up."

"You mean, when you've used up the local population. Fancy trading women in exchange for your safety."

Grinning uneasily, the Sibornalan said, "You barbarians of Campann-lat, you don't value your women."

"We value them highly."

"Do they rule?"

"Women don't rule."

"They do in some countries of Sibornal. In this settlement, see how well we take care of our women. We have women priests."

"I haven't seen one."

"That's because we take care of them." He leant forward. "Listen, Laintal Ay, I understand you are not a bad fellow, all things considered. I'm going to trust you. I know the state of affairs here. I know how many scouts have gone out and not returned. They've died of the plague in some miserable thicket and had no burial, their corpses probably devoured by birds or Others. It's going to become worse, while we sit here. I am a religious man, and I believe in prayer; but the bone fever is so strong that even prayer cannot prevail against it. I have a wife I love dearly. I wish to strike a bargain with you."

As Skitosherill spoke, Laintal Ay stood on a low eminence, looking down a miserable bit of ground which sloped towards a stream; stunted thorn trees grew along the watercourse. Among the stones littering the slope, the prisoners were slinging back earth, while seven cadavers —the Sibornalan corpses wrapped in sheets—lay in the open awaiting burial. He thought to himself, I can understand why this overweight lump wishes to escape, but what is he to me? He's no more than Shay Tal, Amin Lim, and the others were to him.

"What's your bargain?"

"Four yelk, well fed. Me, my wife, her maidservant, you. We leave together—they'll let me through the lines without difficulty. We ride back with you to Oldorando. You know the way, I protect you, see to it that you have a good steed. Otherwise you'll never be allowed to get away from here—you're too valuable—particularly when matters get worse. Do you agree?"

"When do you plan to leave?"

Skitosherill buried his nose in the posy and looked up searchingly at Laintal Ay. "You say a word of this to anyone and I'll kill you. Listen, the crusade of the phagor kzahhn, Hrr-Brahl Yprt, is due to start passing here before Freyr-set, according to our scouts. We four will follow on afterwards—the phagors will not attack us if we are in their rear. The crusade can go where it will; we shall progress to Oldorando."

"Are you planning to live in such a barbarian place?" Laintal Ay asked.

"We shall have to see how barbarian it is before I answer that. Don't try to be sarcastic to your superiors. Do you agree?"

"I'll have a hoxney rather than a yelk, and choose it myself. I've never ridden a yelk. And I want a sword, white metal, not bronze."

"Very well. You agree, then?"

"Do we shake hands on it?"

"I do not touch other hands. Verbal agreement is enough. Good. I'm a godfearing man, I'll not betray you; see you don't betray me. Get these corpses buried while I go to prepare my wife for the journey."

As soon as the tall Sibornalan had gone, Laintal Ay called the captives to halt their activity.

"I'm not your master. I'm a prisoner as much as you. I hate Sibornalans. Throw those corpses in the water and cover them with stones— it'll save you labour. Wash your hands afterwards."

They gave him suspicious looks instead of thanks, he in his grey woollen garments, tall, standing above them on the bank, he who talked with the Sibornalan guard on equal terms. He felt their hatred and was unmoved by it. Life was cheap if Shay Tal's life was cheap. As they scrambled among the corpses, they brushed the sheet from one of them, so that he glimpsed an ashen face underneath, frozen in its anguish. Then they had the body by feet and shoulders and tossed it down to the stream, where dashing water seized ravenously on the covering, moulding it round the body, which it began to roll unceremoniously downstream.

The watercourse marked the perimeter of New Ashkitosh; on its other bank, beyond a flimsy rail, no-man's land began.

When their task was over, the Madis considered the prospect of escape by fording the stream and running away. Some advocated this course of action, standing on the edge of the water and beckoning their fellows. The more timid hung back, gesticulating towards unknown dangers. All kept glancing anxiously at Laintal Ay, who stood where he was, arms folded. They were unable to make up their minds whether to act individually or corporately, with the result that they did nothing but argue, starting up the bank or down into the stream, but ever returning to a common centre of indecision.

There was reason for their hesitation. The no-man's land on the far side of the river was filling with figures that moved westward. Birds made uneasy by constant disturbance flew up before them, wheeling in the sky and then attempting to realight.

The land rose to a low horizon in the middle distance, where it dropped sharply to reveal a line of drums, the crowns of ancient rajabarals which emitted steam. Beyond their vapour, the landscape continued on a grander scale, revealing hills, stacked distant and serene in misty light. Stone megaliths stood here and there, curiously incised, marking land- and air-octave lines.

The fugitives heading westward turned their faces away from New Ashkitosh, as if fearing its reputation. They were sometimes solitary but more often in groups, frequently large groups. Some drove animals before them, or had phagors with them. Sometimes the phagors were in control.

Progress was not always continuous. One large group stopped on a slope some distance from where Laintal Ay stood. His keen eyes made out the signs of lamentation, with figures alternately bowing down or stretching upward in sorrow. Other groups arrived or passed; people ran from group to group. The plague travelled among them.

He found himself searching the more distant landscape for sight of that from which the refugees fled. He fancied he saw a snow-covered peak between the fold of two hills. The quality of light on it constantly changed, as if shadowy beings sported on its upper slopes. Superstitious fears filled his mind, clearing only when he realised that he was seeing not a mountain, but something closer and entirely less permanent: a flight of cowbirds, converging as they streamed through a pass.

Then at last he broke his reverie. Turning away from the protognostics, who still quarrelled in their ditch, he made his way back to the guard buildings.

It was clear to him that these refugees, many already infected by the plague, would descend on Oldorando. He must return as soon as possible, to warn Dathka and the lieutenants; otherwise, Oldorando would sink under a tide of diseased humanity and inhumanity. Anxiety for Oyre tugged at him. He thought of her too little since the days of his snoktruix.

The suns shed warmth on his back. He felt isolated, but there was no remedy for that at present.

He kicked his heels at the guardhouse, listening for music from the church, but only silence came from that direction. Being uncertain whereabouts on the wide perimeter Skitosherill and his wife lived, he could only wait for the couple to appear. Waiting increased his foreboding.

Three scouts entered the settlement on foot, bringing with them a pair of captives, one of whom collapsed immediately, to lie in a heap by the guardhouse. The scouts were sick and exhausted. They staggered into the guardhouse without a glance at Laintal Ay. The latter looked indifferently at the prisoner who remained on his feet; prisoners were no concern of his anymore. Then he looked again.

The prisoner stood with his feet apart in a defiant attitude, although his head hung as if he were tired. He was of a good height. His thin stature indicated that he also had survived bone fever. He wore clumsy black furs which were draped loosely about his body.

Laintal Ay put his head round the guardroom door, where the newly-arrived scouts were leaning on a table drinking root beer.

"I'm taking the prisoner outside to work—he's needed immediately." He retreated before they could answer.

With a curt order to the man, Laintal Ay directed him to the Church of the Formidable Peace. Priests were inside at a central altar, but Laintal Ay led the captive to a seat against the wall where the light was dim. The man sank down thankfully, subsiding like a bag of bones.

It was Aoz Roon. His face was gaunt and lined, the flesh of his neck hung like a wattle; his beard had turned almost entirely grey; but, from the knit of his brows and the set of his mouth, there was no mistaking the Lord of Embruddock. At first, he would not recognise the thin man in Sibornalan cloth as Laintal Ay. When recognition came, he gave a sob and clutched him close, his body shaking.

After a while, he was able to explain to Laintal Ay what had happened to him, and how he had come to be stranded on a small island in the middle of a flood. As he recovered from his fever, he realised that the phagor stranded with him was starving to death. The phagor was not a warrior but a humble fungusmonger, by name Yhamm-Whrrmar, terrified of water and consequently unable or unwilling to eat fish. In the anorexia that seized those who recovered from the fever, Aoz Roon himself needed almost nothing to eat. The two of them had talked across the intervening water, and eventually Aoz Roon had crossed to the larger of the two islands, to strike up an alliance with his erstwhile enemy.

From time to time, they saw humans and phagors on the banks and shouted to them, but no one would cross the rapid-gliding water to aid them. Together, they tried to build a boat, which took many vexatious weeks.

Their first attempts were useless. By intertwining twigs and lining them with dried mud, they finally constructed a vessel that would float. Yhamm-Whrrmar was persuaded to climb into it, but leaped out again in fear. After much argument, Aoz Roon pushed off on his own. In the middle of the river, the mud all dissolved and the coracle sank. Aoz Roon managed to swim to a bank some way downriver.

It was his intention to find a rope and return to rescue Yhamm-Whrrmar, but such things as he met were either hostile or fled from him. After many wanderings, he had been captured by the Sibornalan scouts, and dragged to New Ashkitosh.

"We'll go back to Embruddock together," Laintal Ay said. "Oyre will be so delighted." Aoz Roon made no response at first.

"I can't return. . . . I can't . . . I can't desert Yhamm-Whrrmar. . . . You can't understand." He rubbed his hands on his knees.

"You're Lord of Embruddock still."

He hung his head, sighing. He had been defeated, had failed. All he wished for was a peaceful refuge. Again the uncertain movement of hands on knees, on shabby bearskin.

"There are no peaceful refuges," Laintal Ay said. "Everything's changing. We'll go back to Embruddock together. As soon as we can."

Since Aoz Roon's will had deserted him, he must make his decisions for him. He could obtain a suit of the Sibornalan cloth from the guardroom; so disguised Aoz Roon could join Skitosherill's party. He left Aoz Roon with disappointment. This was not what he had expected.

Outside the church, another surprise awaited him. Beyond the wooden buildings that circled the church the members of the colony were gathering. They faced outwards silently, looking across the settlement towards open country, anonymous in their drab greys.

The crusade of the young phagor kzahhn was about to pass.

The flight from the advance of the crusade still continued. An occasional stag plunged along amid the humans and protognostics and Others. Sometimes, the fugitives walked beside groups of the phagors who formed part of the van of Hrr-Brahl Yprt's army. There was a certain blindness about the procession, about its seeming blunders. It was impressive for its numbers rather than its discipline.

Seemingly at random, in fact under control of air-octaves, groups of phagors studded uncounted acres of wild territory. Everywhere, they progressed at their slow remorseless pace with their slow unnatural stride. No haste glowed in their pale harneys.

The way through mountain and valley from the almost stratospheric heights of the Nktryhk down to the plains of Oldorando was three and a half thousand miles. Like any human army travelling mainly on foot over rough terrain, the crusaders seldom averaged better than eleven miles a day.

They rarely marched more than one day in twenty. Most of the time was taken with the customary diversions of large armies: foraging off the land and resting up.

In order to acquire supplies, they had laid siege to several gaunt mountain towns near their path, allying themselves to rocks and crags while waiting for the sons of Freyr inside the town to open their gates and throw down their arms. They had pursued nomadic people, on the threshold of humanity, still ignorant of the power of the seed, and therefore condemned to a life of wandering, tracking them up perilous paths to acquire a few head of scraggy arang for the mess pot. They had been detained at the start by snows and, towards the end, more seriously, by immense inundations crashing towards lower ground from the flanks of the shrinking Hhryggt.

The crusaders had also suffered illness, accident, desertion, and raids by tribes through whose territory they ventured.

Now was the Air-turn 446 according to the modern calendar. In the eotemporal minds of the ancipital race, it was also Year 367 After Small Apotheosis of Great Year 5,634,000 Since Catastrophe. Thirteen air-turns had passed since that day when the stungebag horn had first sounded along the icy cliffs of the home glacier. Batalix and louring Freyr were low in the western sky and close together, as the crusade plodded on the last stage of its journey.

This terrain was soft as a woman's lap compared with the higher lands of Mordriat already traversed, and spoke less nakedly of savage forces. Yet it was scoured and scooped. True, the season had patched it with trees, the acid-green leaves of which spread their points horizontally, as if compressed by invisible air-octaves, but no foliage could disguise the great geological anatomy beneath; that anatomy had been corroded too recently by centuries of frost. It was a land fit to support without sustaining the restless soul of life, in whatever form that soul was cast. It constituted the unedited manuscript of Wutra's great story. The chunky bodies of the phagor army were autochthonous manifestations of the place.

By comparison, the grey-clad inhabitants of the settlement were shadowy things, more transient than those who passed their borders.

Laintal Ay walked along the curved street formed between the church and the surrounding offices, guardrooms, and stores, carrying a suit of Sibornalan clothing for Aoz Roon. As he went, he caught glimpses of the scene between buildings.

All the inhabitants of New Ashkitosh had gathered to watch the crusade pass. He wondered if they waited there from fear, to test whether the human tribute they had paid the ancipital force had indeed secured their safety.

The silent white brutes went by on either side of the settlement. They moved with precision, looking incuriously ahead. Many were thin, their coats moulting; their naked heads by contrast looked enormous. Above them flew the cowbirds, setting up a great racket. Many cowbirds broke ranks, to dive on manure piles lying about the settlement, fighting for them with screams and beating wings.

The people of the settlement sent up their own sound, as if in opposition. As Laintal Ay emerged from the church, the massed ranks broke into song. The words were not Olonets. They carried a harsh yet lyrical texture matched by a powerful melody. The song breathed some grand elusive quality between defiance and submission. Women's voices floated clear above the bass, which developed into a slow chant much like a march.

Now among the ragged army of brutes streaming by could be discerned some on kaidaw-back—not so many kaidaws now as there had been at the start, but enough to make a showing. In the centre of a more orderly phalanx stepped Rukk-Ggrl, red head held low, bearing the young kzahhn himself. Behind the kzahhn came his generals, then his private fillocks—of whom only two survived, and they now haughty gillots. Human prisoners plodded along amid the throng, bearing loads.

Hrr-Brahl Yprt held his head high, his face crown glinting in the sickly light. Zzhrrk fluttered above him like a banner. The kzahhn did not deign to cast his regard upon the human settlement that paid him tribute. Yet the throaty song that rolled out across the land to greet him roused a feeling of some kind in his eddre for, when he came to a point that might be regarded as level with the Church of Formidable Peace, he raised his sword above his head in his right hand—whether as greeting or threat could never be determined. Without pause, he continued on his way.

Seeing that Aoz Roon kept by his side, Laintal Ay led him to the guardhouse. There they waited until Skitosherill arrived, bringing along his wife and a maidservant loaded with baggage.

"Who's this?" Skitosherill demanded, pointing to Aoz Roon. "Are you breaking your side of our bargain already, barbarian?"

"He's a friend of mine, let that suffice. Where are your phagor friends going?"

The Sibornalan shrugged one shoulder, as if denial was hardly worth two.

"Why should I know? Stop them and ask, if you're curious."

"They are heading for Oldorando. Don't you know that?—you brigands, so friendly with the brutes, singing a song to their leader."

"If I knew where every little barbarous town in the wilderness stood, I should hardly rely on you to show me the way to one of them."

They were confronting each other angrily when Skitosherill's wife pushed forward and said, "Why are you arguing, Barboe? Let's get on with the plan. If this man says he can lead us to Ondoro, then encourage him to do so."

"Of course, dear," Skitosherill said, sketching a rictus of a smile in her direction. Scowling at Laintal Ay, he made off, returning very soon with a scout who led several head of yelk. His wife contented herself with surveying Laintal Ay and Aoz Roon in silent contempt.

She was a sturdy woman, almost as tall as her husband, shapeless under her grey garments. What made her remarkable in Laintal Ay's eyes was her fair straight hair and her light blue eyes; despite her harsh expression, they had a pleasant effect. He said to her cordially, "I will take you to Oldorando in safety. Our town is beautiful and exciting, and boasts geysers and stone towers. The Hour-Whistler will amaze you. You are bound to admire all you see."

"I'm not *bound* to admire anything," she said severely. As if regretting this response, she asked his name in more cordial terms.

"Let's move, sunset's upon us," said Skitosherill briskly. "You two barbarians will ride yelk—no hoxneys available. And this scout will accompany us. He has orders to be firm with any trouble."

"With any trouble at all, really," said the scout, from under his cowl.

As Freyr sank to the horizon, they moved out, six of them with seven yelk, one used for baggage. They passed the sentries at the western entrance of the settlement without incident. The guards stood there dejectedly, shadowy in the declining light, staring into the gathering gloom.

The party entered the wilderness, following the last of the kzahhn's shaggy army. The ground was trampled and fouled from the passage of many feet.

Laintal Ay led the others. He ignored the discomforts of the yelk saddle. A suffocating weight lay on his heart and eddre as he thought of the savage phagor army somewhere ahead of him; with growing certainty, he believed that they would encompass Oldorando on their route, whatever their ultimate destination. It was up to him to spur on as fast as possible, outflank the crusade, and warn the city. He kicked the yelk in the ribs, heaving it on by mental force.

Oyre and her smiling eyes represented all that was dear in the city. His long absence was nothing he regretted, since it had brought him new understanding of himself, and new respect for her insight; she had seen his lack of maturity, his dependence on others, and had wished better for him, perhaps without being able to articulate that wish. His return would bring her at least something of those necessary qualities. Provided he arrived in time.

They entered into a murky forest, through which a faint trail glimmered, as Batalix set in golden sheen. The trees were young as yet, growing like weeds, thir crowns scarcely higher than the heads of the riders. Phantoms moved close by. A thin trail of protognostics wended its way eastwards; by holding to its own mysterious octave, it had somehow managed to evade the kzahhn and thread its course through his ranks. Haggard faces moved palely among the eclipsing saplings.

He hunched his thin frame in the saddle and looked back. The scout and Aoz Roon brought up the rear, hardly distinguishable in the twilight. Aoz Roon's head was down; he looked lifeless and broken. Then came the maidservant with the baggage yelk. Directly behind Laintal Ay rode Skitosherill and his wife, their faces shaded by grey cowls. His gaze sought her pale face. Her blue eyes glinted, but something frozen in her expression frightened him. Was death already creeping up on them?

Again he kicked the slow-moving yelk, forcing it towards the dangers ahead.

XV
THE STENCH OF BURNING

Silence reigned over Oldorando. Few people walked in the streets. Of those who did, most carried some nostrum or other to their face, sometimes keeping it in place with a mask over nose and mouth. Herbs were most highly regarded for this purpose. They fended off plague, flies, and the stink of bonfires.

High over the houses, the two sentinels, only a hairsbreadth apart, glared down like eyes. Beneath the tiles and slates, the population waited. Everything that organisation could do had been done. Now only waiting remained.

The virus moved from one quarter of the city to another. One week, most deaths would be confined to the southern quarter, the so-called Pauk, and the rest of the city would breathe more freely. Then the district across the Voral would be chastised—to the relief of the other districts. But in another few days, the plague might make lightning visitation to its previous haunts, and lamentations would burst out from streets, even households, where similar cries had only recently been heard.

Tanth Ein and Faralin Ferd, lieutenants of Embruddock, together with Raynil Layan, master of the mint, and Dathka, Lord of the

Western Veldt, had formed a Fever Committee, on which they themselves sat, together with useful citizens such as Ma Scantiom of the hospice. Aided by an auxiliary body formed by the pilgrimage from Pannoval, the Takers, who had stayed in Oldorando to preach against its immorality, laws had been passed to deal with the ravages of the fever. Those laws were enforced by a special police contingent.

Notices were posted in every street and alley, warning that the penalties for concealing dead bodies and for looting were the same: execution by phagor bite—a primitive punishment that sent refined shudders through the rich merchants. Notices posted outside the city warned all who approached that the plague ruled. Few of those fugitives who came from the east were rash enough to ignore the warning: they ringed their foreheads and skirted the city. It was doubtful whether the notices would provide such effective protection against those with evil intentions towards the place.

The first carts ever to be seen in Oldorando, clumsy things with two wheels, pulled by hoxneys, rumbled through the streets regularly. On them went the day's crop of corpses, some left shrouded in the street, some thrown unceremoniously out of doorways or dropped naked from upper windows. No mother or husband or child, however beloved in life, but caused sickening revulsion when dying, and worse when dead.

Though the cause of the fever was not understood, many theories existed. Everyone believed that the disease was contagious. Some went so far as to believe that the mere sight of a corpse was sufficient to turn one into the same state. Others who had listened to the word of Naba's Akha—suddenly of persuasive power—believed that venery brought the fever on.

Whatever their beliefs, all agreed that fire was the only answer for corpses. The corpses were taken in carts to a point beyond the city, and there thrown into the flames. The pyre was constantly being rekindled. Its smoke, the smell of its black fats, drifting across the shuttered streets, reminded the inhabitants of their vulnerability. In consequence, those still surviving threw themselves into one or other—and sometimes both—of the extremes of mortification and lechery.

No one as yet believed that the fever was at its height, or that there was not worse to come. This dread was counterbalanced by hope. For there was an increasing number of people, mainly young, who survived the worst that the helico virus could do, and who, in slimmed down shapes, moved confidently through the city. Among them was Oyre.

She had fallen in the street. By the time Dol Sakil had taken her into her care, Oyre was locked rigid in pain. Dol looked after her without fear for herself, with that listless indifference which was an established part of Dol's manner. Despite the prognostications of friends, she did not fall ill herself, and lived to see Oyre come through the eye of the needle, looking slender, even skeletal. The only precaution Dol had taken was to send her child, Rastil Roon, to stay with Amin Lim's man and his child. Now the boy was back.

The two women and the child spent their time indoors. The sense of waiting, the sense of an ending, was not unpleasant. Boredom had many mansions. They played with the boy, simple games that took them back to their own childhood. Once or twice Vry joined them, but Vry had an abstracted air these days. When she spoke, she told them of her work, and of all that she aspired to do. On one occasion, she broke out into passionate speech, confessing her involvement with Raynil Layan, of whom they had previously nothing good to say. The affair vexed her; she often felt disgust; she hated the man when he was absent; yet she flung herself on him when he appeared.

"We've all done it, Vry," Dol commented. "It's just that you're a bit late, so it hurts you worse."

"We haven't all done it enough," Oyre said quietly. "I have no desires now. They've gone from me. . . . What I desire is desire. It may return if only Laintal Ay returns." She gazed out of the window at the blue sky.

"But I'm so torn," Vry said, unwilling to be distracted from her own troubles. "I'm never calm, as once I was. I don't know myself any longer."

In her outburst, Vry said nothing of Dathka, and the other women evaded that issue. Her love might have brought her more ease if she did not worry about Dathka; not only was he on her conscience, but he had taken to following her obsessively. She feared for what might happen, and had easily persuaded the nervous Raynil Layan that they meet in a secret room, rather than in their own places. In this secret room, she and her fork-bearded lover had daily tryst, while the city waited on the disease and the sound of saddle animals drifted through their open window.

Raynil Layan wished the window closed, but she would not have it.

"The animals may convey the illness," he protested. "Let's leave here, my doe, leave the city—away from the pest and everything else that worries us."

"How would we survive? This is our place. Here in this city, and in each other's arms."

He gave her an uneasy grin. "And suppose we infect each other with the pest?"

She flung herself back on the bed, her breasts bouncing in his sight. "Then we die close, we die in the act, knotted! Maintain your spirit, Raynil Layan, feed on mine. Spill yourself over—over and over!" She rubbed her hand along his hairy loin and hooked a leg about the small of his back.

"You greedy sow," he said admiringly, and he rolled beside her, pressing his body to hers.

Dathka sat on the edge of his bed, resting his head in his hands. As he said nothing, so the girl on the bed did not speak; she turned her face from him and brought her knees up to her chest.

Only when he rose and began to dress, with the abruptness of one who has suddenly made up his mind, did she say in a stifled voice, "I'm not carrying the plague, you know."

He cast her back a bitter look, but said nothing, continuing hastily to dress.

She turned her head round, brushing long hair from her face. "What's the matter with you, then, Dathka?"

"Nothing."

"You're not much of a man."

He pulled on his boots, seemingly more concerned with them than with her.

"Rot you, woman, I don't want you—you're not the one I want. Get that into your skull and shift yourself out of here."

From a cupboard fitted into the wall he took a curved dagger of fine workmanship. Its brightness contrasted with the worm-scored panels of the cupboard door. He stuck it in his belt. She called to ask where he was going. He paid her no further attention, slamming the door behind him and clattering down the stairs.

He had not wasted the last few bitter weeks since Laintal Ay left and since he had discovered what he regarded as Vry's betrayal of him. Much of his time had been spent building up support among the youth of Oldorando, securing his position, making alliances with foreign elements who chafed at the restrictions Oldorando imposed on them, sympathising with those—and there were many—whose way of life had been disrupted by arduous work patterns imposed by the introduction of a native coinage. The master of the mint, Raynil Layan, was a frequent butt of his criticism.

As he strode into the alley, all was quiet and the side street deserted except for a man he paid to guard his door. In the market, people were about of necessity, attending to their day's requirements. The little apothecary's stall, with its pots ranked imposingly, was doing good business. There were still merchants with bright stalls and bright robes on their backs. Equally, there were also people moving by with loads on their backs, leaving the threatened city before things got worse.

Dathka saw nothing of it. He moved like an automaton, eyes fixed ahead. The tension in the city was one with his personal tension. He had reached a point where he could tolerate it no longer. He would kill Raynil Layan, and Vry too if need be, and have done with it. His lips curled back from his teeth as he rehearsed the fatal blow over and over in his mind. Men started away from him, fearing his fixed look presaged the onset of fever.

He knew where Vry had her secret room; his spies kept him informed. He thought to himself, If I ruled here, I would close down the academy for good. Nobody ever had the courage to make that decision final. I would. Now's the time to strike, using the excuse that classes at the academy spread the pest. That would really hurt her.

"Take thought, brother, take thought! Pray with the Takers to be spared, hear the word of great Naba's Akha. . . ."

He brushed by the street preacher. He would have those fools off the street, too, if he ruled.

Near the Yuli Lane hoxney stables, he was approached by a man he knew, a mercenary and animal trader.

"Well?"

"He's up there now, sir." The man signalled with his eyebrows towards the garret window of one of the wooden buildings facing the stables. These were mainly hostels, rooming houses or drink shops, which acted as a quasi-respectable front to the music rooms and bawdy houses ranged behind them.

Dathka nodded curtly.

He pushed through a bead curtain, to which fresh orling and scantiom had been tied, and entered one of the drink shops. The cramped dark room was empty of customers. On the walls, animal skulls gave dry, serrated smiles. The owner stood against his counter, arms folded, gazing into space. Already primed, he merely lowered his head so that his double chins spread on his chest, a signal to Dathka to do whatever he wished to do. Dathka passed him by and climbed the stairs.

Stale smells greeted him, of cabbage and worse things. He walked by the wall, but the boards still creaked. He listened at the end door, heard voices. Being of nervous disposition, Raynil Layan would be sure to have barred his door. Dathka knocked on the cracked panels.

"Message for you, sir," he said in a muffled voice "Urgent, from the mint."

Smiling a ghastly smile, he stood close, listening as the bolts were drawn inside the room. As soon as the door opened a crack, he burst in, flinging the door wide. Raynil Layan fell back, crying in terror. At the sight of the dagger, he ran to the window and called once for help. Dathka grasped him by the neck and flung him against the bed.

"Dathka!" Vry sat in the bed, pulling a sheet over her nudity. "Get out of here, you rat's eddre!"

For answer, he kicked the door shut without looking round. He went over to Raynil Layan, who was picking himself up and groaning.

"I know you're going to kill me, I can see it, I can tell," the master of the mint said, putting out a tremblingly protective hand. "Spare me, please, I'm not your enemy. I can help you."

"I'm going to kill you with as much compassion as you killed old Master Datnil."

Raynil Layan rose slowly, hiding his nudity, keeping a wary eye on his attacker.

"I didn't do that. Not myself. Aoz Roon ordered his death. It was legal, really. The law was broken. Killing me isn't legal. Tell him, Vry. Listen, Dathka—Master Datnil gave corps secrets away, he showed the secret book of the corps to Shay Tal. Not all of it. Not the worst thing. You ought to know about that."

Dathka paused. "That world's dead, all that corps scumb. You know what I think of the corps. To fessups with the past. It's dead, as you will be."

Vry seized on his hesitation. She had recovered her nerve.

"Listen, Dathka, let me explain the situation. We can help you, both of us. There are things in that corps book that Master Datnil did not dare reveal even to Shay Tal. They happened long ago, but the past is still with us, however we might wish it otherwise."

"If that were so, then you would accept me. So long I longed for you."

Raynal Layan drew his robe round himself and said, mustering his wits, "Your quarrel is with me, not Vry. In the various corps books are records of Embruddock in past time. They prove that this was once a phagor city. Possibly the phagors built it—the record is broken. They certainly owned it, and the corps and the people in it. They kept people as slaves."

Dathka stood regarding them darkly. All he said in his head was, We are all slaves—knowing it to be stupid.

"If they owned Embruddock, who killed them? Who won it back? King Denniss?"

"This happened after Denniss's time. The secret book says little; it records history only incidentally. We understand that the phagors simply decided to quit."

"They were not defeated?"

Vry said, "You know how little we understand the brutes. Perhaps their air-octaves changed and they all marched away. But they must have been here in strength. If you ever studied the painting of Wutra in the old temple, you would know that. Wutra is a representation of a phagor king."

Dathka rested the heel of his hand on his brow. "Wutra a phagor? It can't be. You go too far. This damned learning—it can make white black. All such nonsense stems from the academy. I'd kill it. If I had the power I'd kill it."

"If you want power, I'll side with you," said Raynil Layan.

"I don't want you on my side."

"Well, of course . . ." He gestured frustratedly, tugged the twin points of his beard. "You see, we have a riddle to resolve. Because it seems that the phagors are returning. Perhaps they will reclaim their old city. That's my guess."

"What do you mean by that?"

"It's simple. You must have heard the rumours. Oldorando's alive with the rumours. There's a great force of phagors approaching. Go and talk to the people passing outside the city. The trouble is, Tanth Ein and Faralin Ferd will not protect the city, being too involved with their private interests. They're your enemies—not I. If a strong man killed the lieutenants and took over the city, he could save it. That's just my suggestion."

He watched Dathka scrupulously, seeing the play of emotions on his face. He smiled encouragingly, knowing he had talked his way out of being killed.

"I'd help," he said. "I'm on your side."

Vry said, "I'm on your side, too, Dathka."

He shot her one of his darkly glittering looks. "You'd never be on my side. Not if I won all of Embruddock for you."

Faralin Ferd and Tanth Ein were drinking together in the Two-Sided Tankard. Women, friends, and toadies were with them, enjoying the evening.

The Two-Sided Tankard was one of the few places where laughter could be heard nowadays. The tavern was part of a new administrative building which also housed the new mint. The building had been paid for mainly by rich merchants, some of whom were present with their wives. In the room were furnishings that until recently were unknown in Oldorando—oval tables, sofas, sideboards, rich woven rugs hanging on the walls.

Imported drink flowed, and a fair foreign youth played the hand harp.

The windows were being closed to keep out the chill night air and to shut out an odour of smoke from the alleyways. On the central table, an oil lamp burned. Food lay about, uneaten. One of the merchants was relating a long tale of murder, betrayal, and travel.

Faralin Ferd wore a jacket of suede, untied to reveal a woollen shirt underneath. He rested his elbows on the table, half-listening to the story while his gaze roved about the chamber.

Tanth Ein's woman, Farayl Musk, padded quietly about, ostensibly to see that a slave was securing the shutters correctly. Farayl Musk was distant kinswoman of both Tanth Ein and Faralin Ferd, being descended from the family of Lord Wall Ein Den. Although not exactly beautiful, Farayl Musk had wit and character, which commended her to some people and not to others. She bore a candle in a holder, which she shielded against the draft of her progress with one hand.

The light made her face glow, throwing unexpected shadows on its contours, lending her mystery. She felt Faralin Ferd's eyes on her, but forebore to return his gaze, knowing the value of feigned indifference.

He reflected as he often had done before that he deserved Farayl Musk, rather than his own woman, who bored him. Despite the dangers involved, he had several times made love to her. Now time was short. They might all be dead in a few days; drink did not drown that knowledge. He lusted after her again.

Rising, he stalked abruptly out of the room, casting a significant glance in her direction. The long story was reaching one of its periodic excitements, involving the smothering of a prominent man with the carcass of one of his own sheep. Laughter rose from round the table. Nevertheless, watchful eyes saw the lieutenant disappear—and his fellow lieutenant's woman made her exit after a discreet interval.

"I thought you wouldn't dare follow."

"Curiosity is stronger than cowardice. We've only got a moment."

"Do it with me here, under the stairs. In this corner, look."

"Standing, Faralin Ferd?"

"Feel this, woman—is it standing or is it not?"

She sighed and leaned against him, clutching what he offered with both hands. He recalled from previous occasions how sweet this woman's breath was.

"Under the stairs, then."

She put the candle down on the floor. Ripping open her bodice, she revealed her majestic breasts to him. He set an arm about her and dragged her into the corner, kissing her excitedly.

There they were caught when a party of twelve men under Dathka came in from the street with torches burning and swords naked.

Despite their protests, Farayl Musk and Faralin Ferd were brought forth. They barely had time to draw their clothes together before they were thrust back into the meeting room, where the rest of the lieutenants were already confronted by sword blades.

"This is all lawful," Dathka said, eyeing them much as a wolf regards kid arang. "I am taking the rule of Embruddock into my own hands until such time as the rightful Lord of Embruddock, Aoz Roon, returns. I am his deposed but oldest-serving lieutenant. I mean to see that the city is properly guarded against invaders."

Behind him stood Raynil Layan, his sword sheathed. He said loudly, "And I support Dathka Den. Hail, Lord Dathka Den."

Dathka's eye had found Tanth Ein, lost in the shadows. The older of the two lieutenants had not risen with the rest. He sat still at his place at the head of the table, arms resting on the chair arm.

"You dare defy me!" Dathka cried, leaping forward with his sword raised, to confront the seated man. "Get to your feet, scumb!"

Tanth Ein never moved, except that a rictus of pain traversed his face as his head jerked back. His eyeballs started to roll. As Dathka kicked at the chair, he slid stiffly to the floor with no attempt at breaking his fall.

"It's the bone fever!" someone shouted. "It's among us!"

Farayl Musk began to scream.

By morning, two more lives had gone, and the smell of burning once more tainted the air of Oldorando. Tanth Ein lay in the hospice under Ma Scantiom's courageous care.

Despite the dread of contagion, a large crowd gathered in Bank Street to hear Dathka's public proclamation of his rule. Once on a time, such meetings would have been held outside the big tower. Those days had passed away. Bank Street was more spacious and more elegant. On one side of it, a few stalls dotted the bank of the river. Geese still strutted there, aware of their ancient rights. On the other side was a line of new buildings, with the old stone towers rising behind them. Here, a public platform stood.

On the platform stood Raynil Layan, shifting his weight from foot to foot, Faralin Ferd with his arms bound behind him, and six young warriors of Dathka's guard, armed with sheathed swords and spears, grimly regarding the crowd. Bouquet sellers roved through the people, selling protective nosegays. The pilgrim Takers were there too, dressed in their distinctive black-and-white garb, holding banners urging repentance. Children played on the edge of the crowd, sniggering at the behaviour of their elders.

As the Hour-Whistler blew, Dathka climbed onto the platform and began immediately to address the crowd.

"I am taking up the burden of authority for the sake of the city," Dathka said. It seemed his old silence had dropped from him. He spoke with eloquence. Yet he stood almost motionless, not gesturing, not using his body to help carry his words, as if the habit of silence had quit nowhere but his tongue. "I have no wish to supplant the true ruler of Embruddock, Aoz Roon. When he returns—if he returns—then what is rightfully his will be rightfully handed back to him. I am his lawful deputy. Those he left in command have abused his power, have cast it in the gutter. I could not stand by and see it. We will have honesty in these bad times."

"Why's Raynil Layan beside you then, Dathka?" called a voice from the crowd, and there were other remarks, which Dathka tried to override.

"I know you have complaints. I'll hear them after—you hear me now.

Judge Aoz Roon's usurping lieutenants. Eline Tal had the courage to go into the wilderness with his lord. The other two creatures stayed at home. Tanth Ein has the fever as his reward. Here stands the third of them, the worst, Faralin Ferd. Look at the way he trembles. When did he ever address you? He was too busy about his sly lascivious ways indoors.

"I'm a hunter, as you know. Laintal Ay and I tamed the Western Veldt. Faralin Ferd will die of the pest like his crony, Tanth Ein. Will you be ruled by corpses? I won't catch the plague. Intercourse passes on the plague, and I'm free of it.

"My first deed will be to restore guards all round Embruddock, and to train a proper army. As we are at present, we are ripe to fall to any enemy—human or inhuman. Better die in battle than in bed."

This last remark caused a groundswell of unease. Dathka paused, glaring down at them. Oyre and Dol stood among the people, Dol clutching Rastil Roon in her arms. Oyre cried out loudly as Dathka paused, "You are a usurper. How are you any better than Tanth Ein or Raynil Layan?"

Dathka went to the edge of the platform.

"I steal nothing. I picked up what was dropped." He pointed at Oyre. "You of all people, Oyre, as the natural daughter of Aoz Roon himself, should know that I will return to your father what is his when he returns. He would wish me to do this."

"You cannot speak for him while he's away."

"I can and do."

"Then you speak wrongly." .

Others to whom this wrangle meant little, and who cared little about Aoz Roon, also started to shout, calling out complaints. Someone threw an overripe fruit. The guard jostled the crowd, without effect.

Dathka's face grew pale. He raised his fist above his head in passion.

"Very well, you scumble, then I will tell you publicly what has always been kept silent. I'm not afraid. You think so greatly of Aoz Roon, you think he was so admirable, I'll tell you the kind of man he was. He was a murderer. Worse, he was a double murderer."

They fell quiet, their faces upturned to him in a cloud of flesh.

He was shaking now, conscious of what he had started. "How do you think Aoz Roon gained power? By murder, bloody murder, murder by night. There are those of you who will remember Nahkri and Klils, sons of ancient Dresyl, in the days bygone. Nahkri and Klils ruled when Embruddock was just a farmyard. One dark night, Aoz Roon—young then—threw the two brothers off the top of the big tower when they were in their cups. A foul double deed. And who was there as witness, who saw it all? I was there—and so was she—his natural daughter." He pointed accusingly down at the thin figure of Oyre, now clinging in horror to Dol.

"He's mad," a boy shouted on the edge of the crowd. "Dathka's mad!" People were leaving at a run, or running up. General confusion was breaking out, and a struggle developing in one corner of the mob.

Raynil Layan tried to rally the crowd, bringing up his powerful pale presence to shout in a large voice, "Support us and we will support you. We will guard Oldorando."

All this while, Faralin Ferd had been standing silent at the rear of the platform, arms bound, in the grip of a guard. He saw his moment. "Throw Dathka out!" he shouted. "He never had Aoz Roon's approval and he shall not have ours!"

Dathka turned about with a hunter's rapid movement, drawing his curved dagger as he did so. He flung himself on the lieutenant. A high scream came from Farayl Musk, somewhere in the crowd, at the same time as several voices took up the cry, "Throw Dathka out!"

They fell silent almost immediately, stilled by Dathka's sudden action. In the hush, smoke drifted across the scene. Nobody moved. Dathka stood rigid, back to his audience. For a moment, Faralin Ferd was also still. Then he threw up his head and gave a choking groan. Blood gushed from his mouth. He sagged, and the guard let him fall at Dathka's feet.

Then there was uproar. Blood gave the whole crowd voice.

"You fool, they'll slaughter us," Raynil Layan shouted. He ran to the back of the platform and jumped down. Before anyone could stop him, he was disappearing down a side street.

The guard ran about, ignoring Dathka's commands, as the mob closed on the platform. Farayl Musk was screaming for Dathka's arrest. Seeing that it was all over, he also jumped from the platform and ran.

At the rear of the crowd, by the stalls, the small boys jumped up and down, clapping their hands in excitement. The crowd began to riot, finding rioting more lively than death.

For Dathka, there was nothing but to make an ignominious escape. He ran panting, gasping, muttering incoherently, through the deserted streets, his three shadows—penumbral, umbral, penumbral—changing their topology at his feet. His scuttling thoughts similarly dilated and shrank, as he tried to evade the knowledge of his failure, to retch up his disaster from inside him.

Strangers passed him, their belongings loaded on an archaic sledge. An old man, helping a child along, called to him, "The fuggies are coming."

He heard the sound of people running behind him—the mob, avenging. There was one place he could go to for refuge, one person, one hope. Cursing her, he ran to Vry.

She was back in her old tower. She sat in a kind of dream, aware—and frightened of her awareness—that Embruddock was moving to a crisis. When he hammered on her door, she let him in almost with relief. She stood there with neither sympathy nor derision as Dathka collapsed weeping on her bed.

"It's a mess," she said. "Where's Raynil Layan?" He went on weeping, striking the bedding with his fist.

"Stop it," she said mildly. She walked about the room, gazing up at the stained ceiling. "We live in such a mess. I wish I were free of emotion. Human beings are such messes. We were better when the snow contained us, frozen, when we had no . . . hope! I wish there were only knowledge, pure knowledge, no emotion."

He sat up. "Vry—"

"Don't speak to me. You have nothing for me, and never had, you must accept that. I don't want to hear what you have to say. I don't want to know what you've done."

Geese set up a great honking outside.

He sat on the bed, yawned. "You're only half a woman. You're cold. I've always known it, yet I couldn't stop feeling as I did about you. . . ."

"*Cold?* . . . You fool, I steam like a rajabaral."

The noise in the street was louder, loud enough for them to catch the note of individual voices. Dathka ran to the window.

Where were his men now? The people who poured out of nearby alleys were all strangers to him. He could not see one familiar face—none of his men, no Raynil Layan—not that that surprised him—not even one citizen he could identify. Once on a time, every face had been known to him. Strangers were calling for his blood. Real fear entered his heart, as if his only ambition had been to die at the hand of a friend. To be hated by strangers . . . it was intolerable. He leaned from the window and shook his fist in defiance, cursing them.

The faces tipped upwards, opening in the middle almost in unison, like a shoal of fish. They roared and jibbered.

Before that noise, he dropped his fist and shrank back, not meaning to be quelled but quelled nevertheless. He leaned against the wall and examined his rough hands, with blood still moist in the nails.

Only when he heard Vry's voice below did he realise she had left the room. She had flung open the door of the tower and was standing on the platform, addressing the people. The mob surged forward as those at the rear pressed in to hear what she said. Some called out mockingly, but were silenced by others. Her voice, clear and sharp, flew above their tousled heads.

"Why don't you stop and think what you're doing? You're not animals. Try to be human. If we are to die, let us die with human dignity, and not with our hands round one another's throats.

"You are aware of suffering. Both the suffering and the awareness are your badges of humanity. Be proud, rot you—die with that knowledge. Remember the waiting world of the gossies below, where there is only gnashing of teeth because the dead feel disgust for their own lives.

Isn't that a terrible thing? Doesn't it seem to you a terrible thing, to feel disgust—disgust and contempt—for your own lives? Transform your own life from within. Never mind external weather, if it snows or rains or shines, never mind that, accept it, but work to transform your inner self. Create calm in your soul. Take thought. Would Dathka or his murder have the power to cure your personal predicament? Only you have that.

"You think things are going badly. I must warn you that more challenges are to come. I tell you this with the full weight of the academy behind me. Tomorrow, tomorrow at noon, the third and worst of the Twenty Blindnesses is due. Nothing can stop it. Mankind has no power over the skies. What will you do then? Will you run madly through the streets, cutting throats, smashing things, firing what your betters built—as if you were worse than phagors? Decide *now* how filthy, how low, you will be tomorrow!"

They looked at one another and murmured. No one shouted. She waited, instinctively seizing on the right moment at which to launch in again on a new tack.

"Years ago, the sorceress Shay Tal addressed the inhabitants of Oldorando. I remember her words clearly, for I revered everything she said. She offered us the treasure of knowledge. That treasure can be yours if only you will be humble and dare to reach out your hands for it.

"Understand what I tell you. Tomorrow's blindness is no supernatural event. What is it? It is merely the two sentinels passing one another, those two suns you have known since birth. This world of ours is round as they are round. Imagine how large a ball our world must be for us not to fall off it—yet it is small compared with the sentinels. They look small merely because they are so far away.

"Shay Tal, when she spoke, said that there was a disaster in the past. I believe that is not the case. We have added to her knowledge. Wutra has disposed of his world so that everything works through continuous action in all the parts. Your hair grows on your head and body as the suns rise and set. These are not separate actions but one in Wutra's eyes. Our world travels in a circle round Batalix, and there are other worlds like ours which behave likewise. At the same time, Batalix travels in a greater circle round about Freyr. You have to accept that our farmyard is not at the centre of the universe."

Their murmurs of protest grew louder. Vry overrode them by pitching her voice higher.

"Do you understand that? Understanding is harder than slitting throats, isn't it? To comprehend fully what I tell you, you must first understand and then grasp the understanding with your imagination, so that the facts live. Our year is four hundred and eighty days long, that we know. That is the time we take on Hrl-Ichor to make a complete circle about Batalix. But there is another circle to be made, the circle of Batalix and our world about Freyr. Are you prepared to hear the word? It takes eighteen hundred and twenty-five small years. . . . Imagine that great year!" They were quiet now, staring at her, the new sorceress.

"Until our day, few could imagine it! For each of us can expect only forty years of life. It would take forty-six of our lifetimes to add up to one whole circle of this world about Freyr. Many of our lives find no echo, yet are part of that greater thing. That is why such knowledge is difficult to grasp and easy to lose in time of trouble."

She was seized up by her new power, seduced by her own eloquence.

"What is the trouble, what is this disaster of which Shay Tal told us, large enough to make us mislay such important knowledge? Why, simply that the light of Freyr varies according to the time of the great year. We have come through many generations of poor light, of winter, when the earth lay dead under snow. Tomorrow you should rejoice when the eclipse comes—the blindness, when distant Freyr slips behind Batalix—for it is a sign that Freyr's light grows nearer. . . . We enter spring of the great year tomorrow. Rejoice! Have the sense, the knowledge, to rejoice! Throw away the mess of your lives that ignorance causes, and rejoice! Better times are coming for all of us."

Shoatapraxi deflected them. The woody grass had been growing in clumps as they approached lower ground. The clumps became thickets. Now they tried to find their way through a region choked with it.

The vegetation rose above their heads. It was broken only by drumlins, up which it was possible to climb occasionally in order to get a bearing. With the shoatapraxi was entwined a thin-stemmed bramble, making progress both difficult and painful. The phagor army ahead had travelled another way. They were forced to follow the more meandering tracks of animals, yet the going remained bad for the yelk. They were nervous of the grass, as if disliking its pungent scent; their sweeping horns caught on the hollow stems, and the thorns underfoot penetrated to the softer parts of their hooves. So the men dismounted, leading their necrogenes as they progressed on foot.

"How much farther, barbarian?" Skitosherill asked.

"Not far, " Laintal Ay responded. It was his stock answer to the stock question. They had slept uncomfortably in the forest, rising at dawn with frost in their clothes. He felt refreshed, still rejoicing in his lighter form, but he saw how weary the others were becoming. Aoz Roon was a shadow of what he had once been; in the night, he had called out in a strange language.

They came to marshy ground, where, to everybody's relief, the shoatapraxi thinned. After pausing to see that all was quiet, they moved on, scattering flights of small birds before them. Ahead loomed a valley, with soft mounds rising on either side. They went that way, rather than moving on to higher ground, chiefly because of their fatigue; but as soon as they entered the neck of the valley, they were assailed by a chill wind, which rushed at them like an animal and bit to their bones. It was a time for struggling on grimly, with the head down.

The wind brought fog with it. The fog curled about their bodies, though their heads were above it. Laintal Ay understood the wind, knowing that a layer of cold air poured down like water from the distant mountains on their left flank, down over the mounds into the valley, seeking lower ground. It was a local wind; the sooner they left its numbing grip, the better.

Skitosherill's wife gave a faint cry and halted, leaning against her yelk and burying her face against her arm.

Skitosherill returned to her concernedly and placed a grey-clad arm round her. The icy air wrapped his cloak about his leg.

He looked worriedly up at Laintal Ay. "She can't go on," he said.

"We'll die if we stay here."

Dashing the moisture from his eyes, he looked forward. In a few hours, he realised, the valley would be warm and harmless. At present it was a death trap. They were in shadow. The light of the two suns slanted across the left slope of the valley above their heads; the light lay in thick vertical bars, where the shadows were cast of giant rajabarals which stood on the opposite crest. The rajabarals were steaming already in the morning sunshine, the vapour pouring up into the sky, casting a rolling shadow.

He knew this place. Its configurations had been familiar to him when snow clothed it. It was normally a welcoming place—the last pass before a hunter gained the plains on the edge of which Oldorando stood. He was too cold even to shiver, body heat snatched by the wind. They could not continue. Skitosherill's wife still leaned sickly against the flank of the necrogene; now that she had given way, her maid-servant also felt able to release her miseries and stood screaming with her back to the tide of air.

"We'll get up among the rajabarals," he said, shouting the words into Skitosherill's ear. Skitosherill nodded, still involved with his wife, whom he was trying to help up into the saddle.

"Mount, all of you," Laintal Ay called.

As he shouted, a flutter of white caught his eye.

Above the hillside on their left flank, cowbirds appeared, fighting the cold downdraught, their feathers flickering from white to grey as they rode in the shadows of the rajabarals opposite. Below the birds was a line of phagors. They were warriors; they carried spears at the ready. They moved to the edge of the mound, to poise themselves there as steady as boulders. They looked down at the humans embroiled in the tumbling mists below.

"Fast, fast, up, before we're attacked!" As he shouted, he saw Aoz Roon was staring up at the brutes, without expression, making no move.

He ran to him, clouting him across the back.

"Up. We've got to get out of here."

Aoz Roon said something harsh in his throat.

"You're enchanted, man, you've learnt some of their accursed language and it's rendered you powerless."

By force, he heaved his friend into his saddle. The scout did the same with the servant woman, who was sobbing in terror.

"Up the slope to the rajabarals," Laintal Ay shouted. He slapped Aoz Roon's mare across its shaggy rump as he ran back to mount his own. Reluctantly, the animals started to climb. They made little response to heels in their ribs; a hoxney would have been lighter and faster.

"They won't attack us," the Sibornalan said. "We'll give them the maidservant if there's trouble."

"Our mounts. They will kill us for our mounts. To ride or for food. You stay behind and haggle if you wish."

With a sick look, Skitosherill shook his head and swung himself into his saddle.

He went first up the slope, leading his wife's beast. The scout and the maidservant followed close behind. Then there was a gap as Aoz Roon listlessly rode his yelk, allowing it to stray away from the others, despite Laintal Ay's shouts to keep together. He brought up the rear with the pack yelk, frequently casting glances back at the eminence behind them.

The phagors did not move. It would not be the cold wind that worried them; they were creatures of the cold. Their immobility need not imply decision. It was impossible to know what the brutes thought.

So they mounted the rise. They were soon out of the wind, to their great relief, and tugging with urgency on their reins.

As they came over the brow of the hill, the sunlight shone into their eyes. Both suns, near enough to look amid their dazzle as if linked, glittered between the trunks of the great trees. Just for a moment, dancing figures could be seen in the heart of the gold, lightly tripping—Others at a mysterious festivity; then they vanished as if the acid glory of light had inexplicably dissolved them. The party drew into the protection of the smooth columns, still gasping with cold. With the canopy of steam overhead, it was almost as if they had entered a hall of the gods. There were about thirty of the massive trees. Beyond them lay open ground and the way to Oldorando.

The phagor detachment moved. From complete immobility, it sprang into total action. The brutes came plodding concertedly down the slope on which they had remained poised. Only one of their kind was astride a kaidaw. He led. The cowbirds stayed shrieking above the valley.

Desperately, Laintal Ay looked about for a refuge. There was none, except that offered by the rajabarals. The rajabarals themselves were emitting internal rumbling. He drew his sword and spurred over to where the Sibornalan was lowering his wife from her mount.

"We'll have to stand and fight. Are you prepared for that? They'll be on us in a minute or two."

Skitosherill looked up at him with agony etched in every line of his face. His mouth was open in a kind of snarl of anguish.

"She has the bone fever, she will die," he said.

His wife's eyes were glazed, her body stiffly contorted.

With an impatient gesture of dismissal, Laintal Ay called to the scout, "You and I then. Look lively—here they come."

For answer, the scout gave him a villainous grin, at the same time making a gesture with his finger of slitting windpipes. Laintal Ay was grimly encouraged.

He cast about furiously by the base of the trees, looking for earths down which the Others had disappeared, thinking that here somewhere near at hand might be refuge—refuge and a snoktruix; but never *his* snoktruix, never again.

Despite their abrupt retreat, the Others had left no trace. Well, then there was no alternative to fighting. No doubt they must die. He would not expire until his breath could escape from every wound he received from the spears of the ancipitals.

With the scout by his side, he went to the edge of the mound to challenge the enemy as they appeared.

Behind him, the rumble in the rajabarals grew louder. The mighty trees had ceased to pour out steam and were making a noise like thunder. Below him, the first slanting rays of the linked suns had penetrated almost to the bottom of the valley, where they lit the spectacle of the phagors fording the katabatic wind, their sturdy bodies enmeshed in writhing fog, the stiff hairs of their coats stirred in their progress. They looked upwards and gave a churring cry at the sight of the two humans. They began to move up the hill.

This incident was witnessed from the Earth Observation Station and, a thousand years later, by those who came on sandalled feet to the great auditoria on Earth. Those auditoria were fuller now than they had been at any time over the last century. People who went to view that enormous electronic recreation of a reality that had not been real for many centuries were wishing in their hearts that the humans whose lives they had followed would survive—always using the future tense, which comes naturally to homo sapiens, even for such events as this, so long past.

From their privileged viewpoint, they saw beyond the incident among the grove of rajabarals, across the rolling plain where Fish Lake had once enshrined its terrifying statuary, to Oldorando itself.

And all that landscape was dotted with figures. The young kzahhn was preparing at last to descend upon the city that had torn both life and tether from his illustrious grandstallun. He awaited only the sign. Although his force was arrayed in no great military order, but rather disposed itself like so many herds of cattle, not always looking to the front, numbers alone made it formidable. It would roll across ancient Embruddock, and then roll remorselessly on towards the southwest coasts of the continent of Campannlat, to the very cliffs of the eastern Climent Ocean, to cross if possible to Hespagorat, and the rocky ancestral homelands of Pagovin.

Because of this nonhomogeneous disposition of the phagor crusade, it was still possible for travellers—refugees mainly—to move among the various herds and components without molestation, while hurrying in the direction from which the crusade had come. Generally, these fearful parties were led by Madis, sensitive to the air-octaves avoided by the hulking beasts under Hrr-Brahl Yprt's banner. One such party had the fork-bearded Raynil Layan pushing a timid Madi before him. It passed close by the young kzahhn himself, but the latter, immobile, gave no flicker of interest.

The young kzahhn stood against the eroded flanks of Rukk-Ggrl and communed with those in tether, his father and his great-grandstallun, hearing once more their advice and instruction in his pale harneys. Behind him stood his generals and then his two surviving gillots. He had serviced the gillots rarely but, given favourable fortunes, the time would come again. First must the two future octaves of victory or death be unravelled; if he travelled down the octave of victory, there would be music for mating.

He waited without motion, occasionally sliding his milt up the slots of his nostrils under the black fuzz of his muzzle. The sign would come in the heavens, the air-octaves would convulse themselves into a knot, and he and those whom he commanded would surge forward to burn down that ancient damned city, once Hrrm-Bhhrd Ydohk.

Across this ancient battlefield, where man and phagor had encountered each other more frequently than either side knew, Laintal Ay and the Sibornalan scout stood with their swords ready to greet the first phagors to climb the mound. Behind them, the noise of the rajabarals was like thunder. Aoz Roon and the maidservant crouched by one of the boles, supinely awaiting whatever befell. Skitosherill laid down the rigid body of his wife tenderly, tenderly, shielding her face from the blinding double sun now climbing towards zenith. Then he ran to join his two fellows, drawing his sword as he did so.

The uphill climb disrupted the line of phagors, the fitter arriving at the top first. As the leader charged into view, head and shoulders appearing over the slope, Laintal Ay ran forward. In despatching them one by one lay their only hope—he had counted thirty-five or more of the brutes, and refused to reckon the hopeless odds.

Up came the phagor's throwing arm. It bent back to what to a human was a disconcerting angle, but Laintal Ay dived under the point of the spear, rendering it useless, and stabbed with a straight arm. His elbow took the shock as the blade grated against rib. As yellow blood spurted from the wound, to his mind came the old hunters' tale that ancipital intestines were situated above their lungs; he had proved its truth when he skinned the phagor to deceive its kaidaw.

The phagor threw back its long boney head, lips peeling back from yellow teeth in a gesture of agony. It fell, and went rolling down the slope, to lie at the bottom in the dispersing mists.

But the other brutes were at the breast of the rise now, closing in. The Sibornalan scout was fighting valiantly, every now and again gasping a curse in his native tongue. With a yell, Laintal Ay flung himself into the fray again.

The world exploded.

The noise was so sharp, so close, that fighting immediately stopped. A second explosion came. Black stones flew overhead, most of them landing somewhere on the far side of the valley. Pandemonium ensued.

Each side was governed by its own instincts: the phagors became immobile, the two humans threw themselves flat on the ground.

Their timing was perfect. Concurrent explosions sounded. The black stones flew everywhere. Several hit phagors, carrying them immediately over the brink, scattering their dying bodies. The rest of the phagors turned tail and ran back into the valley for safety, rolling, slipping, sliding, in their haste to escape. The cowbirds flew screeching across the sky.

Laintal Ay sprawled where he was, hands over his ears, looking upwards in terror. The rajabarals were splitting from the top, cracking and peeling open like exploding casks, their staves falling. In the autumn of Helliconia's last great year, they had retracted their enormous fruit-bearing branches into the top of their trunks, sealing the crown over with a cap of resin until the vernal equinox. Over the winter centuries, internal heat pumps, drawing up warmth through the root system from rocks far below, had been preparing the way for this mighty explosion.

The tree above Laintal Ay burst with furious noise. He watched the seeds expelled. Some flew upwards, most were shot out on all sides. The force of the ejaculation threw the black projectiles as much as a half mile away. Steam rolled everywhere.

When silence fell, eleven of the trees had exploded. As their blackened casings peeled back from the top, a more slender crown thrust up inside, whitish, topped by green growth.

That green growth was destined to spread until the grove, which had consisted merely of polished columns, became roofed over in brilliant green foliage, shielding the roots from the more savage suns that were to come, in the days when Helliconia moved close to Freyr—too close to be comfortable for man, beast, or vegetation. Whoever lived or died under their shade, the rajabarals had their own form of life to protect.

These rajabarals formed part of the vegetation of the new world, the world that came into existence after Freyr swam into the clouded skies of Helliconia. Together with the new animals, they were set in ceaseless ecological competition with the orders of the old world, when Batalix ruled in isolation. The binary system had created a binary biology.

The seeds, a mottled black in colour, designed to resemble stones, were each as big as a human head. Over the course of the next six hundred thousand days, some would survive to become adult trees.

Laintal Ay kicked one carelessly away, and went over to see to the scout. The latter had been wounded, pierced by a sharp-edged phagor blade. Skitosherill and Laintal Ay helped him back to where Aoz Roon and the maidservant stood. He was in a bad way, bleeding freely. They squatted helplessly by his side as the life drained from his eddre.

Skitosherill began to go into an elaborate religious ritual, whereon Laintal Ay jumped up angrily.

"We must get to Embruddock as soon as possible, don't you understand? Leave the body here. Leave the woman with your wife. Press on with me and Aoz Roon. Time's running out."

Skitosherill gestured to the body. "I owe him this. It will take a while but it must be done according to the faith."

"The fuggies may return. They don't get scared easily, and we can hardly hope for another turn of fortune like the last. I am going to press on with Aoz Roon."

"You've done well, barbarian. Go forward, and perhaps we will meet again."

As Laintal Ay turned to go, he paused and looked back. "I'm sorry about your wife."

Aoz Roon had had the sense to keep hold of two of the yelk when the rajabarals exploded. The other animals had galloped away in fright.

"Are you fit to ride?"

"Yes, I'm fit. Help me, Laintal Ay. I'll recover. To learn the language of the phagor kind is to see the world differently. I'll recover."

"Mount and let's be off. I'm afraid that we may be too late to warn Embruddock."

They rode off rapidly, one behind the other, leaving the shade of the grove where the grey Sibornalan knelt in prayer.

The two yelk proceeded steadily, heads held low, eyes staring vacantly forward. When they dropped their scumble, beetles emerged from the ground and rolled the treasure to underground stores, inadvertently planting the seeds of future forests.

Seeing was bad, because of the way the plain rippled with ridge after ridge. More stone monuments dotted the landscapes, ages old, their circular signs eroded by weather or ripicolous lichens. Laintal Ay pressed ahead, alert for trouble, ever turning back to urge Aoz Roon to keep up.

The plain contained its travelling groups, moving in all directions, but he gave them as wide a berth as possible. They passed fleshless corpses to some of which garments still clung; fat birds sat by these memorials to life, and once they sighted a slinking sabre-tongue.

A cold front rose like a shawl behind their shoulders to the north and east. Where the sky remained clear, Freyr and Batalix clung together, their discs inseparable. The yelk had passed the site of Fish Lake, where a cairn had been erected to mark Shay Tal's miracle in the vanished waters, many winters ago; they were climbing over one of the tiresome ridges, when a wind rose. The world began to grow dark.

Laintal Ay dismounted and stood fondling the muzzle of his yelk. Aoz Roon remained despondently in the saddle.

The eclipse was beginning. Once more, exactly as Vry had predicted, Batalix was taking a phagor bite from the brilliant outline of Freyr. The process was slow and inexorable, and would result in Freyr's being lost entirely for five and a half hours. Not so many miles away, the kzahhn had his needed sign.

The suns were devouring their own light. A terrible fear took hold of Laintal Ay, freezing his eddre. For a moment stars blazed in the day sky. Then he closed his eyes and clung to the yelk, burying his face in its rusty pelage. The Twenty Blindnesses were upon him, and he cried in his heart to Wutra to win the war in his heavens.

But Aoz Roon looked up to the sky with awe blunting his thin features, and exclaimed, "Now Hrrm-Bhhrd Ydohk will die!"

Time seemed to cease. Slowly, the brighter light faded behind the duller. The day took on the greyness of a corpse.

Laintal Ay pulled himself from his dread and took Aoz Roon by his skeletal shoulders, searching that familiar but transformed countenance. "What did you say to me then?"

Aoz Roon said dazedly, "I'll be all right, I'll be myself again."

"I asked you what you said."

"Yes. . . . You know how the stench of them, that milky smell, clings to everything. Their language is the same. It makes everything different. I was with Yhamm-Whrrmar a half air-turn, talking with him. Many things. Things of which my Olonets-speaking intelligence can make no sense."

"Never mind that. What did you say about Embruddock?"

"It is something that Yhamm-Whrrmar knew would happen as certainly as if it were past, not future. That phagors would destroy Embruddock—"

"I must go on. Follow if you wish. I must return and warn everyone. Oyre—Dathka—"

Aoz Roon grasped his arms with sudden force.

"Wait, Laintal Ay. A moment and I'll be myself. I had the bone fever. I knocked myself out. Cold nailed my heart."

"You never made excuses for others. Now you make excuses for yourself."

Something of the older man's qualities returned to his face as he stared at Laintal Ay. "You are one of the good men, you bear my mark, I have been your lord. Listen. All I say is what I never thought of till I was on that island half an air-turn. The generations are born and fly their course, then they drop to the world below. There's no escape from it. Only to have a good word said after all's over."

"I'll speak well of you, but you're not dead yet, man."

"The ancipital race knows that their time is done. Better times come for men and women. Sun, flowers, soft things. After we're forgotten. Till all Hrl-Ichor Yhar's frame is empty."

Laintal Ay pushed him away, cursing, not understanding what was said.

"Never mind tomorrow and all that. The world hangs on now. I'm riding to Embruddock."

He climbed again into the saddle of the yelk and kicked it into action. With the lethargic movements of a man rousing from a dream, Aoz Roon followed suit.

The greyness was settling in thicker, like fermentation. In another hour, Freyr was half-devoured, and the hush became more intense. The two men passed groups petrified by dusk.

Later in their progress, they sighted a man approaching on foot. He was running slowly but steadily, arms and legs pumping. He stopped on top of a ridge and stared at them, tensed to run away. Laintal Ay rested his right hand on his sword handle.

Even through the twilight, there was no mistaking that portly figure, the leonine head with its forked beard dramatically flecked with grey. Laintal Ay called his name and moved his mount forward.

It took Raynil Layan some while to be convinced of Laintal Ay's identity, still more for him to recognise the skeletal Aoz Roon with no sparkle in his eyes. He came cautiously round the antlers of the yelk to grasp Laintal Ay's wrist with a damp hand.

"I shall be one with our forefathers if I take another step. You've both endured the bone fever and survived. I may not be so lucky. Exertion makes it worse, they say—sexual exertion or otherwise." He held his chest and panted. "Oldorando's rotten with pest. I've failed to escape in time, fool that I am. That's what these revolting signs mean in the sky. I've sinned—though I'm by no means as bad as you, Aoz Roon. Those religious pilgrims spoke true. It's the gossies for me."

He sank to the ground, puffing and holding his head in misery. He rested an elbow on a pack he had been carrying.

"Tell me what news of the city," Laintal Ay said impatiently.

"Ask me nothing, let me be. . . . Let me die."

Laintal Ay dismounted and kicked the lord of the mint in the buttocks.

"What of the city—besides the pest?"

Raynil Layan turned his red face upwards. "Enemies within. . . . As if the visitations of the fever were not enough, your worthy friend, the other Lord of the Western Veldt, has been trying to usurp Aoz Roon's position. I despair of human nature."

He dipped his hand into a purse hanging by his belt, and brought out some bright gold coins, roons freshly minted at his mint.

"Let me buy your yelk, Laintal Ay. You're within an hour of home and scarcely need it. But I need it. . . ."

"Give me more news, rot you. What of Dathka, is he dead?"

"Who knows? Probably so by now—I left last night."

"And the phagor components ahead? How did you get through them —buying your way?"

Raynil Layan gestured with one hand while he tucked his money away with the other. "Plenty of them between us and the city. I had a Madi as a guide, who avoided them. Who can tell what they may be up to, filthy things." As if struck by a sudden recollection, he added, "Understand that I left, not of course for my own sake, but for the sake of those I had a duty to protect. Others of my party are behind me. We had our hoxneys stolen almost as soon as we set out yesterday, and so our progress—"

Growling like an animal, Laintal Ay seized the other's coat and dragged him to his feet.

"Others? Others? Who's with you? Who are you running away from, you bladder? Is Vry there?"

A wry face. "Let me go. *She* prefers her astronomy, I'm sad to relate. She's still in the city. Be grateful to me, Laintal Ay, I have rescued friends and indeed relations of yours and Aoz Roon's. So bestow on me your insufferable yelk. . . ."

"I'll settle with you later." He pushed Raynil Layan aside and jumped on the yelk. Spurring it fiercely, he crossed the ridge and rode forward to the next one, calling.

On the syncline of the ridge, he found three people and a small boy sheltering. A Madi guide lay with his face buried in the bank, still overcome by the stigmata in the sky. Beside him were Dol, clinging to Rastil Roon, and Oyre. The boy was crying. The two women gazed at Laintal Ay in terror as he dismounted and went forward to them. Only when he clung to them and called their names did they recognise him.

Oyre too had been through the eye of the fever needle. They stood and surveyed each other, smiling and exclaiming at their skeletal selves. Then she gave a laugh and a cry at the same time, and snuggled into his arms. While they stood together, faces against each other's flesh, Aoz Roon came forward, clutched his small son's chubby wrist, and embraced Dol. Tears poured down his ravaged face.

The women related some of the recent painful history of Oldorando; Oyre explained Dathka's unsuccessful attempt to take over the leadership. Dathka was still in the city, together with many others. When Raynil Layan had come to Oyre and Dol, offering to escort them to safety, they had accepted his offer. Though they suspected the man was really fleeing to save his own skin, such was their fear that Rastil Roon would catch the pest that they accepted Raynil Layan's offer, and had left hurriedly with him. Because of his inexperience, their goods and mounts had been stolen almost immediately by Borlienian brigands.

"And the phagors? They're going to attack the city?"

All the women could say was that the city still stood, despite the chaos within its walls. And there had certainly been massed ranks of the dreadful fuggies outside the city as they slipped away.

"I shall have to go back."

"Then I return with you—I'm not leaving you again, my precious," Oyre said. "Raynil Layan can do as he pleases. Dol and the boy stay with father."

As they stood talking, clutching each other, smoke drifted across the plains from the west. They were too involved, too happy, to notice.

"The sight of my son revives me," Aoz Roon said, hugging the child and drying his eyes on his sleeve. "Dol, if you are able to let the past die, I'll be a better man to you from now on."

"You speak words of regret, Father," Oyre said. "I should be the first to do that. I know now how wilfully I behaved to Laintal Ay, and almost lost him as a consequence."

As he saw the tears come to her eyes, Laintal Ay thought involuntarily of his snoktruix in the earth below the rajabarals, and reflected that it was only through Oyre's nearly having lost him that they were now able to find each other. He soothed her, but she burst out of his grasp, saying, "Forgive me, and I'll be yours—and wilful no more, I swear."

He clasped her, smiling. "Keep your will. It's needed. We have much else to learn, and must change as times change. I'm grateful to you for understanding, for making me act."

They clung lovingly together, clutching each other's skeletal bodies, kissing each others' fragile lips.

The Madi guide began to come to his senses. He got up and called for Raynil Layan, but the master of the mint had fled. The smoke was thicker now, adding its ashes to the ashen sky.

Aoz Roon started to relate his experiences on the island to Dol, but Laintal Ay interrupted.

"We're united again, and that is miraculous. But Oyre and I must return to Embruddock in all haste. We'll surely be needed there."

The two sentinels were lost in cloud. A breeze was rising, troubling the plain. It was the breeze, blowing from the direction of Embruddock, which carried the news of fire. Now the smoke became denser. It became a shroud, dimming the living beings—whether friend or foe—scattered across the expanses of plain. Everything was enveloped. With the smoke came the stench of burning. Flights of geese winged eastwards overhead.

The human figures clustering about two antlered animals represented between them three generations. They began to move across the landscape as it faded from view. They would survive, though everyone else perished, though the kzahhn triumphed, for that was what befell.

Even in the flames consuming Embruddock, new configurations were being born. Behind the ancipital mask of Wutra, Shiva—god of destruction and regeneration—was furiously at work on Helliconia.

The eclipse was total now.

END OF VOLUME ONE

. . . Alternatively, you may believe that all these things existed before, but that the human race was wiped out by a burst of fiery heat or its cities were laid low by some great upheaval of the world or engulfed by greedy rivers which persistent rains had driven to overflow their banks. All the more reason, then, to concede my point and admit that an end is coming to earth and sky. If the world was indeed shaken by such plagues and perils, then it needs only a more violent shock to make it collapse in universal ruin.

Lucretius: *De Rerum Natura*
55 BC

ACKNOWLEDGEMENTS

My thanks for useful preliminary discussions go to Professor Tom Shippey (philology), Dr. J. M. Roberts (history), and Mr. Desmond Morris (anthropology).

I must also thank Dr. B. E. Juel-Jensen (pathology) and Professor Jack Cohen (biology) for indispensable suggestions. But most gratitude is reserved for Professor Iain Nicolson (cosmology and astronomy) and Dr. Peter Cattermole (geology, climatics); the great globe itself, yea, all which it inherit, is largely their work.

My debt to the writings and friendship of Dr. J. T. Fraser is apparent, I hope.

Thanks are also due to Jennifer Elton (typing beyond the call of duty), to David Wingrove (for being protean), and to my wife, Margaret (for being herself).

In a career spanning a quarter of a century, Brian W. Aldiss has written more than two dozen books, many of which have come to be recognized as classics of science fiction. His novel *The Long Afternoon of Earth* won a Hugo Award in 1962, *The Saliva Tree* a Nebula Award in 1965, *Starship* the Prix Jules Verne in 1977. In 1969 he was voted Britain's most popular science fiction writer and the following year he received the Ditmar Award as the World's Best Contemporary SF Author. One of his most influential books is *The Billion-Year Spree*, a history of science fiction. *Helliconia Spring* is the first volume of a trilogy, his most ambitious undertaking. Mr. Aldiss lives in Oxford, England.